mk

SECRET ADMIRER

An unputdownable psychological thriller with a
breathtaking twist

PATRICIA
MACDONALD

Revised edition 2022
Joffe Books, London
www.joffebooks.com

First published by Warner Books in
the United States in 1995

Cover art by Nick Castle

ISBN: 978-1-80405-261-7

AUTHOR'S NOTE

Please note this book is set in the 1990s, a time before smart phones and when social attitudes were very different.

PART ONE

December, New Year's Eve

CHAPTER ONE

A slice of moon glided between bare tree branches, and brittle tufts of brown grass crunched beneath her feet as Laura Reed crossed the Village Green. Tiny white Christmas lights were still suspended in the trees. By next week the diligent Cape Christian Parks Department would have them all down, but for now they were a twinkling reminder of the holiday just passed. Laura shoved her hands deep into her coat pockets and shivered. She was used to tramping around town in her parka, a heavy sweater, and boots in this weather. But she and her husband, Jimmy, had plans for a New Year's Eve dinner, so she was wearing stockings and heels, a silk blouse, and a skirt under her good wool coat. The December chill seemed to cut right through her.

Despite the cold, she loved to walk through town. Cape Christian, a little jewel of preserved Victoriana perched on the southern tip of the New Jersey shore, was picturesque at any time of year. The branches of huge shade trees arched over the quiet streets and screened the rows of old homes that were fastidiously maintained and festooned with intricately carved gingerbread. From almost any corner on Main Street you could catch a glimpse of the ocean, just visible beyond the promenade that formed the eastern border of the town.

In the summertime huge crowds of tourists flocked here to drink in the quaint atmosphere of another century while they vacationed at the beach. Jimmy Reed had been born and raised in this town, and when he'd brought Laura back here, he'd promised her she would soon grow to love it. He was right. She did love Cape Christian at any time of year, but, like a native, she loved it most in the dead of winter, when the streets were deserted and the town was steeped in silence beside the beating heart of the sea.

She passed by the Gothic-style Catholic church. The crèche was still set up out in front of the church, a spotlight illuminating the tender scene. She was reminded of the first time they were here for a visit—the Christmas when their son, Michael, was two. She was looking in a shop window when he left her side and toddled over to the manger scene, proudly lifting the baby Jesus from the manger and coming back toward her, his eyes alight. "My baby," he crowed, to the indulgent amusement of passersby, as Laura hurried to replace the little figure in the manger.

Laura smiled, remembering, and continued walking between the rows of gaily painted, clapboard-sided stores that made up the shopping area of Main Street. All the windows were ornately decorated. The Christmas season in Cape Christian was almost as busy as a month in summer. In the weeks preceding Christmas Day, visitors came to tour the Victorian guest houses, which were candlelit, garlanded, and tasseled to the hilt. Laura sometimes wondered how people found the time to go touring in the Christmas season. It was all she could do to finish all the baking, shopping, and wrapping that needed to be done.

But once Christmas Day came and went, Cape Christian returned to its winter slumber. Reed's Gallery, in the third block of Main Street, was dimly lit. There was no danger of any business at six o'clock in the evening on New Year's Eve. Jimmy had gone in late in the afternoon to finish up some framing projects, which was the only reason the gallery was open at all. Laura pushed open the front door of the gallery, and a bell tinkled as she walked in.

Only a few of the track lights in the gallery were lit, although the golden glow from Jimmy's frame shop upstairs spilled down the stairwell. A gaunt-looking man with a thatch of gray hair sat in a wheelchair beneath one of the spotlights, turning over a book in his large yet delicate hands. He looked up as the door opened. His skin was unlined, and his face was youthful. Two spots of color appeared in his wan cheeks. "Laura," he exclaimed.

She smiled at the sight of him. "Hi, Gary. What a nice surprise."

"Jim and I had some business to discuss—the fellowship."

Laura nodded. Gary Jurik was a local artist and a friend. Jimmy had convinced Gary to apply for a prestigious fellowship that would mean a year of both teaching and studying at the Boston Museum of Fine Arts.

"I know you're going to get it," she said.

"I never had any formal training," Gary protested.

"Yes, and look at all the success you've had that other artists only dream about."

Gary's face turned pink with pleasure at her words. "I suppose," he said.

"Is he upstairs?" she asked.

Gary Jurik nodded and pressed the book down in his lap.

Laura walked to the foot of the staircase, noting as she passed by that some new paintings had been hung, and many of the paintings displayed proudly wore the blue stickers that indicated they were sold. Jimmy's timing in opening this gallery had been fortuitous. In these last two years there had been an explosion of interest in art among both tourists and locals and a steady stream of eager customers.

"Hey, babe, it's me," she called out.

"Be right with you," he yelled back.

Laura nodded and returned to where Gary sat. She pulled up a low, rolling stool and sat down beside him. Gary had once mentioned that he hated having to look up at people all the time when he talked to them. Laura could understand that. It seemed a small enough concession to his comfort to

4

sit in his presence. "Whatcha got?" she asked, pointing to the book in his hands.

"Doesn't it look familiar?" he asked, extending it to her.

Laura accepted it from him and looked at the spine. It was her new book, *Raoul and the Horse from the Sky*, the fourth in her well-received series for children about Raoul and his otherworldly friends. "No dust jacket?" she said.

"It must be around here somewhere," said Gary, avoiding her gaze. "It's Jimmy's copy. I think it's your best as far as the illustrations. The horse has such life to him," he said earnestly.

"Well, thanks, Gary," she said, genuinely pleased. "That's a real compliment coming from you."

Gary smiled and blushed again. He was a little younger than Jimmy, about thirty, but from a distance, with the wheelchair and his gray hair, he looked much older. Jimmy told her that Gary's hair had turned gray when he was seventeen, in the year following the accident. Yet when he smiled like that, Laura thought, he looked positively adolescent.

She pointed to a new painting of his on the wall, a lyrical, light-suffused watercolor of the Dormley, a grand old Victorian hotel on the beach. "That is a beauty," she said. "How do you remember the light like that?"

"It's always summer in my head," he said.

Laura laughed appreciatively, and Gary turned away, wheeling his chair around with a frown as he examined some of the other paintings. "Jim's got some promising people here."

Laura smiled and shook her head. Gary knew perfectly well that none of these painters was any competition for him, but an artist's ego was always fragile. Gary was Jimmy's one certified find at the gallery. They had been friends since boyhood. Gary had always dabbled in art, but after the auto accident had confined him to the wheelchair, he had become intent on his work.

When Jimmy returned to town and opened the gallery, he immediately recognized the commercial potential of Gary's lovely watercolors of the many splendid Victorian buildings in this town. It was Jimmy who conceived of the stationery, the calendars, and the mugs that were printed with Gary's different paintings. The series was becoming virtually synonymous with a visit to Cape Christian, the way a box of Fralinger's saltwater taffy was the de rigueur souvenir of a visit to Atlantic City. Their collaboration had been a financial success for both of them.

"You think he's going to replace us?" she asked Gary bemusedly.

Gary looked at her, startled. There was something innocent about him, which never failed to touch Laura. "Do you think so?"

"I'm kidding," she said. "Although it probably *is* time for him to be finding another protégé. He can't help himself. It's in his nature."

Gary nodded. "He was born to be a patron of the arts."

"Wait a minute," said Laura. "That suggests somebody with money."

"You're right. A mentor, I guess you could say."

"I know I would never have dreamed of doing these books without him pressuring me," she said, laughing. It was true. She had studied art in school, but always with a practical eye to becoming an art teacher. It was Jimmy who bullied and encouraged her until she got her first book together, Jimmy who sent it to agents and publishers. With every rejection she received, she became more hopeless and he became more determined. And in the end, his faith in her work proved justified.

"He's very sure of his taste," said Gary.

"Well, if he likes something, he figures it's just a matter of time until the world follows suit," Laura said wryly.

Gary gazed around at the walls. "It must be wonderful to have such confidence," he said.

The doorbell tinkled again, and the door opened. A middle-aged woman, bundled up in a scarf and tweedy coat, entered the gallery. She had a haggard complexion and thin salt-and-pepper hair carelessly pinned up in a knot. Her mournful gaze fell on Laura and Gary. "I'm done shopping," she said without preamble.

"Hello, Mrs. Jurik," said Laura. Every time Laura saw Wanda Jurik, she felt sorry for her. Wanda always seemed distracted and on the verge of tears. Laura knew from Jimmy that Wanda had borne the whole burden of supporting them when Gary was young and caring for Gary after the accident. Gary's father, Karl Jurik, had been a shiftless charmer, an alcoholic who came and went as he pleased, never taking responsibility for his family. He took off for good several years after the accident. A lot of people seemed to fault Wanda, to think she was overprotective, including Jimmy, but Laura could not help but imagine how she would feel if she were in Wanda's position—if something like this had happened to her own son, Michael. How could a mother ever accept it?

"Hello," Wanda said shortly. "Gary, I'll meet you around back."

"Okay," he said.

Without another word, Wanda turned and left. Gary seemed embarrassed. "Mother brought me down today," he explained. "My van's in the shop." Gary had a customized van equipped with hand controls so that he could drive. "I have to be going," he said, searching for his coat.

Laura spotted it hanging over a nearby chair and handed it to him. "It was good to see you," she said. "Come for dinner next week? How's Tuesday?"

"I'll check," he said gruffly. "It sounds nice. How's Mike?"

"He's fine." Laura smiled.

"Tell him I'll be over to take him for a spin." Michael loved to ride in Gary's lap in the wheelchair, always urging him to go faster. Laura had been appalled when Michael first clambered up and insisted on a ride, but it just made Gary laugh. He seemed to enjoy it.

Gary pulled on his coat and began to wheel his chair toward the back door. Jimmy had had ramps installed, both at the gallery and at home, so that Gary could visit easily. He stopped the chair briefly at the foot of the stairs. "Good-bye, Jim," he called up. Then he headed for the back door.

"Keep her in the road, man," Jim called back. "Now, Laura," he commanded, "close your eyes and don't open them until I say."

"Why?" Laura giggled, but she did as she was told.

She heard Jimmy's heavy footsteps on the stairs, inhaled the fresh, masculine scent of him passing by her, and then heard the *thunk* of something being placed on the desk. "All right," he said. "You can open them."

Laura looked and then exclaimed with pleasure. He had taken the dust jacket from her new book, flattened it out, and framed it.

"Belated Christmas present." He sighed. "I didn't get a chance to finish it before. I was so busy trying to finish up the orders."

Laura smiled at her husband. He was a rugged-looking, broad-shouldered man, with the easygoing self-assurance of one who had always been abundantly loved. He was one of Cape Christian's favorite sons, who had triumphed both academically and on the football field, in high school and college, and he'd been on his way to becoming a power player in the business of museum art collections when she'd met him out in San Francisco. Everyone was amazed when he decided to abandon his promising career and return to the East Coast to start a little gallery in his hometown. But he had applied his huge capacity for work and his shrewdness about art to the gallery. It was no wonder he had been successful.

"This is great," she said. "Thank you." She got up from the chair and kissed his bearded cheek. She loved his new beard. She thought it looked sexy, and he never complained about shaving anymore. She turned back to her gift and ran her finger lightly over the frame. "You did a beautiful job."

Jimmy looked over her shoulder. "Nice picture of you." The author photo used on the jacket was one he had taken last summer at the beach.

Like most people, Laura was critical of her own image. But she did like this particular photo. "It is nice," she admitted.

"Hardly does you justice, though," he said.

"By the way," said Laura, "Marta called me today." Marta Eberhart was Laura's editor, who three years ago had lifted her manuscript and illustrations from the obscurity of the slush pile and turned her into an author. Laura felt a deep sense of loyalty and gratitude to Marta.

"Really," said Jim. "What did she want? How's the book doing?"

"It seems to be doing pretty well," said Laura. "She seems pleased."

"Great."

"She met a guy from *Book World* last month who wants to do a story on me," Laura said, proud of her news. "Some guy named Bob Gerster. He wants to come down, get pictures, do an interview . . ."

"That's great," said Jimmy, shamelessly welcoming an opportunity for publicity. "We can have him at the house, the gallery, the whole works!"

"Well, wait and see," Laura cautioned. "He hasn't called yet. Maybe he's changed his mind by now."

"I don't know," Jim said teasingly. "On second thought, I'm not sure I want some other guy taking pictures of you. All those book lovers drooling over you."

Laura raised an eyebrow at him. "Flattery will get you . . . a very special evening," she said.

Jimmy smiled. He loved to look at his wife. He always said that he had fallen in love with her at first sight. In fact, the first thought he ever had about her was that he wished he were talented enough to paint her. She had opalescent skin, smoky gray eyes that always looked calm and thoughtful, high cheekbones, and a generous mouth. It was a haunting face, made even more arresting by the silver-blond hair that fell in a shining curve to her shoulders.

"Well," she said, blushing under his admiring scrutiny, "this is a far better present than that fishing tackle I gave you for Christmas . . ."

"Hey, that was just what I wanted. I only hope I get a chance to use it this summer . . . get out on the boat with you and Michael."

Laura understood. He had bought a fishing boat when they moved back here, but summer was his busiest time. He hardly had a chance to go out on it. Jimmy was busily putting things away on his desk, straightening up from the day. "I'm almost ready to go," he said. "I made a reservation at Marie's."

"Good. I'm ready for some Italian food."

"Did you take Michael to Mom's?"

"Sidney came and got him," she said. Sidney Barone was Jimmy's stepfather. James Reed Sr. had been a policeman here in Cape Christian who had dropped dead of a heart attack when Jimmy was three years old. Jimmy's mother, Dolores, had supported and raised him alone. She didn't marry Sidney, a kindly widower with a linen supply business that served the hotels and restaurants of Atlantic City, until Jimmy was sixteen. Jimmy never could regard Sidney as a father figure, but to Michael, he was the only grandfather he had ever known—his beloved Poppy.

"I saw Gary for a minute," she said. "And his mother."

Jimmy's brow darkened. "I can't stand that woman," he said. "She treats Gary like he was a child in a stroller, not a grown man."

"Whenever I see her, I always think of that old saying, 'Be careful what you wish for,'" Laura mused. "I mean, every mother wishes at one time or another that her little ones would never leave her. But not like that. What you really want is for them to grow up and be happy and make their dreams come true . . ."

"That's what *you* want," said Jimmy. "Not everybody is like that. The thing is, he could leave her, and live a pretty normal life, but she makes it too difficult for him. Sometimes I think she likes things this way."

"Isn't that a little unfair?" she said.

"I don't know. Maybe. Look, ummm . . ."

"What?"

"Richard stopped by today . . ."

"And?"

"And he asked me if we were going out tonight . . ."

"Don't tell me . . .," said Laura.

"He and Candy want to join us . . ."

"Oh no. Jimmy . . ."

"What could I do? He trapped me into it."

"You could have told him that it was New Year's Eve and you wanted to be alone with your wife."

Jimmy nodded. "You're right. I'll call him."

Laura sighed. She knew she was putting him on the spot. Richard Walsh was their lawyer and Jimmy's partner in the art gallery. He was a local boy, another childhood friend of Jimmy's, who had exhibited a breathtaking knack for making money. His business was the law, but his hobby and preoccupation was investing, and he seemed to be spectacularly successful at it. It was all he ever talked about. Still, he had a sense of humor, and Laura liked him well enough. But she could barely tolerate his wife, Candy.

Candy was a former beauty queen whose chief pastime seemed to be sitting alone in their big modern house in Rock Harbor, the next town over, and buying jewelry off the Home Shopping Network or working out on her NordicTrack. There was no one Laura felt less like spending the evening with than Candy Walsh.

"What's his number?" Jimmy mumbled aloud. Laura knew that Jimmy felt indebted to Richard. He had insisted on investing in the gallery, and Richard's money provided the financial boost Jimmy needed to outfit the place so that it drew every passing eye. She hated to put Jimmy on the spot.

"All right," she said. "Let's just go."

"Are you sure?" he asked doubtfully.

"Yeah, yeah. But let's hurry before I change my mind."

Jimmy looked at her gratefully. "I'll make it up to you, babe."

"You better," she said.

CHAPTER TWO

Candy Walsh stretched like a cat and purred. "This time next week I'll be working on my tan. Just me in my thong bikini, soaking up the rays." She glanced over at Jimmy and Richard, expecting a salivary response to the image of her, half naked and prone under the sun, but the men had their heads together as Richard punched numbers into his pocket calculator. Candy pouted.

"Where are you going?" Laura asked dutifully.

"Nassau. We always go there. It has the best shopping. You wouldn't believe the china and crystal," announced Candy, who didn't cook and never entertained. "And the jewelry. I got this watch there." She held out a soft, slender hand, weighed down with a diamond-studded timepiece.

"Very nice," Laura said without enthusiasm.

"And, of course, the casinos. We go there so often, Richard's even thinking about buying us a condo down there. Aren't you, honey?"

Richard paused in his explanation of investment strategies and beamed at his wife. Candy gave him half a wink, careful not to smudge her mascara. Laura sighed.

Candy misinterpreted the sigh. "I guess you two don't get away very much, between the kid and the little gallery and all," she said sympathetically.

"For me, traveling around isn't all that tempting," said Laura. "I spent my whole childhood traveling. My father was in the navy, and every year or two we had to move. All I ever wanted to do was to stay put."

"Well, moving with your parents would be a drag," said Candy. "But vacationing in the most beautiful spot in the world is different. Where do your parents live now? Any place good you could visit?"

"They're dead," Laura said bluntly. "Plane crash." She felt a little perverse satisfaction at Candy's gasp of dismay. Picturing herself on that plane to Nassau, no doubt.

"That's too bad," said Candy.

Laura shrugged and finished the last of her coffee, staring bleakly over the rim of her cup. Jimmy glanced at his wife and then at his watch. "We'd better wrap this up," he said.

"Well, I'll think of you," Candy said gaily, "when I'm out there on the beach."

"Great," Laura said flatly. Jimmy came around and pulled out her chair.

At the door, Marie Vanese dislodged two wine-dark roses from the vase on the table and, as was her custom on special occasions, handed one to each of the departing women.

"A rose for the lovely ladies," she said in her gravelly voice.

"Thank you, Marie," exclaimed Laura, accepting the long-stemmed bloom and sniffing the velvety, blood-red petals.

"Ouch," Candy complained, licking the top of her perfectly manicured index finger. "That thorn pricked me. Here, Richard, you hold it."

Richard took the rose in his meaty hand and tried to juggle it while he enveloped Candy in her fur coat.

"Everything was great, as always," said Jimmy to Marie, shrugging on his overcoat. "Thanks for fitting us in."

Marie's olive-skinned face wrinkled into a gentle smile. "I'm glad you enjoyed yourselves," she said hoarsely. Marie's candlelit trattoria was always popular, but especially so on cold winter nights when most of the other restaurants were closed for the season and Marie's spicy cooking seemed to soothe the soul. Marie came from a restaurant family. Her brother, Dominick, owned a famous restaurant reputed to be a hangout for organized crime figures in Atlantic City, but no one ever breathed a word about it in front of Marie, whose dignified manner and genteel habits were pure Cape Christian. She lived quietly with another woman, a retired librarian, and they kept three cats. When she wasn't at the trattoria, Marie was collecting shells on the beach for the collages she liked to assemble and display in the summer craft shows.

"Now bundle up out there," she said as she ushered them out into the chilly December night. "And come back soon."

Candy had pulled on her leather gloves and retrieved her rose from Richard, brushing it fetchingly against her cheek and smiling at Jimmy.

"Well," Richard said heartily, "what do you say we shoot up to Atlantic City to ring in the new year. Have a few drinks, maybe catch a show?"

Laura knew from Jimmy that Richard had a fondness for the action in Atlantic City. To her there was nothing more tedious than an evening feeding quarters into a slot machine, watching other people squander their money on blackjack and craps. She gave her husband a warning glance.

"We can't, Rich. We've got to pick up Michael at my mother's," said Jimmy.

"On New Year's Eve? It's only ten o'clock. Come on," said Richard. "Your mother will keep him overnight."

Jimmy shook his head. "No, no, we have to go get him. The life of a parent, you know."

Candy looked at them pityingly.

"All righty," said Richard. "We'll have to go it alone. It was great seeing you guys."

Laura forced herself to smile.

Candy stamped her Ferragamo-shod feet. "I'm freezing, Richard. Let's go."

There were good-nights all around, and Laura huddled up against Jimmy as they hurried to the car. Her teeth were chattering as she got onto the front seat and closed the door.

"It'll be warm in a minute," said Jimmy, turning on the engine and pushing up the heat. "Good dinner, didn't you think?"

"Delicious," Laura agreed. "Although I was afraid for a minute that we were going to end up ringing in the new at Trump's Castle."

Jimmy laughed. "Thank God for Michael. I almost felt guilty using him as an excuse."

Laura shook her head. "Did you see that look she gave us? As if you had said we were going to go and have root canal without novocaine."

"You know, I think Richard would really like to have kids, but it's going to be a hard sell with Candy."

"It's probably a mercy for the kids," said Laura.

"I'm sorry we ended up with them tonight, babe," he said.

"It's all right."

"I wonder if Michael will be asleep. I kind of hope so," he said. "Maybe we can have champagne in our boudoir." He raised his eyebrows suggestively.

"Drive on," she said.

They drove the short distance to the Seashell Condominiums in companionable silence. The condos were in an enormous, seaside shingle-cottage-style building that had once been a summer hotel. Dolores and Sidney had a comfortable two-bedroom apartment. One of the bedrooms was outfitted for Michael with every amenity a boy his age could desire.

"It's better than my room at home," he said once, to Laura's irritation. She knew he didn't mean anything by it, but it rankled all the same. She always felt as if she were in some unwholesome competition with her mother-in-law. It had been that way from the moment they'd met.

Jimmy rang the doorbell, and Dolores buzzed them in. She was waiting at the apartment door, dressed in an aqua jogging suit and pristine white sneakers. Her frosted hair was styled in a stiff, layered bubble, and her square, perennially tanned face was carefully made up. On top of her head was a gold foil party hat. She blew on a noisemaker as she opened the door.

"Happy New Year!" she proclaimed. She held out her arms to Jimmy, and he embraced her, towering over her like a bear.

"Not till midnight, Ma," said Jimmy. "I'm superstitious."

Laura edged past them into the apartment.

Sidney was seated on a bamboo-framed barrel chair, reading the *Atlantic City Press*. He also had on a party hat, tipped at an awkward angle on his balding head. Behind him, in the corner, their Christmas tree still blazed with colored lights. Sidney looked up over his reading glasses. "Hello, Laura. How was your dinner?"

"It was good," she said. "Richard and Candy Walsh joined us."

"That Candy is a beautiful girl, isn't she?" said Dolores, walking in with her arm linked possessively through Jimmy's. Her bracelets jingled like sleighbells. "She always looks so turned out. So well groomed."

Laura was immediately conscious of the run that had developed in her panty hose and the fact that she had not reapplied her lipstick after dinner.

Sidney interrupted smoothly. "Hey, Jim, you think the Flyers are going to get rid of that coach?"

"If they want to win a game again, they'd better," Jimmy replied. Jimmy often said that he wondered why Sidney liked sports so much since he did not seem to be a very astute analyst of any game. What Jimmy did not seem to notice, Laura thought, was how mildly Sidney managed to stitch the year together with his stepson. Baseball to football, basketball to hockey, team by team, player by player, Sidney maintained the dialogue between them that was peaceful and of objective interest to them both. It must have been a necessary tactic when he entered this household, wedging himself in between Jimmy and his mother.

16

"How was Michael?" Laura asked.

Sidney chuckled indulgently. "He was on a tear tonight." Like Dolores, he delighted in the happy tumult of Michael's frequent visits.

"I hope he didn't give you too much trouble."

"He was no trouble. He was an angel," Dolores declared indignantly.

"Is he asleep?"

"Conked out in his room," she said. "Dead to the world. Why don't you leave him here tonight?"

"He's got Sunday school tomorrow," said Laura.

"So, can't I get him to Sunday school? I got my son off to Sunday school every week for twelve years, And to regular school every day. And I went to work every day at the same time."

Laura recognized the criticism implicit in her words. Dolores considered her children's books little more than a frivolous pastime, an excuse not to get a job, especially now that their only child was in school. It was true that Laura didn't make a fortune from her books, but she did have an income. Besides, she liked to be home to take care of their household. But what was the use of defending herself? If she had a regular job, Dolores would probably suggest that she was neglecting her family.

"You two should get over there to Marie's," said Jimmy. "That's a great restaurant."

"That kind of food gives me heartburn," Dolores declared.

Laura stifled a groan. She could not understand why her mother-in-law had to contradict or find fault with everything that was said. Although it never seemed to bother Jimmy. It rolled right off him. He would laugh and say, "That's just the way she is."

"Did Michael eat?" Laura asked.

"Did he eat?" Dolores laughed. "Did he ever. We had our own New Year's Eve party. First he ate hot dogs, then popcorn, ice cream, cake. What else, Sid?"

Sidney shook his head. "A jelly doughnut."

"Oh, yeah, left over from breakfast. He ate like he hadn't had a square meal in days."

"I hope he doesn't get sick from all that," Laura said irritably. More than once, after a visit to his grandmother's, Michael had complained of a tummy ache.

"He won't get sick," Dolores said airily. "It's good for him to have some food he likes once in a while. All that health food isn't good for them, either. Besides, grandparents are supposed to indulge them. Right, Sid? We're the only grandparents he's got."

Sid nodded and patted her leathery hand on his shoulder.

Laura wanted to scream. Dolores always acted as if there were something suspect about Laura's parents because they had died before she'd ever met Jimmy. It's not as if that were their first choice, Laura wanted to say to her. Dolores had demanded to know why Laura used her maiden name on her books. When she tried to explain that it was a way of honoring her parents' memory, Dolores had looked skeptical. Well, what good does that do? Dolores had asked. They're dead. How about honoring your husband and your son, who could appreciate it?

"I've just got some coffee made," said Dolores. "Why don't you sit?"

"I don't think so, Ma," Jimmy said. "We've got to get up early. You know."

"All right, all right," said Dolores.

Jimmy touched Laura lightly on the arm. "I'll go get him."

"I'll get his stuff," said Dolores, following her son. "You'll never find it in the dark."

Laura sat down opposite Sidney. She knew that Jimmy still looked upon Sidney as something of an interloper in the family. Just the way Dolores saw her. It made her feel a kind of kinship with Sidney. He seemed to be the most affable, self-effacing of men. She sometimes marveled at what a feat it must have been for him to win Dolores's affection. She

18

was sure there were depths of determination in him that few people recognized. Laura couldn't imagine why he had been so determined to have Dolores in the first place. Well, that was not exactly fair. Dolores was a woman of enormous drive and energy. She loved the men in her life with a fierce loyalty. It was just her daughter-in-law she could do without.

"That boy of yours," said Sidney. "I feel twenty years younger when I'm down on the floor playing with him."

Laura smiled. "He's a bundle of energy all right."

"Yeah, I feel twenty years older after he leaves," Sidney admitted.

Laura laughed.

"And you know, he's starting to read pretty well. He was helping me read his bedtime story tonight. I guess they start them early these days."

"Oh yes," said Laura. "They know their alphabet in preschool."

"He's a great little guy."

"He really loves his Poppy," Laura said sincerely.

"Well, I love him, too," said Sidney.

Fleetingly Laura wished she could talk with her mother-in-law with the same ease she talked to Sidney. With Dolores it was more like sparring than conversation.

She stood up as Jimmy entered the room, their five-year-old son asleep on his shoulder. Michael's red Phillies baseball cap, which Jimmy had bought him at a game last summer, perched at a crooked angle on his soft brown hair. Laura walked up to him and ran a finger down Michael's flushed, round cheek. She frowned. He felt warm to her touch. She decided not to mention it.

She reached for his Donald Duck backpack, which Dolores was carrying. "Thanks for keeping him tonight, Dolores," she said.

"What? He's my grandson. I'd keep him forever if I could. I just wish there were three more just like him."

Laura turned away from the familiar refrain, which she recognized as an accusation. "Good night, Sid," she said.

Jimmy leaned over and kissed his mother's cheek.

"Start the new year right. Shave that beard off, will you?" Dolores said. "It makes you look like a bum."

Jimmy chuckled. Laura opened the door and escaped into the hall.

CHAPTER THREE

While Jimmy was taking a shower, Laura rummaged in her lingerie drawer for something sheer and lacy. She usually slept in a flannel nightshirt in the winter. The drafty old farmhouse-style Victorian that they'd bought when they came to Cape Christian to live had once been a summer home. Even though it was now winterized, it was not a house built to hold the heat. It had lots of windows and multipaned doors that rattled with the wind. Still, Laura loved this house. It seemed somehow fitting that she and Jimmy had used her modest inheritance to put a down payment on the one material thing she had craved since childhood—a home she could call her own.

Laura reached back in the drawer and pulled out the silky black nightgown that Jimmy bought her after Michael was born and she lost her pregnancy weight. At the time he gave it to her she remembered joking with him that if she wore this nightgown, she'd be pregnant again in no time. But it hadn't turned out that way. The doctors told them there was no medical problem. Their advice was not helpful. Maybe you're just trying too hard, one of them said callously. He offered no answer as to how you stopped trying hard for your heart's desire. To everyone who asked, and there were plenty of people who did, they simply said, "We hope to have another child." But Dolores was unconvinced. Last Thanksgiving Laura had walked into the kitchen and overheard Dolores saying to her sister-in-law, "She had no trouble getting pregnant the first time—when she was trying to trap my son into marrying her."

Laura slammed the drawer shut and sat on the edge of the bed. There was no appeasing that woman. She would never forgive Laura for "stealing" her son behind her back. Laura and Jimmy met in San Francisco when they were introduced by a mutual friend. She was working as a junior high school art teacher, and Jimmy was an assistant curator for one of the city's major museums. She was reluctant to meet him at first. She pictured a kind of wispy guy in a bow tie and was pleasantly surprised to find that he looked more like the defensive lineman he had been in college than an art historian. His easygoing, expansive personality was well suited to wooing patrons into parting with their collections, and Jimmy was considered a comer in the business of art.

Laura was drawn to his warmth and his self-assurance, and their relationship blossomed in an easy way. But when, despite precautions, she got pregnant, Jimmy did not hesitate. He insisted that nothing but marriage would do, and the sooner the better. For her part, Laura didn't care about a fancy wedding. She was an only child, and her parents had been killed two years before. There was no one to enjoy a wedding or fuss over it with her. But she wondered, at the time, if it wasn't going to hurt Jimmy's mother not to be included. Jimmy promised her that he would explain it all to his mother later, and within weeks they were married at City Hall. But shortly thereafter, the phone call to Dolores was explosive. Jimmy assured Laura that Dolores would get over it. Why did I ever listen to him? she wondered now.

It was Jimmy's idea to come back to Cape Christian and open the gallery. He had been losing patience with the politics of the art world for a long time, and by the time Michael was three, Jimmy was fed up with city life and with feeling cut off from his wife and child by the increasing demands of his job. He told Laura that he wanted to be his own boss, raise his son in a small town, and pursue a hands-on interest in art. He was a little worried about her reaction, but Laura was delighted with the idea. They had made one Christmas visit to Cape Christian, to bring Michael to meet his grandparents, and Laura had loved the place. Dolores had been frosty to her, but this seemed to be the perfect way to heal the old wounds. Reveling in her own happiness, Laura naively thought that her mother-in-law would be pleased and all would be forgiven. But it hadn't turned out that way.

In retrospect, Laura could understand why Dolores had reacted as she had. Any mother would be upset that her son had gotten married, had a child, and decided to ditch his career, of which she was so proud, without asking her opinion one way or the other. It was easier to blame it on the wife than to admit that her son had chosen a new life without her approval or even her knowledge. So despite what Jimmy told her repeatedly, Dolores maintained her belief that Laura had gotten pregnant, forced Jimmy to marry her, and then proceeded to sabotage his career.

Ugh, don't think about her, Laura told herself. It'll ruin the mood. She took off her clothes and pulled the slinky nightgown over her head. Even though the cold room gave her goose bumps, the nightgown felt delicious against her skin. It didn't matter what anybody said or thought. She and Jimmy had done the right thing, made the right choice. Their marriage was solid and happy, and they had a son they adored. Jimmy enjoyed having his own business and working right down the street from their home. The three of them often spent time together in the gallery in the summer, and in the winter there was a lot of free time in which to huddle in front of the fire or go out tramping in the snow. She looked forward to each day with her husband, and she had the home and family she had always dreamed of.

Laura pulled back the covers on the bed and turned down the lamp so that the room was dim. She slipped under the sheet and flicked one of her spaghetti straps off her shoulder as she heard his footsteps in the hall. My husband, she thought. And her heart seemed to well up with her love for him.

Jimmy came into the room, rubbing his clean-shaven jaw. Laura sat bolt upright in the bed and stared at him.

"Well," he murmured, eyeing her nightgown and untying his robe. "What have we here?"

Every amorous impulse had fled from her at the sight of his beardless face. "You shaved off your beard," she said accusingly.

"Yeah, I decided I was tired of it. It wasn't really me." He climbed into bed and leaned on one elbow, nuzzling her shoulder with his freshly shaven cheek.

"No, don't," she said coldly, recoiling from him.

Jimmy sat up. "What's the matter? You're not wearing that for some other guy, are you?" he asked teasingly. Laura remained stubbornly silent. "Come on," he said. "What is it?"

"You shaved it off because your mother said to, didn't you?"

"No, of course not. Don't be silly." He tried to reach for her hand, but she drew it away. Suddenly she was freezing. She crawled over the covers and reached for her heavy chenille bathrobe at the foot of the bed and put it on. "Don't you think it's a little odd that as soon as your mother says get rid of the beard, you go in and shave it off?"

Jimmy flopped back on the pillow. "She's been saying that for the last six months, if you'll recall. I just didn't feel like having a beard anymore. Am I suddenly so repulsive without it?"

"That's not the point and you know it."

"What is the point?"

"You're thirty-three years old, and you're still doing whatever your mother tells you."

Jimmy sighed. "Do we have to start on this again?"

"Why not? It's always open season on me as far as Dolores is concerned."

"It's because you take everything she says to heart. And you think I do, too. But I don't take her that seriously. I know she doesn't mean most of what she says. She's outspoken . . ."

"That's a nice way to put it," Laura fumed.

"Look, I know the things she says hurt you sometimes. Okay, she's tactless. What can I say? I grew up with her. I've seen her in action all my life. She doesn't think before she speaks, the way you do. She just blurts everything out. But she doesn't mean any real harm."

"She hates me, and she always has."

"She does not hate you."

"She blames me that you're not the next Thomas Hoving. She still thinks I trapped you into marrying me and ruined your life."

Jimmy rolled up on one elbow and smiled at her. "Sweetie, what difference does it make what she thinks? I hated all that sucking up to rich collectors just to snag a painting. And I loved you. And I still do. She can think anything she wants."

"But why can't you make her understand that?" Laura pleaded.

"Because she'll never change," he said calmly. "I guess because of what we went through when I was little—my father's death when I was so small—she's more possessive than some mothers might be. She would have found something wrong with any girl I fell in love with. She can't help herself. But I always knew that. When I met you, and I realized that I had found the one and only girl for me, I did the only thing I could. I talked you into marrying me, and then, when I was ready, I dealt with the fallout. There is no other way with Dolores. I've handled her this way all my life. I listen to her, and tweak her cheek and say yes, and then I do what I want anyway. It's always been that way. It always will be."

Laura felt her anger ebbing. She knew it was true. He was as stubborn as his mother, and as single-minded. In a way, it was that bulldozer quality of his that had attracted her, and that same quality was probably the result of years of dealing with Dolores. If he'd been any different, she wouldn't have loved him. She looked over at him, at his sparkling brown eyes, at the bemused smile on his broad, rough-hewn face.

"I told her I liked that beard. I should have known better," Laura said ruefully.

"Will you get off the subject of the beard? It was itchy. I was getting a rash from it. Besides, I thought you were just humoring me when you said you liked it."

"No," Laura protested. "I really did like it."

Now Jimmy was grinning. He reached over and pulled her to him. "Well, there will be some new whiskers coming in tomorrow. If that's what turns you on . . ."

"It does," she said, pretending to resist.

"But I thought in the meanwhile . . ." He tugged gently at the sleeves of her bathrobe until it dropped, in a heap, on the floor beside the bed.

She slid into his arms. "You're so easy to fight with," she said, laughing.

"I'm easy, period," he said, starting to kiss her.

The familiar warmth of his lips, the exciting pressure of his body against hers, began to block out the day, the world around her. She was sinking into him, enjoying the tenderness of his touch. All of a sudden, a cry interrupted their lovemaking.

"Mommy . . . I don't feel good."

Laura pulled away from Jimmy and glared at him, but there was a smile on her lips. "Your mother's junk-food diet has just kicked in."

Jimmy shook his head. "The long arm of Dolores, reaching across town, into our bedroom."

Laura sighed and got up, tying on the warm bathrobe and shuffling into her old ballet slippers. "I'm sorry, darling. I'll be back as soon as I can."

Laura started down the hallway. Michael's bedroom was at the other end of the house. "I'm coming, honey."

When she got to his room and turned on the Winnie-the-Pooh lamp beside his bed, Michael was sitting up, his face squinched into a grimace. She sat beside him and brushed his soft hair back off his forehead.

"Whatsa matter, honey?"

"I feel sick."

"Your tummy?"

"It hurts," he said.

"I heard you ate a lot of stuff at Grandma's."

Michael nodded solemnly. His eyes were like chocolate kisses, his hair as soft as silk. "I don't feel good."

"Okay, look. I'm going downstairs and get you some of your special tea, okay? Then I'll rub your tummy."

"Okay," he said pitiably.

Laura started for the stairs. Jimmy leaned against the door frame in their room, wearing just his pajama bottoms, his bare arms crossed over his wide, muscled chest.

"Tummy ache," she said. "I'm going to make some tea. This could take a while."

Jimmy nodded. "I'll go see him for a minute." As Laura started down the stairs he called after her, "Rain check?"

She looked up at him and nodded.

"Love you," he said.

"You too." She smiled and then started down to the kitchen.

* * *

The herbal tea with honey seemed to help, as it always did when Michael had an upset stomach. More than anything else, Laura suspected, it was the sugary warmth of it, the fact that Mom got up and made it for him that made him feel better.

She put the empty cup on the nightstand, plumped up his pillows, and crawled into the narrow bed beside him. He snuggled down under his quilt and rested his head against the bulky warmth of her old, familiar bathrobe. Gently she rubbed a circle on his tummy, round and round. Michael relaxed and nestled against her.

"Mommy, sing 'Thumbelina,'" he said in a drowsy voice.

Still rubbing his stomach, she began to sing softly. She couldn't help but enjoy this—not that he was sick, of course—but just that he wanted to be cuddled and comforted. He had become so independent lately that times like these were precious. For just a little while, he was her baby again.

"Sing it again," he whispered when she finished.

"How's the tummy?"

"Better," he said. "Will you sing it?"

She squeezed him and kissed the top of his head. "Sure," she said, and yawned.

She closed her eyes and began to sing again, her voice drifting off key every so often when drowsiness overcame her. Michael would pipe up with a phrase when she faltered. She heard his breathing grow deep and steady. Somewhere, in midverse, her voice trailed away and she too fell asleep, still cradling him in her arms.

She could not tell exactly what it was that woke her. Whether it was a strangled cry, a loud crack—something made her sit up in Michael's bed, alert and filled with a sense of dread. Michael rolled over, warm and heavy, deep asleep.

She sat there in the dark, the headboard uncomfortable against her neck, waiting for another sound. Had Jimmy heard it? she wondered. He was a sound sleeper. To her, his deep, untroubled slumber was just further evidence of that confidence he had. He worked hard, played hard, slept hard. That was Jimmy. But that crack was loud, she thought. It might have been enough to wake even him. Surely he would get up and check. She listened intently, but there was no other sound. Maybe she had imagined it. Or dreamed it. But she knew with a sickening certainty that the sound had been real.

Well, it didn't have to be something bad, she told herself. A squirrel landing on the roof. The wind, causing the door of the outdoor shower to open and shut with a thud. A passing car backfiring. Or it could be something . . . someone. She wanted to forget it, to sleep again, but her whole body was tense by now. Besides, she should go back to her own room. She would wake Jimmy. No easy matter. But he would go downstairs and check. He wouldn't want her to do it. Yet even as she decided to get up, Laura hesitated, her heart racing, a sickish feeling in her stomach. She extricated the folds of her bathrobe from under Michael's little, curled-up body and climbed out of his bed. The motion did not disturb his slumber. The clock on his bureau read 2:30 a.m. Laura tiptoed out of his room and pulled the door shut behind her.

Other than the dim glow of the night-light emanating from the bathroom, the hallway was dark. She started down the corridor to their room. As she reached the top of the staircase she looked down. There was a stained-glass window over the first landing that let in a little moonlight. Otherwise the downstairs was dark and quiet. She listened for a moment, then started toward their room. Just as she passed the top of the stairs, a dark figure appeared, stepping out of their doorway and into the hall.

Laura let out a gasp, a little shriek, at the sight of the man in the hall. Her heart beat furiously, and her scalp prickled with fear. "Jimmy," she whispered, but she knew it was not Jimmy. "Who is that?" she demanded, but it sounded more like a whimper.

The man approached her. He was dressed in black and wearing a ski mask over his face. As he drew near she saw that he was holding something in his gloved hand. Laura shrank back, her eyes wide, her limbs frozen with fear. "Jimmy," she cried, her voice weak. "Help."

Before she could move or think, the man was upon her. She tried to back away, groping for the banister, but the open stairwell was behind her. Swiftly he raised his arm and struck. She felt a blow to her head. She clutched at the railing, missed it, and began to fall.

CHAPTER FOUR

Laura opened her eyes, felt an acute throbbing in her head, and when she tried to move, pain ripped through her ankle. She was crumpled on the first landing, a third of the way down the stairs. The house was still dark and silent. She could feel something wet and sticky on her forehead and the side of her face. Even in the darkness she could see dark blotches down the front of her old white bathrobe.

For a moment her mind was in a fog. Then, suddenly, the image of the intruder seized her heart. She gasped, remembering, then stifled it. What if he were still here and he heard her? What was he doing here? Where was Jimmy? Why didn't he come? And Michael. Oh, my God.

The thought of her helpless child propelled her to her feet, the pain causing her to cry out as she scrambled up. She gripped the banister for support and hauled herself up the next step. Jimmy, Michael. She whispered their names like a prayer as she pulled herself up the rest of the way. At each step she looked behind her, down the dark stairwell, expecting to see him there, a figure dressed in black, looking up at her with his invisible eyes. Was he still here? her heart kept thudding. Is he here? Is he in the house? Her thoughts careened to Jimmy. Why hadn't he come? If he could come

30

to her, wouldn't he have done it? She wanted to call out his name, but she didn't dare. The man could be downstairs. He would hear her. And come back.

Laura reached the top of the steps and stopped, torn in two directions. Her room was closer, where Jimmy must be. Had to be. Could be sleeping. Or hurt. Or . . . She didn't allow herself to think further. Her heart went first to her child, her baby, the most vulnerable one. It was far down the hall, but there was a railing on this side that she could lean on. It wasn't really a choice. She had to get to Michael.

After propelling herself slowly forward along the banister, she reached the end of the hall and lunged forward, falling against the door frame of Michael's room. He was there, in his bed. Quickly her eye searched the corners of the room. They were dark, filled with indistinct shapes that could be toys or furniture, or something else. She thought how he would sometimes cry out, afraid that a monster was lurking in those corners. And she and Jimmy would throw on the light and show him there was nothing to fear. Her fingers trembled on the light switch, but she did not dare push it up. If the man were still in the house, the sudden illumination might catch his eye. She limped over to the bed and threw herself on it. Michael stirred and murmured, "No . . ." His breath was as sweet as spring on her face. She buried her face in his little pajama top.

"Thank God," she whispered. "Thank you, God."

She looked up, around, but the room was still. For a moment she just gripped him, felt his breathing, blessed him. Then she shook him and whispered, "Michael, honey, wake up. You have to come with Mommy."

Michael groaned in protest at being awakened, and then he opened his eyes.

Laura tried to smile at him. "Come on, honey," she whispered. "You have to get up."

He blinked at her and rubbed his eyes. "Why are you whispering?" he asked in a normal voice.

"Hush, baby," she said urgently. "Please, be quiet. Come with Mommy."

Still half asleep, he obediently climbed out of bed. "Where are we going?" he asked loudly.

"Honey, quiet," she pleaded. "I need your help. You have to help me walk down to Mommy and Daddy's room. I hurt my foot."

He nodded soberly. "I need my bear," he said seriously.

"Okay, get your bear. Come on," she whispered urgently.

He tucked a furry teddy bear under one arm and took her hand. Together they moved slowly down the hall. Laura grimaced with every step. Finally they reached the doorway to her room. The door was ajar, but she could not see inside.

"Okay," she said. "Michael, stop here. You wait right here for Mommy where I can see you. And don't move."

He started to protest, but she crouched down, gripping his arms and glaring into his eyes. His protest died in his throat. "Okay," he said.

With a trembling hand, she pushed open the door and looked in. The top drawers of the bureaus were open. Her jewelry box was overturned. Moonlight spilled in the windows, across the bed. Jimmy was lying on the bed. One leg was over the edge. His arms were outstretched, his face turned to the window. He never slept that way.

Maybe he did, she thought. Maybe he does. Maybe when she was asleep he turned that way every night. A little, frightened voice inside of her was crying *No, no*, but she drowned it out with a desperate chant. Maybe he did, maybe he's sleeping. Or maybe the burglar knocked him out, too. Hit him in the head and knocked him unconscious, too, so he could rob them. Yes, that had to be it. She tried to ignore the icy claw gouging at her heart. She tried to ignore the hairs standing up on her neck, the sick feeling in her stomach. She tried to ignore the presence in the room.

Not the intruder. She could see well enough in the moonlight, and he was no longer there. It was another presence—still, empty, and final. Laura refused to acknowledge it. She dragged herself over to her husband's side, pleading in her mind, bargaining with God. Let him be all right. Let him be unconscious, just asleep, and I will be . . . do . . . anything, everything . . . promise . . . anything.

His eyes were open, staring. The side of his head and the pillow were a dark, sticky mass. She touched his face, and it was cool. "Jimmy," she whispered. "Darling. It's me. It's Laura. Talk to me." His bloodied head lolled like a rag doll's. His lifeless eyes looked past her, into the next world. Suddenly the sight of him filled her with terror. She shook her head and began to back away. "Nooo . . ." she started to scream. "Nooo . . . Jimmy, nooo . . ."

"Mommy." Michael's white, frantic face in the doorway, the sound of his high, frightened voice, was like a slap in her face.

"Mommy, what's the matter? What's wrong with Daddy?"

She turned and saw him coming into the room. It was like slow motion, the sight of him pushing back the door, starting toward her, the bear dangling from his hand, as he called out for his father. Instinctively, not even feeling the pain in her ankle, she crossed the room, lunged at him, tackling him to the floor so he would not see.

"What's wrong with Daddy?" he was pleading.

One thought burned in her mind. She had to get him out of there. She had to get him out of the room. She couldn't let him see. There was a phone right there, beside the bed, beckoning to her, but if she reached for it, Michael would break free, and he would see his father. Lying there, like that, in the blood. A sight that would terrorize him for all his life. Think, she told herself. For Michael.

Part of her wanted to grab that phone. What if the man were just there, outside the door, waiting for them to emerge? But Michael was crying now. Struggling to get to Jimmy. Wriggling out of her arms. She gripped him until he yelped, "You're hurting me."

"Help me," she whispered. "Mommy needs your help." There was a phone in the next room, her studio. "Help me up. Hurry," she whispered.

"Let's wake up Daddy," he cried. "Daddy can help you."

"No, only you. Help me next door," she insisted. "I can't walk without your help."

"Why not?"

"Michael, now!" she shrieked.

Tears were running down his cheeks. Her own were dry. Her father was a military man from a long line of military men, who had systematically shamed and bullied her out of her tears—robbed her of the natural release of weeping. She knew he hadn't done it to be cruel. It was the only way he knew to behave. And she'd been dry-eyed at his funeral, as the commander would have wished. But Laura had vowed never to do that to her own child.

So, as Michael sniffled, he let her lean on his shoulder, gripping her bathrobe in his little fist. She limped into the studio, satisfied herself that no one was in that room, and locked the door behind them. She stumped over to the desk and switched on the lamp that swung out over her drawing board.

"Mommy, you're all bloody!" Michael screamed.

"Come here to me," she said. He shook his head. Now that he saw it, he didn't want to get near the blood on her bathrobe. She sank onto her desk chair, gripping his little hand, and picked up the phone.

"Don't move," she ordered him. She could feel him trembling all over.

She punched 911. "How may I help you?" said a woman's voice.

For a moment Laura thought she was going to faint. She held Michael's gaze with her own. He was sobbing now, his little shoulders heaving. Her mouth was so parched that she was not, at first, able to speak.

"May I help you?" the voice repeated.

"Help. My husband," she whispered. "Someone broke in. He's bleeding. I think . . . I think . . . he's dead."

CHAPTER FIVE

Vincent Moore turned over in his warm bed and threw an arm over Ingrid, his sleeping wife. The shrill ring of the phone woke him. He opened his eyes and tried to collect his thoughts for a moment before he reached for it.

Katy, he thought with a sickening sense of dread. His daughter, who lived in Albany, was four months pregnant and having a terrible time of it. Bleeding, bed rest, the works. Vince picked up the phone.

"Chief?"

Vince was relieved to hear the voice of Jerilyn Conlon, the seasoned dispatcher at the police switchboard. Vince squinted at the digital clock beside him: 3:45 a.m. It had to be serious if they were calling him at this hour. It wasn't a fire. The horn would be blowing. New Year's Eve. Probably a car wreck. Some reveler who'd had too much to drink, no doubt. "Yeah, what is it?" He struggled to a sitting position on the side of the bed.

Ingrid rolled over and blinked at her husband in the darkness. "Is it Katy?" she whispered fearfully.

Vince shook his head and switched on the bedside light.

"Thank God," said Ingrid. She sat up and clutched the covers to her chest, watching her husband's face turn ashen.

"Okay," Vince murmured. "Okay. The EMTs are there now? . . . Good. Call Ron Leonard, the investigator from the DA's office, and tell him to meet me there ASAP. And the coroner . . . He is? Okay, good. I want every available man fanned out in that neighborhood. I want the suspect and the weapon . . . What? . . . An hour ago? Oh, my God. All right. And Jerilyn, this is important. I want you to get Bobby McCandless to go and pick up the Barones. They live at the Seashell Condominiums on the Beach Road. Tell him no sirens. They'll be scared as hell as it is when they hear the doorbell."

Ingrid gasped.

"That's right," Vince continued. "He's the best one. He's known the family for years. Okay. I'm on my way."

Vince hung up the phone and climbed out of bed, fumbling for his pants on the chair.

"Why are you sending Bobby for Dolores?" Ingrid asked urgently. "What's happened, Vince?"

"Jimmy Reed's been shot and killed," Vince said bluntly.

Ingrid let out a terrible cry.

"I have to go," said Vince.

* * *

"Mrs. Reed," said the female paramedic in a firm, loud voice. Laura was lying on a gurney where they had lifted her. "We're going to be taking you to the emergency room in a few minutes. Do you understand?"

The house was ablaze with light now and urgent activity. The sound of footsteps thundered up and down the stairs. Three people were working around her, a young man and two women. They were taking her vital signs, immobilizing her foot. Laura reached up and clutched at the parka of the EMT who was cleaning the wound on her head. Her name tag said Kara. "My husband," Laura tried to say, but her teeth were chattering. "Michael."

"Put another blanket on her," said Kara to the man behind her. "Her pressure's dropping. We don't want her going into shock." The woman looked calmly into Laura's eyes. "Your son is right here, with your neighbor, Mrs. Garrity. She's going to look after him."

Pam Garrity's face swam into view above Laura. Laura was vaguely aware that Pam was wearing her magenta parka over her nightgown. Tears stood in Pam's eyes as she searched Laura's face worriedly.

"Laura," she said gently, "I'm going to take Michael next door. We'll put him in Louis's room." Louis, Pam's son, was Michael's best friend. "Don't you worry about him. We'll take good care of him. We won't leave him alone for a minute."

A police officer loomed over Pam's shoulder. "We'll station a man outside the Garritys' house. They'll be under constant guard."

Laura shook her head. No, she wanted to say. Stop. What's going on? But it was all very vague and far away. They had given her a shot, and everything was fuzzy.

"I want to stay with Mommy," she heard Michael cry.

Laura twisted on the stretcher to see him.

"Your mommy has to go to the hospital so we can take care of her," the paramedic explained. Then she turned to Laura. "We checked him out. He's perfectly fine. He wasn't injured in any way."

Laura reached for Michael, and he put his arms around her, put his head on her cheek. Concentrate, she thought. For Michael. "You go with Pam now," she whispered through cracked lips. "Play with Louis till I get back."

His tears were wet on her face. Pam squeezed her hand. "I'll take good care of him," she said fiercely.

Laura nodded, feeling as though she were drifting away from them on an ice floe. "Go on, sweetheart," she whispered to her son, and she felt his small hands detaching from her.

"Let's get her out of here," said the EMT named Kara, and suddenly straps were being fastened around Laura and she felt the gurney being lifted.

"Let's move," said the young man at the foot of the stretcher.

"Noooo . . ." Laura wailed as they bumped along, ignoring her feeble cries. She was being carried to the stairwell. She turned her head and saw police clustered around her bedroom door and flashbulbs going off inside the room. Men were talking in angry murmurs.

"Jimmy," she cried. He was still in there. She knew it. Still lying on their bed, all alone, while these strangers milled around their room.

Then she felt herself tilting, and she was being carried down the stairs. From this angle she could see a piece of wallpaper peeling off the uppermost corner of the stairwell ceiling.

Jimmy will have to use the extension ladder to paste that back, she thought. And then it hit her again, a blow to the chest. Nevermore, nevermore.

"Easy around this corner," said the young man in front. "It's steeper down here."

They bumped down the stairs, and Laura's teeth seemed to rattle with every bump. There was a band of pain around her head. The drugs had loosened it, but it was still there. Her eyes were gritty, but she could not cry.

"Clear the way, please," the EMT shouted at the officers by the door. A path between them suddenly appeared.

"Just a minute." The paramedics stopped short, and Laura saw a familiar face looming above her.

She licked her parched lips and whispered, "Chief Moore." She reached up and tried to grip his sleeve, but her fingers were too numb to close.

"Is she sedated?" the chief asked Kara.

"Yessir, we gave her a painkiller and a sedative. She was hyperventilating. We have to watch her closely because of that head wound."

Another man had stepped up beside the chief. He was younger and wearing a gray suit and a dark tie. There was a strange expression of misgiving in his eyes as he stared down at Laura. The chief bent down and peered at Laura. "This is Detective Leonard. He's gonna help us find the guy who did this," he said grimly. He enunciated his words slowly, as if she were deaf.

Suddenly the man in the gray suit pulled Vince to one side and spoke in a low voice. Chief Moore grimaced, as if with distaste. Then, grimly, he nodded. He turned around and spoke to Kara, the head of the EMT team. "We need to bag her hands up," he said. "Have them do a paraffin test at the hospital."

Kara raised her eyebrows and looked down at Laura quizzically. She stepped aside as Detective Leonard crouched beside the gurney and affixed plastic bags around Laura's hands, taping them at the wrist. "Does that feel okay?" he asked Laura.

She nodded at him, numb, not feeling anything.

Kara bent down and replaced Laura's hands underneath the thin blankets.

"I'll come and see you at the hospital," Vince said. He gave Laura a pat on the shoulder and straightened up.

"All right, take her on," he said.

Laura felt herself moving again. The front door was opened, and she could feel the blast of cold air mingling with the warmth of her foyer. As they started to carry her outside, the doorway was suddenly blocked. Dolores and Sidney, clothes and hair disheveled, appeared there, followed by Officer McCandless.

Dolores looked, wild-eyed, at Laura strapped to the gurney, her foot encased in a molded plastic cast, her face nearly as white as the bandage on her head. At the sight of her, Dolores's eyes filled with tears. Tenderly she brushed back the damp hair on Laura's clammy forehead. "My poor girl," she whispered. Her eyes fearfully scanned the phalanx of police officers in the house and came to rest on the chief, who had seen them arrive. He stood facing them.

"Where is my grandson?" she demanded.

"He's with the neighbor, Mrs. Garrity, next door. He'll be quite safe. The house will be guarded all night."

Sidney let out a groan, as if it were all beginning to sink in.

39

"Oh, Vincent," Dolores cried, reaching out to grip the hand of her old friend. "Dear God, tell me it's not true."

All his years of training deserted the chief. "I'm sorry, Dee," he said, and tears filled his eyes.

CHAPTER SIX

It was morning by the time they finished with her in the emergency room and wheeled her up to a private room. A nurse helped her out of the wheelchair and in between starchy sheets. Laura saw that the day was gray and bleak before the nurse pulled the blinds. A policeman was visible at the door to the room as the nurse left.

She lapsed into a half sleep of violent apparitions. The nurses shook her every time she began to nod off, for some reason having to do with her head wound. She willingly swallowed whatever pain-deadening drugs they offered and turned away the bits of soup and Jell-O that arrived. The doctors came and went, examining her, asking her questions. Groggily, with numb disinterest in her own condition, she cooperated.

Sometime during the day that seemed all twilight, Chief Moore arrived, sat by her bed, and asked her to tell him what happened. While she recounted the events, a doctor stood grimly at the foot of her bed, monitoring her strength. Haltingly Laura told the chief about the noise, and the man in the darkness, and the blow to her head. When she got to the part about finding Jimmy, she began to have trouble breathing. At the doctor's insistence, the chief let her skip over it. Then she told him about Michael and about calling 911. It was as if she were telling about something that had happened to someone else. Chief Moore did not stay long. When it was over, the doctor ordered her another painkiller.

She was allowed no visitors, but during the evening she spoke to Michael on the phone. His little voice sounded as if it were being beamed to her from another planet. She crooned something to him. A song or something. When she was done, the phone dropped from her hand.

The waking dream state continued until the middle of that night, when they finally let her fall asleep, the danger point for her head injury having passed. Her sleep was a black void, where no sound or sensation entered.

* * *

"Wake up, dear," said the nurse. Laura opened her eyes and looked around the room. Gray light filtered in through the blinds, which had been opened slightly. A day had begun. The new year. Her heart shriveled at the prospect of this day. Of this year. Of the years to come. Of her life now. Her life without Jimmy. Just a day ago she was a normal, happy woman. And now her life as a widow had begun. Laura turned her face to the pillow, wishing the oblivion of sleep would return. Blot it out.

"Oh, no, you don't," said the nurse. "Got to get yourself prettied up. You've got company coming."

"I don't want any company," Laura said dully.

But at the nurse's relentless behest, Laura got up and made some superficial effort to clean up, stumping along on her cast and crutches. Exhausted, she slumped back into the bed and sipped warm water through a straw from the cup on her bed table. The nurse gathered up crumpled towels and linens and backed out the door, making some flirtatious joke with the cop on guard.

Laura lay back in the bed and stared blankly at the blinds, wondering how she was going to manage. How to work? How to live? How to raise her son without a father? Their lives had revolved around Jimmy. They were his planets. He was their star. Their source of warmth and light. She closed her eyes and saw his face. All of a sudden the door to her room opened. Laura turned her head to look.

Chief Moore came into the room, followed by a young, uniformed female officer and a man in a suit who looked vaguely familiar.

"Mrs. Reed, how are you feeling?" asked the chief.

"Laura," she reminded him, feeling vaguely confused by his formal tone.

The chief nodded. "This is Officer Hale. She's going to be recording our conversation here." The female officer nodded to her and sat on a chair in the corner of the room, removing some sort of equipment from a briefcase.

"And this is Detective Leonard," the chief went on, indicating the man with blond hair combed back and sober gray eyes.

"You were at my house," she said dully.

Detective Leonard nodded.

"Did you catch him?" Laura asked, feeling a little spark of something—anger or vengeance. "The man who did it?"

"Not yet," the chief said uneasily.

Laura sank back against the pillow. He was on the loose. Some monster who had entered their house like a wild animal, tearing her life to shreds, and he was still free. How could she sleep there anymore? Where would she ever feel safe again? She realized, almost with a sense of shock, that she wanted him dead. She had never thought of herself as a vengeful person, but now she knew the truth. She wanted him gone, whoever he might be. Eliminated from the earth.

"Laura," said Chief Moore, "we're here because we need to clear up a few things."

Laura sighed and nodded. "Okay," she said. "Anything that can help."

"Mrs. Reed," said Ron Leonard, "why is it that you were not in bed with your husband when this incident occurred?"

His harsh tone was like a bucket of ice water in her face. Everyone had been kind to her since it happened, treating her gently, as if she were made of glass. This man was different. He seemed hostile. As if she could have prevented Jimmy's murder if she had only been in her own bed. And was it true? she wondered. Would it have turned out differently? Would Jimmy still be alive? Her voice was shaky as she replied, "I told the chief. My son was sick. I was in his room with him."

Ron nodded. "How sick was he? Was he, say, throwing up?"

"No, he had a tummy ache. I was rubbing his stomach."

"So, he wasn't sick enough to call the doctor, for instance."

Laura smiled weakly. "No. You don't call the doctor in the middle of the night for a tummy ache. Not unless it's something really serious."

Ron Leonard frowned. "So if it wasn't serious, why were you sleeping in the child's room?"

"I fell asleep cuddling him. Do you have kids, Detective Leonard?"

The detective ignored her question. "So it wasn't because, say, you and your husband were having a fight?"

Laura shook her head, insulted by the question. She felt suddenly defensive, remembering the business about his beard, about Dolores. God, it seemed so petty now, so sad somehow. Their very last moments together . . . and some of those moments were wasted, bickering about his beard. "No. I mean, we'd had a little argument, actually, but it was nothing." She looked to Vince for understanding. He avoided her mournful gaze. "It was nothing. We were . . . making up when Michael called out to me."

Ron Leonard looked at a pad of notes. "We spoke to a Mrs. Candy Walsh. You and your husband had dinner with the Walshes on the night in question."

"Yes."

"Mrs. Walsh said you might have been quarreling with your husband—you were in a bad mood, she said."

44

Laura's face turned hot with indignation. Fury, almost. And at the same time she wanted to laugh. "Candy Walsh," she exclaimed, shaking her head. "That . . ." She prevented herself from calling Candy an ugly name. "That figures," she said. Candy would never see herself as the cause of anybody's irritation.

Before she could explain further, Detective Leonard said, "Were you and your husband getting along?"

"Yes, of course," Laura said angrily. "Why are you asking this stuff? How is this going to help you to catch this killer?"

"Do you know of anyone who might want to kill your husband?"

"No," Laura said flatly. "No one. My husband was . . ." The band of pain tightened around her head again. She could not summon the relief of tears. "Everyone loved him," she finished hurriedly.

"Other women?" he asked blandly.

Laura sat up and glared at him. "No, of course not." She turned and punched her pillow up behind her.

"You know, if you don't mind my saying so, I'd expect to see you weeping over such a loss, Mrs. Reed," Detective Leonard said.

Laura looked at him furiously. "I do mind. I mind very much. If I could cry, believe me, I would."

Quickly, smoothly, he changed tack. "Do you know what this man was doing in your house?"

"Do I know . . .?" Laura asked, confused, her mounting anger at this man turning to sarcasm. "I guess he was robbing us. I'm just going by the fact that he had a gun, that he was wearing a mask, and that our house was ransacked and my husband killed."

"Technically, your house was not ransacked. A few drawers were opened and so forth. Do you and your husband have a lot of expensive jewelry?"

Laura stared at him, then shook her head. "No."

"Do you own a gun, Mrs. Reed?"

"No, I don't."

"Do you know how to shoot a gun?"

Laura's flesh began to prickle. "What difference does that make?"

"Do you?"

Laura looked at Chief Moore. She did not know the chief well, although they had a social acquaintance. He and his wife were old friends of Jimmy's family. She felt he should be stepping in here, for Jimmy's sake, if not for hers. This detective didn't seem to grasp the fact that she had just lost her husband. "Chief Moore, didn't you tell this man what happened?"

Chief Moore avoided the familiarity in her tone. "Detective Leonard and I . . . we have some confusion about the facts surrounding your husband's murder. Mrs. Reed, before we go any further, I want to inform you that you are entitled to have a lawyer present during questioning. If you want an attorney, we can hold off until we get one up here."

"A lawyer," Laura exclaimed. "I don't need a lawyer. Don't be ridiculous. Why would I need a lawyer?"

"Then let's continue," said Ron Leonard. "Do you know how to shoot a gun?"

"Yes, I do," Laura said defiantly. "My father was a commander in the navy. He taught me how to shoot a gun when I was ten years old. And if I'd had a gun, I would have shot that bastard in the face."

"Which bastard?" Ron Leonard asked.

You, Laura thought. She bit her tongue not to say it. "How dare you?" she said bitterly.

Ron Leonard nodded and then looked at her coolly, his gray eyes implacable. "How do the doctors say you're doing?"

Laura was flustered by his sudden change in tone. "All right. I'm hoping I can go home . . ." She thought of the house, without Jimmy. "Get back to my son," she mumbled. "Maybe today."

"We understand you have a sprained ankle."

"Yes, when he pushed me down the stairs."

"And a head wound. Superficial."

46

Laura looked at him with narrowed eyes. "You might not say that if it was your head."

Ron Leonard chuckled but did not look amused. "That's the medical diagnosis."

"There was blood everywhere. I was knocked unconscious."

"Scalp wounds tend to bleed a lot, no matter how minor. And you say you were knocked out because you hit your head when you fell. That, in fact, you must have been out cold for nearly an hour. I mean, we have an hour here that's unaccounted for between the time your husband was killed and the time you called 911."

"So?" Laura demanded.

"So, this killer . . ." He drew out the word. "He shot your husband point-blank, but he only gave you a tap on the forehead, and then you fell and did the rest."

Laura turned to Chief Moore. "What are you saying here? Am I to blame for how hard the guy hit me? Do you think I want to be alive?" Her voice rose to a cry. And then she thought of Michael and felt guilty. Yes, I want to live for Michael.

"Look," she said more calmly, "I don't know why he didn't kill me, too. Maybe he was in a hurry, maybe he meant to. I don't know. I don't know what this man was doing . . ."

"If there was a man," said Ron Leonard.

She stared at him. Her blood seemed to freeze in her veins.

"If?" she said.

"Do you know how much your husband's life was insured for, Mrs. Reed?"

"*If* there was a man . . .?"

"I'll tell you how much he was insured for. James Reed Jr. was recently insured for five hundred thousand dollars. That's a lot of insurance for such a young man. With a small business."

Laura's head was spinning. "Richard advised us . . . it was term insurance. Richard Walsh . . . he said it was important that we be protected, while Michael was young. Ask him. He'll tell you."

"We did speak to Mr. Walsh. He said that your husband was reluctant to buy that much insurance, but that you convinced him to do it . . ."

"Because he convinced me," Laura cried. "Richard said it was the responsible thing to do, for Michael's sake . . ."

Ron Leonard appeared to be calculating on his pad. "Now murder is considered an accidental death. With double indemnity, that's a million dollars, Mrs. Reed. You're quite a wealthy young woman."

Laura looked at Chief Moore, but his normally friendly face was somber. She looked back into the cool eyes of Ron Leonard. Her heart was thundering. She could feel the blood rising, like a tide, to her face. "What are you saying?" she asked. But she knew. Her mind could hardly grasp it, but she did know.

The expression on his face was impassive, but there was a steely edge to his voice. "I'm saying, Mrs. Reed, that we have a few problems with your story."

"My story?" she breathed. As if it were some fiction she had created. Laura clutched the sides of the bed. The room was beginning to spin.

CHAPTER SEVEN

Vincent Moore, chief of the Cape Christian Police Department, cradled the phone receiver on his shoulder and beamed down at the photographs of a sleeping infant.

"I got the pictures this morning," he told his wife, Ingrid, on the other end of the phone connection. "What a little doll. How's Katy feeling today?" Ingrid was up in Albany, helping out Kate, who, after her risky pregnancy, had just given birth without complications to her second child, a little girl. Their son, Robbie, who lived in Philadelphia, had one son, so this made three grandchildren for Vince and Ingrid.

Ingrid reassured him that Kate was doing well, but that she was sleeping at the moment. "Tell her I'll call her later," said Vince. He wished he could be there to see the new baby, but it would have to wait until his vacation in September. May was the beginning of high season in a resort area like Cape Christian. He could not possibly slip away. "When are you coming home?" he asked Ingrid wistfully.

His wife promised it would just be a few more days. As she was describing her plans for the next few days, Vince took a sip of coffee from a cardboard cup, and his eyes scanned the squad room. All of a sudden he saw a familiar figure in the doorway.

He straightened up on his seat and wiped off the coffee ring on his desk with a paper napkin. "Honey," he interrupted Ingrid, "I gotta go. Dolores is here." Ingrid understood, and they said a quick good-bye as Vince motioned for Dolores to come into his office.

Vince Moore had known Dolores, and her late husband, Jim Reed, since they were children together. He remembered their parents. He'd attended their wedding, and he could still recall the night when Jim Jr. was born. The death of Jim Reed Sr. had been like the loss of a brother to him. He and Ingrid tried to remain close to Jim's widow and young son. Ingrid and Dolores used to take their kids to the beach together in the summer and sit under neighboring umbrellas while Jimmy, Robbie, and Kate played in the sand.

Vince sighed. He hated to see Dolores coming toward his desk. He hated to face her empty-handed yet again. He knew what Dolores was seeking, but so far he could not act. He could not make an arrest.

Vince, Ron Leonard, and the county DA, Clyde Jackson, a handsome black man with a Princeton education and a penchant for custom-tailored suits, had spent endless hours poring over the evidence they had. To varying degrees they all held the same suspicion, but officially Laura's version of the story stood. Officially they were seeking a masked intruder who had entered the Reed house through an unlocked window and shot James Reed Jr. in his bed, stealing a Rolex watch and a few pieces of jewelry in the process. They had no witnesses, and they had never found the murder weapon, a .38-caliber Smith & Wesson revolver. Dutifully the local press reported the story of a random burglary turned to murder. And for weeks afterward Vince had had to employ extra men to see old ladies home at night, to investigate every noise outside every open window.

But many people in the town of Cape Christian seemed to have absorbed, almost instantly, the secret suspicions of the law enforcement officers on the case. Jimmy Reed had been a local boy, and his widow was an outsider. He had been murdered in his bed, and she had been left virtually unharmed, to enjoy a million-dollar windfall. It was axiomatic in law enforcement that the premier suspect in such a killing was the spouse. No one in the neighborhood had seen any suspicious persons in the area. There was no evidence in the house of the mystery intruder—no fibers, no hairs. A killer who had left no trace of himself was an oddity indeed. An hour had elapsed between Jimmy's murder and Laura's call to the police. An hour in which, Ron, Vince, and Clyde Jackson all suspected, the murder weapon and a small cache of jewelry had been tossed into the sea and carried off on the outgoing tide.

But there was no proof. No evidence to take to trial. A paraffin test they did on Laura's hands suggested that she had not fired a gun. At least not without gloves on. And against the advice of her attorney, Laura had submitted to a lie detector test and passed. She expected the results to clear her in the minds of the police and the people in this town. She was wrong about that.

Dolores settled herself on the chair beside Vince's desk and placed a square of crumb cake wrapped in waxed paper on his blotter. "Here," she said. "For your diet."

"Thanks a lot," Vince said ruefully, patting the roll around his middle. Dolores often brought him something when she came by the station these days. She no longer came every day, but she was still vigilant. In those first weeks after Jimmy's death, Dolores was a fixture here, sobbing and railing by turns, demanding information, while her second husband, Sidney, supported her quietly. These days she was as neatly coiffed and as turned out as ever, but there were dark circles under her eyes that were not camouflaged by her careful makeup. She seemed to have shrunk lately, aging years in only months. Everybody knew how she had mourned her son, was still mourning him.

"Is Ingrid still up in Albany with Kate?" Dolores asked.

Vince nodded. "I got these in the mail this morning," he said proudly, passing the Polaroids across the desk.

Dolores studied them avidly. A smile played on her lips, but her eyes were sad. "Isn't she beautiful," she exclaimed. "That's your third?" she asked.

Vince nodded.

Dolores sat back and sighed. "That's wonderful."

"How's your grandson doing?"

Dolores pressed her lips together. "Michael? He's an angel. He's doing okay. Of course, you know kids. They're little actors. They can keep the worst things hidden, as if nothing had happened."

Vince nodded grimly. "Don't I know it."

"We're trying our best to help him. All of us. My husband and I. Our friends. You know."

"Your daughter-in-law is agreeable to visits?"

Dolores's face turned to granite at the mention of Laura. "Sidney picks him up. I don't speak to her. Sidney has been the go-between. He's a saint. I don't know how he can stand to even talk to her, but he does it so that I can see Michael."

Vince was well aware of how Dolores felt. At first she resisted the notion that Laura might be guilty. Laura was a wife and a mother. It was unthinkable. But something inside of Dolores was deeply shaken at her son's funeral when his widow did not weep. People tried to explain it to her. Shock, they said. She's in a daze. Laura herself apologized, saying that her father had abhorred weeping and had conditioned her to hold in her tears. But Dolores could not accept that. She had been a young widow once. She knew about heart-broken grief. Then, alerted by the probing questions of Ron Leonard, she had begun to wonder about Laura's story. She had gone over it with the police, and then with Sidney, until he was weary of her suspicions. But with each passing day her suspicions grew firmer. Now her heart was hardened against her daughter-in-law.

For his part, Vince was dragging his feet. He knew the facts as well as anybody, but a part of him wanted to believe the girl. She was quiet and serious, although it was hard to tell what she had been like before this tragedy. It was true that no one ever saw her weep, even at the funeral, but he was convinced that she was grieving. Whenever he saw her after Jimmy's death, he always thought of that phrase from "*La Belle Dame sans Merci*," "alone and palely loitering," because it seemed to suit her. Of course, when he mentioned it to Ingrid, who had been a high school English teacher, Ingrid reminded him in her tactful way that the phrase referred to the knight in the Keats poem, not the woman. It was the man who had been abandoned and was pining for the cruel maiden.

"Laura was in to see me a little while ago," said Vince. "Just wanted to know if we had anything new."

Dolores's eyes blazed with anger. "I'll bet she was."

Vince pretended not to understand her meaning. Laura had not been charged with any crime. He had to maintain an appearance of objectivity. "The posters have been bringing in some calls. That big reward is very tempting to people," said Vince. Laura had offered $250,000 of Jimmy's life insurance money as a reward for information leading to the apprehension of Jimmy's killer. Gary Jurik had designed the posters, and they were extremely eye-catching. Lots of people had called in tips. So far, all the tips had proved useless.

"Yes, well, she's pretty safe offering that reward, isn't she? I mean, it's not like she has to worry that anyone will ever claim it," Dolores said bitterly.

"Dolores," Vince said, patting her hand gently. "You mustn't give up hope. If that guy is out there, we will find him one of these days."

"And if there is no guy?"

"This is an ongoing investigation," Vince said firmly.

"Well, I wanted to stop by today before I left. Sidney and I are going away for a few weeks. One of his big customers, the guy that owns Stella di Mare in Atlantic City, offered us the use of his condo in Florida, and Sidney says if I don't go and get a rest, he's going to divorce me," she said with a hollow chuckle.

"That sounds like a good idea," Vince said sincerely. "Get away for a while. Get a change of scene."

Dolores handed him a slip of paper. "This is the phone number of the place in Florida. If there is any news . . . any-thing . . ."

Vince closed his hand over hers as he took the paper. "I will call you at once. I promise you that, Dee."

"All right, Vince," she said wearily, standing up. "I've got to go home and finish packing."

Vince stood up and took her hand. "You try and enjoy yourself, and I'll manage things at this end. Your Jimmy is always on my mind. We're never gonna rest until his killer is locked up. Okay?"

"Neither am I," she said grimly.

"Thanks for the cake," said Vince.

"Give my love to Ingrid and Katy when you talk to them."

"I will," said Vince.

He watched her walk away, her shoulders stooped as if under a great weight, and he felt a familiar anguish. Sometimes in the past he'd felt bored by the job, and he used to daydream about retirement and the RV he and Ingrid were going to buy. But ever since that horrible New Year's Eve, all his daydreams were about finding that elusive, crucial piece of evidence that would bring to justice the killer who had stolen the life of Jimmy Reed. If it was Laura Reed, they would find a way to prove it. He owed it to Dolores and to her grandson, and to the memory of his long-lost friend, Jim Reed. This crime sickened him, outraged his every instinct, as a police officer and a human being. An innocent man should not be killed in his bed and no one made to pay.

CHAPTER EIGHT

The spring day clamored at the window, now opened to the air. Sun and the song of birds poured in, and the scent of lilacs wafted through the screen. Come out and play, the day cajoled her. Inside the house, most persistent of all, was Michael, reminding her that she had promised to take him to the marina to see the boats. Finally she had agreed. She had made a plan. This was the day.

Laura squinted out the window at the unwelcome sight of the sun. The winter had been perfect for her, a thin gray cloak she could wear, shivering. She went out only for the most urgent purposes, to get food, to pick up Michael at school. It usually took her most of the day to summon the will to leave the house. Then, in the cold and early darkness, she could bundle up, hiding herself from the narrowed eyes, the whispers that hissed in her wake. But ever since the first weak sunny days in April, her depression seemed only to increase. The light of day seemed to dawdle on endlessly, and she felt vulnerable, being around town without the armor of a heavy coat, a hat pulled down low on her head. People were free to study her face, to see her flinch from their cold stares. It was heartache enough to be a widow, to face each long day without Jimmy. But to be suspected . . .

The ringing of the doorbell made her jump. "I'll get it," Michael cried, but Laura leapt up and pulled him back.

"No," she barked. Then she said more calmly, "I'll get it."

It was broad daylight on Chestnut Street. It was a beautiful day when people were out strolling. She wondered if she would ever feel safe again. Certainly not in this house. For the first two months she had hired a security guard to watch the house at night. She had moved to the bedroom across the hall from Michael. She'd talked to Richard Walsh about putting the house up for sale, but he'd advised her not even to try it right now. She would be besieged by the curious, the voyeurs, but no one would want to buy it. Everyone knew it was a tainted place. A house where a man had been murdered in his own bed.

Laura opened the door a crack and saw a boy holding a small bouquet of flowers in a glass bowl. The truck from Scott's Flower Shop was idling at the curb. Laura tipped the boy and thanked him, taking the flowers inside and placing them on the hall table. She opened up the card, but she knew what it would say: "From a friend." She had been receiving these bouquets twice a month since Jimmy's death. When the first bouquet arrived, she had been puzzled, even frightened for an instant, by the anonymous message. Then, almost immediately, she'd recognized the printing on the card and was consoled. Gary Jurik was one of the only people in town who was still kind to her—who did not seem to assume she was a murderess. But when she'd tried to thank him, he'd reddened and pretended to know nothing about the flowers.

Maybe we should stop by his house on the way to the marina, she thought. The last time they'd spoken he had asked her to come by and see his new paintings before they went to the gallery. Richard Walsh managed the affairs of the gallery these days. That was fine with Laura. She could not bear even to go in there anymore. But she knew Gary would genuinely appreciate her opinion. Without Jimmy's encouragement, they were both unsteady, missing their most trusted critic and supporter. For her part, Laura had not picked up a pen or paintbrush since the day Jimmy died.

"Maybe we'll stop by and see Uncle Gary on our way," Laura said to Michael.

"Okay," said Michael. "Can we go now?"

Laura sighed. Two stops would not seem like a major project for most people, but to Laura it was a complicated mission. All morning Michael had played quietly, not wanting to upset her, to send her back into her shell. They had talked about going to the marina the night before, and Laura had even washed her hair in preparation. Often she'd neglected to wash it for days on end in these last months. But when this morning came, she had almost backed out of the plan again. Michael had coaxed her, using all his childish wiles.

She had put on a long gray dress with a small print of flowers. It was Jimmy's favorite spring dress of hers. The day was fine. There was no excuse to delay it any longer. She tied on a wide-brimmed straw hat that hung on a hook there. When Michael saw her adjusting the hat in the hall mirror, he jumped up from his train set, grabbed his baseball cap, and jammed it on his head.

Suddenly the phone rang, and they both looked at it. Then they looked at each other, Laura with a weary expression in her eyes, Michael with a determined set to his jaw. Michael jumped up, ran to pick up the receiver, and said abruptly, "We can't talk now. We're going out."

"Michael," Laura protested, "give me that phone."

Reluctantly Michael handed her the receiver.

"Hello?" Laura said tentatively.

"I can see I called at the wrong time," said Marta Eberhart.

Laura smiled at the sound of her editor's voice. Luckily Marta was the sort of person to be amused, not offended, by Michael's maneuver.

"I've been promising him we'd go to the marina," said Laura. "He's sure I'm going to back down." Laura and Marta's business relationship had long encompassed an easy friendship, albeit at long distance. "Are you home?" Laura asked, picturing Marta in her one-bedroom apartment on East 65th Street, chicly decorated in shades of white and beige, with Marta's clothes, shoes, and books strewn over the expensive furnishings.

Marta sighed. "I'm home. Just wishing some hunk like Michael would want to take me to a marina. Instead, I'm going to an all-girls aerobics class run by a former marine drill instructor. Listen, I'm not going to keep you. I just wanted to see how you were feeling."

Laura glanced at Michael, who had sat back down on the floor and was crashing soldiers together with an angry look on his face. "I'm doing okay. I haven't done any work yet . . ."

"I didn't call about that. It's Saturday. I'm off duty. Listen, you get going. I know that little guy of yours is getting impatient."

"It's true," said Laura, wishing she could be magically transported to the island of Manhattan, where she could just flop down on Marta's couch, drink some wine and talk for hours, go out to dinner, and then fall asleep on Marta's foldout sofa. Once or twice, when Jimmy was alive, he had urged her to do just that, and it had been a sybaritic getaway from her everyday life. I need that now, Laura thought wistfully. How I would love to get away from here. From this town. From everything.

Everything but my son, she thought, looking sadly, lovingly, at his head bent over his warring soldiers. "I'd better go," she said.

"You take care," Marta said before they hung up.

"Okay," Laura said softly to her little boy, crouched among his toys. "I'm ready."

Michael looked up and then smiled broadly. "All right." He scrambled to his feet and slipped his hand into hers, as if for courage. Together they started out the door.

* * *

The house where Gary Jurik and his mother lived was gray, with weathered cedar siding, and it sat isolated on a spit of land overlooking Cable Bay. It was a large rancher built in the fifties, but it had been completely renovated to accommodate Gary's needs. It was a much nicer house than the one Gary had grown up in. The insurance settlement from the accident enabled them to move here. There had been four boys in the car on the snowy night of that accident. Jimmy and another boy had escaped unhurt. The driver had been killed, and Gary had been permanently disabled. Gary's lawsuit had dragged on for several years, but now he and his mother lived in relative comfort here. Laura knew that some people even envied them this house, whispered that he'd done all right for himself. The people in this town could be so cruel and small-minded, she thought. As if a check could compensate for the loss of your limbs or your loved one.

She knocked on the door while Michael fidgeted on the steps. Wanda Jurik answered the door, looking as disheveled as if she had been torn away from doing demolition work, although Laura could hear the television running in another room, a morning talk show playing. Wanda looked blankly at Laura, as if she did not recognize her. That was nothing unusual for Wanda. She seemed to be in a constant state of preoccupation.

"Is Gary here?" Laura asked.

"Where else would he be?" Wanda asked accusingly.

Lots of places, Laura thought irritably. He's in a wheelchair, not an iron lung. She remembered Jimmy's assessment of Wanda. She likes to keep him helpless, he had said. Jimmy was usually shrewd about people, but in this case Laura thought he'd missed the mark. Wanda never seemed very happy with this life they led. She always acted as if she were doing a life sentence of hard time.

Laura sighed. "May we see him?" she asked.

Wanda looked away from her. "He's in that studio of his," she said.

Laura had only been in the house once or twice before. She looked around uncertainly, and Wanda pointed toward

59

the back of the house. Laura shepherded Michael in front of her, deciding to find her way rather than inquire further from the unwelcoming Wanda.

But the studio was not hard to find. It took up an area that must once have been a deck but was now enclosed. The walls of windows looked out on the water. Behind the house was not so much a yard as a dune, stubbly with rocks and beach grass. At the edge of it was a dock that jutted out into the gentle waters of the bay. Today those waters were deep blue, and seagulls wheeled above, their cries audible through the panels of windows. Gary, who was sketching at his desk as they came in, turned and greeted them with a shy but delighted smile. Michael ran over to him and began to clamber onto his lap.

Laura winced. "Michael, don't," she said, but Gary was happily pulling the bill of the boy's cap over his eyes and tickling him under the arms. Michael's squeals of protest filled the quiet room. Laura smiled. Gary picked up a box of markers and handed it, and a piece of paper, to Michael. "Here," he said. "Make me a picture of that lighthouse down there."

Michael peered across the bay to where Gary was pointing and then, sprawling out on the floor, set to work.

"We're on our way to the marina," Laura explained casually. "I thought we'd stop by and see the new paintings."

Gary nodded. He understood the life she was leading these days—the confinement of it. Laura was speaking as if it were a normal thing for them to be on an outing. Once upon a time it had been. But not since Jimmy died. "It's good you're getting out," he said. "I know it's hard when you feel like everybody's looking at you—pointing at you behind your back. And you don't feel much like leaving the house to begin with."

Laura looked at him gratefully. She realized they were alike in a way, their lives circumscribed by one violent incident they'd had no control over. "How come you don't look at me like the others do?"

Gary shrugged and wheeled his chair over to some canvases by the far wall. "I know you," he said. "I know how you are."

Laura followed him and sat on a wooden ladderback chair by the wall. She studied the new paintings. Instead of the usual light-filled architectural watercolors, these were beautiful but gloomy views of the wetlands that abounded in the area. Land turned to water, then melded into the sky. It was lonely marshland, populated by shore birds, protected from trespassers by the treacherous changeability of its deceptively placid surface.

"What do you think?" he said.

"Well, they'll never replace the building series in popularity," she said.

Gary stared at his work, trying to stifle the urge to defend it.

"But I think these are the most beautiful paintings you've ever done."

He looked at her, his face alight, his cheeks as pink as a child who'd just gotten a puppy.

"Well, don't look so surprised," she said. "You must know how good they are."

"I wasn't sure," he said.

"Well, they are," Laura said gently. "Although they're very somber, compared to what you usually do."

"There's something very moody and sad about the wetlands. I park the van down at the bird sanctuary. There are never any people around. Although I have to be a little careful about rolling up on those wooden bridges over the marshes. If I get stuck in that spring mud, I could be there for a week until somebody found me," he said with a laugh.

"Maybe you shouldn't go by yourself," she said.

"I like being by myself," he said firmly.

Wanda Jurik entered the studio and looked around. "I'm making tuna fish for lunch," she said flatly. "Do you want white bread or rye?"

The color faded from Gary's face. "Do you two want to stay for lunch?" he asked hopefully.

Laura jumped up. She could see Wanda purse her lips at this disagreeable suggestion. "We've got to be going. Come on, Michael."

Michael picked up his piece of paper and waved it at them triumphantly. "Look at my picture."

Gary took it and studied it. "That's very good, Michael."

"White bread or rye?" Wanda demanded.

"Rye," Gary said quietly, not looking at her. Wanda turned and left the studio.

"Thanks for showing me the paintings," said Laura.

"When are you going to have some work to show me?" Gary asked gently.

Laura shook her head. "I don't know. Marta just called me this morning, although she always is careful not to ask. I have another book due on this contract, but I'm just too numb, Gary."

Gary nodded. "I know. But if you tried doing some work, it might take your mind off of things. I'd be glad to look at sketches. It's not the same as Jimmy, but . . ."

"Oh, I would welcome your help," she assured him. "Maybe you're just what I need. And I'm sure you're right. You know, these books about Raoul all come out of fantasies that I had as a child. I mean, I was a lonely kid. My father was a lot older than my mother, and he was . . . well, he didn't mean to be harsh, but he was a stiff person, very demanding, I guess you could say. I know he loved me—I never doubted that—but life in our house was never fun or lighthearted. And since we moved all the time, I rarely had a friend that got very close. So I lived in my own little world a lot of the time. And that was a happy place for me. But it's one thing to slip into that world as a child. It's another as an adult."

"Sure. I understand."

"I'm just trying to get through the days now."

"Well, if you get anything started, I'd love to look at it. Life has to go on, you know."

"That's what they say." She sighed. "But really, Gary, thanks. Thanks for being a friend through all this."

For a moment there was an awkward silence. Then Laura said, "Well, we'd better be going. Michael, say good-bye to Uncle Gary and come on."

"I'm going to hang this on my bulletin board," Gary said solemnly, still holding Michael's picture. "You two have a good time at the marina. Or I could come with you if you want."

"This is something I have to do alone," Laura said grimly.

"Oh, I wasn't suggesting . . .," he said hurriedly.

"I just have to do it," said Laura. "To prove that I can."

"I understand," he said.

I know you do, she thought. Michael kissed Gary on the cheek and bolted for the door. Laura leaned over and kissed him on the other cheek. "Maybe next time," she said. Just then Wanda walked back into the room.

"Good-bye, Mrs. Jurik," said Laura.

"Good-bye."

After Laura and Michael were gone, Wanda looked at her son. "Do you want to eat here or in the kitchen?"

"I'll come in the kitchen," he said.

"You know, you're wasting your time being nice to her and that boy. You act like a little puppy dog when she's around."

"Mother, they are my friends. It's none of your business."

"People say she killed him. I say, so what if she did? The world's better off without him."

"Don't you dare say that," Gary snarled.

"Why shouldn't I say it? It's the truth. Jimmy Reed as good as put you in that chair you're sitting in."

"It was an accident, Mother. I don't want to listen to this."

"It is true, and you know it," Wanda cried. "He ruined all our lives, and then he went off on his merry way. He never cared about what happened to you. If you ask me, Jimmy Reed got what he deserved."

"I didn't ask you. And don't ever say that again," said Gary, gripping the arms of his chair until his knuckles turned white.

Wanda shook her head. "You'll never learn," she said.

CHAPTER NINE

Michael broad-jumped along the planks of the pier, exclaiming joyously at the sight of the boats, although his shouts of glee also had something to do with the beauty of the day and the fragile presence of his mother walking slowly along behind him. The sky was pastel blue, hung with soft tendrils of clouds. The water was deep sapphire, and the boats, anchored side by side down the docks, gleamed dazzling white against its dark, shimmering surface.

Michael stopped to wait for Laura. When she reached him he said, "I wish we still had Dad's boat."

"I know," she said. Dad's boat, Dad's smile, Dad's life. We would like them all back, please. "But Michael, I don't know how to run a boat. And you're a little young to be captain yet."

"Yeah, I know," he said.

Laura had not been trying to sell the boat after Jimmy's death. She had been altogether too numb and disoriented to make any moves at all. But Richard Walsh had been looking for a boat like Jimmy's for his dad, and he'd offered a fair price, so Laura had agreed to the sale. She'd given a thought to saving it for Michael, for when he grew up, but Sidney had pointed out gently that it would be easier to buy another boat when the time came than to store and maintain Jimmy's boat all those years.

"I'm sure when you're big enough, we can get another boat," she said, trying to sound positive.

Michael nodded, his buoyant mood deflated.

"You want an ice cream?" Laura asked impulsively, goaded by the look of sadness in his eyes.

Michael looked astonished. "Before lunch?"

"Sure," she said. The prospect of ice cream distracted him from thoughts of the lost boat. In truth, they'd hardly ever used the boat. They'd hardly had a chance. "Come on," said Laura, and he took her extended hand amiably.

They walked down the pier to Boat People, a general supply store that had made a tidy fortune for its shrewd, hard-working proprietors, Wendell and Fanny Clark. Laura hesitated before going in. Wendell and Fanny had been in Florida all winter, but they had been back since April. No doubt they had heard everything, made up their minds about her by now.

Stop, she told herself. Your son is sad and wants an ice cream. That's all that matters. She pushed open the screen door for Michael and waved to Wendell Clark, who was behind the counter.

Wendell seemed to blanch at the sight of them. He began to busy himself with the shelves behind him, as if hoping they might leave without his having to speak to them. But Michael marched right up to the ice-cream case.

"Hi, Mr. Clark," Michael said unselfconsciously.

Wendell, a grandfather himself, turned and looked sadly at the boy. "Hello, Michael," he said. Then he grimaced at Laura, trying to smile. Laura recognized his awkward expression. Sometimes it wasn't hostility. Sometimes it was just that people had trouble knowing what to say to her.

"Beautiful day, isn't it," said Laura.

"Indeed it is," said Wendell, seeming relieved. "Can I get you anything?"

Laura ordered Michael an ice-cream cone and handed it down to him.

"On the house," Wendell insisted, and would brook no protest.

Laura thanked him and turned to Michael. "Don't let it drip," she said.

"I won't," Michael promised gravely. "Can I go outside?"

Laura hesitated. Just then Fanny Clark emerged from the storeroom. She looked at them and then at her husband, her eyebrows raised like two little warning flags. "Hello, dear," she said to Michael. "Hello, Laura. How are you?"

"Hi, Miz Clark. Can I go out, Mom, please?"

Already the ice cream was beginning to ooze over the edge of the cone, and Laura glanced worriedly around at the sturdy but deceptively expensive merchandise in the store. She wanted to flee from the store, and Michael's dripping cone was the perfect excuse. We have to go now. Excuse us, please. But a stubborn little voice inside was insisting. *You don't need to make excuses. You were the victim of a horrible crime. Do you want your son to see you slinking away from people? As if you and he were somehow to blame?* No, she thought. Never.

"You may go out and sit on the bench in front of the store and eat that ice cream," she said calmly.

"Okay," he agreed.

"I'll be right out. You stay on that bench, hear me?"

"I will," he said, slamming the screen door behind him. She followed him almost to the door and watched him settle himself contentedly on the bench, swinging his sneakered feet, watching the boats down the docks bobbing lazily in their slips.

Fanny came out from behind the counter. "He just gets bigger every time I see him. He looks more and more like his father."

Laura nodded. "Yes, he does. He's a great comfort to me."

"We were terribly sorry to hear about Jimmy," said Fanny.

"Thank you. The flowers you sent were lovely."

"Least we could do. We've known Jimmy all his life." Fanny shook her head. "It's hard to believe something like that could happen."

Why did it sound like an accusation? Laura thought. It was just a statement. And it was true. She could hardly believe it herself.

"I know. It's been a nightmare for us."

"Right here in Cape Christian. It's the kind of thing you'd expect in Philadelphia or something. But not here." Fanny shook her head. "He broke in your house and just shot Jimmy in his bed, they say."

"That's right," Laura said uneasily.

"I don't know how you can continue to live in that house. If that happened to Wendell, I'd be out of there the next day. Nothing would make me stay there."

Unless I killed him, right? Laura wanted to ask. She could feel the anger rising in her again. And where would you have me go? she wondered. Who would I go to? "It has not been easy," she said with all the dignity she could muster, "but we are doing the best we can."

"You're looking well," said Fanny, and this time there was an unmistakable note of disapproval in the older woman's voice.

"Thank you. Did you have a good winter?" Laura asked politely, determined not to flinch.

"Oh, you know, we love it in Florida. The kids all came down, and it was fun. But we're always glad to get back. I get bored. I miss the store."

Laura smiled thinly and nodded. "Well, I promised Michael we'd look at the boats," she said, turning toward the door. She could hardly wait to get away. She edged out to where she could get the bench into her view. She glanced around and did not see her son. She rushed to the door and pushed it open. The bench was empty.

"Michael," she cried.

"What is it?" Fanny asked.

"He's gone," Laura cried. "Michael," she wailed. Her heart began to pound as she bolted out the door. The sunshine reflecting off the water was blinding after the dimness of the store. Laura shaded her eyes and looked frantically up and down the pier. There was no sign of him. "Oh, God, no," she whispered weakly. No, she thought. This can't be happening.

"Take it easy," said Fanny, right behind her. "Sometimes they wander off."

"He can't swim," Laura cried. "Why did I let him sit out here? Oh, God, please, no . . ."

"I didn't hear a splash," Fanny said sensibly. "We would have heard a splash, or heard him yelling." Wendell, noticing the anxiety in their voices, came outside and joined them on the pier.

The sunny skies seemed to mock her. Am I cursed? Laura wondered. Is this it? Will this place take everything I love from me? Is this the day I lose everything I have left? It was possible. It could happen. The unthinkable could happen just like that. She knew all too well. "Michael!" she shrieked. She turned to Wendell and grasped his shirt. "Help me," she cried. "Do something. Call the police."

"Calm down," said Wendell, but his face was dead white. "He'll turn up. Michael!" he bellowed, and his voice shook.

"Here I am, Mom," called a little voice.

Relief flooded through Laura, making her weak. It was not the end of the world. Life would go on. It was the first moment she was glad of that in months. She whirled in the direction of the voice as Wendell patted her arm and turned back toward the store. Michael was standing on a seat in the stern of an enormous sailboat, in a slip halfway down the second dock off the pier.

Laura rushed down the dock toward him. "What in the world are you doing on that boat?" she cried. "Get off of there."

"He asked me," Michael said, pointing to a man emerging from the enclosed, windowed cabin. Laura lifted Michael off the boat and squeezed him fiercely for a moment before setting him down on the dock. Then she turned and stared at the man in the cockpit. He had a taut, muscular body and moved with an air of tension unusual in a sailor. His eyes were bright blue, and his black hair was shot through with silver. He wore a khaki workshirt and jeans, and his forearms were tanned, his face lined with exposure to the weather. For a moment she thought she might know him. Something about him sounded in her like a few notes of a vaguely familiar melody, and then it was gone.

"I'm sorry, is something the matter?" he asked. "Your boy was admiring my boat, so I invited him aboard to have a look around."

Laura clutched Michael close to her. "You invited him aboard? What's the matter with you?" she demanded. "Are you crazy? This is a five-year-old child!"

The man made a helpless gesture. "He said you were right in that store. It's not like I was going to take him out for a sail . . ."

Laura began to shake. "Did it ever occur to you, even for a moment, that I might be missing him?"

"I'm sorry," said the man. "Really, I didn't think . . ."

"You certainly didn't," Laura said. "For all I knew, he'd fallen in the water and drowned." Her voice cracked.

The man watched her warily.

Laura forced herself, as she had been taught, not to cry. She crouched in front of Michael and stared him in the eyes. "I told you never, ever to go off with a stranger."

"I didn't go off," Michael protested.

"Don't you dare pretend you don't know what I mean. I have told you a million times, and the minute my back is turned . . ."

Michael hung his head. "I'm sorry . . ."

"Did he do anything to you?" she demanded.

"Hey," the sailor protested angrily.

"No," Michael said miserably. "He was just showing me the boat."

"Well, he's okay," Fanny said firmly, smoothing Michael's hair. "That's the main thing."

"Come on," Laura said shortly. "We're going."

"But the boats," Michael cried.

69

"Don't argue with me. We're going. You've seen all the boats you're going to see for this day."

"Mom," he pleaded.

"Don't 'Mom' me. Come on."

Laura turned to Fanny but could hardly manage a smile. "Thank you for helping me," she said stiffly.

"It's all right," Fanny murmured. "I'm just glad everything's all right."

Laura shook her head and began to hurry away with Michael in tow.

The man climbed out of his boat and up onto the dock next to Fanny. He watched Laura fleeing with Michael, a troubled look on his face.

"Don't take it personally," Fanny advised. "She's not thinking straight."

"I really didn't mean any harm," he said. "I guess it was stupid, but the boy said his mother was right here . . ."

Fanny sighed as Laura and Michael disappeared from view. "It's not really your fault. She's very high-strung. She's been through a lot. Her husband was murdered this past winter. On New Year's Eve. You might have read about it in the paper. James Reed was his name."

"No, I've been in the Caribbean," said the man. "My God, that's terrible."

Fanny nodded, savoring the effect of the gruesome information. People were always so shocked when they heard it. "Shot to death in his bed. She was the one who found him."

"The poor woman," he said.

Fanny nodded. "Well, yes. Of course, some people say . . ."

The man looked at her curiously. "Say what?"

"Some say she did more than just find him . . ."

"What do you mean?"

Fanny shrugged. "She says there was a burglar with a gun, but . . . nobody's ever been arrested."

The man stared at Fanny and then looked back to where Laura and Michael had disappeared. "You mean . . . they think she killed him? That lovely woman?"

Fanny shook her head. "People talk. You know. It's a small town."

"Is that what you think?" he asked with a trace of disapproval in his tone.

"I think you never know about people," Fanny said firmly. "In any case, that boy is all she has left. You can see where she'd be uptight."

"Well, yes, of course you would. I didn't realize," he said.

"No. How could you know? You were just being friendly."

"Still," he said. "I feel bad."

"Oh, don't bother yourself about it. By the way, my name's Fanny Clark. My husband and I own the store up there. I noticed you come in the other day. That's quite a boat you've got there. Tartan 3800, isn't that? We don't often see them that big around here."

"Yes, thanks," he said distractedly, still staring down the dock as if he could still see Laura.

"Where'd you sail from?"

The man forced himself to focus on Fanny. "I came up from Barbados," he said. "I've been sailing the islands this winter." He extended his hand to Fanny. "Ian Turner," he said.

"Nice to meet you, Ian," she said. She was accustomed to the easy familiarity of the boating fraternity. "Are you going to be around for a while?"

Ian looked back up toward the pier. "I don't know," he said. "I'm taking it day by day. You know, there was something about that woman. I felt as if I knew her."

"She's not from around here," said Fanny.

"Neither am I," said Ian.

"Where you from?" Fanny asked pleasantly.

"Connecticut, actually. Although I bought the boat in Bridgetown, in Barbados, and I'm sailing back up the coast."

"Well, anything you need, Wendell and I can fix you right up."

"Thank you," said Ian.

"Why don't you come on up and meet Wendell, my husband?"

The man nodded and pressed his lips together. "I could use some batteries."

"Any size, any voltage. We got 'em," said Fanny. "And stop looking so worried. Laura's just come unglued from all that's happened. Anybody else would have realized you were just trying to be nice."

"I suppose," he mused. "She just looked so . . . familiar to me. I knew a girl when we were children . . . Her name was Laura, too. Laura Hastings."

"That's her," Fanny said excitedly. "She writes books, children's books, under that name."

The man stared at Fanny in amazement. Then he gazed back down the empty dock, where Laura had disappeared. "It can't be. I can't believe it. The same girl?"

"Oh, yes," Fanny said with satisfaction. "That's her." She leaned toward him with a wicked grin. "Did she seem like the kind of little girl who might grow up to shoot her husband?"

"Laura Hastings." Ian shook his head in disbelief. Then his expression changed, and he looked at Fanny with such enmity that she immediately regretted her suggestive remark. "I hardly think so," he said coldly. "Laura Hastings saved my life."

CHAPTER TEN

Laura sat on the edge of Michael's bed and brushed his soft hair back off his forehead tenderly. By the dim glow of his night-light she could see his dark eyelashes fluttering against the soft curve of his cheek. Ever since Jimmy died, he had insisted on having the night-light, even though he had never before been afraid of the dark. He also wanted her to stay in his room with him until he fell asleep each night, and Laura was glad to do it, although she hated that moment when she left his room and went downstairs to the lonely, empty house, the silence.

"Sleepy?" she murmured.

"A little," he admitted.

"I'm sorry our trip to the marina turned out that way today. But I was really scared when I couldn't find you."

"I know it," he said.

"Do you understand why it was wrong to get on that man's boat? It's not just getting into cars with strangers that is dangerous."

"I know, Mom," he said gravely. "I'm sorry you were scared. I won't ever do it again."

"Promise?"

"Promise."

She lifted him up and embraced him, feeling a pain in her heart that the world had become such a perilous place. Her gaze fell on the little framed picture of his father that he kept by his bedside, ever since that night. "I love you more than anything," she said. His little arms held her tightly. She didn't want him to see the anguish on her face. "We'll go again soon," she said. "And we'll have a much better time. Okay?"

Michael nodded, clearly drowsy.

"All right now," she said as he sank back against his Aladdin pillowcase. "You get to sleep."

He turned over under his covers and rustled around until he was comfortable. Laura waited until his eyes closed and the rise and fall of his breathing filled the room. At least Michael was able to sleep. Her own nights were torturous. She would lie there, eyes wide open in the dark, thinking about the sleeping pills she tried not to rely on. Michael's peaceful slumber was something to be grateful for.

When he gave the shuddering sigh that announced, as it had since infancy, that he was deeply asleep, she got up carefully from the bed, pulled his door to, and gazed at him one more time. "Sleep tight, my angel," she whispered, and then left his room and started down the stairs.

The grandfather clock in the hall ticked loudly, and otherwise the house was silent as usual. She went into the living room and looked with disinterest at the pile of books she intended to read. She felt unaccountably restless, as if she would not be able to sit on the chair for any length of time. She glanced at the TV program guide and tossed it down impatiently. There were chores she could do, of course, but she was too weary. She walked over to the desk and riffled through the bills on the blotter. I guess I could pay these, she thought. Get that done. With a sigh she switched on the lamp under its fringed silk shade and pulled out the leather desk chair.

Just as she was about to sit down, the ringing of the doorbell made her jump. The sound of the doorbell made her afraid. Sometimes even the phone ringing filled her with fear.

Stop it, she thought. Get a grip. But she wondered if it would always be so. If she would always expect to turn a corner in her own house and see a stranger there—someone evil who had entered unnoticed. Don't wake Michael, she thought angrily as the bell chimed again. Through the stained-glass lights surrounding the front door she saw the shape of a man she didn't recognize. Her heart leapt with fresh fear at the idea of a stranger at her door, and then, suddenly, she realized who it was.

Laura opened the door and stared, without speaking, at the man on her doorstep. The man from the boat. He had on a clean shirt, and his hair shone under the porchlight. He smelled of soap.

He attempted a smile. "I hope I'm not disturbing you. Fanny Clark told me where to find you," he said.

Laura did not answer. After a moment's hesitation he went on, "I should introduce myself properly. My name is Ian Turner."

It sounded more like a question than a statement, and he was looking at her expectantly, hopefully. Laura gazed back at him blankly.

Seeing that she did not recognize his name, Ian frowned. "I came over because I wanted to apologize again, about this afternoon."

"You apologized already," she said coolly. "There's no need for further apologies."

"I think there is," he said stubbornly.

"I'm sure you were just trying to be nice to my son," Laura said. She did not add, "Despite your bad judgment," but she might as well have. She twisted the brass doorknob impatiently in her hand.

"That's true, but I felt as if I'd really done something stupid. And then Fanny told me about your husband."

Laura's pale cheeks colored with anger. "What about my husband," she said flatly. Did she tell you I shot him? Laura wanted to ask. Did you want to get a closer look at a possible murderess?

"I just thought that, you know, having suffered such a shocking loss like that . . . might have made you more protective . . ."

Laura looked at him with narrowed eyes. "You mean I overreacted?"

"No, not at all. I just meant—"

"For your information, one has nothing to do with the other. I'm a parent. Michael is my child. Any parent would have reacted the same way." She felt exasperation rising in her. This was a man who spent his time cruising around on a boat. How did you explain to someone like that about the responsibility, the imagination for danger, that comes with being a mother? "Never mind," she said wearily. "Let's just consider the whole thing forgotten." She forced herself to dismiss him politely. "It was nice of you to come by."

"Look," he said, "I'm . . . I can see you're about to close the door on me, and the truth is, well, I did come to apologize but, I . . . I have another reason."

Laura looked at him warily.

"I have the idea that we might have met before."

"Don't I know you from somewhere?" Laura said sarcastically. But her sarcasm covered the fact that something in his persistence made her feel a little afraid.

"I know," he said. "It sounds like the tiredest of all pickup lines, but I'm serious. Do I seem familiar to you?"

Laura shook her head. But even as she was denying it, she remembered that she had thought so, briefly, this morning at the dock.

"Did you ever live in New Brighton, Connecticut," he asked, "as a little girl?"

Surprised, Laura studied his face and nodded. "But I lived all over," she demurred.

"Fanny told me that you're an author. That you write books under the name of Laura Hastings. I knew a girl named Laura Hastings. I mean, years ago. When I was just a little kid. And her hair and eyes . . ."

Laura peered at him, trying to lift the curtain of time, but it was no use. There were elements to his face, but they were jumbled, as if she were seeing him through a kaleidoscope. A broken image from somewhere in the past.

"This is a little embarrassing to admit," he said. "I was in trouble once . . . I fell . . . and this little girl . . . Laura Hastings . . . you . . . found me."

Suddenly it came back to her. No wonder she did not recall those dazzling eyes. He wore glasses. His head was covered with a dark, fuzzy crewcut. A little thin boy in a filthy striped T-shirt, his pinched face blotchy with dirt and tears. "The boy in the pit," she exclaimed.

Ian nodded, his face breaking into an enormous smile. "You do remember," he cried exultantly. "When Fanny said your name it just blew me away, because I was so sure, from the minute I saw you. I mean, I don't want to say you haven't changed a bit, but that hair, and that beautiful face . . . I was so thrilled to see you."

Laura stared at him, shaking her head. She couldn't have been more than six years old at the time. She was alone, playing in some wooded acreage near her house. She was often alone as a child. No brothers and sisters. A series of far-flung rented houses. She lived in her imagination most of the time. And those nearby woods were the perfect place to play out your fantasies. And then she heard those strange, pitiful cries that scared her half to death. It took all her childish courage to go toward them, not to run away. "It was getting dark out, and I heard you calling."

Ian smiled and concurred enthusiastically. "I didn't think anyone would come. I was out exploring, and I'd fallen in and broken my leg. I'd been there for hours, it seemed, calling out for help. And then you were looking down at me, with that same white hair. I thought you might be an angel or something."

Laura laughed, remembering. "Your mother gave me a dollar for finding you."

"That sounds like my mother," he said, shaking his head.

"Yes, of course," she said. She leaned against the door frame and stared at him, filled with amazement that this man, this person from the dim past, should have crossed her path this way. "What an odd coincidence," she said.

"I know," he said eagerly. "I couldn't believe it myself. What are the chances . . .? That's why I had to come by tonight . . ."

"That was a long time ago," she mused. "You were ahead of me in school. Ian . . . that's right. You were brainy."

"Don't be kind. I was the class nerd. Hey, would you mind if we sat down and talked for a while? I'd love to catch up with you a little bit."

Immediately Laura was wary again. Yes, she did remember now. But he was still a stranger. "I don't know," she said. "It's late."

Ian looked at her tenderly. "Well, whatever you think. I wouldn't impose on you for the world. After all, I owe you my life, Laura Hastings," he said lightly.

In spite of her apprehensions, his words touched her, filled her with gratitude that this man remembered her for something good. That he remembered her as an angel, come to his rescue. She was so used to being seen as a villain lately.

"It's just that it gets awfully lonely on that boat," he said wistfully.

Lonely, she thought. You don't know the half of it. The silent house loomed behind her like a threat. She made up her mind. "Okay, why not. Please," she said. "Sit down."

"You better get a jacket," he said. "It's beautiful, but it's cool." There was a note of protectiveness in his voice that she started to protest but then didn't.

"I'll be right back," she said. She went into the foyer, took her embroidered blue jean jacket off its hook, and glanced into the mirror as she got it. Her face was flushed, her eyes were bright and anxious. She ran her fingers through her hair and pulled on the jacket. She was so unused to company, she thought. She had become like a hermit in these last few months.

When she returned to the porch he was seated on the railing, looking out over the quiet street. He looked at once tense and tired, a feeling she knew well. It seemed strange in a man who spent his days knocking about in a sailboat. He was not classically handsome, but his features had a weary grace that drew the eye. Laura sat down on the rocker and felt his gaze on her. She shivered. "It is a little cool," she said, thrusting her hands into her jacket pockets. "Can I get you a drink or something?" she asked.

"No," he said. "I won't stay long."

She felt at once relieved and disappointed.

"I feel a little funny now," he said, "knowing that when you look at me you're seeing that little skinny kid with the glasses and the broken leg."

Laura smiled. "Does your family still live in New Brighton? You had a brother, didn't you? He was my age."

Ian nodded. "Jason. He still lives there. He's a fireman. He's got two kids. My mom lives with them."

"And your father? I don't remember . . ."

Ian's expression changed. His eyes became instantly stony. "He's dead," he said shortly. "He was the music teacher at the high school."

"That's right," said Laura. "I'm sorry." She could picture Mr. Turner vaguely. A heavyset man with a very pale complexion. The same dark hair as Ian's.

"What about your family?" he asked. "You moved away. Wasn't your dad in the navy?"

Laura nodded and counted on her fingers. "Second grade. We moved to Virginia. And then to Texas. And California. And on, and on, and on."

"And now? Where are they now?"

"They died in a plane crash," said Laura.

Ian frowned. "That's too bad. You're really all alone, aren't you?"

She felt suddenly, absurdly grateful to him for understanding that. She felt as if she were the one in the pit and he was looking down at her now, his eyes full of sympathy.

"Yes," she said. "I really am."

There was a silence between them, and she knew he wanted to ask about Jimmy, about what had happened. She didn't want to get into it.

"Where are you sailing to?" she asked.

He looked away, frowning. "I'm just sailing," he said. "No particular destination."

Laura nodded. "Well, that's a nice way to live if you can do it." She tried, in vain, not to sound disapproving.

"I thought it would be," he said. "It seemed like the right thing to do at the time."

Laura looked at him curiously. "You haven't always been a boat person?"

He looked over at her and caught her glance. "No," he said. "I used to be a real person."

Laura blushed at the rebuke. "I didn't mean it like that," she said.

"That's all right," he said. "It's true."

"Well, lots of people dream of getting on a boat and sailing away," she demurred. "I think it's a common fantasy to want to escape. To fly away or sail away, or whatever. Most people don't really do it, though. They just fantasize about it, and it gets them over the rough spots. What were you when you were a real person?" she drawled with a little smile.

There was an awkward silence. Then he said, "I worked at the base in New Brighton. I'm a scientist. Nuclear physicist, actually."

"What a coincidence," Laura said teasingly. "So am I!"

Ian smiled a little sheepishly. "It is kind of specialized . . ."

"So you just decided to chuck physics for a life on the seven seas?"

"Not just like that," he said. "I lost my . . ."

She could see he was struggling with the words, and all at once she felt alarmed, as if she had waded too deep into the tide.

"My wife and my son died. He was only seven years old. I couldn't see the use of it anymore . . ."

Laura felt her face flaming. "Oh, God," she said. "I'm so sorry." She felt so ashamed of her flippancy. For telling him that only a parent could understand . . .

"I didn't mean to be depressing," he said.

"No, no," she said. "I shouldn't have said anything."

"I just wanted you to understand . . . when you couldn't find your boy today . . . I did know how you felt. And about your husband. I'm not just some beach bum, sailing around . . ."

"God, I feel awful, Ian," said Laura. "Please forgive me."

"Don't," he said. "I just didn't want you to think . . . I don't mind talking about it . . . with you," he added.

Part of her wanted to jump up from the chair and flee from him. Before Jimmy's death, she might have fled. But she was schooled in suffering now. It did not scare her the way it did those whose lives were still untouched. Some people treated the grief of others like a disease that you could catch if you got too close. She knew better. She knew that it was a club that no one ever joined by choice. A club whose members had shared the most brutal of initiations.

"When did this happen?" she asked quietly.

Ian sighed, then frowned, as if calculating. "Phillip died . . . in September. He and my wife were killed in a fire that destroyed our home. There was a serial arsonist in the New Brighton area. They finally caught him, but . . ." He hesitated, as if he were about to explain further and then decided against it. "Anyway, Gabriella died in the blaze. Phillip lingered for a while in the burn center." He nodded, the way people did when they tried to pin their thoughts to a fact, to prevent tears. "Afterward I kept thinking about all the things we had planned to do together when we had the time . . ."

"How terrible for you. I'm so sorry," said Laura.

There was a silence between them, but it was no longer awkward. It was as if they were both gazing into the same

81

dark cave. "Well," he said abruptly, "how did I get started on this?"

"You were telling me about the boat," she said gently.

"Right. Well, everyone tried to convince me not to quit work, but I kept thinking that life is too short, that you have to live now, seize the day, if you will . . . So, at the end of November I went to the Caribbean and I bought a boat. And I've been sailing ever since."

"And are you glad you did it?" she asked.

Ian gave her a rueful smile. "Well, you can't sail away from your heartache."

"No," Laura agreed. "No, I guess not. Although I wouldn't mind trying."

"It has certain things to recommend it. I've seen lots of gorgeous sunsets. Read a lot of good books. And you meet interesting people."

Laura leaned her head back on the rocker and closed her eyes, pretending to relax. In the quiet darkness she felt acutely alert, and she was still shivering, although it was not cold. "It sounds like you did the right thing," she said.

"That's what I used to think," he said. "But now I'm beginning to tire of it. Too much freedom is its own kind of cage."

"Mmmm . . ." She began to drift off into her own thoughts. The conversation had taken a decidedly somber turn, and she didn't know how to change it. "Aren't we a cheery pair?" she said, attempting to smile.

"Well," he said abruptly, "I'd probably better be getting along. I've bent your ear for long enough. I didn't mean to get into all of this. I just had to come and find out if you were the real Laura Hastings. The girl who saved me."

Laura smiled. What a relief not to be seen as a black widow, a pariah. "I'm glad you did," she said sincerely.

"Thanks for your hospitality," he said, unfolding his muscular frame from his seat on the porch rail.

Laura felt flustered and laughed weakly. "What hospitality? You didn't even get a comfortable seat."

"It was fine. Believe me."

She watched him walk down the porch steps. At the bottom he turned and looked up at her. "Tomorrow," he said, "if you'd like to bring your son for a visit to see my boat, I'd be glad to show him the whole thing. I'll take you both out for a sail. I mean, boys like boats and it would be fun for me, too. I would really enjoy his company. And yours."

For a moment her heart lifted and she thought, *Yes, okay.* Then her enthusiasm shriveled. "No, I can't," she said.

He looked at her calmly. "Why not?" he asked. "You worried about what people will think?"

She recognized the absurdity of it the moment he said it. The people in this town couldn't think any worse of her than they already did. And there was something about the fact that she had known him in childhood that made their acquaintance intrinsically innocent. Michael would like it. Just a few hours out of the house. It would do them good. It was not as if it were a date. It was something friendly, an outing for Michael's sake.

"Come at eleven," he said. "The tide will be right." He frowned at her ballet slippers. "Wear rubber soles."

I don't know, she thought, watching him turn away. Maybe I shouldn't do this. He looked back at her, observing the conflict in her face. "You do have sneakers, don't you?"

Laura laughed in spite of herself. "Yes, I have sneakers."

"Well then, see you tomorrow," he said.

"All right," she said helplessly. "Tomorrow."

CHAPTER ELEVEN

She was standing on the top of a hill, looking down on a flowering meadow of honeysuckle, clover, and wild roses. The sun blazed in a perfect sky, and she was perspiring from the heat of it. At the foot of the hill was a lake, a blue mirror of the sky, which beckoned to her, cool and clear. As she stared at its surface, she saw that someone was swimming there. He looked up, and waved to her. It was Jimmy. Her heart began to sing. Barefoot, like a child, she began to pick her way down the hillside. She went slowly at first, and then, reckless with the desire to reach him, to plunge below the inviting surface of the water and join him, she began to run. She was almost to the edge, arms outstretched to dive, when suddenly she heard a shout.

The shout was not in the dream. It was outside the dream, at her ear, loud and desperate. Laura sat up in bed like a shot, sweat broken out all over her. "What?" she cried, frantically searching the dark corners of her bedroom, her eyes trying to focus in the darkness.

There was no one in the room. She was alone. Her heart was pounding with fear. Michael, she thought.

She jumped up, grabbed her robe from the foot of the bed, ran to the bedroom door, and threw it open. The house was silent. Awkwardly she pulled the robe on over her night-gown and rushed across the hall to her son's room.

She opened the door and looked in. He was asleep on his back, his mouth open, his arms lifted over his head in an attitude of surrender. She crept over to the bed and knelt beside him, stroking his hair, kissing his firm, rounded cheek. Michael stirred but did not awaken.

It wasn't Michael, she thought, the wild racing of her heart calmed somewhat by the warmth of him, the knowledge that he was safe. What was it? Just a dream, she told herself. Just a weird dream. Maybe somebody passing by in the street who shouted. And you heard it in your sleep. In the warm weather there were always intermittent bursts of noise outside, the ebullient yelps of young people coming home from bars and dance clubs late at night. That's probably it. She forced herself to let go of her son and walked over to the window, pulling back the homespun cotton curtain.

The street was empty. There was a pattern of leafy shadows on the pale gray of the macadam thrown by the moonlight and the gaslit street lamps. Beyond the street lamp's arc, houses, shrubs, and trees were steeped in inky darkness. There was no one there. She was about to turn away from the window when she caught sight, from the corner of her eye, of a movement in the hedges across the road. Her heart leapt up again, and she gripped the curtain fabric, twisting it in her fingers. She peered into the darkness, but could see nothing. Who's out there? she demanded silently, but there was no further movement, no sign of life. No one, she chided herself, trying to calm the racing of her heart. Probably just a cat or a dog passing by. You're spooked by that dream. All right, she thought. Whatever it was, it's gone now. Go back to bed. But she did not move away from the window. She stood for a long time, staring out, the echo of the shout still sounding in her head.

* * *

"I thought you wanted to go out on the boat," Laura said in a low voice as she gripped Michael's hand and hurried down the dock. Michael had dawdled getting ready and made them late. Laura passed the Clarks' store and glanced in but was relieved that neither of them was in sight. She had prepared her story—Ian's invitation was to make up for yesterday's scare with Michael. And it was true, essentially. But it felt false, and she didn't want to have to say it. In the clear light of day she had to admit that it might seem like a date, and Michael had sensed it, for he had been positively balky all morning.

Ian stood on the deck and waved to them as they approached. Laura had thought that maybe, without the moonlight, he would look different, unattractive. But the first sight of him punctured that hope and filled her with an unwelcome flock of butterflies in the stomach. The blue water sparkled beneath the boat, and the sun rested on his wide shoulders like a mantle. He squinted at them, shielding his eyes with a brown hand.

"Come aboard, you two," he called.

Although Michael had clearly intended to be stubborn, the first sight of the enormous sloop was an irresistible temptation. With Ian's help he clambered on board and asked if he could go below. "Go ahead," said Ian. Then he held out his hand to Laura.

She waved his hand away. "I'm all right," she said.

"Watch your step," he said as she descended into the cabin where Michael had already disappeared.

"This is where you live?" she asked lightly.

"Home sweet home," he said.

The main cabin was surprisingly roomy and comfortable looking. There was a galley kitchen, two wide berths on either side, and a table between them. There was a shelf of books behind the sofas and cabinets above. All the wood was glossy with polished care.

"This is beautiful," Laura said honestly. "What's in the cabinets?"

"They're called lockers," he said. "More books, clothes, stuff, you know. Everything has to have a door, or it'd all fall out of the shelves in rough seas."

"Oh, right," she said, trying out the various seats. "This is comfortable, too."

Ian sat on one of the berths. "It's not bad," he said.

"I always kind of pictured these cabins as so little and cramped that you had to walk in a crouch," she admitted.

"It would be a hard way to live, unless you were Quasimodo," he said.

Laura laughed. "Where do you sleep?" she asked.

"In the forward cabin," he said, pointing toward the bow of the boat. "I think Michael's up there trying out the bunk. I've also got another pint-sized cabin back here," he said, indicating a darkened area behind the galley. "Up here is the head. Everything you need but a tub . . ."

She followed him, peering around him into the tiny bathroom. Michael bobbed up out of the darkness of the sleeping quarters. "Mom, this is so cool. It's like a pirate ship."

"It is, isn't it," she murmured.

"Glad you like it," said Ian. "Michael, how about helping me get her under way."

Michael's eyes were wide. "All right."

He followed Ian back through the cabin. Laura brought up the rear. As she passed the shelf of books, she automatically perused his book titles. There was some nonfiction and a few Tom Clancy novels. There were also a number of books on Eastern religions that looked particularly well thumbed. Beside them she noticed a single framed photograph of a beautiful, raven-haired woman and a small boy with dark brown hair in a bowl-shaped cut and a great, gap-toothed smile. Gabriella and Phillip, she thought, and her heart turned over with pity at the sight of their bright, untroubled faces.

She came up the ladder and took a seat in the cockpit, watching as Ian buckled Michael into a life jacket. Then, as

Ian explained each step of the process to Michael, he rigged the jib and unwrapped the mainsail. Then he freed the boat from the dock and started the motor they would use to negotiate the channel. Michael exclaimed at every familiar landmark and waved at other boats. The sun was warm on Laura's face, and the combination of the quiet hum of the motor and her fretful night's sleep made her feel drowsy, although there was an undeniable buzz in her nerves.

Once they were out in open water, Ian called to Michael. "This rope here is called a halyard," he said to the boy. "Give me a hand with it and we'll raise the mainsail." As they pulled together, the huge white sail unfurled upward, and Michael let out a whoop and looked at his mother, wide-eyed with delight at his new role as first mate. Laura smiled back at him and closed her eyes, feeling better now, feeling glad they'd come. The day was beautiful, and the water had a soothing roll to it.

Then Ian cut the engine. "Now we catch the wind," he said with satisfaction, and the boat began to cut silently through the water, the only sound being the occasional flap of the sails. Ian held the tiller and smiled at Laura.

His smile made her uncomfortable again. "It seems so calm out here," she said, looking away from him, toward the shore. "How do you know which way the wind is blowing?"

His fingers grazed her cheek and neck and made her gasp. She turned on him sharply.

"You feel it on your cheek and neck," he said innocently. "It's a sensitivity you develop."

"Don't get too far out here," she said. "We can only stay out here for a little while."

"I know," he said. "We'll be back in an hour or two."

"Okay," said Laura, settling back on her seat. "Just so you understand."

"I understand," he said.

It was a perfect day for a sail. The sky and the water were dazzling in their bright shades of blue, and the rest of the world seemed far away. Laura was taken with the peacefulness, the solitude, of it. Ian answered all of Michael's eager questions as she leaned back and let the breeze and the sun envelop her.

"You're a very patient instructor," she observed. "You must get that from your father."

Ian's smile disappeared. "I don't think so."

"I just assumed . . .," Laura said awkwardly. "Since he was a teacher."

"Perhaps what little patience he had was exhausted by his students," Ian said bitterly. "We saw a different side of him at home."

She could tell by the look on his face that this was something of an understatement. She decided not to pursue it. "Well, I'm sure you were a very patient father," she said.

"I wanted to be a good father. Different from my own. But I failed my son in the end," he said.

His reaction did not make her uncomfortable. She understood now that people needed to talk about their tragedies, not be treated as if their lives were unspeakable. "I saw all those books you had on philosophy and Eastern religions," she said. "Are you trying to make some sense of what happened to you?"

Ian squinted at the sunny skies. "I'm interested in the idea of determinism and free will. How much do we control our fate? Or do we just have to learn acceptance?"

"I used to think I had some control of my fate," she said. "But now I wonder . . ."

"I think we have to try to shape our destiny," he said. "No matter what. I'm a scientist, you know. I'm accustomed to controlling the variables. I don't like the idea of being tossed about by circumstances."

"Or even by the wind," she observed. "You have to harness the wind to travel."

"That's true," he conceded. "Some carefree sailor I am . . ."

"I wasn't really fooled," she said.

Ian winced, as if caught out in a lie. "I'm transparent," he said.

She looked at him sympathetically. His life had been ripped away from him, and he was trying to get back in charge. She could understand that. She could easily understand it. "Well, being on this sailboat makes me feel as if I chose to make the absolute best of a beautiful day," she said agreeably.

"I think so, too," he said, visibly more cheerful.

There was something timeless about it, Laura mused, letting the wind propel you, harnessing an invisible element to get where you wanted to go. And Ian seemed to work the wind effortlessly. The boat never lost speed, and if the sails shuddered, it was only a scant moment before he had them adjusted. It was an ancient means of travel, impractical in this day and age. But it was undeniably romantic to eschew the motor for the sail.

They sailed for another half an hour, enjoying the breeze, chatting lazily as they went. Several times Laura caught him gazing thoughtfully at her, and she smiled, but it made her uneasy all the same. She tried to return the conversation to the impersonal. "I can see why you like sailing," she said to him as their eyes met once again. "My husband had a fishing boat, but . . ."

"Powerboats," Ian scoffed. "There's no mastery in that. Just turn on the engine and go."

Laura sat up, feeling irritated. "He just wanted to fish. He wasn't into the whole mariner thing. Jimmy had mastery in a lot of other areas." She wrapped her arms around her chest.

"What's the matter?" he asked.

"I'm feeling chilly," she said. "I think it's time to go back."

Ian looked at her in surprise. "Already?"

"Yes. Now."

"Hey, don't take offense," he said. "All sailors talk that way about powerboaters. It's sort of a tradition. Like a rivalry between schools. It wasn't anything personal about your husband."

Laura rummaged in her canvas pack and put on a pair of sunglasses.

"I'm sorry," he said. "That was thoughtless of me. I didn't mean to offend you. That's the last thing I wanted to do."

She shook her head. "It's not that. I just started thinking of Jimmy . . . I feel tired all of a sudden. Please take us back."

"Are you sure?" he said.

Laura did not reply.

Ian sighed. "Coming about, Michael," he called out. "We're headed in."

"Already!" the boy protested, and Laura had to smile.

The trip back to the dock went swiftly. Ian was silent on the ride. Now that their outing was almost over, Laura felt embarrassed for having taken offense at his casual remarks. They reached the marina, and Ian maneuvered the boat carefully back into the slip. Laura took off her sunglasses and replaced them in her bag. She gathered up their sweatshirts and put them in the pack also. While she sat in the stern, Ian climbed out and, still explaining everything to Michael, secured the boat to the dock. Then he climbed back aboard to where Laura was seated. Michael gamboled joyously on the shining deck while Laura called out to him to be careful.

"It's good to see him so happy," she said.

Ian nodded. "I'm sorry I spoiled the trip," he said.

"You didn't spoil it," she said. "I'm sorry you went to all that trouble and then we had to come back so quickly. I . . . I wasn't quite up to it, I guess."

"You were perfect," he said. "You are perfect."

Laura looked at him, surprised by the intensity of his tone. He was looking at her with an unabashed admiration. Maybe he still saw her as the helpful schoolgirl she had been, but it didn't matter. It felt good to have a champion, someone who saw her as worthy. She felt a rush of warmth for him, for their ancient connection. "Ian," she said, "I just want you to know how grateful I am . . ."

"I'm the one who's grateful," he said. "That you came with me."

"There, you see. My good deed of long ago paid off. I had a chance to spend this lovely, carefree day, when I really needed it."

"We can have lots of days like this," he said.

"But you've got to be on your way soon. Many ports of call left to visit," she said lightly.

"No, I don't," he said. "I make the rules. I can stay as long as I like."

A knot formed in Laura's stomach at his words, and she shook her head. "Ian, look, this was wonderful. But I don't want you to get the wrong idea . . . about me. There's really no possibility—"

All of a sudden she heard Michael cry, "Dad's boat, Dad's boat." Laura leapt up, expecting against all reason to see him, to see Jimmy, and looked around. A motor launch was cruising gently past them. The gray-haired man at the wheel was clearly puzzled, staring at Michael, who was waving at him. Behind him was a young couple, seated in the stern. The woman was dressed from head to toe in a lavender parachute silk outfit and looked terminally bored. The man was talking on a cellular phone. Laura recognized Richard and Candy Walsh, out for a ride in the boat Richard had bought for his father. Richard's eyes met hers, and he stared. Laura raised a hand weakly in greeting. Candy sat up and gaped.

"That's Dad's boat," Michael cried.

"Yes, it is," Laura agreed stiffly. Richard's father returned his attention to the channel, and Richard pretended to resume his phone call, but Candy swiveled around and stared as they chugged out of the harbor.

"Friends of yours?" Ian asked.

Laura nodded. "He's our lawyer," she said. "He was my husband's close friend. He manages my finances."

Ian nodded. "Is this awkward for you?"

Laura shook her head wearily. "It doesn't matter. We need to get going now." The yacht rocked as she climbed up on the dock. Ian was still in the cockpit.

"Don't rush off," he said. "Let me finish up here and we can all have lunch."

"No," said Laura. "It's time to go. Michael, say thank you to Mr. Turner."

"Laura, what's the matter?" Ian said.

"Nothing," said Laura. "Thank you for the sail. Come on, Michael."

"Thanks," said Michael.

"No problem. We'll do it again," said Ian.

Michael began to skip up the planks of the dock as Ian climbed out of the boat.

"I'm thinking of staying for a while," Ian said softly.

Laura understood, and it alarmed her. "Don't stay on my account," she said sharply, hating the way she sounded.

"I like it here," he said. "It's the loveliest place I've ever seen."

Laura felt her face flaming. She rushed after Michael like someone pulling away from a riptide. As she reached the pier she saw Fanny Clark, standing in the doorway of Boat People, her hands on her hips, her mouth set in a thin, disapproving line. Laura tried to force a smile, but Fanny turned her back on her and disappeared inside the store.

CHAPTER TWELVE

Laura set two plates of macaroni and cheese on the kitchen table with two glasses of milk. Michael and Louis were seated across from one another, their kid-size forks at the ready. "Eat that up," said Laura. "Your mom's going to be back soon."

Pam had come by earlier with a toothache and an offer from the local dentist to fit her in. Laura readily agreed to take care of Louis. Michael and Louis enjoyed playing together, and the two women often traded baby-sitting back and forth. Pam's husband, Duane, was in the Coast Guard and was away from home more often than not. Laura felt there was a definite hostility in Duane's attitude toward her since Jimmy's death, but when she asked Pam about it, Pam told her she was imagining things.

It was a little white lie, and Pam knew it, but she had no intention of hurting Laura's feelings. As devoted as she was to Duane, Pam prided herself on her independent thinking. She took Louis to church, even though Duane didn't like to go, and voted Republican even though her husband was a Democrat. So when Duane suggested, though Pam would never admit it to Laura, that she find someone else for Louis to play with, Pam had tartly told him not to interfere.

The two boys set about eating their macaroni with a good appetite, and Laura looked disinterestedly in the refrigerator for something to eat herself. A knock on the front door interrupted her ruminations. In spite of herself, she felt her heart do a little anxious flip. It wasn't Pam or Gary. Both of them came around to the back door.

"You two finish eating. I've got Oreos for anybody with a clean plate," she promised as she headed out of the kitchen.

It's probably the paper boy, collecting, she told herself. But she undid her ponytail and tried to fluff out her hair as she hurried to the door and opened it.

"Good evening, Mrs. Reed."

Laura's heart sank. It was Detective Leonard. He was dressed in his usual gray suit, which matched his eyes, and she felt certain that he never removed that jacket and tie while he was working, no matter how the temperature soared. His blond hair was neatly combed back, and his expression was impassive.

She did not ask him in. There was no pretense of friendliness between them. She had felt his distrust of her from the moment they'd met. His suspicions pressed on her. "What can I do for you, Detective?"

"May I come in? I'd like to ask you a few questions."

She turned and walked into the living room, not even bothering to reply. He would come in if he wanted to. She had always been law-abiding, always trusted the police. She'd never felt much connection with the teenagers, the urban poor, the black males who claimed that they were hounded for no reason by the cops. But now she understood what it was to have the police harass you, not because of what you'd done, but simply because of who you were.

Laura indicated a chair for him and sat on another. "What do you want?" she asked bluntly. No use pretending this was a friendly visit.

"I've had a report that you were seen yesterday in the company of a man, a stranger here in Cape Christian. I wondered if you could tell me about him."

"Who told you that?" Laura demanded.

"I'm afraid that's no concern of yours."

"Am I not allowed to have friends?" Laura asked. "I mean, is it illegal for me to spend an hour with a friend?"

"We know this much—that his name is Ian Turner, and that he has a slip for a rather large and expensive sailboat down at the marina."

"I can't believe this," Laura protested. "How did you . . .? All we did was go for a sail. That was all."

"Can you tell me a little bit about your relationship? How long have you known this man?"

"Fanny Clark," Laura said flatly. "Has to be. Well, if she told you his name, I'm sure she also told you how we met."

Detective Leonard did not bother to confirm or deny her suspicion. "You claim to have known each other for a long time. Are you and Mr. Turner having an affair? Were you having an affair while your husband was alive?"

"No," Laura cried. "We met down at the marina two days ago. I haven't set eyes on Ian since we were children. And no, we are not having an affair."

Detective Leonard gazed at his notes, and the expression on his face did not change. "Were you lovers in the past, when you knew each other?"

"We were five or six years old, Detective. We went to the same grammar school for a year or two."

"Is Mr. Turner married or single?"

"Why don't you ask him?"

"Are you expecting him?"

"No," Laura said defiantly.

Ron Leonard cocked his head thoughtfully. "Well, why don't I just wait here. See if he shows up."

Laura sighed in exasperation. "Mr. Turner is a widower from New Brighton, Connecticut. He's lived there all his life. He's a physicist. He worked at the navy base. His wife and child were killed in a fire last year."

The detective raised his eyebrows.

"There's a serial arsonist doing three life terms in Lansdale Prison right now as a result. Are you satisfied?"

"I'll check on all this, of course. And you maintain that you were not having an affair with this man while his wife, or your husband, was still alive?"

Laura clenched her teeth. It was like having someone hurl buckets of swill all over you, to be seen in this way. She was sick of being cast in this loathsome light. "You know, Detective Leonard, I am the victim here. I am the one who lost my husband, lost my peace of mind, forever. I am the one who has been waiting for you to find a killer. You can't know how furious it makes me to have to answer your ugly insinuations when I can see that you are wasting both our time . . ."

Ron Leonard snapped his notebook shut and stood up. "I guess that will give me a place to start," he said.

"Why don't you try to find the man who killed my husband," she cried hoarsely.

The detective opened the door and stepped out onto the porch. "Your flowers are lovely," he said, nodding at the arrangement on the hall table. "Did Mr. Turner bring you those?"

She wanted to slam the door on him, but she resisted the urge. "No," she said coldly. I don't have to tell you who sends me flowers, you bastard, she thought. He looked as if he were ready to ask, then thought better of it. She waited until he was down the walk and heading for his car before she closed the door and leaned against it, her eyes shut.

Michael came out into the hallway. "We ate it all, Mom," he said. "We're ready for Oreos."

"And more milk, please," said Louis behind him.

Laura sighed and pushed herself away from the door. "Okay," she said. She went into the kitchen and began to get the boys their treat. Michael and Louis saw the scowl on her face and remained unusually quiet. When she put down the plate of cookies, they fell on them as if they were starving.

Laura tore off a paper towel, wet it under the tap in the kitchen sink, and pressed it to her forehead, which was beginning to throb. She poured herself a glass of Coke and swallowed it quickly. Sometimes a little caffeine helped her head. All at once the back door opened, and Pam breezed in, her right cheek swollen.

Laura looked up. "How was it?"

"Brutal. Don't ask."

"Hi, Mom," Louis crowed, his teeth blackened with the cookies he was eating.

"They're almost done," said Laura.

"Can we go outside?" Michael asked.

"Sure. Just stay in the backyard," Laura said wearily.

Pam wiped some crumbs off the kitchen chairs and sat down. Laura went about cleaning up the kitchen. "Something to drink?" she asked Pam.

Pam rolled her eyes and touched her tender jaw. "I'll pass." She watched Laura putting plates in the dishwasher, running water in the pot where she had cooked the noodles. "Laura, what's the matter? Did Louis behave himself?"

"Oh, Louis was great," said Laura. "They both were. I've just got a headache coming on."

"Let me help you," said Pam.

"No, no, you just sit. Nurse that jaw. Did he give you something to take for the pain?"

Pam nodded. "I stopped at the drugstore on the way home." She hesitated, seeing the distracted expression on Laura's face. Then she said, "I thought I saw that Detective Leonard driving up the street as I was coming in. He wasn't here, was he?"

Laura sighed. "Oh, yes," she said.

"What now?" Pam cried.

"Michael and I went sailing yesterday with a man we met at the marina. And the police want to know why," Laura said flatly.

"Does this have anything to do with the guy you were talking to on the porch the other night?" Pam asked.

Laura turned, the bag of cookies in her hand, and looked at Pam with raised eyebrows. "Are you keeping an eye on me, too?" she asked, bristling.

Pam was not ashamed of her curiosity. "Listen, if I so much as hear a bird chirp these days, I'm looking out the window." She shook her head. "If only I had been so nosy that night . . ."

Laura sighed. Then she nodded. "Yes. As a matter of fact, it was the man on the porch. His name is Ian Turner. We met him when we went to look at the boats. It turns out we knew each other as children. So, he invited us for a sail."

"Attractive guy," said Pam.

"Pam!"

"What? I got a pretty good look at him when he left."

"Well, I don't really care whether he's attractive or not. I just went with him 'cause I thought Michael would enjoy it. And because I knew him once . . . you know."

"Right," Pam murmured. There was a silence between them as Laura put the cookies in the cupboard and shut the door with a crack. "Is he married?" asked Pam.

"No, but what would that have to do with anything?" Laura asked irritably.

"Well, what did the police want?" asked Pam.

Laura leaned back against the kitchen counter and folded her arms over her denim shirt. "They wanted to know if I was having an affair with him. A man I met two days ago."

Pam shook her head in sympathy. "That's ridiculous," she said.

"Actually they wanted to know if we were having an affair *before* Jimmy was killed."

"Oh, Laura!"

"I know," said Laura. "It's disgusting. It's vile."

"Well, do you like this guy?" Pam asked.

"Like him!" Laura sputtered in exasperation. "Even if I did . . . Look, he's a nice man, but I am not in the market for a romance. And the way the police scrutinize my every move . . . Well, I'm not going to see him anymore, and that's that. I don't need the harassment."

"I don't blame you," said Pam. "I just think it's a sin the way they hassle you. It's just not worth it. Besides, Jimmy's only been . . . gone for a short time. You're not ready yet for another relationship. It takes time . . ."

"That's right," Laura said defensively.

The doorbell rang, and Pam and Laura exchanged a glance. "Expecting someone?" Pam asked.

"No," Laura said pointedly as she went to answer it.

Ian stood on the front porch, holding a brown paper bag with a white flyer stapled to it. "I got take-out Chinese, but it doesn't come in any single-serving sizes," he said. "Would you be interested . . .?"

Pam drifted into view behind Laura.

"I'm sorry," said Ian. "You have company."

"I was just leaving," Pam said.

"Would you like some Chinese food?" Ian asked politely.

Pam cupped her swollen jaw in her hand. "Emergency root canal," she explained. "It's soup night for me. I'll keep an eye on the boys out my back window," she said to Laura. She passed by Ian in the doorway and glanced back at Laura, who felt her face flaming.

Ian looked at Laura. "Gung pao chicken," he said hopefully.

"I told you I couldn't see you anymore," she said.

"I brought chopsticks," he said.

CHAPTER THIRTEEN

Laura turned her back on him and walked into the house. He came in behind her and shut the door.

"Is there someplace I can set this stuff out?" he asked.

Laura walked into the living room, flopped down into a chair, and sat stiffly, her hands gripping the armrests, her expression hard and unsmiling.

"How about the coffee table?" he said, carefully moving aside some magazines and setting the bag down gingerly, as if it might be explosive.

He opened the bag and reached inside. "Egg roll?" he asked.

Laura finally looked at him. "Don't you know how to take no for answer?" she said coldly.

Ian put the egg roll back in the bag and wiped his fingers absently on a paper napkin. "I probably should have called," he said.

"You shouldn't have come at all."

"I wanted to see you," he said quietly.

"And I told you, I can't," she cried.

Ian studied her face without speaking. Laura shook her head and looked away from him. "Why are you so angry?"

he asked. "Did I do something to offend you? I mean, is it the Chinese food? Are you allergic to MSG or something?"

She knew what he was doing. That he was trying to tease her into a better frame of mind. But he was ignorant of the issues here, she thought. She looked at him without smiling. "The police were here today," she said.

"The police? What for?"

"Someone saw me out sailing with you and informed the police. Now my shadow, Detective Leonard, wants to know all about you. He wants to know if I am having an affair with you. If we were lovers before my husband died. Or your wife, for that matter."

Ian paled. "You're kidding."

Laura shook her head. "A lot of people in this town—especially this particular detective—think I was the one who shot my husband."

"Why in the world do they think that?" he said.

"Do you want the whole story?" she asked bluntly.

"No," he said. "No. It doesn't matter."

"Well, I would if I were you," she said belligerently. "Because they're probably going to investigate you now. Check your background. The whole nine yards. How many dates can you say that about?"

Ian frowned. "Just because we went sailing together? Who told them that, anyway?"

Laura sighed. "I don't know. Well, actually, I could guess, but . . . what's the difference? It's a commonly held opinion."

Ian sat silently for a minute. Then he looked up at her. "Have you got some plates we can use for this? It's getting cold."

Laura gazed at him ruefully. "Did you hear what I'm saying?"

"Yes, and I don't care," he said, standing up. "Is the kitchen back here?"

Laura remained on the chair, shaking her head. Ian disappeared for a few moments and returned with two plates and two teacups. He unpacked the food and spooned it out onto the plates. He poured tea from a paper container into the teacups. Then he placed two chopsticks on her side and began to eat with his own.

"I don't see why their suspicions should affect us," he said. "We have nothing to hide. We only met the day before yesterday. Try some of this. It's good."

Laura picked up the chopsticks and held them limply in her hand. She studied him as he deftly lifted a slice of water chestnut from his plate. There was a quiet, calm quality about him, as if nothing worried him in the least. She felt soothed by his presence, as if he promised all the answers and she had only to trust him.

It was strange, she thought, to know someone in childhood and then meet them again as an adult. All the coping mechanisms, the self-control a person learned throughout life, seemed like a mask, a facade imposed on the ingenuousness of that long-lost child. This self-contained man who sat in her living room, eating Chinese food, was a far cry from the hysterical boy she had found, broken in that pit, in the dark forest twilight. Where did that child go? she wondered. What changed you so much? Or is that terrified child still in there? Are you really as aloof from the world as you seem? Or have you just learned how to put up a convincing front?

"How long were you married?" she asked abruptly. "How did you meet your wife?"

He looked up, startled by the question. "That's quite a change of subject," he said coolly.

"Do you mind my asking?" she said.

A frown crossed his face. "No," he said. "No." He sat thoughtfully for a moment, as if considering his reply. Then he said, "I met her in Rome, when I was studying there. She was a student at the university. We were married for eight years."

"What was she like?"

Ian sighed. "Gabriella . . . Gabriella was like a beautiful, exotic plant that should never have been transplanted. She never took to life here. She never bloomed here. She had come to Rome from a small village, and in her heart she always longed for home."

Laura took a sip of tea and set her cup carefully on the table. "She must have loved you very much, to leave her country and come here with you."

Ian pressed his lips together. "She had a very tender heart. Sometimes I think she loved us too much, Phillip and me. She was uneasy whenever we were out of her sight. She was forever fearful of life here. Of what could happen . . ."

"Maybe she had a premonition," said Laura.

"Maybe she did," he agreed. He sipped some tea. Then he said, "I used to scoff at things like premonitions. But no more . . ."

She looked at Ian thoughtfully. Their paths had crossed once, long ago, and then diverged. But their dreams had been mangled in a similar way. It was as if they had been living parallel lives. Of course, in her case, it was a little different. In her case, she was still suspected of engineering her loss.

"Look, Ian. I'm not trying to be coy. Believe me. I like you. I'm . . . glad we met each other again. I like talking to you. But I just think it would be best for both of us if you continued on your trip," she said carefully.

Ian put down his plate and reached for her hand. His touch felt like an electric shock. "I don't think so," he said. He gazed at her intently, and she shivered. She pulled her hand away from him and looked away.

"The police are going to poke through your life. It's no fun, I assure you."

"I'll take my chances," he said.

Laura avoided his penetrating gaze by looking at her watch. "It's late. I have to call Michael in," she said, standing up abruptly.

Without waiting for him to respond, she turned and walked through the house to the back door of the porch and opened it. "Michael," she cried. "Time to come in. It's getting dark."

"Five more minutes, Mom," his little voice called back.

"Now," she insisted. "Right now." She heard Ian's footsteps behind her and felt his gaze, steady on her, like a warm hand massaging the base of her neck. Hurry, she thought. I mustn't be alone with him. She stood at the doorway, looking out, until, with relief, she saw Michael's little white face coming toward her, glowing in the gathering darkness of the yard.

* * *

"I think maybe she did kill him," Candy said airily, waving her hand in front of her to dry the polish on her nails. She was lying on a leather chaise in the den. Richard was seated at his huge mahogany desk, working feverishly at the laptop computer open in front of him.

Richard rubbed his eyes and looked over at his wife. "What are you talking about?"

"Laura, who else?" asked Candy, gingerly lifting a copy of *Elle* from the chrome rack beside her and propping it open against her perfect thighs. "With a hunk like that waiting in the wings, who could blame her?"

"Candy," Richard said in a warning voice, "I have work to do."

"So do your stupid work. Who's stopping you?"

Richard stared at the screen, and the computer whirred quietly. The figures in front of his eyes caused him to press his lips together anxiously. His hands felt clammy on the keyboard. The pages of Candy's magazine riffled through her fingers. Richard looked over at his wife. She was expecting a concession. He tried to get by on the minimum. "You don't really think that, do you?"

Candy shrugged and did not look up.

He kept his gaze on her, waiting for her to respond, but she was carefully turning pages with her fingertips. Then she lifted the whole magazine to her face and inhaled the scent from a perfume ad. She was getting pissed at him. The chill was beginning to set in. He had to try to change her mood. But he was clumsy at this. He never seemed to get it right. Maybe if he changed the subject . . .

"I think my dad's really getting a kick out of that new boat. That was a great idea you had to buy it for him," Richard said. It was stretching the point to say that it was Candy's idea, but he was in a tight spot.

"I noticed," Candy drawled. "I thought we'd never get off that goddamned boat."

Richard sighed. She was determined to talk about it. She wasn't going to be nice if he didn't give in. He leaned back on his chair and crossed his arms over his chest, trying to look wise and legally astute. "The thing is, I did advise them to get that insurance. It wasn't her idea. So as far as I could see, she didn't really have any motive. Besides, she and Jimmy seemed very happy together . . ."

"Oh, Richard, how do you know whether they were happy or not?" Candy said scornfully. "Men never know these things."

"You don't really think there was anything to that guy and her, do you?"

Candy looked up. "No. I think she's taking sailing lessons."

Richard clenched his jaw and stared off into the distance. "Well, it's none of our business if she has a new friend."

"A new friend," Candy snorted. "You're ridiculous, Richard. You think a woman wants to be friends with a stud like that?"

"I don't know and I don't care," Richard said irritably, knowing that she was comparing him unfavorably to the man they had glimpsed on the boat. "What difference does it make to you, anyway?"

"It doesn't make any difference to me," said Candy. "That's up to the police to decide."

"The police? What do the police have to do with this?"

Candy studied a fashion photograph, her head tilted thoughtfully to one side. She held up the magazine and pointed to a photograph of a model in a pale pink organza shirt and palazzo pants. "How do you think I'd look in that?" she mused.

Richard sighed. Once Candy eyed an outfit, it was as good as purchased. "What about the police?" he repeated anxiously.

"I called them and told them about it," she said.

Richard stared at his wife. "You called the police! What would possess you to do such a stupid thing?"

Candy's eyes flashed. "Don't you dare call me stupid, Richard."

"Come on, Candy," Richard wheedled. "She's my client. It's my job to protect her."

"Well, she's not *my* client. And you'd think you'd be concerned. He was supposed to be your best friend."

"You just don't know what's involved here," Richard said in exasperation.

Candy looked at him over the top of her magazine. "What does that mean, Richard? You're sweating like a pig."

"I'm handling her money. I'm . . . I'm responsible for her welfare."

"And what about the welfare of your friend? Your dead friend. Oh, you make me sick, Richard," Candy said dismissively. "If you don't care, I don't know why I should."

"Well, if you didn't care, why did you go and call the cops?" Richard cried.

"Because you'd never have the balls, Richard. God . . ." Candy shook her head in disgust.

Richard frowned and tried to concentrate on the computer screen. Candy was silent, ignoring him. He knew this could go on for hours. When she wasn't pleased with him, she could be very inflexible. But he couldn't worry about her sulking right now. He had other things on his mind. The police. Jesus, Candy. She had no concept, no understanding, of how . . . involved he was in Laura's business affairs. Richard rubbed his forehead, trying to massage away the pain that was settling in between his eyes.

CHAPTER FOURTEEN

Ron Leonard shifted his weight from one foot to another and gazed around the large, thoroughly modern headquarters of the New Brighton police station while he waited for Hal Morgan, the deputy chief of police, to finish his conversation with a pretty female officer who was handing him files and describing the contents of each one. For a brief moment Ron thought about his suit. It was one of three gray suits he wore for work. The best one. He'd bought it in Philadelphia at Boyd's Men's Store, and it was a muted pinstripe that you could wear anywhere and command respect. DA Jackson, his boss, had steered him to Boyd's for his shopping after he came in one day wearing a green plaid suit from Kmart. Clyde Jackson took great care with appearances. He wanted the people from his office to be taken seriously. Ron was glad he'd worn this suit to New Brighton. This was the Connecticut coast, and Chief Morgan looked like something off the cover of the Brooks Brothers catalog.

It was ultimately Clyde Jackson's decision that Ron make this trip to New Brighton. Ron had reported to the DA all that he had learned about Ian Turner and Laura Reed. At first DA Jackson had ordered Ron just to keep an eye on the pair, hesitating to jump the gun. So Ron had staked out the house and, in the past week, had seen Turner coming and going from the Reed house every day, sometimes several times a day. They never went out together, but they were definitely holed up inside that house with one another. When he reported this to the DA, Jackson's response was unequivocal.

"Get up to Connecticut," he said. "Find out all you can about this guy." They were thinking alike—that Laura and Ian Turner had been lying low, and now that Jimmy Reed had been dead for several months, the pair figured it was safe to come out of the woodwork.

Morgan thanked the young officer and turned to Ron. "Sorry to keep you waiting, Detective. Let's go in my office and have a look at these."

Hal Morgan indicated a leather chair and waved the folders at him sheepishly. "All this stuff is on the computer," he said, "but I'm not quite up to speed on the technology. Officer Weller sometimes helps me out by printing up what I need."

"Computer literate and lovely, too," Ron said pleasantly.

Hal Morgan sighed. "Yes, she is. If I don't watch out, she'll have my job. I'm supposed to attend this computer course, but who has time? I'm working overtime as it is. The kids have Little League on the weekend. The house needs painting . . . I can't put it off much longer, though. The computer, I mean . . . or the house, for that matter."

Ron nodded sympathetically. "It's not my strong point, either," he said, although he had taken the course. He did have the time.

"You a married man, Detective?"

Ron shook his head. "Still waiting for Miss Right," he said.

Hal Morgan snorted. "Yeah, well, enjoy it while you can. Okay, let's look at this stuff. Although I'm not likely to forget this case." He put on his half glasses and peered at the top file. He handed a copy over to Ron.

"Stuart Short. By day, a mild-mannered deliveryman for a baked goods company. Lived with his grandmother in one of our less affluent neighborhoods. Paid his bills, sang in the church choir, and played street hockey with some of the kids who lived on his block. By night, Mr. Short was ruthlessly turning houses in the area into raging infernos. He managed to burn down six houses in a year and a half before we caught up with him. It wasn't easy finding him. He'd never been in trouble with the law before. Of course he had set Granny's couch on fire, and her back shed, in past years, but she never reported him. Lord knows how many other little conflagrations he set along the way, before he turned to the big game."

"How many deaths?" Ron asked.

"Four, including Ian Turner's wife and young son. He's doing three life sentences for his work."

"And he's confessed to setting all these fires?"

"No, actually, he's denied any part of it. But we got him dead to rights. Eyewitness identifications, physical evidence up the yin-yang from his house, his car, the works. The jury was out for all of an hour before they convicted him."

"And you're sure the same man set all the fires?"

Hal Morgan nodded. "The MO was identical in every case. Point of origin, means of ignition, the works. Serial arson is a signature crime—as I'm sure you know."

Ron Leonard frowned at the file.

"Why? What's your interest in this Turner guy?" Hal asked.

"He's keeping company with a local widow whose husband was shot in the head in their bedroom on New Year's Eve. She claims there was a masked man, a burglar, but we have reason to doubt her story. The husband was heavily insured. She was home at the time of the murder, was virtually uninjured, the house was not ransacked. You get the picture."

Hal Morgan nodded.

"Then, all of a sudden, she turns up with your Mr. Turner," said Ron. "A recent widower."

"Did he move down to your area after his son died?"

"He claims he's been on a boat in the Caribbean since November."

"Is it true?"

Ron shrugged. "I've talked to some people in Barbados, but I haven't been able to track down anybody who can place him there at the time of the murder. And who keeps track of a guy on a boat? There are airports on every island down there. He could have made a quick trip to take care of Jimmy Reed and been back on his yacht the next morning."

Hal Morgan scratched his head uneasily. "I don't know much about the man. He's some kind of scientist. Worked on submarines, I think. I'll tell you, though. The death of his son was a real heartbreaker around here. The boy was burned from head to toe—eighty-five percent of his body, I heard."

Ron Leonard winced.

"Yeah." Morgan nodded. "I didn't see him, but I understand it was brutal. The kid lingered for a while. Turner moved into the hospital. He was with that boy day and night. There was tremendous sympathy for him around here. Not to mention outrage about the arsonist. Man, they were on our asses. We got lucky not long after that fire and picked him up. Good thing, too. I think I would have lost my job in another month."

"Well, he may be a saint around here, but Turner's the best lead we've got right now in our murder case. There's got to be something about this Reed woman's story that we can crack. And I'm thinking it's gonna be Turner."

"Doesn't hurt to nose around," said Hal Morgan.

"I'm going to spend a few days—talk to his family, his co-workers, see if there's anything . . ."

"Well, we're slow right now. I've got a man here who can go with you. Help you find your way around."

"I appreciate the courtesy," said Ron.

Hal Morgan's phone began to ring. He shook hands with Ron, then lifted the receiver.

"Can I keep this?" Ron asked, lifting his copy of the file.

"Sure." Hal nodded and then waved as he resumed his call.

* * *

"Dr. Kasprak," said Edward Lee, a young man with Asian features wearing a white lab coat, "these are the police officers who wish to speak with you."

Ron and Officer Witkowski, his navigator and driver, made their first stop at the thermonuclear study center at the naval base. They had been welcomed by Dr. Lee and, after some elaborate security precautions, had been ushered through three sets of doors into a large laboratory. Expecting a man, Ron was startled when a tall, fine-featured woman with blond hair worn in a French twist turned to greet them at Dr. Lee's words. My male chauvinist bias is showing, Ron thought. Sure enough, the identification picture on her lab coat read Andrea Kasprak, Ph.D.

Dr. Lee introduced them, and they shook hands all around. Ron looked around the room, which was replete with computers, consoles lit up, and every kind of electronic gadget known to man. The room was abuzz with people at work, most of whom wore glasses, all of whom seemed completely absorbed in their tasks. "Doctor, thank you for taking the time to see me. I'd ask you what it is you do here, but I'm sure I wouldn't understand the answer."

The doctor sighed and then forced a smile. "Perhaps we should skip it, then."

Ron cleared his throat and looked to his notes. "You were acquainted with Dr. Ian Turner and his wife, Gabriella?"

"Dr. Turner was my colleague."

"Did it surprise you when he quit his job and went to live on a boat?"

"Given what happened to his family, no," she said. Ron looked at her expectantly. Reluctantly she continued, "After Phillip died, I think he was too drained, too emotionally worn out, to even think. He probably did the right thing, taking a sabbatical, so to speak. Getting away."

"So, you encouraged him to take this . . . sabbatical," Ron said blandly.

Dr. Kasprak hesitated, and Ron had his answer. But she quickly tried to cover her response. "I think work is good for people when they're . . . distressed. But I'm no expert on these matters . . ."

Ron made a note and nodded. "Did Dr. Turner travel much in his work?"

Dr. Kasprak frowned. "Oh, occasionally."

"Where to?"

"Well, there are scientific conferences we all attend from time to time."

"Can you give me a list of the ones he attended in, say, the last two years?"

Dr. Kasprak looked a little bit put out by the request. "I don't have any such list."

"Did Dr. Turner have a secretary?" Ron persisted.

Dr. Kasprak sighed. "He had an assistant. I'll see if I can get someone to put it together for you. Do you need it right away?"

"I'll be around for a day or two. I can check back," Ron said, pretending not to notice her irritation. "Do you have any reason to suspect that Dr. Turner was carrying on an extramarital relationship?"

Dr. Kasprak looked shocked. "No," she said.

Ron waited for an elaboration that didn't come. "Any reason why you think that?"

"I have no reason to think otherwise," said Dr. Kasprak. "Dr. Turner was devoted to his . . . family."

"Were you social friends with Dr. Turner and his wife?"

Dr. Kasprak hesitated. "No, not really. Mrs. Turner was Italian. Her English was limited. It's difficult to live outside your own country," the doctor said severely.

"So you didn't socialize outside of work . . ."

"Occasionally we would do things that were fun with Phillip. We have a son the same age as Phillip, so we would take him with us on outings." She looked at Ron unwaveringly. A muscle twitched at the corner of her eye, betraying an emotion she did not otherwise reveal. "We had plans to go to a baseball game that very night . . ." Her voice trailed away.

Ron looked at her curiously. "Phillip Turner was supposed to be with you that night?"

"Yes. With us and our son, Zak."

"But he didn't go?"

Dr. Kasprak sighed. "Gabriella called and said he wasn't feeling well. I sometimes think she was a little overly cautious about her son . . . but that's a mother's prerogative," she said stoutly.

"And was Dr. Turner supposed to go with you to the game?" Ron asked.

Andrea Kasprak shook her head. "No. He was working on a project at the lab here."

Ron frowned and felt a little surge of adrenaline. "Did you tell him that Phillip wasn't going with you? That he was going to be at home?"

The woman sighed in exasperation. "I don't know. I don't think so. What difference does it make?"

"Dr. Turner told the police he had to work late at the lab that night," said Ron. "Was anyone here with him?"

"Of course someone was here. We have a rather large security staff, in case you failed to notice."

Yeah, Ron thought. And any guy who's a rocket scientist could figure out a way to evade a few half-asleep security guards. He decided to change his tack. "Did Dr. Turner ever mention a woman named Laura Reed or Laura Hastings to you?"

"No. Never."

"And you have no reason to believe he was involved with someone outside his marriage . . ."

"You already asked me that," said Dr. Kasprak. "Now if you're through . . ."

She was clearly annoyed at the nature of his questions—as if he were making obscene suggestions just to degrade her. "Sorry to offend you, ma'am," Ron said insincerely. "Murder is a messy business."

"Murder?" she cried. "What has this got to do with murder?"

"That's what I'm trying to figure out," said Ron.

CHAPTER FIFTEEN

Gary sat in his chair on Laura's back porch with his eyes closed and let his pale face catch the warmth of the sun. He was always cold. It had been that way ever since he was confined to the chair. Wanda kept the heat on in the house well into June. And he wore a heavy jacket even on a beautiful day like this one. The screen door slammed and Laura came out, carrying a mug of hot coffee and a thin sheaf of paper. He turned his head to gaze at her.

"I'm glad you were home," he said.

"Oh, I'm always home," she said, thanking her stars that his visit had not coincided with Ian's. "What's new with you?" she asked.

"Actually, there is something new," he said. "I'm getting an award."

"An award," Laura cried delightedly. "From who?"

"The arts council," he said. "Some special recognition thing. Artist of the Year for the county. Nothing big."

"Don't be so modest," she said, poking him in the arm. "That's great."

He nodded, smiling bashfully. "It was nice."

"That reminds me," she said, looking at him with narrowed eyes, "did you ever do anything about pursuing that fellowship in Boston?"

Gary sighed. "I . . . I just . . . let it go. Without Jimmy pushing me . . . you know."

"He wanted that for you so much," Laura said kindly.

"Here, let me see what you've done," he said brusquely.

"These are only a couple of sketches," she said, placing his coffee on the table beside him and handing him the pages. "But it felt good to at least be working again."

Gary automatically warmed his hands over the steaming coffee and then took the pages from her and bent his steel gray head over them, studying them. He had showed up unannounced, just wanting a visit, and Laura was glad to be able to have a few drawings to show him. She felt a little awkward with Gary now, especially since she knew how thoroughly he would disapprove of her new friendship if he found out about it. As he sipped his coffee and examined the sketches, Laura glanced at her watch. Michael's bus would drop him at the corner soon. She wanted to be there to meet him. And then Ian would be arriving. She needed to leave enough time for herself to change and comb her hair.

In the past week she had seen Ian every day. They didn't go out. She didn't want to leave Michael with baby-sitters or impose on Pam. That's what she said, anyway. The truth was, she felt more secure staying right there in the house. She could tell herself that they weren't dating, that it was just a friendship. With Michael upstairs there was no chance of anything physical happening between them. And as long as nothing physical happened, she thought, she had nothing to feel guilty about. Although she knew very well that he was attracted to her, Ian didn't pressure her in any way. He treated her as if she were fragile and seemed content just to be near her. She didn't have to face the stares and the gossip they might encounter on the street. She knew she wasn't doing anything wrong, but then again, she knew she hadn't killed Jimmy, either. And it didn't seem to make a whit of difference to anyone else in this town.

So they stayed in. They ate meals, watched TV, played card games and video games, and they talked. When she pressed him, he would talk about Gabriella. But he answered her questions reluctantly. And when she tried to tell Ian about Jimmy, it was clear that he didn't like hearing about her late husband. She remembered Jimmy saying once that he didn't want to know anything about her old flames. He didn't want to imagine her with someone else, even for a moment. If Ian felt that same way, Laura didn't want to acknowledge it.

Seeing Michael at play seemed to remind him of Phillip. He often would share memories about his son, and they would swap stories about small boys that made him laugh, and then, suddenly, he would grow quiet and change the subject. He seemed to derive a special pleasure from playing with Michael that made Laura's heart fill up with gratitude. Sometimes, when the three of them were together, she had to catch herself from calling him "Jimmy."

She'd actually begun to cook again. She and Michael had subsisted on soup and frozen dinners these last few months. Michael hardly cared what he ate, and she never had an appetite. But now that there was someone else at the table . . .

"I like this one," said Gary, handing her a sketch of a small boy nestled under the wing of a giant bird. "That texture in the feathers is great."

"That's my favorite, too," said Laura. "I worked hard on that."

"What got you started again?" Gary asked.

Laura felt her face turning pink. What indeed? The fact that she had begun to feel like living again in the last few days? She couldn't tell Gary that. She spoke carefully. "I'm not sure. Maybe . . . maybe it's the weather."

"Well, I was thinking we could take Michael on a picnic one day soon. Of course, you'd have to be in charge of the food," he said apologetically. "And we can't go anywhere muddy."

Laura nodded. Ian was sure to be gone before long. Each day she half expected him to say it was his last. The thought of his leaving made her melancholy. There was no denying it to herself. "Yes, I think it would be fine," she said.

"You don't look too happy about it," he said hurriedly. "Maybe it's too soon."

For a moment she wanted to confess, to tell him why it made her unhappy, but she immediately thought better of it. She knew that he regarded her as still married to Jimmy. So why burst his bubble? Ian would soon be gone, and Gary would never have to know. She was just glad that Dolores and Sidney were in Florida. She wouldn't ask Michael to lie to his grandparents about Ian visiting them.

"Not at all," she said, covering Gary's hand with her own for a moment. "I think it would be a perfect thing to do. I know we'll enjoy it." She looked at her watch again. "Gary, I'm going to have to go meet Michael's bus in a minute."

"I'm sorry," he said quickly, putting down the sketches. "I shouldn't have come without calling." He wheeled his chair around abruptly and, with one wistful glance back at her, started down the ramp. "It's great to see you," he said.

Laura watched him go fondly. "You're always welcome here," she said. "I'll look forward to that picnic. Michael too."

Gary nodded gravely. "So will I."

After he had rounded the corner by the lilac bushes, Laura picked up his mug and the sketches and hurried back into the house.

She was just about to head out the door when the phone rang. She felt as if the phone were her enemy nowadays. The police invading her life. The ever-present dread of an anonymous caller, enjoying the sound of her fear. She never heard the ring of the phone without thinking of it. But she always answered. A mother whose child was not in the house always answered the phone.

"Yes?" she said with her usual wariness.

"Laura, it's Marta."

With a sense of relief, Laura sank onto the chair beside the phone. Marta. She sometimes felt that her editor was more like a glamorous older sister to her than anything else. She could picture Marta there, at her desk overlooking Sixth

Avenue, her desktop piled with proofs and manuscripts and her ever-present diet Coke. Marta—dressed in something man-tailored and chic, with her shoes kicked off under the desk and her tortoiseshell half glasses perched on her nose, talking on the phone and checking her perfect makeup for smudges at the same time.

"It's good to hear your voice," Laura said sincerely.

"I'm not calling to bug you," Marta said hastily. "This is strictly to see how you are doing. I've been meaning to call for a while, but with the ABA, you know . . ." Marta was referring to a huge booksellers' convention that occurred every Memorial Day weekend and absorbed much of the time and energy of publishers each year.

"Oh, I know," said Laura.

"How's Michael doing?"

"He's doing okay. Looking forward to the end of school, of course."

"Like any normal child."

"Well, you must be psychic. I actually have started to work a little bit these last few days."

"Great. We're talking sketches, I presume," said Marta, who knew that Laura always drew first and then wrote to the drawings.

"A few," said Laura.

"That's good. Does that mean you're feeling better?"

Laura hesitated. She felt a need to confide in someone, tell someone who was on her side. "Something's sort of . . . come up. That's made me feel better . . ."

"Wait, don't tell me. You've managed to meet a single, straight, attractive man in that one-horse town you live in."

Laura laughed in spite of herself. "What makes you think it's a man?"

"What else is there?" Marta asked. She had been divorced after a brief, youthful marriage and was always decrying the shortage of eligible men in New York City. "I'm gonna move there," she said. "I mean, how can this be? I'm here in a city of eight million . . ."

"I knew this guy as a child. We just sort of stumbled across each other."

"The only man I've stumbled across lately was homeless and sleeping in the lobby of my building with flies buzzing around him," Marta said ruefully. "So, is this wedding bells?"

"Oh, Marta, come on. Please. It's just a friendship. Something to take my mind off of . . . everything . . ."

"Hey, if this is a good one, don't let him get away. Listen to your aunt Marta . . ."

Laura sighed. "It's good to talk to you. I wish I could see you."

"Come to New York. Bring your new guy. What's his name?"

"He's not my new guy. And his name is Ian."

"So bring him anyway."

"Maybe I'll get up there one of these days. I've got to run, Marta. I've got to meet Michael's bus."

"Okay, listen, fax me those drawings when you're ready."

"I will."

"And . . . did that Bob Gerster from *Book World* ever get in touch with you?"

Laura looked at the clock. "No . . . who's that?"

"The freelancer who was going to do the story on you."

"No," said Laura.

"Okay. If I see him at the ABA, I'll jog his memory. In fact, I'll make a point of seeking him out. He was cute."

"Well, you have a good time at the convention," said Laura. She was standing up now, ready to put down the phone. She didn't want to be late for the bus.

"I'll call you when I get back."

"Bye." Laura hung up. She was late. She started to run.

CHAPTER SIXTEEN

Michael looked down at his library book, trying to pretend he didn't notice the wads of paper hitting him in the head as the bus rumbled along. He knew only a few of the words on each page of the book, but he was concentrating on those few words as hard as he could. Maybe if he sat very still and quiet, he thought, they would stop. He glanced out the window to see which corner the bus had just passed. Only a few more stops until his street. The ride seemed to proceed with agonizing slowness.

"Hey, toad." Michael felt someone plunk the back of his head hard with a finger. He didn't have to turn around to know who it was. It was the redheaded kid with freckles. He was a big kid, a second-grader, and he and his two friends had lately started to sit behind him and bother him every time they got on the same bus. Michael tried his best to avoid them. He would try to wait, dawdling on the curb, until they got on and sat down, and then he would sit far away from them. But they were wise to him now. As soon as they spotted him, they would move their seats closer to him. Sometimes, when he sat with Louis, Michael could just pretend he didn't hear the big kids. But Louis had gone home early today, and Michael was alone and at their mercy.

"Can't you feel that, toad?" the redheaded kid asked. "Hey, he can't feel it. We better try something else."

Two girls from his class who were sitting in the seats across the aisle saw what was happening and turned away, pretending to look out the window. Nobody wanted to mess with these big kids. Michael's chin trembled, but he was determined not to cry. Mom always said it was okay to cry, but if these big kids saw tears, he knew instinctively, it would be like sharks smelling blood. He looked helplessly up to the front of the bus. The driver was a woman named Audrey who was nice to all the kids. But she was watching the road, and Michael's torment was lost in the general din of excited young voices. Besides, he couldn't go ask a woman to help him. Then they'd call him a wuss forever.

Michael tried to ignore them and craned his neck to see how much farther he had to endure it. One more stop and he'd be off the bus.

Goaded on by the smaller boy's obvious anxiety, the redheaded kid reached out and plucked the Phillies baseball cap from Michael's head. There were loud guffaws from the other boys.

Michael reached up instinctively to try to save his hat and then let out a cry. "Give it back," he said. "That's mine."

The redheaded kid looked the cap over and then tossed it, Frisbee-like, to the boy in the back, who missed it. The red cap fell into the aisle in the bus.

Michael stared at it, tears welling in his eyes. His father had bought him the cap last year, when he took him to his first baseball game. The game seemed very long, and it was hot in the seats, but the hot dogs were good, and the cap was his reward for sitting through the whole nine innings. His symbol of acceptance into the man's world of baseball. It lay on the floor of the bus now. One of the big boys put his foot on it and ground it into the dirty floor. That was too much.

Michael jumped out of his seat and tried to get it.

"Back in your seats," shouted Audrey, stretching up to see them in the rearview mirror.

"Give it," Michael cried as the boy in back flipped it again to the redheaded kid.

Michael spun around and lunged for it as the redheaded kid dangled it over his head. "That's mine. My dad gave me that."

The redheaded kid leaned his face close to Michael's, crammed the hat down crookedly on Michael's head, and crooned, "When was that? Before your mother clocked him?"

He always took the bait. It was why they loved to get on him so. Michael knelt on the seat and faced them, his eyes blurry with tears. "She did not do it," he cried. "You stop saying that."

"You stop saying that," they parroted, poking one another and laughing.

"My dad says she did," said the redheaded kid, putting his face so close to Michael that the younger boy could see each individual freckle.

"Your dad's a stinking jerk," said Michael. He didn't know where the nerve to say it came from. For a brief moment he felt exhilarated and brave.

"Watch your mouth," cried the bigger boy. And then, before Michael could duck or even think of it, a freckled fist smacked him in the nose.

Blood spurted from his nostrils as he toppled back, and kids were screaming. Audrey's voice boomed through the back, ordering them to stop as the bus swerved over to the curb.

"All right, that's enough, that's enough!" Audrey was in among them, examining the damage. Michael could taste the salty blood in his mouth, mixed with tears. The other boys were taunting. The girls were shrieking, and Audrey was ordering everybody to quiet down.

Michael scrambled up and grabbed his books as Audrey gave the redheaded kid stern orders to resume his seat.

"Are you okay?" Audrey asked worriedly, fumbling for a tissue to wipe away the blood.

"Let me go," Michael cried. The tears were flowing now, and he wriggled away from her, wanting only one thing—to get off that bus.

He ducked underneath her arm and ran down the aisle to the door. Audrey marched down the aisle behind him, yelling, "Everybody get in your seats and be quiet!"

"Open the door," he pleaded. He was shaking from head to toe. "Open the door."

Audrey peered out to the curb. "I don't see your mom," she said. Michael's heart sank.

"Let me wipe that mess off your face," Audrey pleaded.

"No, don't touch me," Michael cried, and then, out the window, he saw a familiar face. "Let me off. There's Ian. He came for me." He didn't know if it was true or not, but there was Ian, walking up toward Chestnut Street. "Ian," he wailed through the open window.

Ian looked around, baffled for a moment, and then he spotted Michael in the window of the school bus. He began to stride toward the bus. "Let me go," Michael insisted.

Audrey opened the doors of the bus, and Michael ran down the steps and barreled into Ian. Ian crouched down and looked at him. "What happened to you?" he asked.

"Some big kids took my hat."

Ian looked up at Audrey, who shook her head. "Bullies," she said quietly.

Ian nodded soberly, examining the crumpled dirty cap on the child's head. "Yeah, but you got it back, I see," Ian said admiringly.

"Yeah," Michael admitted through his tears.

"Come on," Ian said gravely, offering his hand to the boy. "You did fine."

Michael reached up and took his hand.

* * *

She was late. Marta's call had kept her just a minute too long, she thought as she saw the bus, Michael's bus, pulling away

124

from the curb. She always met him at the bus, even though it was only two blocks to the corner. She trusted no one, nothing, any longer. She did not want him walking those two blocks alone.

Laura hurried down the front steps and started for the corner. She saw them at once. Ian was holding Michael's hand. There was blood everywhere. On Michael's face, on his shirt. Michael's shoulders were heaving. Laura began to run. She reached them in moments and lifted her son into her arms. "What happened?" she cried. "What's wrong?"

Michael went to her willingly, locking his arms around her neck. "Big kids were picking on me. We had a fight."

She looked frantically over his shoulder at Ian, who shook his head. "He's all right. Just shook him up a little. A bloody nose."

"What happened, honey?"

"He took my hat. So I said his dad was a jerk. So he punched me."

"Why'd you say that?" she asked gently.

Michael straightened up and looked at her with his grave brown eyes, still red rimmed with tears, blood smeared over his face. "Because he took my hat and stomped on it. He was picking on me."

"But why was he picking on you?"

"Because of saying that you clocked Dad."

"Oh, Michael," Laura said, pressing her face into his shoulder. "I'm sorry."

"It's okay," said Michael, childishly patting her back. "It's not your fault. Lucky Ian came along."

"Yes, lucky," she whispered. "Thank you."

"It's all done with now," Ian said. "Let's go home."

It sounded strange to hear him say that. It's just what Jimmy would have said, she thought. She felt as if she should protest, remind him that it was not his home, but the words made her feel so safe. "Yes, let's," she said.

CHAPTER SEVENTEEN

Jason Turner's house was a neat but slightly shabby Cape
Cod prefab, probably built in the fifties, on a quiet street of
large trees and rows of other, similar homes. It was painted
periwinkle blue and had a matching garage set back from the
house. Two little boys were playing on the front lawn, but
when they saw the police car pull up and stop in front of the
house, they ran for the front door, shrieking for their mother
and slamming the aluminum storm door behind them.

By the time Ron and Officer Witkowski arrived at the
front door, a petite woman with cotton-candy-like blond hair
was already there waiting for them. Her features were sharp
and carefully made up. She opened the door boldly as they
approached and waited for them to speak first.

"Mrs. Cheryl Turner?"

The woman nodded.

"I'm Detective Ron Leonard. This is Officer Witkowski.
Could we talk to you for a minute?"

"Sure," she said, gesturing for them to come in.

The two little boys were crouched on the staircase, and
the smaller one started when Ron looked up at them. "Is your
husband home, ma'am?" Ron asked.

"Well, he's sleeping. He just got off his shift a few hours ago."

"I'm only in town for a short time. I'd really like to talk to him."

"Mark, Peter, go wake up Daddy. Tell him there's a policeman here to talk to him," Cheryl said to her sons. The boys whispered and poked each other.

"Go on," Cheryl bawled at them.

A woman with short gray hair and brilliant blue eyes came drifting into the room, clutching a ballpoint pen and a sheaf of coupons as the boys pounded up the staircase.

"Mother, the police want to ask some questions," Cheryl explained to the older woman. "This is my mother-in-law, Edith Turner."

"How do you do?" said Ron. "Are you Ian Turner's mother?"

"Oh, yes," said Edith. "I have the two boys—Ian and Jason."

"Is this about Ian?" Cheryl asked. She lit up an extra-light menthol cigarette and took a drag. "Nothing's happened to him, has it?"

"No, not at all. I just wanted to ask you some questions about him, and his late wife."

Cheryl took another drag off her cigarette and looked at Ron with narrowed eyes. "Why? What's this all about?"

"It's a routine investigation," Ron said firmly.

"We went through all this after the fire," said Cheryl.

"This is another matter. Concerning an incident in New Jersey, where I'm from."

"What kind of incident? Are you sure he's all right?"

"Fine," said Ron. "This concerns a woman he's currently dating."

Cheryl looked surprised. "Oh. Okay."

"Can you tell me, were you close to your brother-in-law? Was his marriage a happy one?"

Edith Turner had settled into a chair with a lap desk and was busily filling out coupons, the tip of her tongue sticking out as she concentrated.

Cheryl shrugged. "Yeah, I guess so. They were happy enough, I'd say."

"You don't seem too sure."

"Well, we weren't that close. I mean, Jason and Ian are close. You know how brothers are. But they lived on the hill, if you know what I mean. Ian's the brain of the family. He's the one with the money. And Gabriella . . . well . . ."

Ron noted the hesitation in her response. "You didn't care for her."

"I wouldn't say that, really. She was sweet. Shy. But, I mean, she never spoke English. I think she could, but she didn't really want to get involved with us."

"Did she speak English to you, Mrs. Turner?" Ron said, turning to the older woman.

"Mother," Cheryl said impatiently.

The old woman looked up from her efforts. "I'm sorry, I didn't hear you. What?"

"Did Gabriella speak English to you?"

Edith frowned. "I guess, once in a while. We didn't see too much of them, you know." She looked at Ron apologetically. "I don't mean to be rude, but I want to finish before the mailman gets here. My contests," she said. "I'm a nut when it comes to entering contests. It's my thing, I guess you could say. But I win a lot of stuff, don't I, Cheryl?"

"Mother, the police don't want to know about your contests."

"I won this lamp, right here," she said, tapping the standing lamp beside her with her pen. "And that CD player. Although don't ask me what a CD is. And . . ." She could see that Cheryl was getting ready to interrupt again. She held up her pen for silence. "And let's not forget the trip to Disney World . . ."

"No, we won't forget that," said Cheryl, stubbing out her cigarette.

Ron looked down at his pad, then turned back to Cheryl, who was waiting patiently for the next question. "Do you think your brother-in-law was faithful to his wife? Would you have any way of knowing? Might he have told your husband?"

"If he told Jason, Jason would've told me. We don't keep secrets. No, I don't think he was screwing around on her. I'm not going to tell you they were the happiest couple in the world. She never wanted to leave the house. It was like she was scared of her own shadow. But he tried. He tried to make her happy."

"So you have no reason to think Ian was involved with anyone else."

Cheryl shook her head, but she appeared to be thinking it over. "No . . ."

"He quit his job to live on a boat. Didn't that seem strange to you?"

"You don't know what he went through . . . with Phillip. You know about Phillip?" The hard angles of Cheryl's face softened. "Ohhh . . ." She let out a little groan. "That little sweet thing. We all loved him. He used to be here a lot. He and my boys were like the Three Musketeers. We loved him like our own."

"And Ian and Gabriella . . ."

"Doted on that kid," Cheryl said with authority. "Adored him."

Edith Turner was frowning at her puzzle. "What's a four-letter word that rhymes with cost?" she wondered aloud.

Cheryl leaned toward Ron. "She's in her own little world."

A slightly overweight, good-looking young man with bright blue eyes shambled down the staircase, rubbing his face as if to revive himself.

"Hey, honey," said Cheryl.

Jason Turner frowned at Ron and Officer Witkowski, who were seated in his living room. "Mark said there were cops here."

Ron stood up and offered his hand. "I'm Detective Leonard. I'm here from the Cape Christian County Prosecutor's Office, in New Jersey."

"What do you want with us?" Jason asked bluntly.

Mark and Peter poked their heads between the spindles of the railing, staring wide-eyed at the policemen in their living room.

"You two," said Cheryl. "Back outside until we're finished here."

"But there's nothing to do out there," Mark complained.

"Shoot some baskets. Do something. Scoot." Reluctantly the boys obeyed.

"I had a few questions about your brother," said Ron. "I've just been asking your wife."

"What about my brother?" Jason said defensively. "I know he's down in your neighborhood. He called me a few nights ago."

"Did he mention what he was doing there?"

"Just spending a few days in port. Why?"

"We are trying to establish if he had a prior relationship with a woman in our county who is now under police investigation."

"My brother's been on a boat for the last six months."

"We know all that," Ron said hurriedly. "Did he ever mention a woman named Laura Reed to you?"

Jason thought it over and shook his head. "Nope."

"Do you have any recollection from your childhood of a girl named Laura Hastings?"

Jason slowly shook his head again. "No," he said, but there was a trace of doubt in his tone.

"They claim to have known each other in grade school. Something about your brother falling into a hole, and she found him."

Jason's eyes widened, and his face turned pale. "Oh, yeah," he said. "Yeah. With the broken leg . . ." He glanced over at his mother, and Ron saw a flash of contempt in his eyes. Edith, who appeared to be absorbed in the jingle she was composing, suddenly stopped writing, her pen poised above the paper. Ron could tell she was listening, but she was pretending not to hear.

Jason sighed. "Yeah. There was a girl, now that I think of it. But she moved away . . . years ago."

"Is that the girl who found him?" Cheryl asked Jason. She was obviously familiar with the story.

Jason nodded grimly.

"Do you know if they kept in contact?"

"No. My brother was married, anyway . . ."

Ron almost had to smile at the assumption this man made, that one circumstance precluded the other. A faithful family man, this Jason. "Mr. Turner, you're a firefighter, isn't that right?"

"That's right."

"Were you present on the night of the fire in your brother's house?"

Jason shook his head. In the corner, Edith raised her hand, as if wanting to be called on in school. "We were in Disney World," she informed him. "Remember I told you I won the trip."

Ron was surprised to see that Jason's eyes were bright with angry tears. "The night he needed me the most . . . the one time I could have repaid him a little for all the things he did for me . . . and I'm in the Magic Kingdom. Life's a bitch."

"Now, Jason," Edith protested. "We had a wonderful time in Disney World. The kids had a wonderful time."

"Stuart Short, the arsonist convicted of setting that series of fires, had a signature means of ignition." Ron consulted his notes. "He used a lit cigarette folded into a matchbook, and he always employed a child's stuffed toy soaked in kerosene." He looked up at Jason. "Kind of a bizarre combination."

Jason shook his head. "Pretty normal for a psycho fire setter. They almost always use matches. It's part of the thrill. As for the toy, well, Stuart was a sick pup . . ."

"Now, these details were kept out of the newspapers."

131

"Well, yeah, to help identify the guy when we caught him."

"Did you ever discuss the arsonist's MO with your brother? You know, how he started the fires. The means he used, his signature, so to speak?"

"No," Jason protested. "Of course not."

"Well, it would only seem a normal thing to do," Ron said smoothly. "I'm sure there was great interest in this area about the arsonist."

"I never told him anything, and he never asked," Jason said angrily. "What are you trying to imply?"

"I'm just asking some questions . . ."

"I'm not going to listen to any more of this crap. Look, I don't know what your problem is, but you lay off my brother. You hear me? He's had enough heartache for one lifetime."

Edith stuffed an envelope, licked it, and sealed it. "Could someone drive me down to the post office with this?" she said plaintively. "I'm afraid if I wait for the mailman, I might not get it postmarked before the deadline."

Jason rose abruptly to his feet. "I'll do it," he said. "Where are my keys?"

Cheryl pointed to a dish on top of the TV. Jason snatched them up and glared at his mother. "Are you ready or not?"

Edith bounced up nervously from her chair. "Pleasure to meet you," she said to Ron and Officer Witkowski.

Ron shook her limp hand and then rose from his chair. "We'd better be on our way, too." Cheryl saw them to the door. As they reached the doorstep, they saw Jason's car roaring down the street, Edith upright as a broomstick on the passenger seat.

"You know, Detective, my husband is very loyal to his brother. He feels very strongly about him."

"I noticed," said Ron. "Well, loyalty is a commendable thing."

Encouraged, Cheryl elaborated. "That time you mentioned. You know, the girl and the pit . . . Jason told me about that. Their father had been looking for Jason to punish him for some stupid thing. He was really cruel to those boys. Ian always tried to stand up to him, protect Jason from him. You know? Well, this particular time, the two of them were hiding out from him in the woods. When they heard the old man coming, Ian boosted Jason up into a tree. The old man caught Ian by the foot and pulled him out of the tree. Broke his leg in the fall. The old bastard left him there. Just collared Jason and dragged him home, and left Ian there with his leg broken. Ian was trying to crawl home when he fell in the pit."

Ron grimaced. "Didn't the mother do anything about it?"

Cheryl shook her head. "You see what she's like. Out there on Planet Edith. Entering contests. She only sees what she wants to see. She tunes out everything else."

"Right," Ron said thoughtfully.

"So, if my husband seems a little . . . protective of Ian . . .," she said apologetically.

"Oh, I understand," said Ron. Better than you might think, he added to himself. Even if Jason knew something about his brother, he'd never tell. Not his wife. Not anybody. "You've been a big help," he said.

CHAPTER EIGHTEEN

The phone rang just as Laura was tucking Michael into bed. The three of them had spent a quiet evening together. Ian had made a fire in the grill, and they'd cooked hamburgers. It had pierced Laura's heart to see him standing there in Jimmy's place, but Michael had been greatly cheered up by a cookout. They'd played cards after supper. Michael had stayed close to Laura, and quiet, all evening long. That was fine with Laura. That was just where she wanted him. Now, as she was about to read him a story, she heard the phone. For a moment she thought of telling Ian to answer it, but then she reconsidered. It could be her in-laws; they were due back any day.

"I'll get it," she called out. She heard Ian coming up the stairs as she kissed Michael and went into her studio to answer the phone. It was Gary.

"Laura," he said, "am I bothering you?"

"No, of course not," she replied. "What's up?"

"Well, you know I told you about the award, from the arts council."

"Right. You distinguished personage, you."

"Right. Well . . ." She could hear a nervous tremor in his voice. He took a deep breath. "The thing is, there's going to be a ceremony at City Hall. I meant to ask you . . . I'd like it, that is, it would make me very proud if you and Michael could come. You know, be my official guests."

"That's so nice of you, Gary. Are you sure you want to be associated with us at a big public event like that?"

"Well, s-sure," he stammered. "I mean, why not?"

"You're a good friend. We'd love to come," said Laura. "When is it?"

"It's next month," he said. "The fifteenth."

"The fifteenth," she repeated. "I'll put it on my calendar."

"If there's a conflict . . .," he said hurriedly.

Laura sighed. No, she thought. I should be all alone again by then. "There won't be," she assured him.

"Is Michael still up?" he asked.

"I was just putting him to bed."

"I'm sorry," said Gary. "You get back to him."

Laura's heart ached for him—he was always so apologetic, so afraid he was bothering her. It was ironic, really, that he should feel that way. Her only real friend. She assured him she was glad of his call and said good night. Then, with a sigh, she padded down the hall to Michael's room. Ian was inside, sitting by the edge of the bed, stroking the boy's hair. She could hear the murmur of his voice, but at first she could not understand what he was saying. Then she was startled to recognize his words as her own.

He was reciting *Raoul and the Giant Yellow Frog*. Michael's eyes were closing, and a smile drifted across his face. Before Ian could finish the story, Michael was asleep. Ian leaned over and switched off the Winnie-the-Pooh lamp. Then he got up and tiptoed toward the door. Seeing Laura in the doorway, he put his finger to his lips. Laura backed out of the room, and Ian pulled the door to as he joined her in the dim hallway.

"He's asleep," he said.

Impulsively she embraced him, resting her face against his chest. He was startled at first, and then, gingerly, he enclosed her in his arms and buried his face in her hair. The

135

feeling of it sent waves of desire rippling through her. For a moment she clung to him. Then, awkwardly, she released him. The expression in his blue eyes was hungry as she let him go. She reached for his hand and held it.

"Thank you," she said.

"For what?"

"For today. For everything. For taking care of Michael. And me."

"It's what I want to do," he said.

She turned and started down the stairs. "Let's not wake him," she said.

Ian followed her to the living room. She sat on the couch, and he sat beside her. He took her hand and lifted it gently to his face, rubbing it against his cheek thoughtfully.

"You were telling him my story," she said, smiling. She took her hand back.

"It's true."

"How did you . . .?"

"I went to your local bookstore and bought your complete collection. I read them all. Several times. They're very good. The stories have a rhythm . . . like poetry. Mesmerizing, really. You're a very talented writer—and an artist."

"How come you never said anything before?"

"Oh, what do I know about it? I'm a scientist. My literary opinion isn't worth much."

"It is to me," she said.

"Well, there it is," he said, smiling. "Who was on the phone? The police again?" He tried to say it lightly but failed.

"A friend of mine," Laura said thoughtfully. "One of the few I have here. His name is Gary. He was one of Jimmy's oldest friends. And one of the only people in this town who has chosen to believe in me. Everybody else around here thinks I killed my husband," she said bluntly. She realized as she said it, she was trying to shock him. But he did not respond.

"How come you never ask me what happened?" she said. "How come you don't seem to have any doubts about me?"

Ian looked at her unsmiling. "That's just it. I have no doubts about you. You don't understand that yet." He could see that she was unsatisfied by his answer. "Maybe it's because I still see the child in you," he said. "That angel's face peering at me out of the gloom. That little voice promising to run for help. You could never kill anyone. Nothing could make me believe that you did."

"I'm not that little girl anymore," she said warningly.

"I noticed," he said, smiling.

Laura got up from the sofa and began to pace restlessly around the room. "I was afraid it was going to be my in-laws on the phone. They're due back from Florida any day."

"You don't like them?"

"My mother-in-law and I never had a good relationship. But after Jimmy was killed . . . well, she needs to blame someone. I understand that. I really do. You don't know how frustrating, how infuriating, it is to have your loved one murdered and not know . . . to have them get away scot-free. Sometimes it's all I can think about. Why don't they catch him? He didn't vanish into thin air. He's out there somewhere. But I feel as if they're not even looking for him. They're just looking at me. And they're not going to find him while they're wasting their time . . ." She could feel herself shaking. "Don't get me started," she said apologetically.

"Why do you stay here?" he asked.

Laura shook her head. "I don't know." She hadn't really given it much thought. Grief had produced a feeling of inertia. "When Jimmy was here, I loved this town, but now . . . Although you know, Ian, I think it wouldn't really matter where I went—this thing would follow me. I feel as if, in no time at all, people would be pointing at me again, whispering that I was the woman who killed her husband." As she said it aloud, she realized that she had known this all along. It had added to her despair about the future. "Until and unless they find the man who killed Jimmy, I will always have this taint on me. No matter where I go."

Ian nodded. "Still, you might be better off far from where this all happened."

"Well, I guess I didn't want to just uproot Michael from the only home he's ever known. He's still in school. Although obviously, judging by what happened on the bus, school is torture for him."

"When is school over?" Ian asked mildly.

"A few more weeks," said Laura.

"Well, when school finishes up, why don't we just leave here? Just get in the boat and go."

"Get in the boat?" she said.

Ian gazed at her. "Yes. You, me, and Michael."

She looked away from him. This was it, she thought. The moment she knew was going to come. He was getting ready to move on. It had to happen. And he wanted to take them sailing before he left. She considered it for a moment. A kind of vacation at sea. It sounded so appealing, in a way. But it was better if he just got going, if they got this over with. Before Dolores even came back.

So soon? her heart cried. But she forced herself to use her head. Dolores would hear about Ian all right. Would hear that her daughter-in-law had kept company with a man. The grapevine would see to that. But at least there would be no ugly confrontations. It was best just to get it over with while it was still innocent. Laura knew she wouldn't be able to enjoy a sailing trip anyway, knowing there was only good-bye and a vague promise to keep in touch at the end of it.

"That's very kind of you," she said. "But I think you should go on right now. Michael has day camp for two weeks after school gets out. I don't want to hold you up all that time."

Ian laughed. "All right. I guess I can wait until after day camp."

"No," said Laura, shaking her head. "You go ahead. This has all been such a . . . lovely time. But we don't want to keep you."

"You don't?" he said. "Well, I want to keep you. Forever, if you let me."

She frowned at him. "Well, sorry . . .," she mumbled.

"You mean you don't want to marry me?"

At first she was too stunned to speak. Then she felt a little angry. "Don't be sarcastic," said Laura. "That's mean."

"Do you think I'm kidding?" he asked.

Laura sank onto the nearest chair. His words took the air out of her, like a blow. "Of course you're kidding . . ."

"Why?" he asked calmly.

Laura threw back her head and stared up at the ceiling. "Why? Because . . ." She couldn't think. Because she hated to admit to herself that she wanted to believe it. And in the same instant she felt as if she were about to be cruelly duped into revealing her own gullibility. She didn't intend to fall for it. "It's just stupid, that's why," she said flatly. "Why in the world would you say such a thing?"

"Because I love you," he said simply. "Don't you know?"

At the sound of those words, her heart turned over and her stomach twisted into a giant knot. I love you! She wasn't all that experienced, but she knew a man didn't just say those words without meaning them. And she couldn't look him in the eye and say that she was completely surprised. But she was. She was.

"I just thought you were lonely," she stammered.

"Did you?" he asked, and she heard a little flash of steeliness in his tone.

Laura shook her head. "No," she said truthfully. "No. But marriage . . . I mean . . . we haven't even . . ."

"Made love?" he asked. "I've made love to you every day, many times a day . . . in my mind."

He was sitting across the room, but his words sent a sexual thrill through her more electric than any touch. She closed her eyes. She had not allowed herself to think of it. But now that she could feel his eyes on her, now that he had said it, she felt almost weak with longing for him.

"I know," she said softly, acknowledging what must have been obvious in her eyes. They sat in silence for a moment, and her mind swarmed over the idea, embracing it, rejecting it. She imagined the people in Cape Christian—how they would react if they heard she'd remarried. They would hang her in effigy. And Dolores. My God. It would be as if she had killed Jimmy all over again. And the police. They would dance a jig. It would be all the proof they needed that she had wished to be rid of her first husband. They would hound her into forever. It would be a complete disaster in every way.

"Oh, Ian," she said. "How can you even think of such a thing? We don't even know each other."

"We've known each other for years," he said.

"Not really," she said. "That's just a technicality. You don't even know what I'm like. You have some kind of idealized memory of me. Some angel who rescued you. That's not me. I'm . . . I'm grumpy when I don't get enough sleep. I . . . I make terrible spaghetti sauce. Everybody says so. You've never seen me cleaning the house in my old sweats, crabbing at Michael. That's who I am, really."

"I have my faults, too, you know."

"I don't know," she cried. "That's just the point."

"We'll find out," he said. "Just say you'll marry me."

"You know, for a scientist, this is not a very scientific way to go about things."

He was sitting tensely on the edge of the sofa. "Have you noticed something?" he asked.

"What?"

"You haven't said no."

Laura felt as though she couldn't breathe. It was true. Why hadn't she just said no? No, I can't marry you. No, this is the most absurd thing I've ever heard. She hadn't said it because the thought of his leaving without her caused her an almost physical pain. Because despite the reckless improbability of it, his proposal was like a life preserver to someone who was drowning.

He slid from the couch to the floor in front of her. "I should have done this on bended knee," he said. "Marry me." He tugged her from the chair to the floor and pulled her close to him. In his arms, pressed against him, she felt dizzy from the feel of his muscled chest beneath his shirt, the sound of his heartbeat, the masculine scent of him, the imagining of them together in her bed.

She pulled away, determined to keep her head. "Michael," she said. "I have to think of Michael. He's just lost his father. It's too many upheavals at once."

"And I've lost my son. He needs a father. And I need a son. It would be a second chance for both of us."

For an instant Laura pictured them, coming toward her from the bus stop, Michael clutching Ian's hand.

"I'll tell you something, Laura. Whatever I hoped to find on that boat, I didn't find it until I found you. I want a home and family again. Is that bad?"

"Oh, Ian, don't. It's a lovely dream. But that's all. You have to go. Think what the police would say if I suddenly married you. They'd look at you the way they look at me. They were already asking questions about you. I couldn't do that to you."

"Let me worry about that," he said. "I'm not worried about what they think. We have nothing to hide. Remember?"

She didn't know whether to laugh or cry. His arms were a haven.

"I sometimes think that I was sent here to protect you," he whispered into her hair. "To save you, the way you saved me long ago."

She pulled away and looked at him searchingly. His gaze was so intense that it was like looking into the sun. There was something thrilling about his resolve. He was a knight-errant, storming a castle to win her. "Even if I knew you better, even if I thought we could . . . it's too soon," she protested.

"That's all wrong," he said. "Life's too short. Who knows that better than we do? There's not a moment to waste. I know that's what my Gabriella would have said. And if Jimmy could talk to you, that's what he'd tell you. That we have to seize the day. That we never know what tomorrow will bring."

The mention of Jimmy brought back the grief. "I loved him so much," she whispered.

For a moment Ian stiffened. Then he put his lips close to her ear. Laura could feel his warm breath caress her ear, like a tropical breeze on a flower. "He would want you to be happy. Every day. The way I can make you happy. Marry me. Right away. Let the whole town buzz about it. Let the cops foam at the mouth. They can't stop us. We'll be long gone."

Laura forced herself to push away from him. To stand up and cross the room. "No. This is too much, too fast."

He scrambled to his feet and came after her. He pulled her to him and kissed her. Bizarre though it was, the thought of Pinocchio in Michael's favorite video flashed through her mind. She felt like the puppet boy at the moment he was touched by the blue fairy. Life poured like honey through her wooden limbs.

"Let me stay," he whispered. "Let me stay with you tonight. Let me show you that this has to be."

"No," she said sharply. "I want you to go."

He let her go and looked at her ruefully. She tried to gaze steadily at him, to reject him and mean it. But it was no use trying to fool him. Despite her words, her eyes softened when she looked at him. He smiled knowingly at her, and her heart flopped over in her chest.

She thought of Jimmy, of the night they had decided to marry. She had known him so well, known his moods and his habits, trusted him completely. It had been an easy choice, the next logical step in their lives together. A baby coming, plans to be made. The approval of friends, the calm steady glow in her heart when she was with him. This man was another story altogether. A stranger. There was something about him that electrified her, but was it love or just the darkness that surrounded them both, the knowledge of suffering they saw in each other's eyes? Wasn't love meant to be joyful? Could they ever get far enough away from the past to find joy in each other? Why are you even considering it? she chided herself. You don't even know this man. How can you even think of it?

Wrapping her arms over her chest as if to protect her heart, she said, "You have to go." When she glanced up and saw the stricken look in his eyes, she said more gently, "I have to think."

"I only want you to think of me," he said.

Laura smiled ruefully. "You can be sure of that."

She walked him to the door. Ian stopped in the hall and kissed her again. She clung to him, drinking him in. Then she pushed him away. He glanced down at the vase of flowers on the hall table. "Who are those from?" he asked. "Do I have a rival?"

Laura shook her head. "Just a friend," she said.

"You're not going to be allowed to have those kinds of friends once we're married," he said.

"I have not agreed to any such thing," she said, sounding prim to her own ears.

"You'll say yes," he predicted. "You will."

She watched him descending the steps, disappearing into the darkness. Tonight he would go to his boat and sleep gently in the nearby harbor. Tomorrow he would return to her. She wondered dreamily what it would be like to go with him, to lie in that bow, to make passionate love, the boat reeling under the stars.

But she suddenly realized, with a cold, awful certainty, that if she said no to his proposal, he would disappear altogether. He was not the kind of man to wait and wait for what he wanted. She knew that much about him. She sensed it. He was offering her hope and a new love. But he would not dangle there indefinitely, waiting for her to decide. If she did not have the nerve to go with him, to choose another life, he would still go. His boat would glide away, to a different future, and she would be stranded here in her loneliness, wondering forever what might have happened if she had been brave.

"Ian," she cried out.

He turned slowly and looked back at her.

"Don't go yet," she said faintly.

He grinned. As he started back toward her, she saw triumph in his brilliant blue eyes.

CHAPTER NINETEEN

Ron Leonard sat stiffly on the backseat of the ancient taxicab as it bumped along the twisted Barbadian roads up into the hills. He'd had the option to rent a car at the airport, but as soon as he realized you had to drive on the wrong side of the road, he'd opted for a taxi instead. The driver had eyed his summer suit and tie and his small overnight bag with a baleful eye. Ron had tried his best to assume a no-nonsense, "I'm the law" posture, but he realized that he looked woefully out of place in this tropical paradise.

Clyde Jackson had listened intently to Ron's report from Connecticut and concluded, with a wince at his budget restrictions, that a trip to Barbados was probably necessary. Ian Turner claimed to be on a boat there on the night Jimmy Reed was killed. They had to find somebody who could confirm or refute that. "I wish I were going," the DA said wistfully. "Debbie and I went to Barbados on our honeymoon."

Looking around as the taxi crawled through the streets of Bridgetown toward the harbor, Ron could imagine that Clyde and Debbie might have felt at home in Barbados. He had never seen such beautiful people—black or white—in his entire life as those he saw from this taxi window. But then again, everything about this place was dazzling to the eye.

He felt as if he had been wearing some sort of gray filter over his eyes until the moment he emerged from that plane. He'd heard the Caribbean was beautiful, but the actual sight of it came as a shock. The colors leapt out at him—colors he'd only ever seen in a crayon box. Ultramarine water and azure sky. Bougainvillea and hibiscus blossoms cascading red violet and orchid wherever he turned his gaze. It was unnerving, in a way, to see people walking around there as if it were normal to live in such an Oz-like place. Ron rolled down the window and gaped as the sultry air caressed his face.

They had stopped first at the marina, and the cabdriver had pleasantly agreed to wait. He was listening to a religious program on the car radio and seemed perfectly at ease, in sharp contrast with Ron's nervous negotiations in this lovely, alien place. It had not taken long for Ron to find Cyril Terry, the bronzed, white-haired Englishman who had sold Ian his boat. Terry had been pleasant and cooperative but had been unable to account for Ian's movements once he'd purchased the boat. But a pretty, albeit leathery-skinned, English girl who appeared to be working for Terry had told Ron that a local man named Winston St. Mercier had crewed aboard Ian's boat for a while. He might be of some help. She'd seen the panic and helplessness in Ron's eyes as she tried to explain the way to St. Mercier's house, so she'd gone over to the cab and together she and the driver had determined the location.

Now they were wending their way through the hills, in search of St. Mercier. As they went, they passed scattered, brightly painted cottages, with white wooden shutters and cool-looking porches, nestled on the hillsides. The homes appeared to be tiny, and Ron wondered how a whole family could live in a place that small. No air-conditioning in this heat, he thought, although he saw the occasional TV antenna as they thudded along. Chickens roamed about, and small children with gorgeous brown porcelain faces looked up, big-eyed, and sometimes waved as the cab rattled by.

Although Ron could see no street signs, or any indication of where they were, the cabdriver announced that they were almost there. They swerved around one more leafy bend in the road, and then the driver pulled up in front of a clearing and stopped. There before them was a small house, painted lavender blue, with a schoolgirl in a simple flowered dress seated on the front steps, reading.

"This is it?" Ron asked. From inside the house came the sound of music with a gentle reggae beat.

"Yes, mon," said the driver.

"You'll wait?" Ron asked anxiously.

The driver leaned over and changed the station from his religious program to a broadcast of local cricket matches. "No problem," he said. He picked up a thermos and poured himself a cup of tea.

Ron got out of the cab and walked up the dirt path to the house. "Excuse me," he said to the girl, who looked up at him with large, black-fringed brown eyes. "Is this where Winston St. Mercier lives?"

The girl nodded and scooted to one side so that Ron could pass her on the wooden steps. She watched him as he walked up on the porch and knocked at the screen door. "Mr. St. Mercier?" he called out.

The small front room was simply furnished with a sofa, a chair, and a TV. A throw rug covered part of the wooden floor. Overhead, a large ceiling fan was running. There was a radio on, from which the reggae music was emanating. A handsome man with brown skin and blue eyes emerged from the dark rooms beyond the living room and asked in a lilting voice, "Who wants him?"

He stopped short when he saw Ron in his suit and tie and dark sunglasses and peered at him suspiciously.

"Mr. St. Mercier, my name is Ron Leonard. I'm a detective from the United States. I wanted to ask you a few questions."

A beautiful woman wearing a turban and a white dress stuck her head into the room and looked at Ron curiously. Winston St. Mercier held open the screen door with one hand. "Questions about what?" he asked warily.

"I was told that you crewed on a sailboat for a while last winter with an American named Ian Turner."

The suspicious look vanished, and a smile broke across the man's face. "Ah, Ian," he said. "My good friend. How is he? He's all right, isn't he?"

"Yes. I just have a few questions about that trip."

Ron could see a struggle in the man's face between his natural friendliness and inclination to be hospitable and his doubts about this foreign policeman. He took off his dark glasses and smiled. "Do you have time for a few questions?"

"Come in," Winston said finally. He indicated a wooden table and chairs, painted apple green, in the corner. "Sit down. Would you like some tea?" He glanced at the woman. "This is my wife, Ava."

She came forward and said shyly, "Some coconut bread?" Her voice was musical.

"No, no, thank you," said Ron. Then he reconsidered. "Maybe a little coconut bread."

She gave him a small slice on a flowered china plate. "What about your driver?" she asked. "Would he like something?"

"He might," Ron agreed. She sliced another piece of bread and headed out the door. Winston sat on the chair opposite Ron's.

"I don't want any trouble, mon," he said. "I met the man at Terry's when he bought his boat. He needed some help at first, you know, getting used to it. He was a pretty good sailor. I only stayed with him a few weeks."

"Mmmm, this is good," Ron exclaimed as the flavor of coconut exploded in his mouth. He brushed the crumbs off his tie.

Winston cocked his head and smiled wryly. "This your first trip here, mon?"

Ron nodded. Is it so obvious? he wondered. He swallowed the bread and tried to reassume an official expression. "We need to account for the whereabouts of Mr. Turner on and about New Year's Eve, of this year."

147

"New Year's Eve," said Winston, shaking his head. "No. I was off the boat by then. I wanted to be back by Christmas, to be with my family. You know."

Ron nodded.

"Why are you asking about my friend Ian? Is he in some trouble?"

"I don't know yet," Ron said cryptically.

The screen door slammed, and Winston's wife reentered the house. Winston looked up at her. "He's asking about Ian Turner. You remember."

She nodded.

"So you were off his boat before Christmas, and that was the last you saw of him. No idea where he was New Year's Eve?"

Winston shook his head. "I saw him from time to time after that. I don't know when he left Barbados."

"Wait, you saw him," exclaimed Ava.

Ron and Winston both looked up at her.

"On New Year's Eve. Remember?" she said. "You told me: you saw him in the harbor, sitting all alone on that boat. And you didn't know whether to wish him a Happy New Year or not?"

"That's right," Winston said excitedly, turning to Ron. "She's right!" Then his whole demeanor turned somber. "You know he lost his whole family last year," Winston said gravely.

"I know," Ron said cautiously.

"Terrible thing," said Winston, shaking his head. "He never mentioned it past the first time. So, yes, I was at the harbor that day, getting some fish for dinner, and I saw him. And I thought, 'How do you wish a man Happy New Year who has lost his whole family?' It was terribly awkward. I spoke to him, though. I asked him to come for dinner, but he declined. I think he was feeling very low. Very low. Yes, I remember now."

"You're sure about this," said Ron, a discernible edge of disappointment in his voice.

"I'm sure, yes. Ava reminded me."

Ron sighed and stood up. "Well, all right. Thank you for your time. You've been very helpful. And your bread was delicious, Mrs. St. Mercier," he said, conscious of his manners, not wanting to seem an ugly American in this strange place.

Winston St. Mercier followed Ron out of the cool, dark house into the brilliant sunshine. Ron stopped on the porch steps and squinted at the little girl who was still sitting, reading, on the steps.

"Got a good book there?" Ron asked pleasantly.

"Show him your book, Sophia," her father said.

The child held up her book. It was called *Raoul and the Giant Yellow Frog*. By Laura Hastings. "That was a Christmas present to her from Mr. Ian Turner, as a matter of fact," Winston said proudly.

Ron's heart did a little flip-flop. "May I?" he said, reaching for the child's book. He turned it over in his hands.

"He knows the author," the child said shyly. "He told me so."

Ron looked up at her sharply and clenched his hands around the narrow volume. "He said he knew her? Are you sure about that?"

The child beamed. "Yes. He told me himself. He said she was a very kind and beautiful lady."

Ron pounced. "Did he say anything else about her? Anything at all?"

The child looked anxiously at her book, clutched in the stranger's hands. Ron followed her glance and handed the book back to her. Then he said, more gently, "I'm just curious. I don't know any authors."

Sophia smiled shyly. "He said she lived in New Jersey of the United States, and that he was going to see her soon. So I wrote her a letter about Raoul so he could give it to her when he saw her. But she didn't write me back yet. Do you think she will?"

"Oh yes," said Ron with a satisfied smile and a distant look in his eyes. "I'm sure she will."

CHAPTER TWENTY

The ceremony was being performed at dusk in the slightly shabby but comfortable living room of a Maryland justice of the peace named Gilbert Trent. A Duraflame log glowed blue in the hearth, even though the windows were open and the evening was mild. A cassette tape of organ music played softly in the background as Justice Trent addressed the nervous couple. Laura wore a beige, antique lace dress that she had found in a vintage clothing store and held a bouquet of pale pink tea roses purchased at a local card shop. Ian wore one of the roses in the lapel of an ill-fitting blue suit he had bought in Harry's, the only men's shop in Cape Christian. He had told the protesting salesman that he had no time to wait for alterations. Ian and Laura were flanked by Mrs. Trent, who had just rushed in from her bridge club, and by Michael, who fidgeted beside Laura, dressed in his Sunday school pants, a white shirt, and a clip-on bow tie. They were halfway through the ceremony.

"Do you, Laura, take this man, Ian—"

"No, no, no . . ." Suddenly childish shrieks of rage ripped through the room, and Michael began to stamp his feet.

Laura turned to her son in amazement as Michael threw himself down and began to pound on the floor. Quickly she shoved her bouquet at the startled Mrs. Trent and bent down beside Michael, trying to get a grip on him.

"Honey, honey, stop. What is it?"

"No, don't. You can't," he began to sob. "Don't get married."

Laura glanced up at Ian, who was frowning at Michael. She gave him a warning look. He couldn't be too surprised. They might have known something like this could happen. "Baby, we talked this all over," she whispered, although she knew in her guilty heart that she had really just sprung it on him, as a fact, only two nights ago. She'd told herself that she didn't want him to have to lie to anyone about it, so it was better if he didn't know until the last minute. He'd seemed to take it calmly. He'd probably just been too stunned to react, she admitted to herself now.

"I don't want you to!" he shrieked.

Laura looked helplessly at Mrs. Trent. "Is there somewhere I could just take him until he calms down a bit?"

"Sure," Mrs. Trent said in an understanding tone.

"I want to go home," Michael cried.

Laura lifted her son in her arms like a toddler. She looked over his shoulder at Ian. "I'll be back," she said grimly.

"Should I come?" he asked. Laura shook her head.

Michael wrapped his arms and legs around her and laid his head on her shoulder. They followed Mrs. Trent into a tiny bedroom with faded, flower-sprigged wallpaper. Laura set Michael on the nubby white bedspread and sat beside him.

"I'll just pop these in the fridge," said Mrs. Trent, indicating Laura's bouquet. "Take your time."

Laura nodded and tried to look sternly at Michael as Mrs. Trent closed the door. But his tears of misery wrenched her heart. "Are you okay?" she asked softly.

"No," he insisted.

"I know this is hard for a little boy to understand. It was all so sudden."

"I don't want you to marry him."

"Why not, baby?" she asked.

151

"I hate him."

A chill ran through her at his fierce pronouncement. His reactions to people were always so honest and ingenuous. But he and Ian had seemed to get along so well together. "I thought you liked Ian, sweetie. You know, the reason we're getting married is because he wants to love us and take care of us."

"You told me not to talk to strangers. And now you're going to marry him. He's a stranger."

"He's not a stranger, now, Michael. We haven't known him a long time, but sometimes people can become very close in a short time."

"We don't need him to take care of us. We can take care of ourselves. Let's go home, Mom," Michael pleaded.

Laura looked away from him. I should have known, she thought. Why did I ever think this would work? Her head was beginning to pound—her usual response to stress. She could feel Ian's gaze beyond the closed door, willing her not to break down. In her lap, Michael was clinging to her, his tears damp on the lace of her dress.

She tried again. "Hasn't Ian been nice to you?" she asked gently.

Michael shook his head miserably. "He's not Dad."

Laura drew him close and hugged him. Ah, this is the heart of the matter, she thought, feeling oddly relieved. She kissed his silken hair. "I know it, honey. But Dad has gone to heaven. He's not coming back."

"I want him to come back," Michael cried angrily.

"I know you do, baby. But he can't come back."

Michael pulled away from her. "You don't want him back. You don't even care. You just want to get married."

Laura shook her head. "Oh, darling, all the wanting in the world won't bring Daddy back. I know this idea of a marriage makes it all seem so . . . final to you. But Daddy can't come back. If he could have, he would have. But he can't. Whether I get married or I don't won't ever change that."

Laura held Michael's face in her hands and wiped a few tears away with her thumbs. "You know that, don't you?"

Michael sighed and nodded miserably.

"We've just been so sad. I thought maybe, with Ian, we'd have a chance to be happy again."

"I'll never be happy again," Michael insisted.

"Don't say that," Laura pleaded. "I know it seems that way sometimes. I thought that, too, but now Ian . . ." She stared at Michael's round, innocent face, saw his sorrow and confusion mirrored in her own heart, and felt her courage seeping away. "I guess I haven't been fair to you. I was hoping to avoid a lot of problems this way, but I can see it's . . . it may have been a mistake to rush into this . . ."

"It *is* a mistake. A big mistake."

Disappointment for herself flickered in her eyes. She had allowed herself to be swept up in a fantasy of a new life. It was stupid to think you could get away from your grief that easily. It was just another version of setting off in a sailboat—trying to avoid your sadness rather than go through it. She sighed. "All right," she said. "I'd better go tell Ian."

Michael studied her face, felt queasy at the sound of her sigh. "Are you mad at me?" he asked.

Laura shook her head. "I'm not mad. I'm just . . . disappointed."

"Why are you disappointed?"

Laura hesitated. "I guess . . . I guess I had my hopes up. You know how that is, when you are excited about something and then it doesn't happen. Like that time we were going to go to that big fair in Millville and then it rained. Well, that's how I feel now. Only a little bit worse."

He did understand. He remembered that time when the fair had been rained out. There were going to be pony rides and a roller coaster and candy apples. He was so mad at his mother and father when they said he couldn't go. He even kicked his father in the leg, he was so mad. Now she was disappointed, and it was all his fault. He had done it. He didn't realize that his outburst reflected her own doubts and fears. He was simply alarmed by his own importance, by his ability to change events so drastically. What if she got mad

153

at him later? What if she stayed sad forever? "I didn't mean it," he said. "You can, I guess . . ."

Laura shook her head and stroked his hair. "You're all confused, aren't you, darling?"

"Yes," he admitted.

"Maybe we better wait."

Michael sat up manfully, wiping his eyes. "No, it's okay, I guess."

There was a soft tapping, and then the door opened. Ian stood in the doorway. "How're we doing in here?" he asked.

Laura felt annoyed by his intrusion. What's the big hurry? she thought. Can't you give us time to think? Why are we not allowed to have time to think? But Michael smiled sheepishly through his tears. "Okay," he said.

Ian came in and sat on the edge of the blanket chest by the bed. "This wedding business is a little like pulling a tooth," he said. "Once it's over, you feel relieved. You feel a lot better."

Michael looked at him seriously. "Louis pulled out one of his teeth when it was loose, and then he got a dollar under his pillow."

Ian nodded. "Maybe you'll get a dollar under your pillow tonight."

Michael's eyes lit up. "I will?"

"First things first," said Ian. "First, the wedding. What do you think?"

Michael sat, staring at his feet, thinking it over. "Okay," he said.

"There," said Ian. "We're all set."

"Magic," Laura said. "Just offer him a dollar . . ." But her disapproval dissolved into relief as Michael's smile returned, like a sunbeam through the gloom.

"Let's do it," said Ian, and he reached for her hand.

She felt shaky inside, like someone who'd been ill on her first day out of bed. Ian's grip was firm, certain, as usual. Michael took her other hand in his soft little fingers. They pulled her to her feet.

154

CHAPTER TWENTY-ONE

"Don't wake him up," Laura whispered.

Ian gently lifted Michael out of the backseat of the car and arranged him against his shoulder. "Let's go," he said.

Together they went up the walk to the porch steps. Ian had wanted to spend their first night as a married couple in a luxurious hotel, but Laura felt it might be too hard on Michael. Besides, there was nowhere she could leave him for the night without having to explain where they were going. She and Ian had told no one else of their plans, not even Pam. Laura didn't want anyone to try to reason with her—to tell her all kinds of logical things about waiting and being careful. They were not in her shoes.

Laura preceded them up the steps and put the key in the lock of the front door. They had already had dinner at a lovely inn in Maryland, where Michael had eaten two desserts. He'd fallen asleep on the backseat of the car before they had gone ten miles toward home.

Laura turned the key on the top lock and frowned. Quickly she tried the bottom lock. Her heart began to pound. She turned to Ian, who was standing behind her, holding Michael in his arms. "The top lock isn't locked," she said. She tried to keep the panic she felt out of her voice.

"Maybe you forgot," said Ian. "In all the excitement of leaving today."

"Of course I didn't forget," Laura cried. "Do you think I would ever forget to lock a door in this house after what happened here?"

"Take it easy," he said soothingly. "You're not alone. I'm with you now. I'll go in first," he said.

"Give Michael to me," she demanded.

Ian hesitated and then placed the sleeping child in his mother's arms.

"Be careful," she said.

Ian pushed open the door and went into the darkness. He flipped on the hall light, and then, after a moment, he called out to her, "Come on in."

Laura clutched Michael to her, his warmth soothing against her chest. She stepped into the house.

The first thing she noticed was the smell.

A delicious floral scent filled the hallway. She walked farther into the house and looked around. The living room and dining room were filled with flowers—gorgeous bouquets of spring blossoms were everywhere. The rooms were a riot of color—beautiful pink and white blooms, spiked with vibrant red tulips, purple iris, orange day lilies, and daffodils.

"Oh, Ian," she cried.

"Like it?"

"It's so beautiful."

"Look upstairs," he said. "Here, give him back to me."

Oblivious of being transferred again, Michael flopped back into Ian's arms as Laura rushed up the stairs. She opened the door to the guest room and frowned. There was nothing in there. For a moment she was confused, and then, with a sick feeling in her stomach, she realized what he meant. She looked down the hall.

The door to her old bedroom stood open, and a glow came from inside. She didn't want even to look. She had not been in that room, except to move her clothes, since that night. She walked down the hallway, half curious, half fearful. As she reached the door she felt almost dizzy with anxiety. She pushed the door all the way open.

She could hardly believe her eyes. There were bouquets of white flowers in cut-glass bowls and vases, all over the room. Dozens of votive candles in frosted-glass holders flickered among the flowers. Champagne waited in an ice bucket. The linens on the bed were all new, a delicate blue-and-white pattern. A white silk nightie and peignoir were draped across the bed.

Carrying Michael, Ian came up the stairs. She turned, and he saw the expression on her face.

"What's the matter?" he said.

She knew that he'd managed this somehow to surprise her. But she couldn't conceal her dismay. It was impossible. "That was our room. The room where Jimmy . . ."

"Oh, God," said Ian. "I just told him to decorate the master bedroom. Of course you wouldn't sleep there anymore. I'm sorry . . ."

Without a word Laura took Michael from his arms, took him into his room, and slipped on his pajamas. She tucked him into his bed, kissed his sleeping face, and closed his door.

Ian was down the hall, staring into the transformed bedroom. She came up behind him but did not look inside.

"How did you do it?" she asked.

He did not turn or look at her. His voice was expressionless. "I've been working on it. With a lot of help from Scott, at the flower shop."

Laura winced at that. Scott loved to gossip. It wouldn't be long before everyone in town heard that she was making love in the bed where her husband was slain. "Ian," she whispered, laying a hand gently on his back. "It's so beautiful. It really is. But, please understand, I can't . . . I just can't . . ."

"I know," he said. He went into the room and blew out each of the candles until the room was gloomy once more. Then he came back to her in the dim hallway.

"I'm sorry," she said.

157

"It's all right," he said, but she could feel his disappointment. "It was a misunderstanding. I just wanted to surprise you."

"I know." She looked away, not wanting to see the expression in his eyes. "We could move everything into the guest room," she offered, but he gave her a reproving glance, and she knew it was no good: his surprise was demolished, and there was no salvaging it.

But somehow, standing there in the ruins of his plans, she felt sure of herself for the first time all day. She took his hand silently and led him down the corridor to the end, where a small step down led to a tiny room, just large enough for a single bed and an old chest of drawers she had found in a thrift shop. "No one's ever even slept in here," she said ruefully.

He looked in at the tiny room, the little window overlooking the backyard. "It looks like a cell," he said.

She turned to him and put her arms around his neck. "I don't need all the trappings," she said. "All I need is you."

"I wanted it to be perfect for you," he said.

"It is perfect."

Ian stared into her eyes. "It's about to be," he said in a husky voice.

She shivered at the intensity of his gaze. She knew what he meant. All she could do was nod and swallow hard as he pulled her down onto the narrow bed.

* * *

Hours later Laura ran her fingers down the arm of her sleeping husband, then extended her left arm and crooked her hand back to admire her new wedding ring in the dim glow of the moonlight. Then she gazed beyond her hand, at the tiny bedroom. The plainness of it seemed just right to her now. Passion, plain and simple. No frills. They were entwined together on the single bed as lovers should be.

Ian grasped her in his sleep, and she traced his face with her fingers. He had loved her like a man possessed. She had been able to forget and be lost with him. But even as she gazed with pleasure at the sleeping man who held her, guilt began to seep into her thoughts. Oh, Jimmy, I betrayed you, she thought. Then she stopped herself. Forced herself to stop. Jimmy was dead. Whether he was dead five months or five years, it wouldn't matter. He would always be with her. But this was a new life, a different life. And it had started off well, all in all, despite a few mishaps, like that business with Michael during the ceremony. And that had worked out okay, too, she thought with a smile. Then she remembered the dollar. A dollar under his pillow. It was the kind of thing an adult might promise without thinking, but a kid was bound to remember. I'd better get one out and put it there, she thought. Or I'll hear about it tomorrow.

Gently she extricated herself from Ian's slumberous embrace and slid out of bed. She crept into the bathroom, found her robe, and pulled it on. She tried to think where her pocketbook might be. Downstairs, she realized. She'd left it there when she'd come in. She knew where there was some money, though: in Jimmy's sock drawer. He'd always kept some cash there for emergencies. It was probably still there.

She crept down the hall to their room and looked in. It really did not look like the same room, she thought. Scott had worked wonders on it. Still, she shuddered as she hurried over to the dresser, opened the drawer, and reached in. There was the old argyle sock he used as a hiding place. Laura pulled out a dollar, tucked it in the pocket of her robe, and slid the drawer shut quietly. As she did it, she glanced at the top of Jimmy's dresser. There was a beautiful arrangement of white roses and baby's breath and a votive candle on its newly dusted surface. Jimmy's leather jewelry box and a can of pip tobacco were still there, also. But something was missing that always sat there: their wedding picture. It was not a formal picture, just a snapshot taken by a friend on the day of their marriage, but there had been joy in their faces, and she had bought a silver frame for it and given it to him as a present. It was always on his bureau. He kept it there. Maybe Scott moved it when he did the flowers, she thought. She looked around the room, on every surface, but it was nowhere to be seen. Maybe someone put it in a drawer, she thought. She slipped open the top drawer again, since that would be the logical place, but the photo was not there. She closed it, frowning. Well, she couldn't go opening every drawer in the room at this hour. I'll look for it tomorrow, she thought, although it upset her to think it was missing.

It's been a long day, she reminded herself. Put the dollar in Michael's room and get some sleep. You'll find it in the morning.

She slipped out of the room and down the hallway. Michael's door was open, and she went in quietly and crouched beside his bed. She placed the dollar gently under his pillow and gave him one last, fond kiss. As she straightened up she looked at the surface of his bedside table. There were, as usual, a couple of action figures, his Winnie-the-Pooh lamp, and one worn-out Magic Marker. But the small picture of his father, which he'd kept there since January, was gone.

Laura felt something cold seize her heart. This was not a coincidence. She left Michael's room, closing the door quietly, and went down the stairs. There were a few places to check, but she already suspected what she would find. She walked into the living room and, from across the room, could see that the Victorian frame was missing from the mantelpiece. She glanced at the top of her desk and noted that the heart-shaped frame that sat beside the fringed lamp was gone. She went into the kitchen. There was only one more place to look. She stood, staring incredulously at the front of the refrigerator. The plastic, magnetized picture frame, with a snapshot of the three of them tumbled together in a hammock, was gone. The list of school lunches that Laura had posted beneath it was moved, sharing a magnet with one of Michael's drawings.

How dare you, she thought. How dare you! Where did you put them?

She began rifling the kitchen drawers, irritated by the clutter inside, groping in the backs of the drawers, and then in the cabinets, for the missing pictures. All of a sudden her gaze fell on the bags in the pantry. She kept her paper grocery bags there, filled with newspaper for recycling. Beside them was a small trash can for glass, aluminum, and plastics. She walked slowly into the pantry and lifted the lid on the can.

There they were. In among the empty wine bottles, the plastic detergent bottles, the empty glass sauce jars. Her pictures of Jimmy. Jimmy, smiling up at her from the debris. Her heart was beating furiously. She lifted out the pictures and took them gently to the kitchen table. From under the sink she got out a spray cleaner and a soft rag and began gently to wipe away the spots and stains. As she finished each one she set it up on the table.

Suddenly her flesh prickled as she sensed someone behind her. She whirled around and saw the shape of a figure in the darkened hallway.

"What are you doing?" Ian asked in a froggy voice. He emerged into the dimly lit kitchen, barefoot, wearing only a pair of pajama bottoms.

She turned her back on him and continued polishing. "What does it look like I'm doing?" she said icily.

"It looks like you're cleaning house. Isn't it a little late for that?" he said.

She wiped off the magnetized frame, took it over to the refrigerator, and used it to post the school menus just as they had been. Then she turned on him. "How could you?" she said in a low voice. "How could you do such a thing?"

"What are you talking about?" he said defensively. "What did I do?"

"You threw away my pictures of Jimmy. You took my belongings, mementos, things I cherish, and you threw them away. What gives you the right?"

"Don't start accusing me," he said. "I don't know what you're talking about."

Laura looked at him with flashing eyes. "I found all of my framed photographs of Jimmy in the trash. The recycling bin, to be exact. Are you telling me you aren't responsible for this?"

Ian rubbed his eyes and then shook his head slightly. "No. Why are you blaming me? Scott must have done it when he was doing the flowers."

Laura frowned doubtfully, thinking of Scott, a pleasant, eccentric man with an earring, whom she scarcely knew. "Scott? I can't believe he would do that—I mean, just trash my belongings. Why would he agree to do this job and then do something so vile?"

"I don't know why he threw these other pictures away. Maybe it wasn't meant to be mean. Maybe he thought you wouldn't want to be reminded . . ."

"The other pictures?" she said slowly.

Ian fidgeted uneasily. "Well, maybe I am responsible, in a way . . ."

Laura stared at him. "What do you mean?" she asked in a small, still voice.

"Laura, I just asked him, if there were any pictures in the bedroom, you know, of Jimmy, to put them away . . ."

"How dare you," she breathed.

"Look, I didn't want to be making love to you for the first time under the watchful eye of your late husband. I thought maybe it would make you uncomfortable, too."

"So you told him to get rid of my pictures."

"I meant, to put them in a drawer or something. He must've misunderstood."

Laura turned her back on him and stared straight at the photo magnet on the refrigerator. "We aren't going to just erase all traces of Jimmy from our lives. No matter what you want. No matter what anyone wants. It doesn't work that way."

"Nobody's trying to erase him. But I'm your husband now." He pointed to his wedding band, holding his hand out in front of her.

"I know," she snapped. "You don't have to say it like a threat."

Ian sat down wearily at the table. "Look, all I wanted to do was surprise you with a beautiful house when we came back. You insisted on coming back here, so I thought, fine. If that's the way it has to be, I'll make it like a fairy tale— the most gorgeous homecoming any bride ever had. But everything I touch seems to go wrong. I just wanted you to be happy." There was a stricken look on his face, like that on the face of a child whose carefully wrought valentine had been ripped up and tossed aside.

Instantly she felt guilty. He was right. Everything he had tried to do had been spoiled. And then their lovemaking came back to her mind. "Not everything was spoiled," she said. He looked up at her warily.

It's not you, she thought. I'm getting mad at you when, really, it's the pictures. It's the people around here, sending me this message, loud and clear. That I've trashed Jimmy's memory in their eyes. And maybe in my own eyes as well. By remarrying so soon. She shivered, although the night was warm. "I can't wait to get away from here," she whispered. "I don't think I can really be happy until we're gone."

"It can't be soon enough for me," he said.

CHAPTER TWENTY-TWO

The van slowed, and Wanda Jurik peered out the passenger window at the short strip of stores they were approaching as Gary signaled for a turn. "What are we stopping here for?" she demanded.

"I want to go to the flower shop," he said.

"I thought you were in such a hurry to get out to the marsh and paint," she said.

"It won't take long," he said.

Wanda pursed her lips in disapproval as Gary swung the van into a space in front of Scott's Flower Shop. She got out of the passenger side to come around and assist him, but Gary had already maneuvered his chair into place and lowered it to the sidewalk. "You don't have to come in," he said.

Wanda glared at him for an instant, then got back into the van. "Fine, I'll wait here," she said.

He rolled the chair into the shop, being careful to avoid upsetting any of the potted plants that were clumped together near the door. Scott DeWitt was wearing a Cape Christian sweatshirt with one of Gary's paintings silk-screened on it. He looked up from the centerpiece he was working on as Gary came in.

"Hey, Gary," he said pleasantly.

"Hi, Scott," Gary said, pretending to look around the shop.

"What can I do for you today?"

Gary gazed into the cold case of cut flowers. Then he said offhandedly, "Just . . . I wanted to send a bouquet—to Laura Reed."

Scott frowned at his centerpiece. "Gary . . ."

"What?"

Scott groped around for the right way to say it. He could tell that Gary didn't know. "You know, Gary, I don't want to talk out of school, but . . ."

Gary looked at him, perplexed by his response. "What?"

"Do you know about the wedding?"

"What wedding?"

The look on Gary's face reminded Scott of a baby squirrel that had fallen out of its tree. He looked so bewildered, so helpless. Do it quick, Scott thought. Put him out of his misery. "Gary, do you know that Laura got married yesterday?"

Gary stared at the florist as if he had suddenly revealed himself to be a space alien. "I want to send a bouquet to Laura Reed," he repeated slowly.

Scott stared back. "Laura Reed got married yesterday to a man named Ian Turner."

"That's a lie," Gary said.

Scott shook his head. "No, it isn't, my friend."

"Well, then . . . you've got it wrong," Gary sputtered.

"Mr. Turner hired me to make ten arrangements for the house. They eloped to Maryland. I had to go over there at eight-thirty and light about two dozen votive candles, put champagne on ice, the works."

Just then a middle-aged woman lumbered into the showroom from the back of the shop. "You can ask Charlotte," Scott offered. "She helped me. We got the whole place ready for them. Charlotte, didn't Laura Reed get married yesterday?"

Charlotte Halley sniffed. She worked part-time for Scott and the rest of her time as a volunteer at the Catholic church.

165

"That's the God's honest truth," she said. "Husband hardly cold in the ground . . ."

Gary shook his head as if he were trying to ward off her words. He turned back to Scott. "Did you speak to Laura about this?"

Scott shrugged. "Well, no. He wanted to surprise her."

"Well, how do you know this guy isn't some crazed maniac? How did you get into the house?"

"With the keys, of course. He has his own keys. Gary, look, it's no mistake. Charlotte had heard Laura was seeing this guy from Fanny Clark, down at the dock."

Gary gripped the arms of his wheelchair and clenched his jaw. Then he turned the chair and began to leave the store.

Scott grimaced at the sight of his anguish. "Shall I skip the bouquet?" he asked. Gary did not look around or answer.

The moment he got back into the van Wanda's eyes widened in alarm. "What's the matter with you?" she asked. "You look awful. Your complexion is all gray."

"I have to go somewhere," he said. "I'll drop you off at home."

"Honey, what's the matter?" Wanda asked gently. "You're scaring me."

"I just heard something . . . from Scott."

"What?"

"He said that Laura has remarried." He spit the word out.

"Well, good for her," said Wanda. "Now you can stop chasing her."

Two spots of color appeared in Gary's cheeks as he looked at his mother. "I don't believe she would do that. Jimmy's only just dead a few months. It would be too soon for her to even start seeing a man. Never mind marry him."

"I guess you missed the boat, honey," Wanda said tartly.

Without thinking, Gary raised his fist, his jaw muscles working furiously.

"Don't you ever raise your hand to me, Gary Jurik," Wanda warned him. "I've sacrificed everything for you. I'll thank you to remember that. She wouldn't have had you anyway. Not the way you are."

Gary stared through the windshield of the van. "I'll drop you at home," he said again.

"Don't go begging and pleading with that woman. Where's your pride?"

Gary put the key in the ignition, not even hearing her.

* * *

In fine weather, the cafeteria doors at Cape Christian Elementary School were left open, and the children were allowed to take their lunches outside and sit on the grassy hillside next to the basketball court to eat their sandwiches. A teacher was always there, roving among them, but it was definitely a better way to spend lunch than eating lined up at the long cafeteria tables.

Michael sat alone, under a budding dogwood tree, and kept looking up at the open doors, hoping to see Louis. Hoping not to see that redheaded kid. A girl in his class named Sara stopped briefly in front of him and offered to trade him an apple for a cookie, but he wanted to eat all his cookies, so she went on her way.

He started to eat his sandwich, but his eyes scanned the hillside constantly, wary of anyone who might be approaching him, coming his way. All of a sudden he noticed the cafeteria monitor, Miss Rogers, standing by the water fountain, talking to two old people. It took him only a moment to recognize them.

"Poppy, Grandma!" he cried. His lunch forgotten, he ran toward them, dodging the other kids in his path.

"We just got back from Florida," Dolores was explaining to the teacher. "We were passing by the school and we saw the kids out here and we just wanted to sneak in a little hug." Then she heard him calling her. She turned and looked and saw him charging toward her. Dolores's face lit up with delight.

"Go ahead," Miss Rogers said indulgently. "I think he's glad to see you."

Sidney had already crouched down, and he received the first burst of affection. Then it was Dolores's turn. She squeezed him tightly. "We missed you so much," she said.

"I missed you, too," he said sincerely.

"Come on, let's sit down over here," said Sidney, pointing out a bench under a leafy plane tree. The three of them sat down, with Michael in the middle.

"Did you finish your lunch?" Dolores asked sternly.

"I ate it," he said.

"I brought you something. Poppy and I went shopping." She reached into a large canvas carryall and brought out a rubber shark.

"Cool!" Michael exclaimed.

"And this," Dolores went on as Sidney beamed at the sight of the boy's delight. She handed him a bag of exotic-looking shells and a book about shells.

"Thanks," said Michael.

"And . . ." She lifted out a neon green T-shirt with a surfing duck on it wearing sunglasses and a logo that read, "I caught the wave at Cocoa Beach."

"Can I wear it now?" Michael asked.

"Not now," Dolores said.

"Why not?" said Sidney. "Let him wear it. Here, pull your other shirt off."

Michael changed shirts enthusiastically, then settled back against the bench, resplendent in neon green, with a piece of pound cake that Dolores also extracted from her bag.

"So, what have you been up to? How's school?" Sidney asked.

Michael's smile disappeared, but he said, "Okay."

"You're almost through for the year," said Sidney.

"Yeah," Michael said. "Can I come over this weekend?"

"Sure. You better," said Dolores. "Here, I'm gonna put this stuff back in my bag and you can get it this weekend."

"Can't I keep it?"

"I'm just gonna hold on to it for you. You can't take it into school," Dolores said sensibly.

"All right," he agreed. The other children on the grass around them were beginning to get up and straggle into the building as the teacher in charge loudly announced the end of lunch.

"How's your mother?" asked Sidney.

Michael looked at his grandfather seriously. "She got married."

Sidney looked up at Dolores. Dolores stared at him.

Sidney ruffled Michael's hair. "You're teasing us, right?"

"No, I'm not. But I might not be supposed to tell," he admitted.

"Michael," Miss Rogers called. "Back in the building. Scrammo."

Dolores held the child's shoulders and looked him in the eye. "Were you making a joke about your mother getting married?"

"No, she married Ian. We eloped in Maryland. Then we went out to dinner and had two desserts. But don't tell Mom I told you. I better go."

Dolores released him, and he ran for the building, turning back to yell, "Thanks for the shark."

Sidney looked worriedly at his wife, who was sitting, dumbstruck, on the bench. "He must be confused," he said. "Honey, are you all right?"

Dolores turned to her husband, her eyes wide, her face chalk white under her Florida tan. She groped for Sidney's arm, for his strength, knocking the canvas bag off the bench as she reached for him. The rubber shark tumbled out onto the grass, teeth bared, at her feet.

CHAPTER TWENTY-THREE

"I hate to admit it," Laura said to Ian, "but I was glad he wasn't there. He probably would have started lecturing me like a schoolgirl." They had stopped by Richard's office to tell him the news of their marriage and to inform him of their plans to leave Cape Christian. They needed him to arrange their financial matters and transfer the money to a joint account. Richard was in court, but his secretary, Adelaide Murphy, had done her best to conceal her surprise at the message by busying herself with the papers on her desk. She didn't even dare to look up into Laura's eyes.

Ian nodded. "These next few days and weeks will be tough, but then we'll be out of here, and it won't matter what any of them have to say." As they drove around the corner onto Chestnut Street, Laura saw Gary's van parked in front of the house and she grimaced.

"What is it?" Ian asked.

Laura sighed. "Gary."

"Who's Gary?"

"He's . . . a friend. He and Jimmy did a lot of work together."

"Well, let's go tell him the good news," Ian said cheerfully.

"He's not going to think it's good news," Laura assured him. "He'll be in the back," she said, noting the van was empty as they turned in the driveway. "That's where the ramp is."

"I noticed that ramp out back."

"It was put in for Gary. He was injured in a car accident way back in high school. This van is specially equipped so he can drive it."

As Laura and Ian were getting out of the car, Laura heard someone call her name. She turned around and saw Detective Leonard emerging from his car, which he had just parked across the street.

"God," Laura murmured. "It's like living in a fishbowl."

"Who's this?" asked Ian as the detective loped across the street and met them on the sidewalk.

"Detective Leonard," Laura said with exaggerated politeness, "I would like you to meet my husband, Ian Turner."

The detective turned pale. "You married him?" he said.

"It's a pleasure to meet you," Ian said pointedly.

"Actually, it's you I was looking for," Ron said to Ian.

"It's not a good time. We have company, Detective," said Laura, indicating Gary's van.

"Well-wishers, no doubt," said Ron, folding a hand over a fist in front of him. "Well, you go ahead and see to your company. I want to speak to your . . . husband." Laura looked anxiously at Ian, but he nodded to her reassuringly. "Go ahead. I'll be with you in a minute."

"Why don't you leave us alone?" said Laura. But Ron was not listening. He was gazing narrowly at Ian, who was returning his stare defiantly. Laura left them on the sidewalk and went in search of Gary.

"So," said Ron Leonard. "You're a newlywed."

Ian looked at him, unsmiling. "What do you want from me?"

"Shall we go inside, sit down?" Ron asked.

"I don't see any reason to," said Ian. "You don't intimidate me, sir. You have harassed my wife to the point where she's afraid of you, but you'll find me quite a different story."

Ron drew himself up as if he were ready to breathe fire on the other man. "I've been very busy lately. Traveling. Doing some research on you. I just got back from Barbados last night."

Ian showed no reaction.

"I spoke to a man named Winston St. Mercier there. Does that name ring a bell?"

"Of course it does," Ian said impatiently. "He's a friend of mine."

"His little girl showed me a book you gave her. A book written by your . . . wife."

Ian's confident expression slipped slightly, and then he recovered himself. "Yes, I gave Sophia a book. So what?"

"You gave her that book shortly before the death of Mr. James Reed Jr. At a time when you and Mrs. Reed had supposedly not seen or spoken to one another since childhood . . ."

"That's right," said Ian.

"And yet you told Sophia that you knew Laura Hastings. That she was a beautiful woman and that you were on your way to see her in . . . how did she put it? New Jersey of the United States."

Ian shook his head as if this claim were somehow pitiful. "Detective, my son was a great fan of Laura's books. I guess I felt as if I knew her. I mean, have you ever read a Stephen King novel? Didn't you ever feel as if you 'knew' a writer, even though you hadn't actually met them?"

"And how did you *know* that this author lived in New Jersey?"

Ian shrugged impatiently. "I probably read it on a dust jacket somewhere. I don't know. I made up a story to please a child. Is that a crime?"

"And yet when you and Mrs. Reed met down on the dock, you professed complete surprise to Mrs. Clark that she was an author, and a girl you once knew. You were flabbergasted, according to Mrs. Clark," Ron said sarcastically.

"I hadn't put two and two together, Detective. It's a common enough name. I may have seen her photo, but it didn't register. We're talking about a child I hadn't seen or thought of for twenty-five years. It wasn't until I saw her on the dock that day, you know, in the flesh, that the slightest bit of recognition occurred. A light bulb went on, so to speak. It simply hadn't occurred to me before, okay? I'm not like you. I don't jump to conclusions."

"I'll tell you what you are," said Ron Leonard. "You're a liar, and I'm going to prove it."

"If you spoke to Winston St. Mercier, if you bothered to ask, then he probably told you that I was in Barbados when James Reed Jr. was murdered. That's what this is all about, isn't it? The murder of James Reed?"

Ron did not reply. He studied the other man with venomous eyes.

"Now leave us alone," Ian said coldly. "We want to get on with our lives. The murder of my wife's first husband was a tragedy. But it has nothing to do with me."

* * *

As Laura came around the large lilac bush on the side of the house, she saw Gary there, on the porch, waiting. He turned at the sound of her footsteps.

"Laura," he cried.

"Hello, Gary." She tried to smile. "What brings you here?" she asked, but her voice was flat. She could tell by the look on his face.

"I just heard the most incredible thing."

Laura came up on the porch and sat opposite him on the porch swing. "You heard I got married," she said.

He stared at her.

"Who told you?"

"I was in the flower shop. Scott . . ."

Laura rolled her eyes. "Ah yes, Scott."

"I was concerned because he told me some strange story about a guy wanting all these arrangements made for your house and how he was supposed to come inside here and light candles and all this . . ."

173

Laura held up a hand as if to stop him. "Gary, it's true," she said.

For a moment Gary stared at her. Then he said slowly, "I thought there must be some mistake."

Laura shook her head. "No. No mistake. Scott was right."

"But you didn't . . . You weren't even . . . dating . . ."

"It happened very quickly," said Laura. "I only met him a short time ago. I wanted to tell you, but . . . honestly, I didn't know myself that it was going to get so serious between us. His name is Ian," she said awkwardly.

Gary shook his head. "It's impossible. How could you do this?" he whispered. "You, of all people, Laura."

"That's not fair, Gary. It's not a crime to get married."

"Who is this guy?" Gary demanded.

Laura clasped her hands together, trying to explain. "Ian and I knew each other as children. We bumped into each other, and—"

"Jimmy's only been dead, what, five months?" Gary interrupted. "I thought Scott was lying or crazy. I mean, who would believe this? Five months! You're not the kind of woman to do that. I thought you were someone special. A cut above other women." Gary shook his head, anguish and disbelief mingled in his face. "I believed in you, Laura. I thought you were better than other people."

"I don't want to be better than anybody. I just want to live my life. I was lonely. It's been awful since Jimmy died," Laura pleaded. She leaned forward, trying to take his hands, but he snatched them away.

"Gary, please don't be like this. There's not a lot of people whose opinion I care about anymore in this town, but I do care what you think."

"You should have thought of that before."

"Please, Gary. Let me explain to you."

"You can't. There is no possible explanation for what you've done." He was looking at her accusingly, and suddenly she realized that his friendship was lost to her. She felt a deep, sudden sense of regret.

"I'm sorry that you're hurt by this."

"Hurt?" he cried sarcastically. "I'm more amazed than hurt. It never occurred to me that you would not even have the decency to wait to jump into bed with another man until your husband—"

"That's enough," Ian said sharply, coming around the corner of the house, his face like a thunderhead. "I've had enough of this. Stop apologizing, Laura. You don't owe this guy any explanations."

Laura stood up, mortified. "Ian, please."

Ian stepped up on the porch, towering over Gary, and pointed a finger at him. "Who do you think you are, talking to my wife that way?"

Gary did not look up. "Please move," he said. "I'm leaving."

"Ian, stop it," Laura demanded. "Gary, stay. Let's talk . . ."

Gary ignored her and Ian. He rolled the chair to the edge of the porch and down the ramp. Laura leaned over the railing. "Gary, come on . . ."

But he was gone. Laura hung her head hopelessly.

"He's the one who sent the flowers, isn't he?" said Ian.

"I'm going to have to get used to this," she said bitterly.

"Why is he so possessive of you?" Ian demanded. "Were you involved with him?"

Laura looked up at him, startled. "You mean an affair?"

"Don't look so shocked. Just because he's in a wheel-chair doesn't mean he isn't perfectly capable—"

"He's a friend of mine," Laura cried. "He was a friend of Jimmy's."

"He acted like he owned you. And you let him—"

"Oh, for God's sake, Ian. Don't I have enough to deal with without some kind of stupid jealousy on your part?"

The back door opened on the house next door, and Pam stepped out on her back porch with a watering can. In a min-ute she'll see us, Laura thought. I can't cope with any more of this right now. I don't want to explain. I don't want to see that look of surprise, that struggle for a smile on her face. You knew this was going to happen, she reminded herself. "I'm going in the house," she said to Ian in a low voice.

"You know, Laura," Ian fumed, "it's no wonder people in this town accuse you of everything under the sun. You act like you're guilty all the time."

"I am guilty," Laura said, glaring at him. "I've done a terrible thing. I deserve their scorn. I don't know what I was thinking. I must have been crazy to marry you like that."

Ian's eyes blazed, but his voice was icy. "Maybe so," he said. "Maybe you just made the biggest mistake of your life."

They stared at each other like the strangers they were. Laura felt as if a flock of blackbirds were frantically beating their wings against her throat, against her rib cage, trying to escape.

PART TWO

Columbus, Ohio, Eight Days Later

CHAPTER TWENTY-FOUR

Rae Noonan's feet were swollen and she had a splitting headache. She knew what that swelling in her feet meant, and it
wasn't good. She wasn't due to get off for three more hours,
and she didn't know, for the life of her, how she was going
to be able to finish this shift. Rae worked in a nursing home
on the outskirts of Columbus. Sometimes she liked being
around the old people. It didn't take much to cheer them up.
A few kind words, sit for a minute and look at their pictures.
And they would always ask about Vicki. They were old, and
they understood the importance of children. It seemed like
no matter what else they had done or been in life, men and
women alike, it all boiled down to children and grandchildren. The future of those who didn't have much future left.

Of course, once the old ones got a hold of you, it was
nearly impossible to break free. Their bony old fingers would
get a grip on a handful of Rae's plump flesh and just hold on
for dear life. Rae didn't mind, though. She always thought
to herself, Someday I'll be old, too.

Rae sighed and continued folding nightgowns. Della
Waters, a friendly black woman who was an RN, poked her
head into the laundry room. "Phone for you, honey. I think
it's Vicki."

"Thanks, Della," said Rae. She put down her laundry and went out into the hall to the phone.

"Hi, Mom," said Rae's twelve-year-old daughter. "I'm home."

"What are you doing?" Rae asked tenderly.

"I got a couple books at the library. I'm gonna read."

Rae could picture her daughter, hair like silk on her shoulders, sitting in the kitchen, her books spread out over the scarred linoleum surface of the kitchen table. "How was school?"

"I got my last report card," said Vicki.

"And?"

"Six A's. One B plus," Vicki exulted.

"Good girl," Rae said, beaming. You won't be like me, she thought. Forced to take whatever you can get. You'll be proud. You'll go to college and you'll have a good job, and you won't be forced to depend on anybody for anything. It was Rae's dream, day and night, for her daughter. A better life.

Vicki's father had left when she was only two, and Vicki didn't even remember him. It had been a tough struggle, but Rae had managed to raise her up, keep a roof over their heads, keep them fed. And Vicki had bloomed somehow in their hardscrabble life and been smart. She was the whole world to Rae.

"I think I'm going to be a doctor, Mama," Vicki said seriously. "Science is my favorite subject. And then I can take care of you."

"That will be just fine, honey," said Rae, forcing herself not to think about how impossible it all seemed. Medical school cost the world. I'll find a way, she thought. "Listen, is Uncle Herman back?" Rae asked.

"No, ma'am. No sign of him," said Vicki.

Rae wanted to say, "Good," but she didn't. "Well, you just have a snack if you're hungry."

"How are you feeling, Mama? You sound kind of tired."

Rae looked down at her swollen ankles. "I'm okay. You just read your books. I'll be home around six. Don't worry about me."

Rae hung up the phone and rose slowly to her feet. As she turned around, Della was standing there, frowning at her.

"Honey, you don't look too good," said Della.

Rae managed a smile. "My head is aching today."

"Come over here. Sit down," said Della. "I want to check that blood pressure of yours."

"Oh, Della, don't fuss," Rae protested, but she sat down as Della rolled the sphygmomanometer over to her and wrapped the cuff around her arm. "It's probably just the weather. My sinuses," Rae said as Della pumped the rubber bulb in her hand and frowned at the gauge.

"Sinuses, my foot," said Della. "Rae, have you been taking your medication?"

"I might have missed today," Rae said evasively.

"Rae, I want you to get home, take your pills, and put your feet up. You're through for the day."

Rae protested weakly, but Della ushered her out, shaking her head.

"You want me to find someone to drive you?" Della asked.

"No, really. You've done enough. I have to admit, I don't mind leaving."

"Go on, now," said Della. "Scoot."

Rae waited patiently for the bus and settled onto a seat. She thought about Vicki's report card again. All those A's. Those little shoulders carried around such a lot of worries. They had managed all right until last year, when one day Rae started feeling nauseated at work and then, on the way home on the bus, her breath got shallow and her chest felt as if a horse were sitting on it and she knew she was having a heart attack. After two weeks in the hospital, Rae's carefully constructed world began to collapse. No insurance, no work, bills piling up. When the landlord told them they had to get out of their apartment, Rae had no choice. She had to turn to Herman. He was her brother, her only living relative, and it was that or be on the street.

So she asked him, and Herman took them in. He had a farmhouse he rented, way off the beaten track. And no wonder. He needed privacy. And Rae knew why. The only good thing about it was that Herman was gone a lot, "on business." A lot of the time they had the place to themselves. When he was home, she just steered clear of him and kept Vicki clear of him. Just lie low, she'd say to Vicki. I'll get us out of here as quick as I can.

She was almost ready to make their move. One of the other aides was getting divorced, looking for someone to share her house. Rae thought it might work out. Herman had left them alone, but Rae didn't want her child in that atmosphere.

The bus rumbled to a stop at the end of the dirt road where Herman's house was located. Rae picked up her shopping bag and got off the bus. She started up the road beneath a tunnel of trees that made the road dark and cool, even in summer. There were only three residences on the road—one house and two trailers. The two trailers were virtually across the road from one another in mirrored clearings. Outside of one was a satellite dish, and from inside, there was the sound of a baby squalling. The other trailer was silent, except for a black dog chained outside that snarled as Rae went by. Rae hated for Vicki to have to walk down the road. She was always afraid that vicious mutt might break free and come after her. Herman's was the house at the very end of the lane.

As she came up to the clearing around Herman's house, she saw his GTO parked in front of the house, and her heart sank. It was not that he was so hard to get along with. The fact was, he barely spoke. He was ten years older than Rae, and she had vague memories of him being kind of a quiet, goofy kid before he went off to Vietnam. He got in the usual amount of trouble, and her father whipped him about the same amount as any boy. But when he came back, he was changed.

Living in his house, she had tried to mind her own business, but it was impossible not to know, after a while, what was going on. At least when he was away, she didn't have to think about it. Didn't have to think about the sorry state

181

of a life when you had to expose your child to a person of Herman's nature.

Rae pressed her lips together and sighed. I'll be okay, she thought. I'll get her out of here. Soon, she repeated to herself. It kept her going.

As she climbed the porch steps, she heard voices from inside.

"Please, Uncle Herman, don't," Vicki pleaded. "Nooo . . ."

Rae threw open the screen door. Herman was straddling Vicki, who was pinned down on the couch, and he was unbuttoning her shirt with a methodical, detached look on his face while the child tried to pummel him with her fists.

Herman's duffel bag was still on the floor inside the door, as if he hadn't bothered to unpack. He had just walked in the door and decided to attack his niece.

For a moment Rae froze, unable even to think. Then she reacted. She reached into the duffel bag, knowing what she would find there. She pulled out a gun, cocked it, and aimed it at her brother's back.

"Get off of her, you dirty scum, or I'll kill you."

Herman looked up at his sister, surprised, as Vicki struggled to free herself from him.

"Put that gun down, Rae," he said.

"Get off my daughter."

Herman pushed himself off his niece and came toward his sister, his belt unbuckled, his fly half unzipped. He was still wearing his combat boots. The sight of him made Rae half mad with rage, with grief and frustration. "I should have known something like this would happen," she said.

"Put that goddamn gun down. What I do in my own house is my own business."

"Vicki, go in our room," Rae cried. "Lock the door."

"Our room. I like that. What makes it your room? You don't pay for it," said Herman. "I'm just trying to collect something for my generosity."

"Don't come any closer," Rae said. Vicki clutched the front of her blouse, trying to button it with trembling hands.

"Vicki, get out of here," Rae cried. Herman was so close that she could smell the beer on his breath.

"Don't hurt my mother!" Vicki screamed, inching up behind him.

"Shut up, shut up, both of you," Herman cried. "I can't stand the noise." He wheeled around and grabbed Vicki by the neck and jerked her off her feet. She dangled in the air, feet flailing, guttural noises coming from her throat.

Rae did not think. She just fired. Herman's grip loosened, and Vicki dropped to the floor and scrambled out of the way, shrieking. Herman staggered and fell. Rae stepped back. She did not fire again. But she didn't put the gun down, either. Or try to help him. She waited and watched, ready to fire again if need be. But Herman was not moving. There was a lot of blood everywhere.

"Mom, you killed him," Vicki whispered. She was shaking all over.

"It's all right. Don't be afraid," Rae said, although her own heart was thudding with terror.

Actually it took him another few minutes to die. Rae held the gun on him. "Call the cops," she whispered to Vicki, gently as if she were reminding her to wear her boots in the rain. "Go on now."

Rae's eyes never left the stricken face of the bleeding man at her feet. She wasn't taking any chances. She wanted to be sure he was dead. Someone so evil should have been harder to kill. "It's all right," she said as Vicki began to cry. "It's all right. He's gone now. It's all for the best. Go, call the police now. I'll keep watch."

CHAPTER TWENTY-FIVE

Wanda Jurik stared out the window as night fell. Where was he? Where could he have gone? She had not seen Gary since the day he'd dropped her off at home and gone on to Laura Reed's house. He'd had his paints with him. When he hadn't returned, she'd assumed he had gone painting. When he hadn't returned by eight o'clock that night, she had called the police. And Chief Moore had told her, with thinly veiled impatience, that a grown man wasn't considered missing if he didn't come home for dinner. That was eight days ago, and there had not been one single trace of him since.

Wanda turned from the window and began to roam the ranch house like a caged cat, looking out every window, jumping at every sound, her heart leaping up with hope and then sinking again.

She went back to the kitchen, where her dinner, hardly touched, congealed on the plate. She sat down and looked at it, then pushed it away. She rested her forehead on the heel of her hand. Whatever had happened to him, it had to do with that woman and her getting married like that. Wanda knew about the flowers he sent her. She knew about his secret dreams for Laura Reed. She knew all that stuff, even though he didn't think so. She could read him like a book. Always could.

There was a sound of gravel crunching in the driveway, and Wanda leapt up from her chair, heart pounding, and ran to the window. She could not see if it was his van. Who else would be here at this hour? she thought, hope shoving reason aside. She opened the back door and stepped out onto the wide, low step. The sea breeze tickled her face. "Gary?" she called.

"No, it's me, Wanda."

Wanda stiffened with anger, her hopes dashed for the hundredth time, as Vince Moore's stolid figure appeared out of the dark and was illuminated in the glow cast by the lights inside the house. Finally, finally, yesterday he had agreed to start making inquiries about Gary.

"What do you want?" she demanded, and then her heart was suddenly gripped with fear. "What is it? Is it . . ."

"I have some good news about Gary. Can I come in for a minute?"

Wanda stepped aside and let him pass into her kitchen. He removed his hat and stood holding it, by the doorway.

Wanda clenched her fists to keep from gripping him by the shirtfront. "What?" she demanded. She noticed him eyeing the kitchen chairs. "Go ahead and sit," she said shortly.

"Thanks," said Vince. "I just wanted you to know that we've contacted the credit card companies and gotten a complete list of the transactions on his accounts. The day he left, it seems he made a large cash withdrawal on his credit card. Nothing since then, but with the amount he took, he'd have money to last for quite a while."

Wanda stared at the chief. "That's it?" she said.

"Well, that seems very promising to me," Vince said. "That's exactly the kind of information we were hoping for."

"He's dead," she said dully. "I know it. I thought when you said news, that you'd found him."

"Dead? Why would you say that? I figure he withdrew the money so he could take off on a little trip. Any day he'll be pulling back in that driveway."

"What kind of hope is that? That means nothing," Wanda scoffed. "He could have been attacked and killed. That card could be stolen."

"He got the money at a local bank, Wanda. The teller said he was in a wheelchair," Vince explained patiently.

"I'd like to take comfort from that," Wanda said with a sigh. She sat back down at the table, and tears brimmed in her eyes. "But I just can't keep fooling myself. If he was alive, he would have called me by now. No. I've been trying not to admit it, but I know my boy. He went off like a wounded animal and took his own life."

"Oh, for heaven's sake, Wanda. Why would he do that?"

"I told you the night I first called you," Wanda cried indignantly. "He was so upset about that Reed woman getting married again. He had kind of a crush on her. But you just paid no attention to me."

"Well, he may have been upset, but that's no reason to kill himself."

"What else did he have to live for, stuck in that chair?" Wanda asked, shaking her head. "I've been afraid of this for years. I did my best to make him comfortable, but what kind of a life was that?"

Vince felt his temper rising. "Well, for one thing, he was a very successful painter."

Wanda waved it away as if it were of no importance. "I'm telling you. I know my son. He wouldn't go anywhere. He never went places. It was hard for him to get in and out of places in that wheelchair. I mean, everything is supposed to be handicapped accessible, but you know as well as I do, nobody enforces that law." She looked at Vince accusingly. "No, he was helpless."

Vince gritted his teeth. He hated the way Wanda talked about her son in the past tense, even though he knew that sometimes people had to voice their worst fears aloud to the police. It was their way of seeking reassurance. Wanda was just such a doom-monger that it was hard for him to sympathize with her. She always put the most negative spin on everything. He hated the way she was always emasculating Gary, belittling his life. As if legs were what made life worthwhile. Vince had had a favorite uncle who spent his adult life in a wheelchair. One of the most powerful, vigorous men he'd ever known. Fathered four children, ran his own company, loved his sports. *You* made him feel helpless, he thought. Who are you to say he had nothing to live for? But then he chided himself. Wanda was suffering in her own way. He could not know what was really in her heart. What was the use of placing blame?

"It's kind of ironic, isn't it," Wanda went on tonelessly. "James Reed put him in that wheelchair, and then his widow drove him over the edge."

"What are you talking about? Jimmy Reed had nothing to do with that accident." Vince frowned at her. He remembered the accident well. His own son, Robby, had been at the basketball game that night. He remembered the fear in his heart when news of an accident involving teenagers came over the scanner.

"Jimmy Reed was the one who talked him into going to that basketball game. During an icy winter storm. Those other boys didn't want him there. But Jimmy Reed convinced him that he had to come. Filled Gary's head with some stupid idea of being one of the guys. It was always that way. Anything Jimmy Reed said was the gospel to Gary. My son had no business being in that car that night. When I tried to tell him that, James Reed said to me, 'You worry too much, Mrs. Jurik.'" Wanda sat back on her chair and stared at Vince, the light of an old animosity bright in her eyes. "Kind of like what you said, the night I called to tell you Gary was missing."

Vince sighed, understanding her implication, but he'd be damned if he'd apologize. "I was only telling you the official policy of the department. A grown man is not considered missing when he doesn't come home for dinner."

"Gary is not a regular man," Wanda cried.

Vince shook his head in disgust. "What a terrible thing to say. I hope you don't ever say that to your son."

"I probably won't have a chance to say anything to my son ever again," she said bitterly.

"You act as if we found his body! For goodness' sake, Wanda, isn't it possible that Gary just needed time to go off and think? If I were you," Vince said pointedly, "I wouldn't be so quick to give up on my child."

They stared implacably at one another for a moment, and then Vince's beeper went off on his belt, breaking the impasse. "May I use your phone, Wanda?"

Wanda shrugged, and Vince went over to the wall phone and dialed the police station.

"I've got a long-distance call for you, Chief," said Jerilyn Conlon. "I'm going to patch it through to you."

"Okay," said Vince, and waited.

"Is this Chief Moore?" asked the caller.

"Speaking."

"Chief, my name is Captain Orrin Evans. I'm a detective with the Ohio State Police. I'm calling from Columbus."

"Yessir."

"Chief, we've got a homicide out here that may be of some interest to you."

Vince grimaced. He had a sudden image of Gary Jurik, pulled from his van at some highway rest stop. Set on by thugs. Unable to run from them. And Wanda, sitting right here beside him. Ready to say "I told you so" and then break apart into a million pieces. Please God, he thought. Not that. "How so, Captain Evans?" he asked.

"A fellow named Herman Powell was shot to death by his sister here late this afternoon. She came home to find him attacking her twelve-year-old daughter, so she shot him with his own gun."

Vince snorted in disgust. "Can't say I blame her."

"No, sir. Anyway," Captain Evans continued, "we found out something very interesting about this Herman Powell. His sister knew about it, or she suspected it, anyway. It seems that Herman Powell was a professional killer. Advertised his services in one of those paramilitary magazines. Some right-wing publication called *Merc*."

Vince frowned in concentration. "A hit man?" he asked.

"That's right," said Captain Evans. "His sister has been very cooperative. She's relieved to have it out in the open. We are just beginning to sort through his things, but we have found a number of items that we think are related to his killings. Luckily for us, he didn't get a chance to put his affairs in order, if you get my meaning. Now, I've already been on the phone with police in Michigan and New York State regarding information he had written down. And among his things was directions to the home of one James Reed Jr. in your town there."

Vince gasped. "Oh, my God," he breathed.

"Was Mr. James Reed Jr. the victim of a homicide?"

"Yes, he was," said Vince.

"I thought so," Evans said with satisfaction bordering on relish. "Was he shot?"

"He was."

"May I ask what the murder weapon was?"

"A thirty-eight caliber Smith and Wesson pistol," said Vince. Perspiration had broken out on his forehead. His hands were clamped to the phone.

"Well, Mr. Powell was in possession of just such a weapon. Although he had several others as well. Chief, I think you may want to come out here and take a look at the gun, and inspect Mr. Powell's effects. We have a cache of jewelry and personal items which Mr. Powell apparently took from his victims. You may want to examine those, too."

Vince glanced at his watch. "I will be on the first plane I can get out of Atlantic City or Philadelphia tomorrow morning. Can you give me the particulars?"

Wanda stood up, curious in spite of herself, and came over to the phone. Vince made a writing motion with his hand, and Wanda fetched him a pad and pencil. As Evans talked, Vince wrote down his directions.

"There will be quite a large group of lawmen here tomorrow," said Captain Evans, as if promising a successful class reunion. "We'll look forward to seeing you."

"I appreciate this," said Vince. He hung up the phone and looked up the home number of Ron Leonard. "I need to make another call," he said.

"What is it?" Wanda asked anxiously. "Is this about Gary?"

Vince was dialing Ron's number as he spoke. "No, it's not," he said absently.

Ron Leonard answered his phone.

"Ron," Vince said grimly, "this is Vince Moore. I just got off the phone with the Ohio State Police. We've got a break in the Reed case."

Wanda's eyes flickered with interest. Vince looked at her warningly, and she backed away from the phone.

CHAPTER TWENTY-SIX

The facade of the Cape Christian County Court House building bespoke an era when grace and spaciousness in public buildings was a norm. The oak double doors with their frosted-glass panes were heavy, as if to convey a sense of the weight and magnitude of the events that transpired within. Once inside the foyer, however, the building appeared altogether different. It had been renovated in recent years, stripped down and modernized. Nothing remained of the ornamental moldings and paneling that had once defined the interior. All surfaces were flat, white, and no-nonsense. Entry to the building was restricted by a guard behind a Plexiglas panel. The marble floor had been covered with industrial carpeting, and the air temperature was climate controlled. Inside, the modernized courthouse was all business.

Dolores and Sidney entered the Cape Christian Court House and identified themselves to the security guard behind the plastic shield. They had been watching TV when the call came from Vince Moore's office, asking them to come down to the courthouse. That is, Sidney had been watching TV. Dolores had been moving around the room, straightening things that were already straight, ignoring his pleas for her to join him on the couch, to relax for a moment.

"DA Jackson is waiting for you," the guard said seriously, and buzzed for the outer door to be unlocked.

Sidney gripped his wife's arm and steered her back to the chief's office. It was strange to be summoned to the courthouse in the evening like this. Dolores had tried to pry information out of the officer who called, but to no avail. "This is something big," she told Sidney when she hung up the phone. "I feel it."

God, please put an end to this, Sidney thought. He could not stand to watch her suffer anymore. She was a wreck all the time now. She hardly slept, she forgot to make meals. It was almost as bad as when Jimmy first was killed. Ever since she'd heard about Laura's remarriage, she'd been like a woman possessed. Sometimes, in the middle of the night, Sidney would wake up with a start and find her side of the bed empty. He would usually find her in the kitchen, drinking coffee and brooding. No amount of cajoling could get her back to bed. And no one could stand that kind of stress indefinitely. Let this be it, he thought. One way or another.

District Attorney Jackson was seated behind his large, gleaming desk. Ron Leonard stood behind him, and Vince Moore was seated to his right. There was also a court officer making a recording. The district attorney indicated the seats in front of his desk. Dolores looked worriedly at Sidney and then sat down. Sidney sat beside her, draping his arm protectively around her chair.

"Dolores and Sidney Barone," said Vince, "this is District Attorney Clyde Jackson."

Sidney rose from his seat and leaned over to shake the man's hand. "We've met," said Sidney. Dolores smiled weakly at the chief prosecutor, not trusting her knees to hold her. They were all here. It *was* something big, she thought.

Vince glanced at the DA, who nodded for him to proceed. "Dolores, Sidney, something has come up regarding Jimmy's murder," said Vince. "I tried to reach Laura, but she isn't at home."

"Out somewhere with her new husband," Dolores said sourly.

"We have men out looking for them right now," said Vince.

Dolores's eyes widened. "What is it, Vince? What's going on?"

Vince cleared his throat and wondered how to begin. Get right down to business, he thought. The district attorney opened the drawer of his desk and pulled out a plastic bag. He pushed it over to Dolores, who took it with a puzzled expression on her face.

"I wonder if you could identify the items in this bag," Clyde Jackson said.

Dolores handled the bag.

"Please don't open it," said DA Jackson. "This is potential evidence in a capital murder case. Just examine the items through the plastic."

Obediently Dolores held the bag under the lamp on the desk and studied the contents. The gold of the watch glinted in the light. She smoothed the plastic over the inscription on the back of the watch case. "From Mother and Sidney," it read, and the year Jimmy received his MFA. Sidney had insisted on this very expensive watch. It was important for a man entering the business world to have the right watch, Sidney said. In the bag also was a ring—a pearl-and-diamond ring that had been given to her by her grandmother when she was a girl. And she had given it to Jimmy, to give to his bride someday. Never realizing . . . Dolores rolled the items in the bag and saw another ring, Jimmy's high school class ring. Through the plastic she fingered the ruby-colored stone in it and traced the numbers of the year, engraved in the sides. On the worn surface inside the ring, even through the plastic, she could just barely make out the initials that she knew so well. Her heart was thudding, and tears rose to her eyes. She clutched the bag in her lap with both hands. As she blinked back tears, her eyes had a faraway look, as if she were seeing the past—a birthday, a graduation, happy times, long ago. Before her world fell apart.

"Do you recognize these objects?" Vince said gently. He already knew the answer. Both Dolores and Laura had described the missing jewelry to him in minute detail. The moment he saw them, tagged and lying across the table in Ohio State Police barracks, he knew.

Dolores nodded. "These are Jimmy's," she said in a quavering voice. "These belonged to my son."

Sidney patted her shoulder. "It's all right, honey," he said. He wrested the bag gently from her and placed it on the desk. Then he gripped her hands, as if to ready her for a hard landing.

Dolores looked up at Vince. "Where did you get them?" she said.

Vince glanced up at DA Jackson, who nodded slightly. Vince licked his lips and spoke carefully. "I went out to Ohio today, with Detective Leonard here. These objects were among the effects of a man named Herman Powell, who was killed there yesterday . . ."

"Killed . . . how?" Dolores asked, confused.

"He was shot in an incident of domestic violence. After his death, certain of his activities came to light. And we were informed by the Ohio State Police. We found these pieces of jewelry in his possession, as well as some papers identifying Jimmy by name. That's how they knew to call us."

"Are you saying . . ." she breathed.

"We have also recovered the gun that killed . . . your son. The murder weapon. Although some further tests are being run."

"Oh, my God," said Dolores. She sat forward on her chair, shock, hope, and confusion mingling in her expression. "He's the one?" She looked down at her hands, locked with Sidney's. She looked up almost shamefacedly. "There *was* a man, then. What she said was true." Everyone in the room knew that she was referring to Laura. "God forgive me, I've been so unfair to her. So this was him. The man that killed my son."

"We believe so, yes," said Vince.

Dolores turned to Sidney, and the relief in her face filled him with joy, even at this grim moment. "Oh, Sidney."

"Thank God," he said fervently.

"I'm afraid that's not all," said Clyde Jackson.

CHAPTER TWENTY-SEVEN

Stars bejeweled the inky sky, and the water was rippling silk in the moonlight. Laura closed her eyes and shivered pleasantly as the cool night breeze caressed her skin. The only lights, beside the moon and the stars, were the red and green lights on the masts and the sides of the boat, reflecting in the water. In the distance Cape Christian resembled a golden, glowing chain, growing nearer.

"What a perfect evening," she murmured. Pam had invited Michael over for grilled hot dogs and a video, so Laura and Ian had taken the opportunity and sailed up the coast to a romantic harborside restaurant. They had dined by candlelight and returned, arm in arm, to the boat as the hour grew late.

"Pretty soon," Ian said, "every night will be like this."

"I can't wait," said Laura. Somehow they had weathered the argument over Gary and made up passionately. In the week since, she had been spending the days sorting through things in the house, with Ian helping her. She wanted all of their belongings packed up in boxes before they left. That way they could just be shipped when they settled down in the fall. "Hey," she said, "is it my imagination or are we stopping?"

"I had an idea," he said. "I thought I'd drop anchor for a while."

"But we're almost in the harbor."

He put his arms around her and whispered into her hair, "You haven't made love until you've done it at sea."

"We can't, Ian. We have to pick up Michael."

"He can stay at Pam's a while longer."

Laura pulled away from his arms. "I can't impose on her like that. Besides," she said more gently, realizing how rigid her response had sounded, "we have all summer to make love at sea."

Ian let her go with a frown. "Are you sure that's the reason?" he asked.

"What?"

"Michael. Or is that just an excuse?"

"An excuse?" she cried. "An excuse for what?"

"To avoid making love with me. I feel like you are holding back with me."

"Oh, Ian, that's ridiculous. I have a small boy who's been through so much. He needs to feel secure, to know that I'm not going to just abandon him. Are you trying to force me to choose between you and my son?"

"No, of course not," he said shortly. But she could see a flash of anger in his eyes.

"How can you doubt me?" she asked. "I mean, I married you in a minute, didn't I? Of course I want to make love with you."

He turned to haul up the anchor, and as he did, she was overcome with a feeling of guilt. If she was perfectly honest with herself, there was some truth to his complaint. It wasn't him—it wasn't his lovemaking. No woman could ask for a more passionate lover. But even in the throes of their rapturous encounters, it was as if a little demon of anxiety got hold of her, making her think of Jimmy. Whenever she and Ian were making love, she felt as if Jimmy were there, looking on balefully. Not in the sense of a ghost or anything like that. It was just some combination of longing and regret, filling her with doubts about . . . nothing, nothing, really. It will go away in time, she told herself. It's only natural, she tried to tell herself. Although who could predict what was natural in their bizarre circumstances? Meanwhile there was Michael to think of. Stick to the practical, she thought. She could not enjoy herself knowing that her son might be anxiously waiting for her.

"All right," he said. "We're on our way in."

"Ian." She wanted to say "I love you." He looked at her expectantly. "Thank you," she said.

Sensing her reticence, Ian clammed up and stared at the glimmering horizon.

"You know how children are. When they're waiting, every moment is like a day to them. I'm sure Phillip was just like that, too."

Ian turned on her, his eyes blazing. Laura immediately felt ashamed of herself for having invoked his son's memory to try to persuade him to her viewpoint. "I'm sorry," she said. "I didn't mean to bring back painful memories."

Ian scowled. "I never forget Phillip. Never for a moment."

She bit her lip and lowered her eyes. She did not want to see the anger on his face. "I'm sorry," she repeated.

"It's because of Phillip that I'm here with you now. Because of Phillip—I knew I had to change my life. You don't have to remind me . . ."

Laura reached out gingerly and put a hand on his arm. His muscles were tense, his back stiff. "You're right. I shouldn't have said that. Darling, we've got our whole lives to love each other. We don't need to rush."

He did not reply but busied himself with starting the inboard motor for the ride into the channel. A cold wind blew up, and Laura shivered as they cruised toward the harbor. "I'm freezing," she said. "Do you mind if I go below?"

Ian shrugged, and Laura sighed. She descended the ladder into the cabin, where one small light was burning. She settled herself into the corner of the futon, wrapping a thin blanket around her. The picture of Phillip and Gabriella stared back at her across the width of the boat. Laura studied their faces and thought about Ian. It was hard for him, too, to start again. You put so much heart, so much effort, into a marriage and children, as if each day you were making headway scaling some lofty peak, and then, suddenly, you find yourself tumbling to the bottom. After a while, with luck, you try to start that climb all over again. But it's discouraging. To begin again. No matter how much you want to.

Were you very happy? she wondered, looking at those smiling faces in the picture. Will you ever let go of him? Will Jimmy ever let go of me?

"Laura." His voice was sharp from above. "We're almost in."

She folded up the blanket and climbed back up onto the deck. Suddenly her eye was caught by a flashing red light on a police car parked near Boat People.

"There's a police car on the pier," she exclaimed.

"So?"

"I don't know. I just have a sick feeling. What if it's Michael?" she said.

"It's not Michael," he reassured her as he turned off the motor and they eased into the slip. "What makes you think it's for us? It's summer. There's a lot of boats coming and going out of here."

"You're right," she said.

But she could not tear her eyes away from the flashing light, and as Ian began to secure the boat she was not surprised—sickened, but not surprised—to see a uniformed officer walking toward their slip. Usually she helped Ian pack up the sails, since she was trying to learn to be a competent crew for their upcoming trip, but this time she climbed right out onto the dock as the policeman approached.

"Laura Reed?" he asked.

Laura's blood ran cold. Turner, she thought, but she did not correct him. Ian stopped what he was doing and looked up.

"Is my son all right?" Laura pleaded.

"I don't know anything about your son," the officer replied. "District Attorney Jackson wants to talk to you and your husband over at the courthouse. Is this your husband?"

Ian finished flaking the mainsail and climbed surefootedly out on the dock. He and Laura exchanged a glance. "Yes," said Laura. Her relief that it was not about Michael turned to sudden irritation. It was more of the same—more questions and intrusions into their fragile privacy. "What is so important that we have to come down there again in the middle of the night?"

The police officer grinned, but it wasn't a pleasant grin. It was more like a leer. "It seems like they found the guy that killed Mr. James Reed," he said.

For a moment her heart stopped. The world stopped. And in an instant, when it started again, anger and gratitude and relief were all pumping inside her. "Oh, thank God. Who is it?"

The officer shook his head. "You'll have to come down to the station."

"Ian, did you hear that?" she cried. "Let's go. Hurry."

"I wouldn't be in such a hurry if I were you," said the cop.

Laura did not hear him. She was running for the car.

CHAPTER TWENTY-EIGHT

A group of reporters and news photographers had gathered outside the county courthouse where the DA's office was. Television vans were clustered at the curb as technicians with videocams jockeyed for a good vantage point. An officer was keeping them at bay, refusing to allow them inside. Laura and Ian emerged from the back of the black-and-white car to the popping of flashbulbs and a cacophony of questions. "I don't know," Laura kept saying as the officer cleared a path for them. "Please, I don't know anything about it yet."

They entered the building and walked up to the shielded window where the security guard sat. He was a burly armed black man, and he was talking on the phone.

"Hey, Marty," the officer said, "buzz us in."

Marty indicated that they should wait a minute until he was through with his call. As he was talking he looked up at the people passing him on his side of the wall and raised his eyebrows.

The door opened into the foyer, and Sidney and Dolores emerged, followed by a pair of officers.

"Sidney, Dolores," Laura blurted out in surprise. "What's going on?"

Laura was struck by how physically diminished Dolores was. They had not met face-to-face since the funeral. Since then Dolores had made her feelings, her suspicions clear by avoiding Laura so completely. Now, however, it seemed they had found Jimmy's killer. Laura was prepared to forgive and forget. It would just be such a relief for them all to have peace of mind at last.

But when Dolores turned and saw Laura, her eyes were filled not with relief, but with hatred. "You," Dolores spat at her. "You evil witch."

"Watch what you say to my wife," Ian protested angrily.

"Dolores," Laura cried, taken aback. "This officer said they found the man . . ."

"Your assassin," said Dolores. "Your hired killer."

"What?" Laura felt her knees buckle, and Ian reached out quickly to steady her.

"Don't play innocent. My God, are you some kind of devil? You will not get away with this. You mark my words. You'll get what's coming to you!"

"Hired killer?" Laura cried.

At the sound of Laura's question, Dolores lunged at her and slapped her face: Sidney and one of the cops reached out to restrain Dolores.

Laura cried out from the shock and the sting. The door from inside the courthouse banged open, and Ron Leonard emerged.

"Let me tell you something," said Dolores. "You may think you got away with this, but God is against you. You thought this guy would just disappear into the woodwork, and for a while you were lucky. But he's been found out. And you're next. They'll find the evidence. And when they do, I won't rest till you go to the electric chair. And him with you," she cried, indicating Ian.

"You're crazy," said Laura.

"And another thing. You will not keep my grandson. No matter how long it takes, I will get him away from you. You will not raise my son's child, after you had my Jimmy killed."

"Stop it," Laura cried. "Stop it now. What are you talking about?"

"Tell her, Sid!" Dolores was screaming, her face blotchy and her eyes wild. "Tell her we will make her pay for this!" All of a sudden she clutched at her chest and a look of fear came over her face, as if she were teetering on the roof of a high building.

"What is it, honey? Help me, help me, somebody," Sidney pleaded.

"You two, inside," said Ron Leonard. "Marty, call up the EMTs. On the double."

"Honey," Sidney was wailing. "Darling, talk to me."

Laura felt herself being carried inside the courthouse like a twig on the current. She could see Dolores being supported by Sidney and an officer, her eyes still wide, her complexion faded to a deathly pallor.

* * *

Duane Garrity followed his wife into the kitchen after she hung up the phone and switched on the little TV in the kitchen to hear the news. He shook his head in disbelief as the reporter outlined the late-breaking developments in the Reed case. "You see?" he said. "I told you. I told you all along."

Pam opened the refrigerator and began getting out the bologna and mayonnaise to make sandwiches for the boys' lunch. "Turn the volume down," she said. "Michael will hear it."

"He's got to know sooner or later," said Duane.

Pam slathered mayonnaise on a piece of bread and slapped a slice of bologna on it. "Well, what did you expect me to do?" she asked defensively. "Tell her I wouldn't keep him tonight?"

"I don't know what he was doing here in the first place," Duane said grumpily.

"I thought you were spending the night at the base," she said. "I didn't expect you home."

"In other words, you were going behind my back."

"No, I was not. It's just when you're not here I don't fix a big meal. I have things the kids like. And besides, I'll invite who I want to my house," she said defiantly.

"Pammy, you just don't realize that this woman is trouble. I mean seriously bad news."

Pam slapped down another piece of bread and began to saw the sandwich in half. She did not reply. The events of the night had shaken her a little. She never would believe it of Laura, but she had to admit, the sudden marriage had taken her by surprise. Of course, she had encouraged Laura to go out on a date, get out of the house. But marriage? And now this. A hit man. Still, it couldn't be . . .

Duane saw the conflict in his wife's face and came over to her. He put his arm around her and hugged her until she gave him an anemic smile. "You're so good. You always want to think the best of everyone," he said gently. "But the world is full of bad people, honey."

Pam sighed and began to make a sandwich for Michael. They were down to the last few days of school, and he would need to have a lunch. She felt so sorry for him. He was the innocent one in all of this. She knew right from wrong, and no matter what else, it was wrong to take it out on Michael.

"Duane, I don't care what you say, I'm not going to treat Michael any different, because he didn't do anything to deserve that." Tears stood in her eyes.

Duane sighed and ate some grapes out of the bowl on the counter. "I guess you're right about that, honey," he said. "When you're right, you're right. But you've got to admit that it looks bad for your friend there."

Pam's hand trembled as she put the mayonnaise back in the fridge. "I just can't believe it," she said stubbornly. "I won't."

* * *

Sidney sat at his wife's bedside and brushed her hair off her forehead with a wet washcloth. All kinds of monitors were attached to her, machines on all sides registering every slight variation in her vital signs.

Her eyes were closed, but she wasn't asleep, despite the drugs they had given her. She was a little less tense than she had been, though. He was grateful for that. He heard the door to the room open, and a young doctor came in. Sidney peered at his name tag, scarcely able to believe that this boy was a doctor.

"Mr. Barone? I'm Dr. Pitkin. We met in the emergency room."

Sidney nodded, although his memory of everything that had happened since Dolores collapsed was a blur.

"How's she doing?" the young man asked pleasantly.

"She seems to be resting," said Sidney.

Dr. Pitkin smiled. Sidney wondered how they managed to smile like that when they were looking into such worried eyes, such frantic faces, all the time. Trick of the trade, he thought.

"Well, the good news is that she didn't have a heart attack. It was an angina attack."

"Oh, thank God," said Sidney, letting out a deep breath.

"It was a severe one, to be sure, and she needs to have further testing done. I want to emphasize to you that this is serious business . . . it can be a warning of trouble ahead."

Sidney nodded. You didn't get to be sixty-five years old without having heard every war story about heart conditions that there was. "You don't have to tell me, Doc."

"We'll keep her here for a day or two, run some tests, and then, when you take her home, you're going have to keep her quiet. Keep her from getting upset."

Sidney sighed. "That's not going to be easy."

"Well, it's very important," said Dr. Pitkin. He glanced over at Dolores and saw that her eyes were open. "How are you feeling, Mrs. Barone?"

"I hear you talking about me," she said.

"No getting upset, you understand?"

Dolores stared at him.

"Thank you, Doctor," said Sidney. "I'm just relieved it wasn't a heart attack."

"Well, it very easily could be. We'll be doing some more tests. Meanwhile, I'm going to give you a special diet to follow, Mrs. Barone. And we'll be giving you medication to take. We'll go over all of this before you leave."

"When do I leave?" she said.

"Take it slow," said the doctor. "Probably the day after tomorrow. Now you get some rest, too, Mr. Barone."

"Thank you, Doctor. Good night," he said as the young man smiled again and waved as he headed toward the hall.

Sidney resumed his seat beside Dolores. "You heard what he said," he told her sternly, knowing it was no use.

Dolores looked at him, and tears of frustration rose in her eyes. She gripped his hand on the blanket, and her fingers were cold and clammy. "She killed him, Sid. She killed him, and she's going to get away with it. You heard them. The police. They can't arrest her. Even though they know she's guilty as sin. They don't have any evidence. They don't have anything linking her to this guy . . ."

"They'll find something," Sidney said soothingly. "If there's something to find."

"'If'?" Dolores cried. "How can you say 'if'?"

"All I'm saying is, it shouldn't be too hard. Now that they know about this hired killer."

Dolores shifted her head on the pillow. "I knew she did it. I always knew. But if this Powell fellow hadn't been killed in a freak way like that, she would have gotten off. She even had the nerve to go and get married to her lover. She was so sure she was home free."

Sidney patted her shoulder anxiously. "But they did find him. And now they're going to find out the rest. You have to leave it to the police. You have to trust them."

Dolores struggled to sit up, leaning on one elbow. All the monitors jumped. "But what if there's nothing left? It was months ago. Almost a year ago. There might not be any way to trace it to her . . ."

206

"Dolores, stop," Sidney pleaded. "You're in the hospital. I thought I lost you."

She looked at him sadly. "I'll be okay. Why don't you go home and go to bed, Sid? I'm just gonna go to sleep."

"No, you're not. You're gonna lie here and think about this until you have another attack."

"You can't expect me not to think about it. He was my baby. My only baby."

Sidney sighed and kissed her forehead. "I know."

A nurse came bustling in with a pill in a little pleated paper cup. "Here you go, Mrs. B.," she said cheerfully. "Something to help you sleep."

Dolores put the pill in her mouth, sipped water through a straw, and swallowed. The nurse took her pulse and her blood pressure and patted her arm. "Okay," she said in an overly loud voice one might use to corral a roomful of children. "That's going to make you drowsy. Your husband should probably be going home now."

Sidney shook his head. As if that pill would be enough to quiet her. She would lie there for hours, going over it all in her head. He leaned over and gently kissed her pallid cheek while the nurse pointedly held the door open.

"I love you," he pleaded. "Try to rest."

"I will," she said.

Sidney shook his head and forced himself to straighten up. But before he could even start for the door, she had turned her head to the wall and he could see her mind working. Ruminating furiously about all she now knew. Despite all the drugs they could give her, her mind, her mother's heart, could not let it go—even if it killed her.

CHAPTER TWENTY-NINE

Richard Walsh parked his Lexus in front of the house. "Are you sure you don't want me to take you down to the marina to get your car?" he asked.

Laura was in the back, leaning against Ian, who sat upright tensely, gripping the inside door handle. "We'll pick it up tomorrow," said Ian. "My wife is tired."

"I'm all right," protested Laura. "Richard, would you like to come in for a cup of coffee or a drink or something?"

Richard glanced at his platinum Rolex. "God, it's nearly three a.m. I better get home." He leaned over the seat and looked at the two of them. "You two look terrible. You need to get some sleep. Where's Michael?"

"At my neighbor's," Laura said wearily. "Thank you for coming down to the courthouse, Richard. I appreciate it."

"Hey, no problem. That's a lawyer's job. And look, things could be a lot worse. I mean, they know somebody paid this guy to kill Jimmy, but they've got nothing concrete on you two. That's obvious. You'd be under arrest by now if they did," he said cheerfully.

"Oh, thanks," said Ian.

"Well, I mean, we have to try to be optimistic. Of course, you have to realize that they're going to make your life miserable. They're going to want every receipt, every bank statement, the works from around that time. Your best bet is to cooperate. Give them everything they ask for. They're going to want to see if they can find evidence of a payment you made to this guy Herman Powell. These hired killers don't work for cheap. They're going to be looking for a large sum of cash, unaccounted for."

"They won't find it," Laura said dully.

"I still can't believe it," said Richard. "A hit man. Who would do that? Who would want to hire someone to kill Jimmy?"

Laura suddenly felt trapped on the backseat of Richard's car. She felt as if she couldn't breathe. "Richard, I think I want to go in now."

"Oh, sure," said Richard, opening the passenger door and shifting back on his seat so they could climb out. "Get some rest now," he said sympathetically. "We'll talk tomorrow."

Ian and Laura walked arm in arm toward the house, her head resting wearily on his shoulder. Richard watched them disappear inside. Then he rolled up the windows, turned on the air-conditioning, and selected a tape for the ride home. The Red Hot Chili Peppers, he thought. Yes indeed. He turned the volume up to the max and headed for Rock Harbor.

* * *

While Ian was in the shower, Laura changed into a nightgown and summer robe. She looked out the window longingly at Pam's house. All the windows were dark, and she was chagrined to see that Duane's car was there. No wonder Pam had seemed so nervous on the phone earlier when she'd called to ask her to keep Michael overnight. Laura knew all too well that this latest development was only going to increase Duane's hostility toward her. How long would it be until Pam started to see it her husband's way?

Well, it was definitely too late to call. Michael will be all right for tonight, she told herself. He likes to stay with Louis. But as she gazed over at Louis's bedroom window, she could not help but remember Dolores's words. She wanted to take Michael away, to punish Laura for something she hadn't done. And, she thought as she heard the bathroom door open, for something she had done.

Ian came into the living room, toweling his hair, wearing just his pajama bottoms. He was so handsome, she thought. So melancholy and so handsome. She had fallen into his arms like a safety net. And now—what would become of them?

Ian poured himself a glass of wine at the oak sideboard. "Do you want one?" he asked. "It might do you good."

She said no, automatically, and then changed her mind. "I could probably use it," she said. He poured another glass and handed it to her where she was, curled up in the corner of the sofa. He sat on a leather club chair by the cold fireplace. Jimmy's chair. His blue eyes were gray, as if a storm were brewing behind them. He stared into his wineglass.

"Ian, I keep thinking about what Dolores said," Laura blurted out. "About taking Michael away from me."

"She can't do that," he said shortly.

She could tell by his tone that he didn't want to discuss it any further. She resented the way he dismissed her concern. But she knew what he meant. Right now there was nothing Dolores could legally do.

And how can you blame him for being impatient? she chided herself. He didn't bargain for all this when he asked you to marry him. He's been pretty understanding, under the circumstances. She stared into the wineglass, feeling the weariness in every muscle after the tension of that interrogation, the shock of those revelations. For a while neither one of them spoke.

Finally Ian took a sip of wine and said, "I'm going to hire another lawyer."

"Another lawyer?" she asked, surprised. "Why? Richard's always handled our business."

"Well, for one thing, this is a criminal investigation, and he doesn't appear to have any expertise in that area."

"That's probably true," Laura said with a sigh.

"And for another thing, I don't trust him. I don't like him and I don't trust him."

"Why don't you like him?" She was surprised at his reaction.

"I don't know. Call it a gut feeling," he said irritably.

"That's not much of a reason," she said. "But if that's how you feel . . ."

"What I feel is that we need a top-notch criminal lawyer advising us. There's a guy in Philadelphia named Curtis Stanhope I've heard about."

"But why do we need this top-notch guy if we did nothing wrong? If we have nothing to hide . . ."

"Laura, this is no time to fool around with some dimwit from the provinces."

But she was following her own train of thought. "Unless you think I did it. Do you?"

"No, don't be ridiculous." He slumped back on the chair. "Laura, innocent people get railroaded all the time. I'm trying to make sure we're protected from that."

"I don't blame you if you do," she said quietly. "You're only human. Everyone else thinks I did it. How long can you be expected to believe in me?"

"That's not it at all," he said. "I blame this on myself."

"On you? How can you be to blame?"

Ian ran a hand through his dark wet hair and avoided her gaze. "Because . . . it's my fault. I came along and insisted that you marry me. If you hadn't married me, they wouldn't be suspecting you. They wouldn't be looking at us in this way."

Laura shrugged. "Well, they always suspect the family first."

"Sure, but a widow who married so quickly. Naturally they're going to think . . . I should have waited . . . been more patient . . . I don't know what I was thinking."

Laura took a sip of her wine. What he said was true, of course. "But we had no way of knowing this would happen. We did it *because* we were innocent. And you didn't force me to marry you. I wanted to . . ." Her voice trailed away.

"I won't let them do anything to you. I swear it," he said. "I'll protect you no matter what. I didn't go through all this just to lose you. I lost everything once. I'm not going to lose everything again."

His vehemence moved her and frightened her at the same time. "Don't say that. You're scaring me."

He came over and sat beside her, enveloping her in his arms. "I'm sorry," he murmured, kissing her hair. "Don't worry. I'll take care of everything. I promise. Everything will be all right."

Laura closed her eyes and tried to believe it. But behind her fears about the police, about Michael, about what Ian might think, another yawning question was tormenting her. A question she did not want to say aloud to Ian. Who hired Herman Powell? Who hired a killer to murder Jimmy?

Ever since the night he died, she had thought it was a random killing, a burglary that got out of hand. No matter what the police might think, she knew for sure that he had been killed by a stranger, an intruder. But now everything was changed. True, the gun had been fired by a stranger, but Jimmy had been murdered by someone he knew. Someone she knew. The thought of it made her quake inside. Ian felt her shudder and tightened his arms around her.

* * *

Candy Walsh sat up in bed, removed her sleep mask, and glanced at the clock. Then she glared at her husband. "Why are you whistling at this hour of the morning? You are a royal pain, Richard." She plumped up her pillow and tried to flop back down into it.

"Aren't you going to even ask me?" he said. He was in the dressing room, draping his pants over the chair even

212

though the room had been designed with every convenience to make hanging clothes easy.

"All right," said Candy, propping herself up on her elbows. "So, did they arrest her?"

Richard swished mouthwash around his mouth and spat it out. Then he patted on some cologne. "No, they did not."

"How'd you manage that?" said Candy.

Richard appeared in the doorway wearing only his silk boxer shorts. "I'm a genius," he said. He began to amble toward the bed.

Candy rolled her eyes. "Forget it, Richard. It's three-thirty in the morning."

Richard crawled under the sheets. "Pwetty pwease with sugar."

"Don't make me throw up," said Candy. "How come she's not in jail?"

"Oh, she will be," said Richard. "She's certainly not going to be setting sail for parts unknown with her new spouse."

"So, why does that make you so happy?"

"Who says that makes me happy?" Richard asked, suddenly wary. He was far from home free. There was still a large amount of money missing from Laura's accounts, and he still had to figure out a way to replace it. When his secretary, Adelaide Murphy, had informed him that Laura was remarried and planning on leaving town with all her money, he'd had an anxiety attack so bad, he'd almost passed out. But now, at least, he had some time on his side. And he could do it. He was good at this. He had skated on thin ice before, and it had always held.

"You're sickeningly cheerful."

"It's just because I wuv my widdle Candy," he said, nuzzling her neck.

"Oh, shut up," she said. And she rammed him in the chest with one perfectly pumiced elbow.

CHAPTER THIRTY

After all too little sleep and a hurried breakfast, Ron Leonard, Vince Moore, and Clyde Jackson had once again convened in the DA's office.

Ron gratefully accepted a cup of coffee from the DA's assistant and tried to shake the cobwebs out of his head. He'd had trouble falling asleep when he had finally gotten in bed the night before. He'd kept seeing Laura Reed's pale face, her tragic gray eyes looking at him beseechingly, as he'd tossed on his pillow. Murderess, he'd told himself. Killer. He'd finally gotten out of bed, drunk a beer, and watched a 1940s detective picture on the cable. At some point he'd fallen asleep in his chair. Vince, despite his greater age, looked exactly the same as he always did: sturdy and steady. "How come you look like you slept eight hours on a bed of rose petals?" Ron asked.

"Clean living and the love of a good woman." Vince grinned at the younger man.

"There must be something to it," Ron said wearily.

"Okay, gentlemen," said the DA. "Let's sort through this mess. Now let's separate what we do know, from what we suspect."

Jackson looked up, and the other two men nodded grimly.

"We do know that someone hired Herman Powell to kill James Reed. We do know that his widow, Laura Reed, inherited a lot of money, and that she remarried, five months later, to this man Ian Turner. Means, motive, and opportunity. So far, except for an acknowledged childhood friendship, we are unable to place them together at any point before this date, when they ostensibly met here in Cape Christian.

"So, our prime suspect is Mrs. Reed. But, if we assume that she hired Powell, was Ian Turner her accomplice, or was the meeting, and the marriage, innocent, as they claim?"

"You know, in a way," said Vince, "this hasty marriage isn't incriminating in my mind. It's just the opposite. I mean, if they had planned it together, if they were guilty, why would they be so blatant? They're practically asking for us to suspect them."

DA Jackson pursed his full lips and looked up at the chief, his root-beer-colored eyes narrowed. "Maybe they couldn't stand to wait any longer. Maybe they figured they'd outsmarted us already, so why wait?"

"I keep asking myself, what if they didn't do it?" Vince said. "Who else stood to gain?"

"Well, that's an important question to ask," Clyde said noncommittally.

"What about that lawyer of theirs?" Ron asked. "I didn't much like the looks of him. Wasn't he Reed's partner?"

"Walsh does have a gambling problem. We know that about him. But I can't see how Jim Reed's death would make much difference to him," said Vince.

"He handles her money, doesn't he?" Ron asked. "Maybe he wanted that extra million from Reed's life insurance to play around with."

DA Jackson shrugged and made a note in his file. "We'll check it out. Meanwhile, what about the guy that's missing? Jurik?" asked the DA. "They were close associates. Like brothers, some people said. And you know what kind of bad blood there can be between brothers. I mean, we dismissed him originally because of the wheelchair. But now that we know it was a contract killing . . ."

Vince sighed. "Well, as you know, Gary Jurik has disappeared—left town without a word to anyone. His mother claims that Gary was distraught about Laura Reed's remarriage. She's fearful that he might try to kill himself."

Ron snorted. "He probably just bolted to get away from his old lady. She's a real peach, I understand."

"This morning we got a lead on his whereabouts," Vince said somberly. "It seems that a gun dealer in the Boston area ran a routine check on him for criminal records. It came up on our computer. I sent a man up there right away to check out the address he gave."

"Uh-oh," said Ron. "Could be Momma was right."

The three men contemplated this possibility in silence for a moment.

"Actually, Wanda Jurik said something weird to me," Vince allowed. "She said she blamed James Reed for the accident that injured her son. Although he was in no way actually responsible. But could she have wanted to get back at him?"

"Vince," Ron said, "that accident happened, what, fourteen years ago? Most people don't like to wait quite that long for their revenge. Revenge tends to be a crime of passion. Am I right?"

"That's true." Vince sighed.

"And speaking of passion," said Ron, making an arc with his coffee cup. "If Gary Jurik was so in love with Jimmy Reed's wife that the news of her remarriage made him suicidal, maybe he was the one who decided to eliminate Jimmy Reed."

Clyde Jackson shrugged. "Possible. Thinking he might have a chance with her with James Reed out of the way. And then, lo and behold, she ups and gets married to another guy. So, he gets a gun, and boom . . ."

"And takes the answer with him to the grave," said Ron.

"Well, it's an interesting scenario," said the DA, "but we don't have any solid reason to think that Gary Jurik is planning to use that gun on himself, number one, and number two, realistically, guys, we all know it's the newlyweds we're looking at."

"Right," Ron said grimly. "Too bad Powell didn't keep a list of his clients."

The three men sat silently for a moment, each one turning over possibilities in his own mind. Vince broke the silence. "Is it possible," he mused aloud, "that Turner did it without her knowledge?"

They all looked at him as if he were speaking in tongues.

"No, hear me out," he persisted. "I mean they admit they knew each other long ago, right? What if he had an obsession with her, and decided that he wanted her for himself? You hear about guys like that."

"You mean he didn't think of her all those years and then, boom, he's obsessed?" Ron asked.

"I know, it sounds strange," Vince admitted.

Clyde Jackson spread his large hands out on the desk. "Why would a guy suddenly become obsessed with some girl he knew in grade school?"

Ron tapped his teeth with his pencil. "He did claim he knew her. He told that little girl in Barbados. He gave me some song and dance about knowing authors by their work, but that kid was very definite about it."

"So," said Clyde, "you're saying that after his wife died, he decided to kill James Reed?"

Vince raised his eyebrows. "Maybe he got rid of his wife first. I mean a guy who's capable of hiring a killer is capable of anything. Right?"

"That's stretching it," said Clyde.

"I don't know," said Vince. "I'm just thinking out loud."

"Do we know everything there is to know about the fire the first wife died in?" asked Clyde Jackson.

"There were things that nagged at me," Ron admitted.

"Like what?" asked Vince.

Ron shrugged. "Well, you know his brother's in the fire department. Which means Turner could have easily found out the MO of the arsonist."

"A copycat crime," said Vince.

Ron nodded. "The brother denies ever having such a conversation. But the brother is indebted to Turner. He'd never admit it to anyone. The thing is, everyone knew Turner loved his son and would never hurt him. But . . . his son was supposed to be at a ball game on the night of the fire. He didn't know that his wife had decided to keep him home."

"Wow," said Vince.

"Doesn't prove anything," Clyde Jackson said abruptly. "Look, I don't care if he did it, she did it, or they did it—what I want is some evidence about who paid Herman Powell. Or, we need a witness. Someone who saw them together before James Reed died. Without one of those things, we can sit here and speculate till their golden anniversary."

"Right," Vince said sheepishly.

"Ron, I want you to get Turner's bank records. Pressure the banks to give you every transaction. Same for hers. And we'll get somebody on that lawyer. There's got to be a trail somewhere . . ." Clyde Jackson sat up straight in his chair. "Gentlemen, we've got a lot to do. Vince, how many men have you got on this?"

"Five, full-time."

"Okay, well, take every man you need from the county. Check their old phone records. Talk to everybody at any hotel, motel, or homeless shelter they might have stayed in out of town. Have you got a record of any business trips or out-of-town gigs either one of them might have made?"

Ron nodded.

"Well, get moving," said Clyde. "This development with Powell has made our cold case hot again. But it ain't gonna last. I got a call from the FBI this morning, and they are already involved out in Michigan and Ohio. I'd just like to keep this local if we could. But we need some answers and quick. So let's get cracking. Now, if you'll excuse me, gentlemen, I'm due in court."

CHAPTER THIRTY-ONE

Aaron Kellerman settled himself on an empty bench, opened his brown-bag lunch, and then lifted his face gratefully to the breeze, the blue sky, and the drifting clouds. He thought about what Henry James had said—that "summer afternoon" were the two most beautiful words in the English language. Certainly true of today, Aaron thought. It felt good to be out of the hospital for a while and to breathe the fresh air. He worked as a nurse in the adolescent psychiatric ward of an exclusive private hospital on Beacon Hill. He loved his kids, wacky as some of them were, but the job took a lot out of a person, and he needed a regular break. In nice weather he always had his lunch here in the Commons. As Aaron unpacked his bag on the bench beside him, he glanced around and saw that the guy in the wheelchair was still there.

Aaron had noticed the man in the wheelchair for a week now. Each day the man sat beside the same tree, across the sidewalk from a group of vendors who sold earrings and incense. He looked as though he were rooted there. He always brought a sketchbook with him, but much of the time it lay unused beside his chair. He had the look of an artist with that gray hair and his pale skin. He stayed mostly in the shade. He never seemed to eat or drink anything or speak to anyone. It was as if he were on a higher plane, mysterious and sad, and Aaron found himself wondering about him.

It was probably his experience as a nurse that made him concerned about the man. He recognized the warning signs from long experience with the kids on his ward: the vacant look, the inertia, the fact that the man seemed oblivious of the beautiful day. Aaron took a bite of his leftover pasta salad and swigged down some Snapple. Mind your own business, he chided himself. Don't you get enough of this at work? He tried to ignore the man, to turn his attention to the people on the swan boats, but it was no use. Since childhood he could never stand to see a creature in pain. His father, whose technique as a plastic surgeon had brought him great glory, took this as a sign that his only son would follow him into the medical profession. He knew his son very little, however, and was mortified when Aaron chose nursing. Aaron's step-mother had been characteristically indifferent to the path he chose, as long as it got him out from underfoot.

Aaron sighed and snapped a breadstick in half. Think about something else, he scolded himself. So, dutifully, he tried. He thought about the walk-a-thon he was going to be in next weekend and wondered if he shouldn't get out by the river this afternoon and clock off a couple of miles. He was supposed to have dinner tomorrow night with friends, a married couple in Cambridge he'd gone to school with. Now would be a good time to go and pick up a bottle of wine. Red or white? he wondered idly. But he didn't do it. Instead, as if drawn by a force, he found himself looking at the man in the chair again. He had picked up his pad and was sketching, although his face remained blank and pale. After gathering up his bag, plastic fork, and napkin, Aaron sauntered over to the can near the man's wheelchair and deposited his trash. Then, after a moment's hesitation, he walked over, crouched beside the wheelchair, and looked at the man's pad.

The man stopped drawing and stiffened at the presence of an intruder. Aaron gazed in admiration at the accomplished sketches of the ancient buildings of Beacon Hill.

"You have a gift," he said sincerely, looking up at the artist.

Gary stared at Aaron as if he were from another planet, waiting for him to leave. Aaron pretended to be oblivious of his cold stare. "May I look at your book?" he asked. "My name is Aaron Kellerman, by the way." Aaron extended his hand awkwardly.

As much to avoid the handshake as anything else, Gary mumbled his name and found himself handing this stranger the book. Aaron opened it and began to examine the sketches. After a few moments he said without looking up, "I've been curious about your work. I've seen you here every day this week. I usually have lunch in the park."

"Today's the last day," Gary said flatly.

Aaron continued gently to turn the pages of the sketch-book. He did not react outwardly to the man's words, but they gave him an unpleasant sensation in the pit of his stomach. He recognized the tone. He had heard it before, at the hospital. He pretended not to understand. "The last day! You mean in the Commons? Do you work in different places around the city?"

Gary looked at the man helplessly. He was a slight man with a neat black beard and soft dark eyes. Gary was non-plussed by the man's interest. People in cities were supposed to leave you alone. Why was this man asking him these things? He wasn't about to start telling him why. "I . . . no. I'll be leaving . . . the city."

"Do you have to go?" Aaron asked innocently.

"Yes," Gary said flatly, in a tone that said "none of your business." The man did not seem to take the hint. He began to pepper Gary with questions about his work, about his background. He even asked him about the injury that put him in the chair. Gary answered in monosyllables as much as possible. Then the man asked point-blank where he lived, but Gary was not about to reveal his home.

"The Golden Pheasant Motel in Chinatown," he said. It was true in a way. It was where he was living now. It was the last place he planned on living.

Unasked, Aaron told him a bit about himself—the loft where he lived in the North End. His job as a nurse. The fact that he was from Florida, but that he had gone to school here in Boston. Gary's stubborn silence did not seem to faze him. He just continued on in his gentle, persistent manner, as if this were the most normal encounter in the world. Finally, regretfully, Aaron announced that he had to leave, to go back to work.

"Will I see you here tomorrow?" he asked.

"I told you," Gary said. "This is the last day."

"Why does it have to be the last day?" Aaron asked worriedly.

"The very last," Gary said. His expression was grim.

"I wish I'd come over sooner, Gary," he said.

"It wouldn't have made any difference," Gary said dully.

Gary watched the man leave, a dark-haired figure dressed in white making his way across the green grass. Every so often the man would turn and look back to wave somberly to him. When he reached the far sidewalk, Gary turned his chair and made his way back to the van. He hauled himself in and started the engine. In spite of himself, he looked back. Aaron was still standing there, watching him. Gary hardened his heart. What's your problem? he thought. Is it help the handicapped week? It had never been his nature to be cynical, but he was cynical now. He turned his attention to the streets. He could feel Aaron's gaze still on him, but he ignored it, carefully pulling his van out into the congested traffic on Boylston Street. It was frightening to drive in a strange city like this. The only place he had ever driven was in Cape Christian County. He still did not know exactly why he had landed in this place. Well, yes, he did, too. Boston was a place he had given much thought to—the museum, the fellowship. But that seemed a lifetime ago. Before everything.

Gary sighed and looked around anxiously. He hoped he could find his way back to that shop. He had stumbled across it by chance in the first place, and he was completely unfamiliar with these streets. He tried to remember turns he'd made before, landmarks he'd noted. But it was difficult. He had not been paying much attention to his surroundings. Actually, he thought as he wove through the busy streets toward the seedy neighborhood in South Boston, it was not as scary as it might have been. After all, he had nothing to lose.

With an ironic sense of victory, Gary recognized the dingy street he had been seeking. There was a building on the corner with a gray brick front and a sign that proclaimed, "Checks Cashed." On another corner there was a tavern and, across from that, a fast-food restaurant. Gary parked the van and let himself down onto the sidewalk. He negotiated his way around an empty beer bottle and rolled over crumpled pieces of waxed paper with the cheese from pizza still clinging to them and cigarettes crushed on the sidewalk. He stopped in front of the shop and peered through the grimy window with its hodgepodge assortment of merchandise. It looked more like the corner of somebody's attic than a store window display. The place sold secondhand garden tools, appliances, and even some children's toys.

Gary rolled into the store and down the cluttered aisle to the glass display case that held the most valuable merchandise in the store, an assortment of handguns and rifles. The proprietor of the shop, a gray-haired man in a newsboy's cap, who was watching a soap opera on a secondhand television, looked up and recognized him the moment he wheeled himself in.

"I believe the waiting period is up," Gary said without preamble.

"Oh, yes," the man said pleasantly. "No problem with your ID. You're clean. Just a moment. I'll go in the back. I have your gun for you."

Gary waited patiently. There was no reason to hurry now.

CHAPTER THIRTY-TWO

Vince got back to his office to find Ron Leonard sitting on his chair with his eyes closed and his feet on the desk. "Make yourself at home, Detective," Vince said wryly.

Ron opened his eyes and dropped his feet to the floor with a sheepish grin. "Sorry," he said. "I had to rest my eyes. I've spent the whole day going over financial records—Laura and James Reed's accounts, the faxes of Turner's bank records that they sent down from Connecticut."

Vince indicated that he should stay on the seat. He was going through his file cabinet, replacing a file he had pulled earlier. "Did you find anything useful?"

"Not so far," Ron said. "Although whatever I'm looking for is bound to be well hidden. I didn't expect to find a check for Herman Powell in the Reeds' joint account. And as for Turner, he liquidated everything before he took off for the Caribbean. He was strictly a cash man after that."

Vince nodded distractedly.

"What's with you?" Ron asked. "Anything new?"

Vince frowned. "I just got a call from Bobby McCandless—the officer I sent up to Boston to look for Gary Jurik. It seems that Jurik got the gun all right, but the local address he gave the dealer was a phony."

Ron winced. "Momma was right. He's up to something . . ."

"I know," said Vince. "But my man doesn't know his way around Boston. He's not going to be able to find Jurik in a strange city. The ground may as well have opened and swallowed him up."

"What are you going to do?" Ron asked.

"What can I do? I told Bobby to alert the local cops and come on home."

Ron nodded in sympathy. The phone rang on Vince's desk.

"Can you pick that up?" he asked Ron. "If it's Wanda Jurik, tell her I'm not here."

Ron answered the phone and asked a few questions. Then he turned to Vince with his hand over the mouthpiece. "This is Dominick Vanese. He owns that big restaurant in Atlantic City."

"Marie's brother? Isn't that place a Mob hangout?" Vince asked. "What does he want?"

Ron shrugged. "Wants to talk to you. Says he has important information about the Reed case."

"They're coming out of the woodwork," said Vince. Cautiously he reached for the phone.

* * *

Entering Dominick Vanese's restaurant, Stella di Mare, was like slipping into one of the dark chambers of the heart. The walls were painted a deep glossy burgundy, and the carpet was another, brighter shade of blood-red. The slippery leather banquettes and booth seats were chestnut colored, but bathed in the glow of candles in their cranberry glass holders, they also oozed a scarlet sheen.

Stella di Mare was one of the most popular restaurants on the boardwalk in Atlantic City. And one of the few that had not been usurped by the casinos. Dominick Vanese had many friends in high places who had been enjoying his cuisine for many years, and when the time came they were as unwilling as Dominick to see his landmark restaurant swallowed up by the new behemoths of the boardwalk. They saw to it that Stella di Mare remained in its comfortable spot. Atlantic City was that kind of town, a town where friendships and loyalty were important to people. Money wasn't the only thing.

Vince and Ron stood in the doorway, framed by the dark, fringed brocade drapes, and peered into the dimly lit room. "Isn't that Gianni di Marco?" Ron asked, naming a known Mob figure.

Vince squinted into the depths of the restaurant. "That's him," he said.

Gianni di Marco, a gray-haired, tonsorially splendid man in his sixties, wearing an Armani suit, sat in a booth at the very back of the restaurant, eating delicately from a small dish. A younger man, dressed in a purple-and-black warm-up suit made out of parachute cloth, sat beside him, tearing bread off the crusty loaf in the basket in front of him.

The haunting prelude to *Cavalleria Rusticana* played in the background as Dominick Vanese, dressed in the dark blue suit and crisp white shirt he always wore, approached the two men in the foyer. "Do you have a reservation?" he asked.

Vince and Ron turned their attention from gaping at gangsters to the small, balding man in front of them. "I'm Chief Moore," said Vince. "This is Detective Leonard from the DA's office in Cape Christian County."

Dominick Vanese's smooth, middle-aged face betrayed not a flicker of surprise. Part of his success was his discretion. Well-known people often met to do business in his restaurant. He merely made sure that they were well fed in the process. Indicating for Vince and Ron to follow him, Dominick led the way through the maze of tables, toward the back. Ron absorbed an impression of table linens that glowed pink, elaborately coiffed women seated with sleek, middle-aged men, and the occasional flash of diamonds as polished silver and goblets of dark wine were lifted to hungry lips.

As they passed by his table, Gianni di Marco looked up at his host.

"Excellent, as always."

Dominick smiled. "*Grazie*. This way," he said smoothly to Vince and Ron as he led them to a door in the back. He opened it and ushered them inside his office.

Ron tried not to stare. Vanese's office was as large as the living room of most houses he had been in, but much more richly furnished. The floor was covered with a Persian rug, and the armchairs and sofas in the room were made of tufted black leather. At one end of the room was a fireplace with a marble mantel, although it was perfectly clean, as if it had never been used. The walls were lined with framed photographs of Dominick Vanese and some of the famous people who had eaten there—Donald Trump, Don King, Charles Barkley, even the Chairman of the Board himself—Frank Sinatra.

Vanese indicated that they should sit. Vince and Ron sat on the leather chesterfield sofa. On a glass-topped table in front of them was a silver tray with several liquor decanters on it and a set of glasses. Vince noted that the consummate host did not offer them a drink. It was a deliberate oversight, Vince was certain. There was no veneer of sociability to this meeting. Vanese waited for the chief to speak.

"Mr. Vanese, Officer Leonard and I are investigating this case together," said Vince. "You realize that if the information you have is relevant, you'll have to give a deposition to the district attorney and we may need you to testify."

Vanese waved a hand as if to say that it didn't matter.

"You said on the phone that you have some information about the Reed case."

Dominick Vanese nodded, gazing toward the door of his office. "That's right," he said. "About the Reed boy. And the hit man . . ."

The skin prickled on the back of Vince's neck, and he sat on the edge of the thickly cushioned sofa. "What about it?" he asked calmly.

227

"I think I know who hired the guy," Vanese said.

Vince raised his eyebrows. "This wasn't local talent, you know."

For the first time, Vanese turned to look at him, his gaze disdainful. "Do you want to know or not?" he said.

"Yes. Sure," said Vince. "Please go on."

"I was watching the news the other night. And I recognized her."

"Who?"

"The wife."

Vince looked over at Ron, who paled visibly at Vanese's words. "Well, perhaps she'd been a customer at your restaurant," Vince said carefully.

"I don't mean that," Vanese said shortly.

"What do you mean?"

"Some time ago . . . last summer, I think it was . . . she came to see me at the restaurant."

Vince watched him warily.

Vanese frowned, as if he were trying to put it together in his mind. "She said she wanted to talk to me. She needed some information and she thought maybe I could help her. She said she had heard certain things about my restaurant." Vanese looked over at Vince and Ron. "You know what I'm talking about. It's common knowledge that I serve a clientele that has a certain . . . notoriety, shall we say."

Vince did not bother to answer.

"Anyway, she knew about Mr. di Marco, and several others who are regular customers of mine, and she was making an assumption."

Ron stifled a sigh of exasperation. Vince shot him a warning look.

"Go on," said Vince.

Vanese looked him in the eye and answered bluntly, "She said she wanted someone killed. She wanted to know if I could tell her who to get to do the job."

Vince felt his heart thudding. This was it. This was the break they had searched for. "And?" he demanded.

"That's it," said Vanese. "I told her she was misinformed, that I knew nothing at all about such things. And then she left."

Neither Vince nor Ron said a word.

"I guess she found someone who could help her," Dominick Vanese said, sitting back on his chair.

"Are you making this up, Mr. Vanese?" Ron asked bluntly.

Dominick Vanese looked at him as if he were a cockroach that had just crawled into his pristine parlor. "Why would I do that?"

"I don't know," Ron said honestly. "You realize this information you have just given us incriminates Mrs. Reed."

"I'm just telling you what she asked me," Vanese said stubbornly.

"What took you so long to come forward?" Vince asked. "James Reed was murdered months ago. If you knew this, why didn't you call us then?"

"I'm a businessman. I have a big restaurant to run. I don't sit around thinking about local crimes. So a guy was killed by a burglar in Cape Christian . . . big deal. I make sure my alarm system is working, and I forget about it."

"The same guy who was married to this woman soliciting a hired killer."

"She didn't give me her name, Officer," Vanese said to Ron coldly. "I'd never seen her before. How'd I know this guy that got shot was her husband? I didn't think about it. I never thought about it one way or the other."

Vince shrugged as if to say that it was reasonable. Vanese took a moment to smooth his ruffled feathers. "Then, the other night, I'm watching the news—that Holly Brody on channel five—I like her—and it says they found out this guy was killed by a hit man, and lo and behold, I see this same woman stepping out of the car, going into the courthouse. And I remembered her. She's a beautiful woman, easy to recognize with that white hair and those big, sad eyes. Son of a bitch, I thought, she went and did it."

"Okay, you saw her on the news and you recognized her. And you remembered her," Ron said impatiently. "So, what made you come forward now? You didn't bother to call us when she came to you looking to find a hired killer. It was your duty to report such a solicitation."

"I didn't know if the woman was serious. I chose to believe she was not. She could have been a nut for all I knew. I didn't want any part of her. I deal with the public every day. You get lots of nuts wandering in. I told her that I couldn't help her, and I asked her to leave."

"So what made you come forward and implicate her now? Surely this is not the first person of your acquaintance who got away with a crime," Ron said sarcastically.

Dominick Vanese glowered at him. "Many of my patrons happen to be of Italian descent, as I am, and they like my cooking. But I don't know anything about the Mafia. I don't know anything about their business. I know the restaurant business. I know food, and wine, and how to set a beautiful table. I keep my ears shut and I mind my own business. What other people do is their business. Now you treat me respectfully or you get out of my establishment."

Ron avoided Vanese's steely gaze.

"You must admit, you could have kept silent, though," Vince said in a placating tone. "A lot of people would not get involved."

Vanese turned to Vince with a look of stubborn defiance on his face, a look that radiated truth. One family man to another. "She killed her husband. They had a child together. Am I correct?"

Vince nodded.

Dominick Vanese's voice rose. "And then she ran off and married another guy. Call me old-fashioned. It's wrong. It offends me. I realized what happened, and I didn't want her to get away with it. Can you understand that?"

"Yes, I can," said Vince. "Yes indeed."

CHAPTER THIRTY-THREE

The Golden Pheasant Motel was situated below and just adjacent to an overpass on the Southeast Expressway, so that the rumble of trucks and speeding traffic was an ever-present reminder to the guests of the lowliness of their accommodations. Gary parked the van in the cracked, rubble-strewn parking lot beside the building. There was a multiracial bunch of teenagers sitting on a low wall at the back of the parking lot, sharing a smoke of something, their hats on backward, their high-top sneakers unlaced. As Gary got out of the van, they eyed his vehicle greedily, hoping, he supposed, to make him uneasy. It's all yours, he thought. He wondered if they would wait until nightfall to trash it or steal it. It was frightening how quickly he had adopted the paranoia of an inner-city dweller. For a moment he thought of leaving the van unlocked, then he decided against it. Let them work for it, he thought. It's the American way.

He rolled into the building through the lobby, with its aqua, vinyl-covered furniture and a jungle of green plastic plants. A man with slicked-back hair, a dingy white shirt, and suspenders was reading a Greek newspaper behind the counter. He eyed Gary suspiciously and grunted in his direction as Gary passed by. Gary continued down the hallway, which was lit by the dimmest of bulbs, until he reached number seven.

He unlocked the door of his room and let himself in. The grimy bamboo blinds were lowered, so that the room was dark and hot. He turned on the bedside lamp, which had a parchment shade shaped like the roof of a pagoda, and stared around at the sparsely furnished room. Two prints that resembled scrolls were hanging on the walls, with Chinese lettering and women in kimonos on them. The bed had a mustard-colored cotton spread, and flanking the window were two chairs that looked as if they had once been office chairs.

A small bedside table held only the lamp, a cardboard calendar from the local liquor store with a Vermont snow scene on it, and a telephone. For a long time Gary looked at the phone, and the phrase *Call for help* seemed to run through his mind like an endless loop of tape. Call who? he thought. And why? What could they tell him that would make him want to continue?

Some shrink who would tell him he was depressed and want to dredge up all his childhood traumas? His life before the accident had been no better or worse than anyone else's. His parents didn't get along, but they didn't really fight. His father would just get up one day and leave. Be gone for longer and longer times. Gary often wondered where he went. Karl never said. Maybe he went to Boston sometimes, Gary mused. Maybe he stayed here, in this very room, on one of his voyages away from them. Maybe he was in Boston this very minute, in that tavern down the street, showing some other drunkard a photo of his son. Saying, "He's an artist, just like me."

I sound like my mother, he thought. That angry sarcasm was the only way she had of dealing with Karl's desertion. He tried to put the thought of Wanda out of his mind. He knew how she would carry on over this when she found out. But finally she would be relieved. How many times had she railed that his accident had ruined their lives? By doing this, he would free her, too, of the burden of him. And Laura? Gary

232

smiled bitterly at the thought of Laura, but the corners of his mouth trembled. No, not Laura. She was on her honeymoon.

Gary opened the box in his lap and examined the gun. It was heavy, much heavier than he had expected it to be. The man at the store had showed him how to load it and warned him to go out to the pistol range and practice before he started toting it around. I don't think I'll need much practice for this, he thought. Now that the moment was here, he felt curiously removed from everything. This whole week, while he had endured the waiting period, he had been readying himself, eating very little, sleeping less, getting himself into sort of a state of removal from day-to-day things. Existing in this room. Going to the park to pass the hours. A fleeting thought of Aaron, the man in the park, crossed his mind. For a passing instant he felt that old curiosity about life, but he dismissed it. It did not bear thinking about. He hardly even felt angry anymore—or sad. It was simply a fact: Laura and Michael were lost to him, despite all his foolish hopes and plans. And what else was there? He had never realized how utterly and completely alone he was until he had confronted her on that back porch, the smell of lilacs in the air, and she'd admitted she had married again. As he drove away from her house, he had seen his own life for what it was. He'd pictured himself going back home to his room and his mother to wait—to wait for what? So he had started to drive. But the feeling had stayed with him. Settled in like a poisonous cloud. Was with him now.

He liked the way this room felt—degrading and foreign. The perfect place for the job. Despite the inner calm he felt, his fingers trembled as he loaded the gun. He put a bullet in every chamber. He was not interested in Russian roulette. This was not a game. It was a logical conclusion, a logical end to his sorry life. He thought of Jimmy Reed. He wanted his last thought to be of Jimmy's face. That was appropriate. For it was the death of Jimmy Reed that had brought him to this place at last. To the place where he could not live with himself for another minute.

Gary snapped the barrel back in place and cocked it. He wondered if he would have the courage after all. The strength to do it. He sat there for a while. He didn't know how long. The last light faded behind the blinds, and then there was only darkness outside and that rumble of traffic. People rolling by, in their hurry to get somewhere. In a hurry to get to someone waiting for them. Something they thought was important. But he knew better. He was already there. The place where we all got to eventually. Finally he could stand the tension of it no longer. It was time to act. He lifted the gun slowly and pressed the cold barrel to the tenderly veined white flesh of his temple. He closed his eyes and tried to think of a way to pray. But he was too empty inside. His finger lightly touched the trigger, and he shuddered.

Suddenly there was a knock at the door.

CHAPTER THIRTY-FOUR

"Let's see those fingernails, buddy," Laura said with feigned sternness as Michael pulled on his pajama top after his bath.

"I washed 'em," he protested.

Laura took his soft little hands in her own and rubbed them absently with her thumbs, pretending to scrutinize his fingertips. There was nothing in the world that felt as gentle, as trusting, as those little hands in hers. Michael knew there was trouble in the air, but he was being brave about it, relying on her to make everything okay. It will be okay, she reminded herself. Nothing could touch her because she had done nothing wrong. "They look pretty good," she said.

"I told you. Mom, can we play Uno tonight? Please?"

"Okay, sure. But put on your slippers before you come downstairs."

Laura left him in his room, hunting for his slippers, and went down to the living room. Ian stood staring into the cold fireplace, one arm leaning on the mantel, his lips pressed together.

"I hope you're up for an Uno tournament," she said.

Ian jumped, startled by the sound of her voice.

Laura came up and put her arms around him, and he drew her sharply to him. "You're a million miles away," she said.

"I've been thinking."

She cocked her head back and looked at him. "Yes?"

"I think we should leave here, just as we planned. I know we were only going to sail for the summer and then settle back in the States, but I've been thinking, why don't we sail down to the islands and live there for a while? There's an island I stopped at called St. Eustatius that would be a paradise to live in. It's in the Dutch West Indies. The climate is perfect year-round. And Michael would love it. It would be like living on Treasure Island. A great adventure . . ."

Laura pulled away from him. "Ian, we can't go. You know that. Not now. Not since they found out about Herman Powell. Until they know who hired him, we can't leave here."

"Why not?" Ian demanded. "Nothing has changed. They can't detain us without any evidence. Why should we live under this cloud? Let's just leave—next week, like we planned. Michael only has a few more days of school."

"I can't," Laura said stubbornly.

"Why? Are you worried about how it will look? It's a little late for that."

"No," she said evenly. "I cannot leave until they have arrested the person who killed Jimmy. It can't take them long to find out, now that they know about Powell. And then I can put an end to this in my mind."

"Jimmy is dead. What difference does it make whether you stay here or you leave? He's just as dead either way. And I want us to start our life. As long as we are here, we're in limbo," he cried.

Laura looked at him worriedly. She was afraid her answer would make him resentful, but there was no use denying how she felt. "Look, I . . . I feel guilty for putting you through this. It's not your . . . loss. Your vengeance, so to speak. But it is mine. It came with me as part of the package. So now it's yours, too. Ian, I have to know. I can't leave until I find out who it was. Don't you see? It's someone I know who murdered my husband. I have to know who it was. I have to know that they will be punished. Surely you can understand that. Didn't you feel relief when they finally arrested Stuart Short? Didn't you want to see him put in jail?"

"Who was put in jail?" Michael asked, shuffling into the room in his slippers, the deck of Uno cards in hand.

Laura reached out and pulled him to her even though Michael squirmed to get away. Ian turned away from them.

"Never mind, sweetheart," said Laura.

"Come on, let's play," Michael pleaded.

"I'll play," said Laura. "Ian?"

Ian came over and sat on the couch. He was so tense that he seemed to vibrate. Laura sat next to him and rubbed his shoulders for a moment.

"Can I deal?" Michael asked.

"Sure, honey," she said absently. With great concentration Michael began to shuffle the cards.

"Don't worry," she whispered to Ian. "It can't be much longer. And then we can go. I don't know about living in the West Indies . . ."

He glared at her. "You don't really want to go. You are stuck in this old life. You can't move. Why did I think I could make it different? I was a fool."

Laura sat back. "That's completely unfair," she said. "I was all set to leave. I've been packing and getting ready. You know I have. But things have changed."

"That's right," Ian said bitterly. "Now they are dead certain it was you. Before, they only suspected."

For a moment Laura was shocked by his words. Then she wondered why she was surprised. He was beginning to crack. She might have known this would happen. "Let's not talk about this now," she said, glancing at Michael.

"Why are you fighting?" Michael wailed.

"I'm sorry, honey. Go ahead and deal. Ian, are you going to join us?"

Ian looked at her with a desperate sadness in his eyes. Before long, he'll leave me, she thought. He'll be all apologetic, and it will be very civilized, but he'll get on that boat and it will be good-bye again. I don't care, she told herself. I have Michael. I'll survive. "Running away won't solve anything," she said quietly. "I have to stay here. But you don't. If you want to go, I understand."

Then Ian reached out and laid his hand gently on her hair. "My guardian angel," he said. "As if I would leave you . . ."

His loyalty chastened her. "Thanks," she whispered. She did not look at him. She looked at the card Michael had given her. She put down a blue five. "It's your move," she said.

Ian sighed and began to play. Michael happily slapped down a card that made Ian lose his turn. "Your turn, Mom," he cried.

They played three games, the atmosphere becoming peaceful as they vied gently for their points. Laura got up and went to the kitchen for some pretzels. "Last game, Michael," she warned him when she returned.

Michael played with all the cunning he could muster and was delighted to shout, "Uno!" as the adults groaned. Then, suddenly, a sharp rap on the door cracked the mood like someone smacking an egg with a mallet.

Laura looked at Ian, who rolled his eyes. "I'll get it," Michael cried, and jumped up to run for the door.

"Don't run in those slippers," Laura warned him as Michael slid around the corner and down the hallway.

Laura got up from the sofa and started after him. "I'd better see who it is," she said apprehensively.

"Tell them to go away," Ian said.

As she followed Michael to the door, she was suddenly overcome with a memory of their old life, of Jimmy, always glad to see a visitor, always ready for a chat and a beer with whoever came to the door. She had found it disconcerting at first. She had not been raised that way. She had grown up in a silent, private home where visitors were unwelcome. But her years with Jimmy had begun to change her. She understood why he loved living here, in his old hometown. To him the city life, the sophisticated world, had been sterile, unsatisfying. Here he knew every face and welcomed every random meeting. And one of those friendly people, unbeknownst to him, was plotting his death, she reminded herself.

Michael opened the door, then jumped back and scampered to his mother with a little cry. Laura frowned at the sight of Chief Moore and two uniformed officers at her door.

"Hello, Chief," Laura said tiredly.

"Mrs. Turner."

Ian came out into the hallway.

"What can I do for you?" Laura asked.

"You're going to have to come along with us."

Laura clutched Michael's shoulders. "Why?"

Vince Moore looked down at Michael. "I don't think you want to discuss this . . . you know . . . here . . ."

"Can't it wait until the morning?" Laura asked.

"I'm afraid not. I have a warrant for your arrest."

"What?" Laura cried. "For what?"

"For murder in the first degree of James Reed Jr.," said Vince.

"Oh, God, you can't . . ." Laura cried.

"This is insane!" shouted Ian.

"I'm afraid you'll have to come now," said Vince. "Please. Take the boy out of here."

"Help me," Laura cried.

"Get out of here!" Ian shouted at the same time.

"Mommy," Michael wailed. "What are they doing?"

One of the officers stepped forward with handcuffs and reached for Laura's hands. Laura felt the world spin out of control around her and realized it was true. They were going to take her away. She had never really been afraid before, because she was innocent. But here they were, like a nightmare come to life. Michael was screaming now, grabbing her legs.

"Honey, no," she pleaded. She tried to bend down to him, but the officer reached under her arm and jerked her back up.

"What proof do you have?" Ian demanded. "You can't just invade an innocent person's home like this. My wife was a victim in this . . ."

"We have a witness who has implicated Mrs. Turner in the murder of her first husband."

"That's impossible," said Ian.

"I don't have to tell you anything," Vince said. "I will only tell you that we have a witness who swears she solicited a contract killer."

Ian lunged at the chief and was restrained by the second officer. "That's a lie!" Ian yelled. His face was purplish.

"Come along, Mrs. Turner."

"I'm coming with her."

Laura looked helplessly at her husband. "You have to stay with Michael."

"Mommy, what are they doing? Don't take my mommy."

"Ian, please," Laura pleaded over the boy's sobs. "Don't cry, baby," she said. "Mommy will be back soon." She felt the hands under her arms roughly lifting her away from her child, her home, her husband.

"This is a terrible mistake," she insisted in a shaky voice.

"Let's get out of here!" Vince roared. The sight of Michael's tragic face was more than he could stand.

They were hustling her along, down the porch steps toward the squad car. Sometime in the evening it had started to rain, and they were all being pelted by unseen raindrops in the darkness. Laura looked back. Michael was pressed against the screen door, pounding on it with his open hands and wailing. Ian was gripping her son by the shoulders, his face slack with shock. Then she felt a hand on the top of her head and she was pushed down onto the backseat of the dark car.

CHAPTER THIRTY-FIVE

Sidney approached his wife gingerly, unsure whether she was asleep on the chair or not. She was very still, wrapped in a heavy robe, not reading or watching TV. But that did not mean she was sleeping. She could be just sitting there, staring out at the rain.

"Honey," he said, "you better take your pill."

Dolores turned her head and looked up at him, her eyes blank. Sidney could hardly bear to look at her. His Dolores was peppy and full of life. This Dolores was like a shell. Since he'd brought her home from the hospital, she hadn't bothered to get dressed. She insisted that she felt all right, but she didn't want to go anywhere. It was as if she were existing on some twilight planet most of the time.

"I brought you some Dr Pepper to wash it down," he said. He handed her the glass, and she took it. The bones in her hand felt fragile to him, breakable. She swallowed the tablet indifferently and handed him back the glass.

"Can I bring you your book or something?" Sidney asked.

Dolores shook her head. "I don't feel like reading," she said.

You don't feel like living, Sidney thought. There was a knock at the door. "I'll get it," he said. "You relax."

Dolores sank back on her chair. She didn't care who it was. She didn't care if she sat on this chair or she went off to bed. It just didn't matter anymore. She heard Sidney's voice rise and turned slightly on her chair. Then she heard Laura's name, and she rose to her feet. She walked over to her husband and heard him say, "No comment."

The young man at the door was wearing a tie and a trench coat. She didn't recognize him immediately, although she had a dim recollection of his face.

"What is it, Sid?" she asked.

"This young man is from the newspaper," Sidney said, trying to sound calm, but there was a suppressed agitation in his voice. "He tells me they've arrested Laura for Jimmy's murder."

"We'd like to get a reaction from you, Mrs. Barone," the reporter said eagerly.

Sidney blocked the doorway. "Mrs. Barone and I have no comment."

"May I come in?" the reporter asked.

"No, I'm sorry. My wife isn't well," said Sidney, closing the door in his face.

He turned back to Dolores, ready to steady her, but she shook him off. Her eyes were ablaze, the color returned to her cheeks. "They arrested her. Finally. How did they do it? Oh, thank God, I knew it . . ." There was a combination of horror and elation in her voice. She floated into the living room and then turned back to Sidney, who was making sure the door was locked.

"They're going to be pestering us all night," he observed.

"Sid, how did they do it? Did he say?"

"Apparently a witness came forward. That's all he told me."

Dolores clasped her hands together and wrung them. "She did do it. I knew it, I knew it. But why? Why? He loved her so. My Jimmy. I hope they put her in the electric chair. How could she do it?" Her mood was careening between sorrow and extreme agitation.

"Take it easy, Dolores. Sit down," Sid pleaded. "You're still not well."

"Oh, I'm better now. Better than I've been in months. Since New Year's Eve, to be exact. Finally, finally, justice for my son." Her eyes welled with tears. "Do you understand, Sid?" She turned to him, her face twisted.

"She will be punished for what she did," he said.

Dolores threw her arms around him, knowing how vehement a remark it was, coming from her mild-mannered husband. For a few moments they embraced, tears running down Dolores's face. Then, suddenly, she pulled back. "Michael," she said.

Sidney frowned at her. "What about him?"

"I want him," she said. "I want him right now."

"I wonder who's taking care of him. Not that Ian fellow, I hope," said Sid.

Dolores shook his arms. "She killed his father. She has no right to him anymore. I'm going to get him away from her, and she'll never see that kid again. Sid, you have to call Frank O'Malley," she cried, referring to their attorney. "I'm going to go get dressed."

Sidney looked somberly into her wild eyes and nodded. "I'll call Frank," he said. "He'll know what to do."

* * *

Laura sat at a narrow table in a cornerless, windowless interview room at the Cape Christian County Court House, awaiting the arrival of her attorney. She was expecting Richard but was informed by the guard that her attorney was a lawyer from Philadelphia named Curtis Stanhope. "They're bringing in the heavy artillery for you," the guard observed with something bordering on admiration in his voice. Beyond that, he had nothing more to say. He stood staring straight ahead with his arms folded at the door. Occasionally he spoke in a kind of incomprehensible code into his two-way radio, but he did not speak to her.

At last there was a knock on the door, and he turned and unlocked it. A paunchy man of about sixty, with thinning strawberry-blond hair and white eyebrows, came in. He was wearing a yellow Ultrasuede jacket and green-and-yellow-plaid pants. He had a green tie with gold pheasants on it. He nodded pleasantly to the guard, who left, locking them inside. Stanhope's cheery outfit seemed horribly out of place, like someone wearing a red dress to a funeral. There must be some mistake, Laura thought. She had been expecting someone sleek, in pinstripes.

"Mrs. Turner," he boomed. "I'm Curtis Stanhope. Your husband contacted me this evening. Dragged me away from one of my wife's hospital fund-raisers."

"Thank you for coming," Laura said automatically.

"Oh, believe me, I'm glad to come. Those things are a crashing bore anyway. Especially nowadays, when nobody drinks anymore!"

Laura closed her eyes. "Can you get me out of here?" she whispered.

Stanhope opened a leather briefcase so glossy that Laura could see her haggard expression in it. He removed a pair of half glasses and perched them on the end of his nose. Then he studied a sheaf of papers. "Well, we'll do what we can. Now, I've spoken to the DA, and I've spoken to your husband. But naturally I want to hear everything that has transpired from your point of view. Before we get to that, though, I want to inform you of what is going to happen to you step by step. Now, we have two hearings this evening. First, in about an hour, we have your arraignment, where bail will be set."

"How much will my bail be?" Laura asked. "Never mind. It doesn't matter. Ian will get the money somehow."

Stanhope looked at her gravely over the tortoiseshell rims of his spectacles. "Mrs. Turner, this is a capital case. Murder in the first degree. I must warn you that it is very likely there will be no bail set in this case."

Laura stared at the man, scarcely able to take it in. "No bail?"

"I will argue that you are no danger to the community. No risk of flight. But frankly, the nature of this crime will be against us. You have no prior arrests or convictions?"

"No," Laura protested.

"Well, that's in our favor. But, you'd be better off if it were a crime of passion. The cold, calculating nature of the crime will influence the judge against you."

Laura gripped the edge of the table instead of doing what she wanted. She wanted to grasp those yellow Ultrasuede lapels and shake the man. "Mr. Stanhope, the thing is, I did not do this. I mean, somebody did, obviously. But it wasn't me. I loved my husband. I don't know why in the world they arrested me. It's unbelievable."

Curtis Stanhope exhaled a tiny sigh. "Well, I just spent a few moments with Mr. Jackson, the district attorney, and he tells me they have a witness—one Dominick Vanese—who claims you solicited a hired killer last summer."

Laura stared at him, trying to absorb what he said. "That's . . . that's an outrageous lie. I don't even know any-one named Dominick Vanese."

Stanhope peered at his documents. "Apparently, Mr. Vanese is the proprietor of a restaurant in Atlantic City called Stella di Mare."

"Oh . . .," said Laura.

"Do you recognize the name now?"

Laura shrugged helplessly. "Well, I recognize the name. I mean, the restaurant is very famous. My husband and I had dinner there once. But I don't know this man who owns it. Why would he say this about me? Why do they believe him?"

"Look, look," said Stanhope. "Calm down. The DA has no corroboration for this, so it was a judgment call on his part. They really had no choice but to arrest you."

"Why? What does that mean?"

"Well, they didn't want to take a chance on your leaving this jurisdiction. You were making plans to leave, were you not?" He did not wait for her to answer. "They figured they could compile more evidence once they had you safely in

custody. And then there was this business of the insurance
. . ."

"I told the police. Our lawyer advised us."

"Hmmm," Stanhope murmured. "Did he advise you against this marriage you've made, considering the continuing police inquiry into your first husband's death?"

"I didn't really give him a chance to advise me," Laura admitted.

"Well, in any case, with the rather hasty remarriage, and the remaining questions about the crime scene, it probably wasn't too difficult to convince a judge to issue a warrant."

"You make it sound like I'm guilty," Laura cried.

"On the contrary, I'm optimistic about your defense. Obviously they don't have much in the way of physical evidence, and no eyewitnesses, or you would have been in jail long ago. No, what they have is circumstantial, and they have the testimony of this witness. It's enough for an indictment, but I don't see how they can hope to convict. We'll just have to go after the witness."

"Does that mean I'll get out?"

"Well, hopefully . . . in time."

"In time? What are we talking about here?"

"The indictment will take two to three weeks. Then, it will be several months before you come to trial."

"Several months?" Laura cried. "I can't stay here for several months."

Stanhope tuned out her protests and continued with the business at hand. "After the arraignment, an emergency session has been scheduled tonight in family court. There is an application for an order to show cause why temporary custody of your child should not be transferred to your mother-in-law."

Laura stared at him, her heart pounding. "What?"

Stanhope looked at her dispassionately. "Your mother-in-law, Mrs. Sidney Barone, wants temporary custody of your son, Michael, pending a final hearing to be scheduled after your trial."

"Well, she can't have him," Laura cried, jumping up from her chair.

The guard rapped on the door, but Stanhope motioned him back. "Sit down, Mrs. Turner," he said.

Laura sat down, but she leaned across the table. "I won't let her have my son. You've got to stop her. They can't just let her take him," she hissed.

Stanhope's voice was coolly contradictory. "I'm afraid it's a virtual certainty that she will be granted temporary custody. You stand accused of murdering the child's other parent. In the case of a child, the judge has to err on the side of caution. The odds are overwhelming that the judge will side with your mother-in-law."

"But that's not fair. I'm not convicted. How can they punish me without proving I'm guilty of anything? Why can't Ian keep him?"

"Your husband is unrelated to the child. He is not even an adoptive father. Besides, your remarriage is an issue in this case that can be raised in family court. The judge is unlikely to award Mr. Turner custody."

"You're supposed to be my lawyer. You're not even trying to help me," Laura cried.

Stanhope was unfazed by her outburst. He had years of experience with confused, frustrated people. "I am telling you the reality of the situation, Mrs. Turner. I'm not going to waste your time or mine trying to give you false encouragement."

Laura was shaking all over. She was beginning to understand that the lawyer's loud, cheerful outfit was deliberately misleading. The man in the costume was steely.

"Now, I will argue that your mother-in-law could prejudice the child against you. I assume, from your reaction, that there is a good possibility of that."

Laura nodded, picturing Dolores. Once she got her hands on Michael . . . "Oh, yes," she said. "She'll convince him I killed his father."

"Well, we'll just have to convince a jury that you did not," he said smoothly.

Laura looked back at the man who stood on the other side of a chasm. He was on the side where Laura had spent her whole life. The side where people were safe, and secure, and called the police only for help. And here she was now. The other kind of person. Someone who was in trouble. Someone people avoided. Warned their children to avoid. Throw me a rope, she wanted to cry out. I belong on your side. Don't leave me here.

Stanhope was calmly making notes that were shielded from her by the lid of the glossy briefcase. He would not let her suck him into the chasm with her needs. He was far too experienced for that.

"Now, let's talk about what happened to James Reed Jr."

"I didn't do it," she said weakly. "Help me."

"That's why I'm here," he said pleasantly.

And she felt the chasm widen.

CHAPTER THIRTY-SIX

"Face the wall, miss."

Laura shuffled into the elevator, her stride shortened by the shackles on her feet, and obeyed the humiliating instructions of the officer accompanying her. Her hands were handcuffed in front of her, and she was shivering in the drab olive-brown jumpsuit she was now required to wear.

The elevator bumped and rose two floors. They rode in silence. The doors opened, and, nudged by the officer, Laura shuffled off. Another uniformed officer stood in the hallway, and he greeted his colleague. Laura might as well have been invisible. Across and diagonal to the elevator were two golden oak doors with a plaque that read "Family Court". Beside her was another doorway.

"You wait in here until they're ready for you," said the officer who had brought her up on the elevator.

Laura was led into a windowless holding cell that had cinder-block walls and nothing but a bench to sit on, a toilet at one end, and a video camera mounted on the wall above her head so that she could be observed from the outside. She sank onto the wooden bench, still reeling from the results of the arraignment.

It had taken place on the first floor of this same building. The whole procedure had been swift and nightmarish, carried out in the incomprehensible language of the law, punctuated by the rap of the judge's gavel and his harsh voice sealing her fate: "Bail denied." Curtis had patted her shoulder in an avuncular manner, whispering something soothing to her. She had no idea what he said. Her perceptions seemed to be tilted and careening around in her head like some out-of-control carousel.

Bail denied. Now she could not leave. Could not go home to Ian and her child. She couldn't quite take it in. She stared down at the chains on her hands and feet. Absurdly, she thought of the chopped meat in the refrigerator that had to be frozen or it would go bad. There was laundry still in the dryer. She couldn't remember if she had put the lids back on all her paints. She would not be allowed to check on anything. She would be herded about by hostile people until . . . until what? Her mind refused to focus on the possibilities.

She heard the beep of the computer access card, and the door of the cell was pulled open. "They're ready for you now," said the young officer. He escorted her to the door of the family court, and the court attendant ushered them both in. The courtroom was like the auditorium of a small school. It had beige carpeting and cream-colored walls. Instead of a stage, there was the judge's huge desk, its wood grain aglow under the recessed lighting, flanked by flags, elevated and imposing, with a high-backed swivel chair behind it.

The officer led her, shuffling, to the desk where Curtis Stanhope was sitting. The courtroom was almost empty— reporters had been barred—and there was only Ian, sitting behind Stanhope. On the other side of the room, behind their lawyer, Frank O'Malley, sat Dolores and Sidney, their hands clasped. Sidney dropped his gaze when Laura looked at them, but Dolores stared back at her, her eyes cold with fury.

As she reached the defendant's seat, Laura turned to Ian, who stood up, leaned over, and tried to grasp her in his arms. The officer separated them. The court attendant, a woman wearing a tie, jacket, and white shirt, announced that the court was in session, Judge Watkins presiding. A door to one side of the desk opened, and the judge came in. She was a well-groomed, middle-aged black woman with grave, intelligent eyes.

"Where is Michael?" Laura pleaded with Stanhope as they all stood up.

"In the judge's chambers. With a policewoman," Stanhope whispered as the judge took her seat and explained why they were gathered here.

"Mr. O'Malley," said the judge, "you may proceed."

Frank O'Malley, a round-faced man with white hair and a rumpled suit, rose to his feet. "Your Honor, my clients are the grandparents of Michael Reed, the minor child the temporary custody of whom we are asking you to decide.

"Michael Reed's mother has been arrested and charged with the crime of murder in the first degree of Michael's father, James Reed Jr. Given these circumstances, my clients, the child's paternal grandparents, request immediate temporary custody of Michael Reed, pending the outcome of Laura Turner's trial. Michael is comfortable with his grandparents, loves them, and is accustomed to being in their care. On the other hand, he barely knows his stepfather, Ian Turner. The prisoner is being held without bail, and has no option to care for the boy herself. Mr. and Mrs. Barone wish to take charge of Michael immediately, and to care for and shelter him until this matter is settled."

Laura tried to stand up and catch the sober eye of Judge Watkins. "I'm innocent. Doesn't that count for anything?" she cried. Even as she was being forced back onto her seat, she realized how hollow the claim of innocence could ring in the great bell jar of the courtroom.

The judge frowned at her. "Sit down, Mrs. Turner. We are informal here, but I will not tolerate outbursts. You'll have your turn. Are you finished, Mr. O'Malley?"

"Your Honor, we feel the circumstances speak for themselves."

"Mr. Stanhope?"

Curtis Stanhope rose to speak. Laura looked over at Dolores, whose face was set in as determined an expression as Laura had ever seen. She tried to feel hatred for her mother-in-law, but she could not. She believes the very worst of me, Laura thought. Of course she wants Michael.

"Your Honor," Stanhope began, "we have no question that Michael's grandparents love the boy. But my client, who expects to be exonerated, does not want her child poisoned against her by the time she goes free. And unfortunately, that is precisely what we expect to happen if Michael Reed is given into the custody of the Barones.

"Mrs. Barone refuses to entertain the possibility of her daughter-in-law's innocence. How can she be expected to be fair? My client fears that Mrs. Barone will attempt to destroy the relationship between my client and her son. And Mrs. Turner will not be in a position to prevent this. Mrs. Turner is not giving up her child. While we are in no way underestimating the seriousness of the charges, we also fully expect Mrs. Turner to be exonerated, and to be able to resume caring for her son. In the meantime, she wants him to live in his own home, and to be allowed to regard her with the same love and affection he always has. To that end, we ask that you award temporary custody to the boy's stepfather, Ian Turner."

Having heard both sides, the judge made a few notes and then looked up. "The circumstances of this case leave little room for doubt. The law in this state has precedents in a case such as this one. The child's mother stands accused of killing his father, and the child's grandparents are ready and willing to care for him. I have talked to Michael in my chambers, and he told me, quite unsolicited, that he wishes to stay with his grandmother and grandfather until such time as he can live with his mother. Therefore I am granting temporary custody of Michael Reed to his paternal grandparents, Dolores and Sidney Barone."

Laura gasped. She'd known it was coming, but she felt the ruling like a blow to her chest. She covered her face with her hands as Dolores yelped in exultation.

"Mrs. Barone," the judge said sternly, "your daughter-in-law's fears are justified in my opinion, and I remind you that she is accused, not convicted. I understand that you have strong feelings in this matter, but I order you to refrain from speaking about them or otherwise making them known to your grandson. To this end, I will have an officer of the court make periodic checks on the boy and question him about this. Any violation of this instruction will jeopardize your custody arrangement, I assure you. If Mrs. Turner is exonerated, she has a right to reclaim her child without having him irretrievably prejudiced against her. Is that clear?"

Dolores looked meekly at the judge. "Yes, Your Honor," she whispered.

"All right, then. Michael Reed will be turned over to his grandparents' custody immediately. Court attendant, can you bring the boy from my chambers?"

Laura felt Ian's hands on her shoulders, pressing against her as if he were trying to hold her together. Now victorious, Dolores refused to look at Laura. The woman in the tie and jacket left the courtroom and returned in a few moments, holding Michael by the hand. The child's gaze swept the courtroom, and he found the face he was seeking.

"Mom," he cried, wriggling from the attendant's grip and running for Laura. Laura rose and tried to shuffle toward him.

A uniformed officer stepped up and quickly apprehended the small boy, lifting him screaming off the ground and curtailing his lunge for his mother.

"Michael," Laura pleaded.

Dolores and Sidney were around the table and approaching the officer. "Come on, honey," said Dolores. "You're coming with Grandma."

"Mommy!" Michael shrieked.

"Your Honor," Stanhope protested, "this is cruel."

Judge Watkins, who had stood up to leave, turned and rapped her gavel. "Officer, let the child have a moment with his mother."

Looking relieved, the young officer set the child down gently and gave him a gentle push in Laura's direction. Michael barreled toward her, and Laura pulled him in, crushed his warm little body to her aching heart.

"Baby, baby," she whispered in a shaky voice. "I love you."

"Come home with me," he pleaded.

"I can't. Grandma's going to take care of you for a little while."

"I want you to take care of me," he said. Tears were forming in his eyes.

"I'm going to," Laura promised. "Just as soon as I can."

"Now," he demanded, rubbing his eyes with his fists.

For once in her life, Laura thanked her stars for her inability to weep. She did not want him any more scared than he already was. "I can't now," she said. "You be a good boy for Grandma and Poppy. I'll see you as soon as I can." It took everything she had to say it. She had to make him think it was okay.

"All right now." She heard voices murmuring around them, felt the frantic beating of his little heart against hers. She resisted the hands tugging at her shoulders, separating them.

"I love you more than anything," she cried. "Be a good boy now. Go with Grandma."

The court attendant led the boy to Dolores, who took him in her arms. The child rested wearily against the familiar shoulder. Dolores no longer looked tired or wasted. She looked strong and full of purpose. Sidney smiled benignly on them both. "Let's go, honey," Dolores whispered to Michael.

Laura stumbled to her feet with Ian's help. He tried again to embrace her, but the officer sharply ordered them apart. Laura looked in Ian's eyes for strength but saw a desperation there that made her look away.

"Bye, Mama," a pitiful voice called out.

Laura looked into the eyes of her departing child. He was holding Dolores's hand and waving back at her.

Mama. He has not called me that since he was a year old. Death could not be worse than this, she thought. How did this happen to me? She clutched Ian's hand and waved to her child. Then, still waving, she felt her fingers being pried from Ian's, felt herself being dragged away, as the courtroom door swung shut behind her son.

CHAPTER THIRTY-SEVEN

The smell of sausages and peppers sizzling on a grill intermingled with the sweet smell of zeppole pillows frying in a kettle and wafted up to the window of Aaron Kellerman's loft. Gary sat at the window, looking down at the twinkling white lights of the street fair below. The street had been closed to traffic for the night, as the parishioners of St. Sebastian's adorned their statuary with flowers and celebrated yet another saint's day with food, wine, and games of chance.

Although he could get in and out of the loft with ease, thanks to the industrial-size elevator in the building, Gary had trouble negotiating the narrow streets of the North End even on an ordinary day, never mind when there was a fair. But the view from the window was a merry one and normally would have filled him with a feeling of well-being. Tonight, however, he was melancholy, for he knew the morning would bring a change. As he gazed out at the street scene, he suddenly spotted Aaron coming down the block, done with the evening shift at the hospital. It was easy to pick him out of the crowd. He had a jaunty walk, his head bobbing around from side to side as if he could not get enough of the sights and smells around him.

Gary pulled his head back. He did not want to be caught watching his friend's approach. It was a long-standing habit—the custom of disguising his interest in the people he was most curious about. It was automatic by now, although it did not seem to fool Aaron. Gary heard the clanking and grinding of the elevator and knew that the next sound would be the door opening on Aaron's floor. Gary turned away from the door as he heard the key in the lock. Aaron came in, holding aloft a bag in his hand.

"Look," he said by way of greeting. "I brought us grinders. We can't fight that smell. We might as well join them."

Gary smiled faintly and shook his head. "These people do love to celebrate."

"They never miss an opportunity," said Aaron. "That's one reason I like living in this neighborhood. It's so full of life." He set his packages on the counter in the kitchen area and got a beer from the refrigerator. "Can I get you one?" he asked Gary.

Gary shook his head and gazed back out the window.

"How was your evening?" Aaron asked.

Gary pointed to a painting in progress on the easel Aaron had set up near the window. "I did some work. I couldn't get out of the building once they started setting up the tables. Too hard to get around. Forced me to work."

"It'll be gone tomorrow," Aaron said apologetically, flopping down on the sofa. "I don't want you to feel like a prisoner in here."

Gary waved it off. He did not feel like a prisoner. On the contrary, he wondered each day when Aaron was going to say that he was too much trouble, that he should go. But Aaron had seemed content to have him there. Gary even dreaded telling him of his plan, for fear he would be misunderstood.

Aaron swigged his beer and stretched out. "God, those kids were rambunctious tonight. They wanted to go to the indoor pool. That's always a real trip. A lot of acting out goes on. Trying to drown each other, or themselves."

Gary nodded. "I'll bet." He wondered where Aaron got the energy to give so much to other people. His work should have been draining, but it seemed to fill him up instead.

"You're quiet," said Aaron, sitting back up and leaning forward. "Anything wrong?"

"I've made a decision."

"Oh?" Aaron asked warily.

"I'm leaving tomorrow. I have to go back."

Aaron sat up and rolled the beer bottle between his palms. "Why?" he asked. "I thought you were going to stay."

"I have to settle some things there."

Aaron studied this statement for a moment, turning it over in his mind worriedly. "I'll go with you," he said at last. "I can get a few days off."

"No," Gary said quickly. "No. I have to go by myself."

Aaron nodded and lay back down on the sofa. They were both silent for a moment. A Neapolitan song, sung in Italian, wafted up through the window. "Are you okay?" Aaron asked.

"It's just something I have to do," said Gary.

"I'm a little concerned about you going back into that atmosphere. To the problems there," Aaron said in a rather clinical tone.

"I'll be okay," Gary said shortly.

"Well, you'll forgive me if I'm a little doubtful," said Aaron.

Gary did not reply. They both knew what he meant. It was Aaron's knock on the door at the Golden Pheasant that had saved his life. That night Gary hadn't been going to answer the door at first, but he'd been afraid it might be the manager or a chambermaid—someone with a key who would let himself in. So Gary had called out to the intruder to go away, and Aaron's gentle, persistent voice had convinced him finally to open up. At least to open up the door—he had not yet been able to open up to Aaron about the layers of grief and deception that had brought him to that state of desperation. But there had been moments . . . when he almost had.

"There are just things I have to get settled before I can . . . come back."

"Why not just leave it behind? Whatever it was, it took you to a bad place. Why go back and stir it all up?"

"I have to," said Gary.

"Closure," Aaron murmured.

"What?"

"It's a shrink phrase." Aaron got up and came over to Gary's chair. He crouched in front of him and rested his hands on Gary's forearms. Gary looked down into his dark, worried gaze. "I just hope you're not going to get caught in some kind of emotional quicksand again."

"I'll try not to."

"Promise you'll come back?" Aaron asked.

Why do you want me to come back? Gary wondered. Why would you want me?

It was as if Aaron could read his mind. "My life's been better since you came here," he said.

Gary blushed with pleasure. He was so used to feeling like a burden. "All right," he said, although he did not look Aaron in the eye.

"You'll leave the gun here," said Aaron.

"I'm going to take it with me," said Gary. "It's not for . . . you know, that. It's just that I'm more vulnerable than most people. On the road."

"I wish you'd get rid of that thing, for good," said Aaron, trying to disguise his anxiety with a cranky tone.

Gary studied Aaron's fine features, his kind eyes. A good man. A genuinely good man. A man who had followed him on a hunch and saved his life. Someone who tried to think the best of people. Who would never think of doing anything hurtful to people. A man who would never use a gun.

"I will," said Gary. "Right after this trip."

CHAPTER THIRTY-EIGHT

A sheen of perspiration covered Candy Walsh's body and made her peacock-blue-and-hot-pink workout suit damp and clingy. She strode the treadmill and worked her arms, facing a full-length mirror. Every few seconds she would glance down from the gauges on her machine to the muscles in her upper arms, obsessively vigilant, looking to obtain the perfect shape, willing to work for it. She was not like some people who watched TV or listened to music while they worked out. For her, this morning workout was a time of concentration, a religious experience, almost.

She heard Richard's heavy tread on the stairs and frowned. He should have gone to work by now. She hated it when he hung around the house. "How come you're not gone yet? Who was that at the door, Richard?" Candy asked, lifting her chin and studying her neck and shoulder muscles. You wanted to keep them firm, but definitely not pumped. That did not look pretty.

Richard came into Candy's exercise room and sat on a bench, his legs sprawled out in front of him. Candy tore her eyes away from her own reflection long enough to glance at her husband. "What are you looking so freaked out about?"

"That was the police," he said.

"Was it about Laura?" Candy asked in a catty tone.

"She's been arrested," he said dully.

"Well, don't sound so miserable. It's about time. Besides, this will be a big case. Big bucks for you."

"She's hired another lawyer," he said.

Candy shook her head. "She's got a lot of fucking nerve. After all you've done for her."

"He's the best criminal lawyer around."

"Well, she'll need him. The little bitch."

Richard did not meet her gaze. "We have a problem, Candy," he said wearily.

Candy jumped off her machine, picked up a towel, and began to pat herself down. "No, we don't," she said playfully.

"Yes, we do," he said grimly.

Candy frowned. She hated problems. Problems were his department. "What is it, Richard?" she said irritably.

"This . . . Stanhope . . . he's going to want to be paid. I didn't think about that. I figured she'd stick with me."

"So?"

"So, he's very expensive, and he'll want a big chunk up front."

"What's a big chunk?"

"Oh, a hundred grand. Maybe more."

"That's not our problem," Candy said airily. "That's her problem. What time is it, Richard? I need to start my free weights."

"I don't know," said Richard.

"Well, look at your watch."

Richard did not answer.

Candy tore her gaze from the mirror and looked at him. "Where *is* your watch?" She suddenly noticed that Richard was holding a paper sack in his lap. "What's in the bag?"

He looked at her with a guilty expression on his face and did not answer.

"Richard," she demanded, "what is it?"

"Candy, I made some bad investments with Laura's money. The police know about it. That's why they were here just now."

261

"What do the police care about that little murderess's money?"

"It's complicated," said Richard. "They know I had some losses at the casinos."

"What do you mean, losses? What kind of losses?"

Richard exhaled a windy sigh. "Some . . . significant losses. They wanted to . . . to question me about it."

Candy looked at him with narrowed eyes. Before he could stop her, she bent down and snatched the bag from his lap. He reached up and then let his hands fall back limply in his lap.

Candy opened the bag and looked inside. At first she seemed perplexed, and then she looked up at him, her eyes blazing. "Here's your Rolex. And this is my jewelry from the safe in here," she said. "Richard, what are you doing with my good jewelry in this shitty little paper bag?"

"We need to raise some money," he said. "Real quick."

"Oh no," she said. "Oh no, you don't. Not my jewelry, Richard. Don't be stupid. We have lots of money. Sell some stock or something."

Richard winced and looked up at her.

"You asshole," she cried, clutching the paper bag to her spandex-covered breast. "What have you done?"

* * *

Dominick Vanese looked on with patient approval as fragrant golden loaves of bread were unloaded from the bakery truck and carried into the kitchen of his restaurant. He could not resist breaking off an end of one loaf and savoring the crunchy crust, the dense, chewy center. "So, Fiona," he asked as the lovely young woman in jeans and a baker's apron finished the last of the delivery and slammed the door on her van. "How's your papa?"

"*Mezza, mezz,*" Fiona answered pleasantly. She was the beauteous result of a union between an Italian father and a Scottish mother. "I told him I'd bring him over for lunch next week."

Vanese nodded. He had been doing business with Fiona's father ever since he'd opened the restaurant thirty years ago. That was not unusual for Vanese. He was a man who valued loyalty above all virtues, in himself and in others. In recent years the old baker had been hobbled by rheumatoid arthritis, but Fiona had ably stepped in, met the orders, and kept up the quality. Her father's life's work would continue in his daughter's hands. Dominick Vanese approved wholeheartedly.

"Hey, we're none of us young as we once were. You bring him over. I'll treat him right."

"I'll do it, Mr. Vanese," she cried. She turned to get back in the van when suddenly a man burst into the dark alleyway behind the restaurant where they stood talking. He blinked several times, as if to accustom his eyes to the gloom, and then spotted the two of them outside the back door of the kitchen. He began to come toward them.

"Dominick Vanese?" the man demanded.

Vanese frowned, squinting down the alleyway. "Who wants to know?"

The intruder had a look in his piercing blue eyes that was wild, like a rabid animal. He strode up to Vanese and grabbed him by the arm. "You lying bastard," he growled. "My wife is innocent and you know it."

"Who are you? Let me go," Vanese insisted, but even as he said it, he knew who this man was. He recognized him right away from the description. The new husband.

Ian grasped the older man's lapels and jerked him close to his face. "I am Laura Turner's husband, and I want to know why you lied about my wife. You put my wife in jail. She never asked you any such thing about any hit man and you know it."

"Mr. Vanese, are you all right?" Fiona asked.

"Calm down," croaked Vanese, his airway slightly strangled by the hold he was in. "Leave me alone, mister. I don't have to answer to you."

"Yes, you do, you miserable little creep," Ian cried. "You think you can ruin my life with your lies and not have to answer for it? You better think again, mister." He jerked at the smaller man again, this time lifting him off his feet so that he dangled inches above the ground.

"All right, that's enough," Fiona said angrily, wiping her hands on her apron and striding over to Ian. "Let him go."

Ian did not even seem to notice the woman tugging at him. His glare was focused on Vanese. He shook the old man, who let out a gasp of pain.

"Stop it," cried Fiona. "Let go of him." She began to pound on Ian's back with her fists, which were uncommonly strong for a woman because of all the kneading and lifting in her work. Still, Ian seemed oblivious of her intervention. His gaze was riveted on Vanese as he tried to shake an admission out of him.

"Help!" cried Fiona. "We need some help out here!"

Two of the cooks in the kitchen heard the commotion and came running out into the alleyway behind the restaurant. One was a muscular, middle-aged black man and the other a stocky young Thai. They saw instantly where their loyalties lay. One of the cooks grabbed Ian from behind, pulling him off Vanese, and the other one punched him in the stomach. Ian doubled over and fell to the ground. He scrambled to his feet and tried to strike back, but the older man pinned back his arms and the young Thai fellow blasted him with a one-two punch to the face that flattened Ian and left him bleeding. It was all over in a moment.

"Are you all right, Mr. Vanese?" Fiona asked worriedly.

Vanese shook himself like a pup and adjusted the cuffs of his shirt. "I'm all right. Thank you, dear," he said in a shaky voice.

"What's his problem?" asked the baker.

As Ian staggered to his feet, one of the cooks drew back his arm to punch him again.

"No," ordered Vanese. "That's enough."

Ian tried to straighten up. There was blood coming from his lip and a dark bruise forming under his eye.

"Now you listen to me, mister," said Vanese, flanked by his glowering, towering kitchen help. "You're all worked up right now. But someday, hey, you never know. You may say I did you a favor. She might have decided she wanted to get rid of you next. This way you're pretty safe."

Ian lunged toward Vanese again, but this time the restaurateur was well guarded. The two cooks stepped forward and detained him. One of them gave him a hard smack on the side of the face, and then they tossed him backward.

"Go on, get lost," said Vanese. "I can't help what she is. Now, go away."

CHAPTER THIRTY-NINE

Laura stepped over to the sink, turned on the faucet, and cupped her hands so that the thin, rusty trickle of lukewarm water pooled in her palms. Then she bent over and splashed her face in a futile attempt to relieve the headache pounding behind her eyes. Except for one fitful hour, she had not slept all night. During the nocturnal hours, the rustling and cursing of the other inmates was punctuated by screams and shrieks and the occasional clanging of a billy club against the bars, meant to silence the insolent. When morning finally came, the screams subsided, and then a high-pitched buzz of insults and manic laughter arose, like steam, through the female prisoners' wing of the county jail.

Breakfast in the bleak common room had been inedible, a pasty blob meant to represent eggs and a muffin as hard as a discus. Then, they had exercise and a mindless work detail. She'd heard the whispering of other prisoners as she'd filed back to her cell, and one tall, muscular woman with crewcut hair had leered at her and said, "Hi, puss. Kiss, kiss." Laura had reentered her cell with a sense of relief.

Laura patted the water on the back of her neck and shook it off like a dog, because she had no towel. Then she sat back down on her cot. She could feel the cold steel coils through the thin mattress. The air in the cell block was warm and stifling. She felt as if she could not catch her breath, and when she did, the smell of perspiring bodies and disinfectant was imposed on it. There was no air-conditioning in the enclosed space. In contrast with the modernized courthouse, the Cape Christian County Jail was run-down and primitive, a symbol of the low regard in which its inhabitants were held.

Laura lay back on the cot and put her hands over her eyes, applying pressure to the pounding in her head. She thought about her bed at home, and lying in it with Ian, the shadows of leaves and glimmers of sunlight shifting on the lace curtains. And across the hall, Michael, still sleeping under his cowboy quilt. She tried to put herself back there in her mind's eye, in that peaceful, happy place, but it kept slipping away. Her mind was at war with itself. One half said, *Innocent people don't get convicted, don't go to jail for life. You will be free again, and soon.* And the other half—the guilty, dark half— was shaking a figurative finger at her. *This is your punishment for remarrying so quickly, for wanting to be happy, for giving in to desire and denying Jimmy the mourning that was due him. This is some kind of cosmic retribution, and you have just begun to pay.*

"Turner," the guard barked.

Laura jumped, uncovering her eyes.

"Visitor."

* * *

"My God," Laura cried as she sat down across from Ian at a visitors table. "What happened to you?"

Instinctively Ian tried to cover his bruised swollen eye. Fresh blood seeped from the corner of his mouth as he pressed his lips together. "I went to see Mr. Vanese," he said.

She felt a kind of hopeless gratitude for his gallantry. "Oh, Ian, you didn't."

"I had to," he said. "This man is lying about you, and I want to know why."

"You had a fight with him?" she asked worriedly. "Oh, Ian, they'll arrest you next."

"Don't worry," he said with a mirthless laugh. "I got the worst of it. And no answers."

He looked exhausted, his complexion gray, his eyes dull with fatigue. His blue work shirt was flecked with blood. She leaned over to touch his face.

"Sit back," the guard ordered her, stepping forward.

Laura sank back onto her chair. "You should go home and try to rest," she said.

"Rest? How can I rest with you in here? I stayed on the boat last night to get away from the reporters, but I couldn't sleep. I've been trying to reach Stanhope, but his secretary keeps giving me the runaround. I think I'm going to just drive up to Philadelphia today and refuse to leave until he sees me. I need to know what he's doing for you. You don't belong in here."

"I'm sorry," Laura said miserably.

Ian grabbed her hands. "No, don't. Don't you be sorry. You're the one who's suffering. I can't stand to think of you being in this place."

Laura wanted to tell him that it wasn't so bad, but she wasn't that good a liar. She groped for something hopeful to say. "Stanhope said he was optimistic, since they have no hard evidence against me," she said.

Ian shook his head.

"Don't you think he meant it?" she asked anxiously.

"No, I do, I do," he reassured her. "But I want to know what the hell he's doing about it. He should have someone looking into this Vanese character."

"Ian," she said, "I want you to know. I mean, you must know, that whatever this man said, I didn't do it. I never did. As long as you believe in me . . ."

"I'll always believe in you," he said. His eyes looked weary and lost.

She leaned back and looked at him as if from a great distance. No, she thought. You're not going to be able to. Not for much longer. And how can I blame you? How loyal can you expect a virtual stranger to be? She could not allow

268

herself to think of his electric body, his desperate kisses. That was not real. That was a pleasure of another life. There was only one thing she had to fight for, and that was a small boy with a round face, and trusting eyes, and little fingers that had been pried from hers. That she could fight for.

"What are you thinking?" he asked.

"I'm thinking of Michael," she replied.

"Time's up," the guard announced, stepping up and rapping on the table with the tip of his club.

"Do you want me to go to Dolores's and try to see him?" Ian asked.

Laura pictured the reception he would get from Dolores and Sidney. It would make Vanese look welcoming. She shook her head. "Thank you, though."

"Don't sound so polite," Ian protested. "I'd do anything for you. I love you."

"Now," said the guard, taking Laura by the upper arm, his fingers gouging her armpit through the slippery synthetic fabric.

Ian untangled his fingers from hers and stood up. Laura looked back at him and felt the fierceness of his gaze in the pit of her empty stomach. Then her shoulders slumped as another guard waiting outside the room started to escort her down the hall. She waited like a schoolgirl while the guard stopped to gossip with a female officer in the corridor. When the guard was good and ready, he turned and prodded Laura as if she had been refusing to move. Laura stumbled forward and walked, waited while the doors to the cell block were unlocked, and then walked again as she was escorted back down the hall. The guard had no sooner unlocked her cell and motioned for her to enter than another officer appeared at the door to the cell block. "Hey," the guard called out, "there's another one here for Turner."

Laura's escort sighed as Laura looked up hopefully. "My son?"

"Some woman," the officer called back.

The guard consulted his watch. "All right, let's go. You got five more minutes."

CHAPTER FORTY

Marta Eberhart sat nervously on the visitor's seat, tapping on the table and giving the guard a feeble, insincere smile each time their eyes met. He looked at her incuriously, like a bug. Marta had to start taking deep breaths like the ones in her yoga class just to keep from snapping at somebody.

I'm going to take this suit to the cleaners, she thought, the minute I get back to New York. It smelled like the Times Square subway stop in this place, and she only hoped they could get the smell out at the cleaners because this was her new Donna Karan. She'd worn it because it made her feel very sleek and in control, and she definitely wanted to feel that way on this, her first jailhouse visit.

The door to the visitors' room opened and Laura was led in. Marta let out a cry of dismay, and jumped up to embrace her.

"Sit," said the guard.

"Arf, arf," Marta responded angrily, resuming her seat.

The guard glared but let it pass. Laura sat on the chair opposite her while Marta watched in disbelief. She reached out and gripped Laura's hand. "Oh, sweetie," she said, "this can't be."

Laura grimaced, unable to muster outrage. She was too tired and her head hurt too much for outrage. She looked at her editor gratefully. "It was good of you to come, Marta. I know how busy you are."

"Oh, Laura, I had to come." Marta leaned forward and whispered, "Are they horrible to you in here?" Her gaze trailed over to the impassive guard.

"No, it's more like I'm not even here," said Laura. "I'm invisible to them. They haul me around from place to place. The contents of cell thirteen-D."

"This is such a nightmare," said Marta, feeling inept and tongue-tied.

"How was your trip?" Laura asked, trying to sound like a normal person. "Did you have any trouble finding the place?"

"I rented a car, although you know me and driving," said Marta, rolling her eyes. She was about to launch into a litany of complaints about the traffic and her own ineptitude at the wheel, but somehow it seemed absurd to be complaining in light of Laura's situation. "It was fine. I remembered my way to Cape Christian from when I came to the funeral, and then I just asked directions to the . . . jail." She mumbled the last word as if it embarrassed her to speak it aloud.

Laura looked fondly at her editor. She still remembered, in the midst of her own grief, how touched she had been by Marta's attendance at Jimmy's funeral. After the funeral service, Laura sat numbly on the sofa with her leg elevated, her crutches beside her. Marta, meanwhile, with her hair by Licari and her nails by Elizabeth Arden, had strapped on an apron and helped fix platters of food in the kitchen to serve to the mourners. "You're always there for me when I need you," Laura said.

"I try," Marta said breezily.

"Well, believe me, it means a lot to me that you came," said Laura.

"I just wish I could do something . . . help you somehow. I feel like you're all alone here."

"I'm not," Laura said more bravely than she felt. "I have Ian."

"He sounds like a great guy," said Marta.

"I thought you might disapprove, you know. We got married so suddenly . . . Everybody else does."

"Disapprove?" Marta laughed. "Honey, you're looking at a woman who had Thanksgiving dinner with a divorced lesbian and an over-the-hill actress on Prozac. If the right guy came along, I'd marry him in two seconds in a barrel going over Niagara Falls. Just tell me this, does Ian have any brothers?"

Laura smiled. "One, but he's married."

"My luck," said Marta.

"I can't wait for you to meet Ian, when this is all over," said Laura.

There was a hollowness in Laura's tone that made Marta wince. She tried to sound optimistic. "I'm looking forward to it."

Laura nodded and looked away.

"Honey, I've got to ask you. Have you got a good lawyer?"

"They say he's the best. His name is Curtis Stanhope. He's from Philadelphia. Ian got him for me."

"Well, that's good," Marta murmured.

"What are you thinking?" Laura asked, noting her editor's frown.

"Nothing. It's just . . . I may need to talk to your lawyer. You can't believe all the calls I'm getting. The media vultures."

"Ian said they've been hounding him, too," said Laura.

Marta shook her head. "They're in a feeding frenzy. Sharon Glassman kept me on the phone for an hour yesterday. She's from the ASM agency in Hollywood. They want movie rights."

"Oh, Marta, no," Laura protested.

"Honey, don't get me wrong. I think it's ghoulish. But maybe I can dump them all in Mr. Stanhope's lap, and he can head them off."

"Well, he's pretty tough. He'll handle them. You do whatever you think best," Laura said wearily. "I don't want to talk to anyone from the press, that's for sure."

"I see Bob Gerster already made his pitch," Marta said disgustedly.

Laura looked at her in confusion. "Who?" She shook her head.

"That freelancer for *Book World*. I assume it was you he was visiting. There can't be two authors incarcerated in this lovely place, can there?" Marta asked with a shudder.

"I don't know what you're talking about," said Laura.

"You remember the guy. He wanted to interview you . . . oh, when was it? Last winter some time?"

Laura narrowed her eyes, a memory returning. "Vaguely," she said. It was hard to think with her head pounding. And it seemed so unimportant now.

"He came to see me, asked me all about you. He was doing some piece on children's book authors. He was a big fan . . . knew all your books."

"Oh, right," Laura said dully. "I remember telling Jimmy that he might be coming down." She felt a wave of sadness, remembering Jimmy's enthusiasm, how she had teased him about his love for publicity.

"I gave him all the information," Marta went on, "and then I never heard from him. I guess he never followed through. But now, of course, with all this lovely scandal, he reappears . . ."

"It figures," Laura said disinterestedly.

"So," said Marta. "What did he want?"

Laura looked at her blankly. "I don't know. I didn't talk to him."

"I saw him leaving the visitors area as I was coming in. I wonder what he was doing," Marta mused. "Well, whatever. I'm glad he didn't get to you. If you want my advice, you keep everything to yourself. Don't talk to any of them."

"I won't," Laura promised. "Believe me."

"I almost didn't recognize him," Marta rattled on. "He's a handsome guy, but he looked like he'd been hit by a truck. He has a bloody lip and a black eye . . . and he looked like he hadn't slept in a week."

Laura felt her heart swoop down in her chest. She stared at her editor. "What?" she said faintly.

"Time's up," said the guard.

Marta leaned in closer to Laura. "I would never forget those eyes, though. Mediterranean blue. With that blue shirt he had on. Yum. You know what I'm saying? The guy may be an opportunist, but he sure is pretty. Well, you don't want to hear about Bob Gerster. You've got a man. It's the deprivation. It makes me crazy."

"Does he have black hair," Laura asked in a flat voice.

Marta raked her fingernails against her temples. "With just a touch of gray. Gorgeous tan. Oh, why do I bother? I mustn't have made any impression on him. He walked right by me today like I wasn't even there. Well, honey, I guess it's adios for me."

Laura clung to Marta's hand. "Wait," she said in a shaky voice.

The guard leaned over and tapped the shoulder pad of Marta's Donna Karan suit. "I said, your time is up."

"All right," Marta said angrily, shaking him off. "Laura, I better go. Listen, if there is anything you need . . . anything at all, I want you to call me . . ." Marta gripped Laura's icy hand and looked worriedly in her eyes. "Are you going to be okay? You look awful. Try not to worry. It will all work out. You'll see."

Laura sat dumbstruck on her seat as the sound of Marta's clicking heels disappeared down the corridor.

"Wake up, Turner," said the guard. "Get on your feet."

Laura did not move.

"Now!" the officer bellowed.

She stared straight ahead as if she didn't hear him. He glared at her and prodded her with his billy club. Numbly, Laura forced herself to her feet.

CHAPTER FORTY-ONE

Wanda Jurik lifted the grocery bag out of the back of her car and trudged up the sandy driveway toward the back door of the house, the rain splattering all over her. She clutched the bottom of the bag, knowing that once it got damp it was likely to bust and things would break and spill all over. And she couldn't cope with that. There was no food left in the house. Yesterday all she had eaten was a can of black olives she'd found in the back of a cabinet. She couldn't go on that way. Then again, she couldn't decide if she wanted to go on.

Today was the first time she had gotten up the will to get to the store in . . . she couldn't remember how long. And it had taken all day to do it. To work up the necessary energy. Since Gary had been gone she had not had the will to do anything. She sat in the gloomy house, no matter how bright the day, her programs running, thinking about him every moment. Sometimes she would weep, certain he was dead. Other times she would begin to wonder if perhaps he was alive and how he was managing if he was. Then rage would consume her, for if he was, why hadn't he let her know? And then, because it was unthinkable that he would stay away like that, feeling certain again that he was dead. It was a vicious cycle of torpor and terror. She wondered, sometimes, how she could go on any longer.

As she rounded the side of the house and started toward the back stairs, a large vehicle loomed there in front of her like an answered prayer. For a moment Wanda couldn't even let out a squeak. Her heart was beating in her throat, and she was flushed as if a dam of blood had been released into her veins. The grocery bag fell from her arms and spilled on the ground, unlamented. She bounded up the stairs like a child and began to scream as she threw open the door.

"Gary, Gary, oh, my baby, where are you?"

She whirled through the rooms, tears standing in her eyes, crying out his name. She could hear the TV running in the living room and, faintly, a voice answering. She rushed in and saw him sitting there, staring at the screen, as if he had never left.

"Oh, my baby," she whispered. She knelt down and crawled over to him, pressing her forehead against his lifeless knees. He reached down and patted her shoulder gently, absently.

"Hello, Mother," he said sadly.

"I thought you were dead," she sobbed.

"I almost was," he said.

"Oh, my darling, you're back. I didn't dare to hope . . ." She sat back on her haunches, clutching the fabric of his pants legs with spiny fingers, her face wet with tears, her eyes swimming. "I've had the police looking for you. Why did you leave like that?"

"I'm sorry you were so worried," he said.

"Was it that woman getting married? That Laura Reed. I told you to forget about her. When will you realize that I know what's best for you? Oh, Gary, I've been in agony. How could you not call me and tell me?"

Gary looked at his mother as if from a great distance. There were spots of color in his smooth, pale cheeks. His steel gray hair was neatly combed. "I should have called you, Mother. You're right. It was wrong of me. It's just that I was close to the edge myself. Very close to the edge . . ."

She covered her face with her hands and began to sob openly, tears streaming down her face, her nose running.

"I'm sorry," he said weakly. "Please forgive me. I didn't know what to do. I had to think . . ."

"Where were you? What did you do? How could you have even lived this long without my help? Oh, God . . ." She shuddered with sobs.

"I guess I was desperate," he said. A wry smile curved his pale lips. "Desperate times call for desperate measures."

Wanda shook her head, liberating some tissues from her pocket and wiping her eyes and nose. Then she began to laugh through her tears. "Oh, it's all right, it doesn't matter. I thought I would be mad, but I don't care. As long as you're back." She embraced his withered calves fiercely, as if it were their very slackness that she loved. Then she looked up at him, her eyes shining.

"You're home. That's all that matters."

"No, Mother. Don't. We should talk," he said weakly.

The look on his face was strange, and she knew it. She chose to avoid it. She rested her cheek on his bony knee and began to hum softly. She didn't even care that she was missing her programs. She could stay like this for hours, just the two of them, safe and together.

"Not now, my poor baby," she crooned. "First let me take care of you. Let me get you a cup of tea. You need to rest. You've been through so much. I must have tea."

For a moment she wondered if she had milk. She remembered the bag of groceries she had dropped in the driveway. She would go out and pick it up. Those waxy cartons were sturdy. It would be all right. She would give him some tea and maybe get him to take one of those Valium that Dr. Ingles had prescribed for her. It would calm him down. Then she could put his things away while he slept. Wherever he had been, it had done him no good. That was for sure.

"You stay right there," Wanda said gently. "I'll bring the tea."

She hurried out to the kitchen and ran water in the kettle. She had to light the stubborn gas jets with kitchen matches that she stuffed absently into her pocket as the burner flared. She could hear the television droning as she searched for a clean cup and saucer. Then she put a teabag in the cup and headed out to the driveway, to pick up the groceries in the rain. She stood there with her hands on her hips, staring at the mess at the foot of the steps. Some of the things were unsalvageable. The strawberries she had bought were squashed and sugared with sand. A bag of rolls had split open, and the rolls were strewn about like golden stones. But she didn't care. She gathered up the cartons and cans in her arms, her heart singing. She was worried about him, still thinking about that Laura Reed. But this had all been so traumatic for him. Once she fed him and got him well, he would forget all that. Meanwhile she was alive again. The rain fell on her head and shoulders like a blessing. He was home again. Their world was complete. It was all that mattered.

Wanda returned to the kitchen, turned off the whistling kettle, and poured the tea. She shelved the various groceries she had salvaged, then poured milk and spooned sugar in his tea, just the way he liked it. Maybe some cookies, too, she thought. She examined the bag. It had a small tear, but the ones on top would still be good. She had bought his favorite kind, out of habit. Out of a mother's hope against hope. And she had been rewarded. Her beloved child was home.

Balancing the cookies on the saucer with the teacup, she carefully made her way back to the dark living room.

CHAPTER FORTY-TWO

"Higher, Poppy," Michael cried.

Sidney obligingly gave the child an extra push that sent the swing soaring up in the air. There was another, older boy in the adjacent swing, and Michael was determined to outdo him.

"Now you pump," Sidney enjoined his grandson. "I'm doing all the work."

Michael laughed, and the sound was balm to Sidney's heavy heart. He's happy here with us, Sidney thought. That's what counts. That and Dolores.

He glanced over at the park bench under the sour-cherry tree. Dolores was sitting very still, facing them, although he could not see her eyes behind the dark glasses she wore. A light drizzle had begun, but still she kept her sunglasses on.

"More, Poppy," Michael pleaded.

"I'm getting tired out," said Sidney. "I'm going to go sit with Grandma. You start pumping. You'll catch him." He winked at the older boy in the neighboring swing. Michael, realizing that his locomotion was lost, began to bend his knees to the task with concentration.

Sidney walked over to the bench and sat beside his wife, taking out his handkerchief to mop his forehead. "Whew," he said. "That'll get the old ticker thumping, half an hour of that business."

Dolores gave him a wan smile and patted his hand as she gazed at her grandson on the swing.

"Shall we take him to the boardwalk for supper?" Sidney asked.

"It's starting to rain," said Dolores.

"It might not," said Sidney.

"No," she said. "I don't think so."

"So we can eat inside. We'll have clams down at the end of the pier. They have that enclosed patio where you can watch the waves."

Dolores nodded. "It sounds good," she said in a hollow tone.

"We have to keep him occupied," said Sidney. "Pretend this is some kind of a vacation, so he won't get too upset."

"You're right," said Dolores.

"This is the best thing for him. He belongs with us. Under the circumstances, he belongs with us."

"Oh, I know," said Dolores. "Under the circumstances."

They sat in silence for a few moments, watching their grandson. Michael had lost interest in the swing now that Poppy was no longer involved. The older boy had brought a basketball and had begun shooting hoops on the blacktop. Michael wandered over and kicked pebbles around at the edge of the court. The older boy caught Michael's eye and tossed him the basketball. Surprised, Michael missed but gamely scrambled after it, then returned to the blacktop. He took aim at the basket.

"Dribble it first," the older boy advised, and proceeded to show him how.

Sidney sighed and nodded. "The best thing this way," he said aloud.

Dolores did not reply. Sidney glanced over at her. He knew he should ask her what was wrong, but the expression on her face filled him with dread. Something was bothering her, eating at her. It had been all day, ever since a reporter had called and mentioned the name of the witness—Dominick Vanese. But why? he thought desperately. Everything was all right for now. Laura was in jail where she belonged, and they had Michael. It was a terrible situation, but it was some resolution, at least. He had thought that Dolores might finally be satisfied. Well, not satisfied, exactly, but more at peace with the situation. He thought she might start to get her spirits back. He had done everything a man could do. And still, there she sat, consumed with anxiety once again.

Sidney thought back to the time before Jimmy died, when their life together had been like a dream of happiness. He had thought, when he took his marriage vows with her, that the "for worse" part would come when they were old and sick and trying to care for one another. But it had come early, with the death of Dolores's son. He wondered, sometimes, if the "better" part was over forever.

I'm not going to ask, he thought. Let us pretend to enjoy this day.

"Sidney," she said, "we have to talk about this."

The tone of her voice made his heart sink. "What is it, my love?"

"You know as well as I do," she said. "The witness. I've been thinking about it ever since we heard his name from that reporter this morning."

Sidney felt a churning in his stomach. "What about him?" he asked mildly.

"We know him, don't we? Vanese?"

Sidney took a deep breath. And nodded. "We know him."

"I've never met him, so it took me a minute to place the name, but then it came to me. He's one of your customers. That was his condo where we stayed in Florida."

Sidney stared at Michael, who was aiming for the hoop, missing by a mile. "That's right."

"Why didn't you say that? Why didn't you tell me that before we went to court? Why didn't you tell the police?"

"I didn't know about it," Sidney protested. "This morning was the first I heard of it. Just like you."

He could sense his wife bristling beside him, although he did not meet her eye.

"Sidney, are you trying to tell me that this man, this old friend of yours, knew about Laura looking for a hired killer all this time, and he never came forward? Why not? He could have prevented our son's murder. What kind of a man is this?"

"Look, I'm not trying to tell you anything. I don't know anything. Vanese told the cops he never put two and two together."

"And you never discussed it with him. The man lent us his condominium, and you never discussed it?"

Sidney stuck out his jaw. "No, we never did. It's not friendship. It was a business thing. The condo. I don't see this man from year to year. He uses my linen service for his restaurant, period."

"This is fishy, Sidney. There's something fishy here."

Sidney did not reply. All of a sudden he stood up and clapped his hands. "Come on, Michael. Let's go. Dolores, let's go. I don't know anything more than you do. Let's get going."

Michael was just about to protest when his grandmother yelled out, "You can still play." Michael beamed at the unexpected extension and turned back to the older boy, clamoring for another shot.

"You sit back down," Dolores said to her husband.

Sidney remained standing, staring out across the quiet gray playground, his heart thudding hard in his chest.

"Now I wasn't born yesterday, and you're going to tell me what's going on here. Why did this man Vanese wait so long to go to the police? I want an answer, Sidney. I demand an answer."

"He didn't know it was Laura who came to him," Sidney sputtered. "That's what he said. I never discussed it with him."

Dolores glared at her husband. "I don't believe you, Sidney. Why are you lying to me? You have never been a very good liar."

Sidney sat back down on the bench and said quietly, "Leave it alone, Dolores. Let it be."

Dolores looked at her husband in amazement. His mild, amiable face was set like stone. "What else do you know?" she demanded. "What else aren't you telling me?"

Sidney considered his options. He knew his wife. Once she got hold of an idea, there was no shaking her loose. He probably should have known she would start to wonder. She had a lot of smarts, and she was the curious sort. He had just figured that when she got what she wanted, she wouldn't start to pick it apart. He had miscalculated. And now that she had this notion in her head, he knew he could not hold up his end of it for long. He knew Dolores. She would hammer at him. He really had no other choice but to confide in her. It would have happened sooner or later. He tried to reassure himself with that thought.

"Honey, look," he said. "I gave this a lot of thought. There was no other way. We both know she did it—had Jimmy killed. But there was no proof. She was about to get on a boat and sail out of here scot-free with our grandson. You know it and I know it. There was no other way to stop her."

Dolores's jaw dropped. Her head felt light and dizzy. "What are you saying? Are you saying Vanese lied about it?"

"He's a good man," Sidney said urgently. "He wanted to help us."

"She didn't come to him about any hit man," Dolores said slowly.

Sidney turned and looked her in the eye. "You believed she did it from the start. I wasn't so sure. Even when she married this Turner guy, and you were going crazy over it, I was still willing to give her the benefit of the doubt. But then, when they found out about Powell—what else could I think? And it was tearing you apart to see her getting away with it. You ended up in the hospital, for God's sake. I felt this thing was going to kill you if I didn't do something . . ."

"You paid him to say it?"

"Money was never involved," Sidney said huffily. "He offered. It was a gesture of friendship."

Dolores sat beside him silently. He glanced at her, but he could not see her eyes behind her dark glasses. "The police are going to find out, you know. If I figured out that about you and Vanese, they're going to figure it out, too."

Sidney shrugged. "Lots of people know Dominick Vanese. Everybody knows him. And the ones who don't know him know of him."

"You could both go to jail for this," she cried.

Sidney gestured for her to keep her voice down. "He's not going to say anything. No one ever has to know."

Dolores stared out at Michael, playing. Sidney waited for her to say something. For a few moments she was silent, and then she reached over and took his hand.

"You're not angry," he said doubtfully.

"You did that for me," she said. "I don't deserve that kind of love."

Sidney felt a lump rising in his throat. "Yes, you do," he croaked.

"But it's not true," Dolores said, shaking her head. "I thought it was true."

"It might as well be. Think of Jimmy," Sidney said fiercely. "She had your son murdered in cold blood. Think of what she did to Michael. His own mother . . ."

Dolores gazed at her grandson, his losses momentarily forgotten in the joy of a game. "I am thinking," she said.

CHAPTER FORTY-THREE

"Come on in," Clyde Jackson called out in response to the rap on his door. He took a bite out of a doughnut and brushed powdered sugar off the lapel of his blue pin-striped suit as Ron Leonard entered his office.

Ron frowned in mock disapproval at his boss. "Does Debbie know you're eating that?" he asked. Clyde's wife, a professor at a local college, was well known to be a health nut who closely monitored her husband's fat intake.

"Debbie had a conference in New York. So I dropped off Clyde Jr. at the sitter's, and then I forgot to have breakfast."

"I'm going to tell on you," said Ron.

Clyde gave a self-conscious laugh and shrugged. "I think she suspects," he said. "So, what's up?"

Ron flopped down on the chair across from Clyde's desk and shook his head, sighing. "Bad news."

Clyde raised his eyebrows and finished off the doughnut. "What?"

"I did some serious nosing around yesterday. It seems our star witness is a longtime associate of Sidney Barone's. The father-in-law. When they went to Florida last month, they stayed in Vanese's condo."

"Barone has Mob connections?" the DA asked in surprise.

Ron shook his head. "He has a linen business in A.C. He services Vanese's restaurant. Has done for years. Barone and Vanese grew up in the same neighborhood."

"Shit," said the DA. He considered the implications of this information. "You think the Barones put Vanese up to this?"

Ron shook his head. "Perjury is serious business. I can't see a smart guy like Vanese getting involved in this if it's not true. I mean, he wouldn't do it for money. He doesn't need the money. But apparently he and Sidney Barone go back a long way. And these people are pretty desperate. I mean, a hired killer? What would you think if you were Jimmy Reed's parents?"

"I'd think exactly what they are thinking," Clyde said grimly. "But if this witness is lying, we have no case against Laura Reed. Or the new husband."

Ron shrugged. "True, and once Stanhope gets wind of this . . . He's bound to find out. I'm surprised his investigators aren't on this already."

Clyde nodded grimly. "Mmm . . ."

The two men sat in silence for a moment, thinking. "The thing is," said Ron, "I know Turner is guilty. I can feel it. He was lying to me the other day when I questioned him. I know it like I know my own name. I'd believe her over him any day. Sometimes I actually think she is telling the truth. But we can't get to him unless she implicates him."

Clyde nodded. "The only way to nail the matched set is to get them to implicate one another . . . I think our only hope is to work on her while we've still got her. Which," he said, glancing at his watch as if it were a matter of moments, "isn't going to be long, if what you say is true about Vanese and the Barones."

"Oh, it's true." Ron sighed.

"We've got to get her in here and work on her," Clyde mused.

"Her lawyer would never go for that," Ron pointed out.

Clyde waggled a hand in the air. "I think we can finesse a little something. Within the bounds of her legal rights, of course."

"Of course," Ron said wryly. "But why would she squeal on him? Vanese didn't say anything about him. And she's claiming to be innocent."

Clyde picked up a pencil and tapped it rapidly on the edge of his desk. "What you said a minute ago gave me an idea. Maybe if she thought we believed her . . .," he said.

"Why would she think that?" Ron asked.

"You just said yourself that sometimes you think she's telling the truth," said Clyde.

"Well, yeah," Ron said cautiously. "Sometimes I do."

Clyde leaned forward across his desk. "So how good an actor are you, Detective? How convincing can you be?"

Ron looked at him warily.

* * *

Lights flashed in the courthouse catacombs, indicating that a prisoner was being moved. Laura kept her eyes down as she shuffled along in the belly chain that kept her wrists and ankles bound in a grim congruence. She did not want to see the looks in the eyes of the employees who stopped to watch her pass. The guards who had accompanied her from the jailhouse ordered her to sit on a bench outside the door of the DA's office, and one of the guards knocked on the door.

"Come," said a deep voice from inside, and the guard stuck his head in to announce Laura's arrival, presumably. She had no idea why she was here. She had no court business today that she knew about. A guard had simply collared her and told her to be ready to go in five minutes.

Gooseflesh rose on her bare arms as she waited on the hard bench. The county jail was stifling, and the two-mile ride over in the back of the van had been even worse, but now, in the cool, white air-conditioned corridors of the courthouse, she was freezing.

The district attorney emerged from his office. "Would you like to wait in here, Mrs. Turner?" he said, indicating the inside of his office with his large, perfectly manicured fingers. "Your attorney, Mr. Stanhope, has been contacted and is on his way down here."

"All right," she said, glad for a chance to get out of the chilly public corridor. She shuffled into the district attorney's office and was led by the guard to the chair in front of his desk. At a nod from the guard, she sat down.

Ron Leonard was seated next to the desk, which instantly made Laura regret her choice to come in. The DA instructed the guard to wait outside. Then he came around and sat on the corner of his desk, clasping his wrist with his other large hand and assuming a posture of casual familiarity.

"Mrs. Turner," he began in an affable tone, "we'd like to talk with you."

Alarm bells went off in Laura's head. "What am I doing here?" she said harshly. "Where is my attorney? I am supposed to have an attorney present."

DA Jackson raised his hands in an attitude of surrender. "Absolutely right," he said. "And, as I said, he's on his way."

Laura looked at him with narrowed yes. She waited without saying a word.

"No," DA Jackson went on, "we don't want to question you. On the contrary, we have kind of a strange agenda today, especially where a murder suspect is concerned. You see, Detective Leonard here has a theory about you that is very interesting. Hard to credit, I admit, but interesting. He thinks Mr. Vanese is lying, and that you're telling the truth. He thinks you're innocent."

Laura felt his words like a blow. She looked at Ron Leonard, who glanced up at her, the usually dispassionate expression in his eyes wavering for a moment as he met her startled gaze.

"Now, I try to be open-minded," said the DA, "but I admit, I need a little help with this one. So, we thought we'd try his theory out on you, see if it rings any bells. I mean, clearly, somebody hired Herman Powell to kill your husband. But let's just say, for a moment, that it wasn't you. Detective?"

Ron Leonard cleared his throat and consulted his notes. Laura tried to focus her attention on him. But in spite of herself, hope was rising in her heart. Could this man who had seemed so hostile finally have realized it was all a mistake? Her mind raced forward, to her release, to her reunion with Michael, to . . . For the millionth time she thought of Marta's visit, of her description of Bob Gerster. It had to be Ian. But how could it be? If it was . . .

The DA noticed Laura's gaze drifting anxiously away. "Mrs. Turner," he asked, "are you curious about this?"

Laura inhaled deeply. "Yes, please," she said, sounding to her own ears like a child in a nursery asking for more pudding. Detective Leonard did not have the smooth, courtroom-honed manner of the DA. He began to put forth his information in a stolid, clumsy tone.

"Do you know that Ian Turner's first wife, Gabriella, and his son, Phillip, died in a fire set, presumably, by a serial arsonist?"

"Detective," the DA said sharply, "no questions, please. We are just putting forth a theory here."

"Of course I know that," Laura said flatly.

"Do you . . ." Ron Leonard regrouped. "Mr. Turner's brother, Jason, is a firefighter. Although he denies it, I have reason to think that Jason Turner may have told his brother all about the arsonist's MO, his signature, so to speak."

"So what," Laura said coldly.

"While Stuart Short, the arsonist who was convicted, denied setting any of the fires, I think it's possible that he did not, indeed, set this particular fire."

Laura stared at him. Her mouth was dry, her heart thundering. They were making it up. They were trying to trick her. "This has nothing to do with me," she managed to say.

"You and Mr. Turner claimed to have met by chance, several months ago, and that he knew nothing about you. But

I have a witness, a man in Barbados, whose daughter received a book from Ian Turner. A book of yours. And Turner told her that he knew you, that he was coming to see you. All this, supposedly before you even met. Now everybody around here wants to think that you and Turner were in cahoots long before Jimmy died. But I say, what if you weren't?"

It took all her will to keep her face impassive. Pictures were rushing through her head. Ian pretending he didn't know she was an author. Ian reciting her story to Michael, claiming to have just bought the book. Marta telling her about Bob Gerster, who had sought out all the personal information he could about Laura Hastings. "So what," she said in a whisper.

Ron Leonard leaned forward and stared at her. "Laura," he said, and the sound of her name on his lips shook her. It sounded like a friend speaking to her. "What if Ian was obsessed with you? What if he eliminated his wife and your husband just so that he could get to you? And you didn't know anything about it."

Laura shook her head.

"Why? Did you ever ask yourself why he was so insistent on marriage right away? He was, wasn't he?"

"Don't answer that, Mrs. Turner. No questions, detective," said the DA piously.

"He had to have you. He was willing to do anything. Remove any obstacle from his path. His wife, your husband . . ."

She tried to look back at him without flinching. "That's ridiculous," she breathed. And then, with a sense of relief, she realized why. "Ian's son, Phillip, was killed in that fire, Mr. Leonard. Now, I realize you don't have any children, but let me just tell you—"

Ron Leonard pounced. "Phillip Turner was supposed to be at a ball game that night. But unbeknownst to his father, Gabriella Turner decided he was sick and kept him home."

Laura stared back at him. The band of pain around her head tightened several notches. She could feel her eyelid twitching from the throbbing behind her eye.

"I'm going to find the money," Ron said. "I'm going to find the way he paid Herman Powell, and I'm going to nail him. But as it stands, it looks as if the two of you were in it together. If you didn't have anything to do with it, you've got to save yourself. For the sake of your son. Why should you take the blame if you didn't have anything to do with Jimmy's death?"

The DA looked at his detective curiously. He was proceeding according to plan, but there was something in Ron Leonard's manner . . . as if he really didn't think this woman was involved. "Detective," he said in an admonishing tone.

"But Ian did," Ron said, slamming his hand down on the desk. "Goddammit, I know he did. Can't you see? If you help us get him, you can save yourself. You and your son can leave here. Can get away from him while you still have a chance."

There was a commotion coming from the outer office and then a sudden knock on DA Jackson's door. A frazzled-looking young woman poked her head in. "Sorry to bother you, sir," she said to Clyde Jackson.

A man was bellowing in the outer office. "Where is my client? I demand to see her at once!"

"It's Mr. Stanhope," the secretary said apologetically.

DA Jackson nodded. "Let him in."

Laura tore her gaze from Ron Leonard's and looked up as Curtis Stanhope steamed through the door, wearing a lime-green-colored linen jacket and a tie with seahorses on it.

"What the hell is my client doing in here, Mr. Prosecutor?" Stanhope demanded. "Is this how you do business in this one-horse county, 'cause let me tell you something—"

"We haven't done anything improper here," the DA said coolly.

Stanhope turned to Laura. "Have they been questioning you?"

Laura hesitated, then shook her head. "Not exactly."

"Why didn't you insist on having me present?" he boomed. Then he shook his head in disgust. "If you've got

291

something to say to Mrs. Turner, you say it through me. I told you I would be here by noon. How dare you bring her in here without me? I'll have this case thrown right out of court. Mrs. Turner, don't you understand your rights?"

"It doesn't matter," Laura said dully.

"You be quiet," said Stanhope. "I'll do all the talking."

"We just wanted to keep Mrs. Turner informed of our thinking," said DA Jackson.

"Well, you can inform me," said Stanhope.

"Certainly, Counselor. We've just uncovered certain things about Mrs. Turner's husband we thought she might want to know."

"In other words, you're trying to get her to squeal on him. Did they offer some kind of deal?" Stanhope demanded, turning on Laura. "You didn't agree to anything with these people, did you?"

Laura shook her head.

"I almost wish you had," cried Stanhope. "Because if they had the audacity . . ."

"Now just a minute," said Jackson.

While the two lawyers argued, Laura looked away. Ron Leonard caught her eye with a warning glance.

Laura knew what he wanted. He wanted her to think about the things he had told her. As if, she thought in despair, she could think about anything else.

CHAPTER FORTY-FOUR

The ride back from the courthouse was a blank in Laura's mind. Before she was led from the courthouse to the waiting station wagon, which was the county car for women prisoners, Stanhope had advised her to disregard everything they'd said, that they were just trying to dupe her. It was the oldest trick in the book to try to get one person to implicate another. Once you admit Ian was in on it, you're both finished, Stanhope said. And the moment Stanhope said that, Laura knew. The lawyer thought she was guilty. He was defending her, but not because he believed in her innocence. For Stanhope it was some kind of intellectual game—to outwit the district attorney. They were playing mind games. A game for which Stanhope would collect a large fee, win or lose. It had nothing to do with guilt or innocence. He thought the same thing the DA thought—that she and Ian had conspired to have Jimmy murdered.

Stanhope had been impatient, angry to be called away from other business to have to come down here for this. His florid face was sweaty. Don't tell them anything, he said. And the next time, refuse to leave your cell until I get here. Or make sure you talk to me. This was a trip for nothing, he admonished her, like an angry parent. They can say anything they want to try to break you. They'll make up things just to confuse you. You just keep quiet. Don't give them any ammunition. She heard herself apologizing to him as he snapped his briefcase shut. And then the guards were herding her toward the garage in the courthouse. She understood what Stanhope was saying. He was the one who did not understand, she thought as the ride began.

Now the car pulled into the bowels of the county jail, and Laura was prodded to get out. Numbly, automatically, she held her breath against the smell of the jail as the door was unlocked. She submitted to a search, shuffled back to her cell, felt herself thrust inside, the cage locked again. It didn't matter to her. Her mind was not there.

Marta's innocent remark yesterday had set off this chain of fear and doubt. And now, all the information dumped on her by Ron Leonard . . . The detective had looked at her so sincerely. Somehow Laura knew that he believed it. That it wasn't a ploy on his part. He had come to see her as innocent. As a victim, just as Jimmy had been. A victim of the man she had married.

Laura tried to think clearly. She thought of Ian, about the way they'd met. That day on the dock. Michael had wandered over to his boat. There was no way he could have arranged that, no way he could have foreseen it. It had seemed so innocent, so . . . so much by chance. It was chance, she told herself. She was satisfied of that. She might never have gone down there that day. He might have sailed off, and they would never even have encountered each other. But, chance or not, there was no getting around it. When they had met, he had pretended not to know her. Even though he'd known who she was. He'd known where she lived. He'd known her books by heart. Even then.

Laura shivered as if the stifling cell were cold. He was Bob Gerster. He had lied to find out about her, lied when he'd found her. If all of that was a lie, then what else? She looked down at her hand. They allowed you to wear your wedding ring in here. She stared at the ring Ian had given her.

294

She pictured his glowing face as he'd pledged himself to her. For better, for worse. And what could be worse than all of this? Ron Leonard's theory pounded in her brain. How much had Ian wanted her? Enough to incinerate his own wife? To accidentally kill his own son? Enough to hire a gunman, to execute . . . No, she thought. *No.* No one could ever want anyone else that much. It was insane.

Insane. The word made the flesh rise on the back of her neck. She thought of the passion with which he made love to her. Madly. Desperately. No. That was desire, not insanity. If he was insane, then she was insane, too. For she had wanted him just as much, thrown caution to the winds just as readily.

And this was Ian. Ian, who believed in her, who was standing by her no matter what the police said. Ian, who refused to credit their accusations. Despite the lies told by Dominick Vanese that had led to her arrest, Ian was steadfast. Even though he hardly knew her, he refused to think the worst of her. Didn't she owe him as much? But even as she thought it, she remembered Michael, sobbing at the wedding. *Why are you marrying this stranger?* And she realized there was one simple explanation for his utter faith in her. The only way he could know for sure that she hadn't done it was if he had done it himself.

She shook her head against it. There had to be some explanation. You read about people like that, of course. A person could present one face to the world and have a secret self. But she had seen his secret self. What could be more secret than the man she saw in the throes of love? Holding her, whispering, crying out in the bittersweet pleasure of their lovemaking. Why shouldn't she just believe that it was his love for her that gave him such conviction, such trust in her? Love was supposed to move mountains. The Bible said, Love bears all things, believes all things, hopes all things, endures all things. So why couldn't she return that love in kind and dismiss these horrible insinuations? They were meant just to undermine her, confuse her. Stanhope said so. Her love must be so weak, compared to his.

Then she thought again of Marta's words. Bob Gerster. He's a good-looking guy, but he looks like he got hit by a truck. The chills were running all through her now. And her stomach was roiling. She crawled to the toilet and waited, feeling the nausea grow, threaten, force its unnatural way up. Then she vomited. Everything inside her turned inside out, into that dingy, stained bowl.

Sweat broke out on her forehead as she struggled to her feet, flushed the mess away, rinsed out her mouth with the rusty stream from the faucet. She was empty inside. Empty. She felt dizzy and groped her way over to her bunk. She lay down on the scratchy blanket, staring at the wall, which had the logos of other inmates scratched into the graying paint job. "R.W. and K.L.," encircled by a misshapen heart. "Dykes 4-ever," scrawled defiantly near the toilet. Laura and Ian, she thought bitterly. Her head was throbbing, and she closed her eyes, to try to blot it all out. She wished she had a sleeping pill. Something, anything, to relieve her feverish brain and allow her to stop thinking. Stop thinking that perhaps, perhaps, all unknowing she had married a murderer.

CHAPTER FORTY-FIVE

"I just want to say three words to you," breathed Daphne, Candy's personal salesperson at Rulene's department store. "White leather suit." She clasped her hands and waited for her words to register.

Candy, who was seated on a pink satin slipper chair in the designer salon, shook her head. "I better not." Then she narrowed her eyes at Daphne. "Soft?" she demanded.

Daphne closed her eyes, smiled, and nodded like a Buddha. "Like butter. Like silk. No one but you could do it justice."

Goddamn Richard, Candy thought. She hated to worry about money at a time like this. When there was something perfect for her in the store, she shouldn't have to haggle with herself over whether or not to buy it. It was demeaning. It was his stupid fault for getting hooked on the casinos. When they got all this mess straightened out, she was not going to let him go back there. But meanwhile, there was the leather suit, and Daphne, waiting. And there was her private account. The secret one she had added to every time he gave her money, for just such a rainy day as this. Candy took a deep breath.

"All right," she decreed. "I'll try it."

Daphne let out a little shriek of pleasure. She loved to wait on Candy, who was a perfect size six and looked absolutely ideal in everything she tried. And when Candy looked that great, she had to have it. Of course the commissions were important to Daphne, but it was the satisfaction of pleasing Candy, the love of her work, as it were, that made her thrill to see Candy coming.

As Daphne disappeared into the back to find the white leather suit, Candy relaxed on the slipper chair and idly assessed the other shoppers in the cushioned silence of the designer salon. You could tell the ones who had stumbled in here by accident. There was a pathetic size fourteen with frizzy brown hair over by the business suits who obviously had taken a wrong turn on her way to the foundation garments department. And a wan, thin girl about seventeen who could be pretty with a lot of help, but who would never be able to afford this stuff. She was fingering the sequined fabric of an evening gown longingly, but she didn't even dare to pull it off the rack and hold it up to herself in front of the mirror. You better not pull that out, Candy thought. You mess up one little sequin on that dress and you're going to be flame-broiling Whoppers at the Burger King until you're thirty-five just to pay for it.

Candy checked her nails for any possible chips in the polish and then glanced around again. There was another woman in there, fortyish, platinum pageboy, well preserved. Good clothes. Probably a tennis player. She at least had the bucks to be here, but it was a shame she was so old. The trick was to be young and have the money. Otherwise it was a waste even to have these great clothes. Who looked at an old hag like that?

Candy frowned, irritated at the thought of the money. And the police. That was even worse. But Richard could get himself out of it. He was just panicking a little bit. The police didn't arrest people like them. They were rich. It was just a little accounting thing. And that was Richard's specialty. There weren't a lot of things he was good at, Candy admitted to herself with a yawn. But he was good with money. Meanwhile she had enough in her own little hideaway account to tide her over. She wasn't about to bail him out. Oh no. But she could cover her needs for the time being.

Daphne emerged from behind a brocade curtain with the white leather suit on a hanger. She held it up, and Candy clapped her hands over her mouth. "Oh, you're right," she said, reaching out her manicured fingers and wiggling them like a child wanting licorice. "Let me try it."

In no time she had sequestered herself in the fitting room, slid the fragrant leather over her silken underwear, and reentered the salon to twirl in front of Daphne and anyone else in there who wanted to know how clothes like this were supposed to look. Daphne nearly swooned at the sight, and Candy giggled at her effect.

"Daphne, you're a witch. All right. You know my card number. Ring it up," she drawled as if the thousand-dollar suit were a pack of gum at the supermarket. She returned to the dressing room to get back into her everyday clothes.

As Candy emerged from the dressing rooms and walked over to the French Provincial desk that served as a counter in the designer salon, Daphne looked up at her with an apprehensive look in her eye.

"I'm ready to sign," said Candy, draping the suit carelessly over the spindly chair beside the desk.

Daphne leapt from her chair and scooped up the suit, gingerly replacing it in a plastic bag and hanging it on a rack near her desk. Candy felt a chill run up and down her spine at the sight. In that instant she knew there was a problem.

"Daphne, what is the matter?" she demanded imperiously.

"Your card's been canceled, Candy," Daphne mumbled, checking the suit through the plastic for any errant traces of makeup or lipstick. "I double-checked."

"Well, that's impossible," Candy protested, but her voice faltered. He didn't, she thought. That son of a bitch. Without even telling me. I'll kill him.

"Let me use your phone," Candy said. She did not like the way Daphne was looking at her. As if her glamour had suddenly crumbled in front of her eyes.

299

Daphne indicated the phone. "I'll just see about this other customer," she said sympathetically.

Candy plunked herself down on the chair and dialed Richard's office. Adelaide Murphy answered, "Mr. Walsh's office."

"Let me talk to that bastard, Adelaide," Candy muttered without preamble, "and don't tell me he's in some goddamn meeting. This is Mrs. Walsh. Get him on the phone now."

"I'm sorry, Mrs. Walsh," said the homely older woman Candy had hand-picked for her husband to avoid the temptation of any office romance. "He left on his business trip. Didn't he tell you?"

Candy felt sweat breaking out on her palms. "What business trip?"

"I don't know. He said he had to meet with a client in Texas. He made all the arrangements himself."

Daphne glanced over at her, and Candy tried to keep her face impassive. "All right. There must be some misunderstanding. I'll look into it." She hung up the phone and sat staring a moment, the phone still in her hand.

Daphne wandered over and cocked her head at Candy. "Everything all right?" she asked.

No, you stupid cow, Candy thought. You can see perfectly well that everything is not all right, and you're loving it, aren't you? Candy smiled at Daphne. "Everything's fine. There's just been some stupid clerical error. Can I make one more quick call?"

Daphne had seen this situation plenty of times before—women cut off by their husbands—and she was ninety-nine percent sure that Candy's shopping days were over. At times like these, Daphne was glad that she had a good job and supported herself. There was a temptation, at such a moment, to make the customer squirm. After all, hadn't Candy Walsh always treated her like one of the queen's peasants? But, you could never be sure. There was always that one percent chance that it was a clerical error. And she didn't want to lose Candy's commissions. No way.

"Of course," Daphne said graciously.

Candy dialed home, but there was no answer. She pressed the code for her messages. Richard's voice, tinny and repentant, came on the line. "Babe, by now you probably know I'm gone. There was too much of a mess for me to ever straighten out, and I just couldn't face explaining it all to you. The cops are all over me because of this business with Laura's money. The shit hit the fan, so to speak. If I stuck around, I'd never get loose from it. I left you a letter here at home, with instructions on what you can sell and what we owe. I'm afraid you're going to come up a little light. But I know you'll be okay, babe. You're a beautiful, fabulous woman, and you'll land on your feet. I know you're going to hate me for this, but I found that little account you had stashed away, and I needed it to get started again. I'm going to miss you like crazy, babe . . ."

Holding the phone to her ear, Candy stared across the inlaid surface of the desk at the white leather suit, hanging in its plastic bag. Furious tears filled her eyes as she gazed at its buttery surface. It might as well have been locked away from her in a steel cage, for all the hope she had now of ever taking it home.

CHAPTER FORTY-SIX

"Laura Turner," the guard said, rapping on the bars of her cage. "The warden wants to see you. Right now."

Laura's eyes shot open, but her head was fuzzy with confusion. How long had she slept? Her mouth was disgusting, furry from the episode of vomiting. She felt too weak to move. What now? she thought. What else could there be?

"Hurry up," he said. "We're taking you down."

Obediently Laura stumbled to her feet. She needed to urinate, but she wasn't about to do it in front of the uniformed man at the door. "I'm coming," she mumbled.

"What does he want?" she asked, splashing a trickle of water from the sink on her face and tucking her hair behind her ears.

"I don't know, lady. He's the warden. He's not my best friend. He doesn't confide in me. Now move it."

* * *

Laura sat on the wooden chair opposite Warden Ferguson and stared at the man in disbelief. Ferguson was a thin, balding man with half glasses. His manner was mild and unthreatening. She had heard that he was severe, brooked no infractions. This was the first time she had seen him. He looked more like a schoolteacher than a prison warden.

"Do you understand what I'm telling you?" he asked.

Laura shook her head.

"This came to me from the prosecutor's office. It's called a complaint." He held out a piece of paper, and Laura stared at it. "The charges against you have been dropped. You're free to go."

"I don't understand," she said. "I was just there this morning."

Ferguson's narrow lips curved into a little smile. "I assume you have no objection to leaving. Most of our guests here don't object to being freed from our hospitality."

Laura knew he was making a joke, but her head was spinning. She felt as if she were being bounced about like a ball on a roulette wheel. "I just . . . How can it be?"

Warden Ferguson, who obviously considered all his words carefully, pondered for a moment and then offered her a minimal explanation. "Apparently, the witness who had identified you came forward today and retracted his statement. He claimed to have made a mistake. The DA was none too happy about it, I understand. But without the testimony of the witness, they don't have enough evidence to hold you. Now, any more than that you're going to have to find out from your own lawyer."

"He admitted he was lying? But why did he say those things about me in the first place?" Laura cried.

The warden stood up. "Mrs. Turner, this piece of paper says you're free to go. I'd get out of here if I were you. You can pick up your clothes and your belongings at the clerk's out front. The guard will escort you. Good luck to you."

Laura rose to her feet, not knowing what to feel. She didn't trust them. It was like a terrible joke, and the punch line was going to hit her in the solar plexus. Just kidding, they would say. Back in your cage.

"Let's go," said the guard, but his tone was less brusque. She was a free woman now. She followed him to the female clerk behind a Plexiglas window and numbly showed the clerk her paper from the warden.

The clerk disappeared for a moment, as if she had been in the post office, looking for some registered mail. My belongings, Laura thought. She remembered that night. They'd been playing a game. Uno. She'd been wearing jeans and scuffed-up Dock-Sides on her feet. She had no belongings, nothing. She had left everything behind. Michael's face swam into her mind, his eyes huge with fear. What have I done to you? she thought.

The clerk returned and shoved a parcel under the window. "Please make sure these are your things before you leave the window," she said.

Laura's hands trembled as she tore open the envelope. There they were, her old faded jeans, her T-shirt, her deck shoes. She had an impulse to embrace them to her chest. It was as if they were old friends, arrived to comfort her.

"Put them on in here," said the guard, indicating a one-person visitors restroom. "You can leave your jumpsuit in the bin there."

No instructions had ever sounded so sweet to her ears. She went into the restroom, and because she could, she locked the door behind her.

When she was dressed, she came out of the restroom and looked around. The guard smiled at the sight of her in her grubby summer clothes. She looked as if she were about to go outside and dig around in her garden. He escorted her out into the waiting area.

"Is there someone you would like to call?" he asked, nodding toward the phone. "Your husband, to come get you?"

"No," she said sharply. Then she looked around. "I don't know," she added helplessly.

"You're free to use the phone," he said. "If you don't have a ride, or any money, a cab can be arranged to take you home at the prison's expense." He extended a hand to her. "Good luck to you."

Awkwardly Laura shook his hand, reflexively unwilling to be rude, even here, even after all this. She looked around, feeling utterly alone, not knowing where she would turn next. Suddenly she heard a familiar voice cry, "Mom!"

She turned and saw him, careening toward her, banging into chairs, panic in his eyes. She stumbled forward, and in a minute she was holding him. She had never felt anything so sweet in all her life. She inhaled the smell of him, his clean hair, his perfect, familiar smell. "Oh, baby," she said. She clutched at his clothes, felt they were damp. "You're wet," she said.

"It's raining," he mumbled into her shoulder.

That's right, she thought. It was beginning to rain this morning, when they drove her back. She had a vague memory of the windshield wipers, clocking off the distance. It didn't matter to her then what the weather was. She wasn't going anywhere, or so she'd thought. And now—now she was holding Michael.

"What are you doing here?" she cried. "How did you get here?"

"Gram and Poppy brought me," he told her, still mumbling into her shoulder.

She looked over his soft hair and saw Dolores, standing in the corner by the pay phone.

Laura looked again, scarcely believing her eyes. She lifted Michael in her arms and carried him over toward Dolores, who met her gaze defiantly. It was the first time they had met face-to-face, except in the courthouse, since the week Jimmy had died.

"Hello, Dolores," Laura said stiffly. "Thank you for bringing Michael."

"Let's get out of here," said Dolores. "This place gives me the creeps."

"Gladly," Laura said with a tight-lipped smile.

Still carrying Michael, nuzzling him reassuringly, she followed her mother-in-law through the foyer and out the door of the county jail. They stood under the portico. It was drizzling outside and gray. Sidney's El Dorado was parked by the curb at the end of the walkway, beyond the impossibly

305

well-kept lawn in front of the jail. Laura glimpsed Sidney, sitting at the wheel of the car, wearing sunglasses. He glanced at them and gave a little wave.

Laura flapped one hand awkwardly. She was still holding her son in her arms.

"Well, you look all right," Dolores said shortly. "We came to give you a ride home."

"Why?" Laura asked. You hate me, she wanted to add. But she didn't, because of Michael. "How did you know I was being released?" she asked, disoriented by her sudden freedom and the totally unexpected arrival of her in-laws.

"Vince Moore called me," said Dolores. "After Mr. Vanese retracted his statement. He figured we'd want to know."

"I don't understand this," said Laura, shaking her head. "I don't understand why Vanese said those things in the first place. Or why he took them back. Did Chief Moore say?"

"Who knows," Dolores said irritably. "He changed his mind."

Laura set Michael down on the ground beside her. He clung to her leg, and she clutched his shoulder. She realized, in amazement, that Dolores was squirming on the subject of Vanese. A cold little knot formed in her stomach. "Dolores? Do you know why?"

Dolores did not meet her gaze. She squinted out across the lawn. She opened her mouth to speak, then hesitated. Then she tried again. Laura stared at Dolores, who was struggling to find the right words.

"I went to see Mr. Vanese," Dolores said carefully. "I wanted to talk to him about all this. But the more we talked, the more he understood that maybe he had made a mistake."

"Wait a minute," Laura said, unable to keep the sarcasm from her tone. "Back up. Are you saying that you talked Vanese into retracting his statement? Excuse me if I find that a little hard to swallow. You were thrilled when they arrested me, and you know it as well as I do. You couldn't wait to take Michael away from me!"

Dolores assumed an injured expression. "I thought about it long and hard. I put my own feelings aside for Michael's sake," she said belligerently. "It's true I've been against you. But you are the mother of my grandson. If Mr. Vanese made a mistake . . . If you did not do what Mr. Vanese said . . ." Her voice trailed away.

"You were the one screaming for blood. You wanted to see me in the electric chair, as I remember," Laura cried.

Standing beside his mother, his face pressed into the leg of her jeans, Michael let out a groan. Instantly Laura was filled with guilt. He is being torn apart, she thought. Stop. Not in front of him. Don't put him in the middle of this ugliness.

Dolores shifted uncomfortably. "What difference does it make who said what? It's all over now."

"What difference?" Laura looked at her with disbelief. Then she lowered her voice. "I intend to find out exactly why that man lied about me!"

"Mistakes were made," said Dolores. She turned and looked Laura in the eye, daring her to contradict. "Mr. Vanese thought he was acting out of friendship. But he made a mistake. And now his mistake has been corrected."

Laura peered wonderingly at Dolores. "Friendship? Friendship for whom?" she asked.

Dolores glared back at her, but her lip trembled.

"For you?" Laura asked.

There was nothing subtle or covert about Dolores. The look on her face was an admission. Laura stifled her first impulse, to grab her by the throat. Her eyes narrowed, piercing through her mother-in-law's guilty defiance. "He's a friend of yours?"

"Of Sidney's. I didn't know it. I didn't know anything about it," Dolores said quickly. "At first I thought Mr. Vanese was telling the truth. But then, when I realized what he was doing, I went and told him we only wanted the truth."

"Sidney's?" Laura cried, wounded afresh by the idea of her father-in-law, the ever-kindly Sidney, orchestrating such a betrayal. "Sidney always seemed like my friend."

"He didn't do it against you, exactly. He thought it was what I wanted," Dolores said shortly. "But I don't want lies. That's not the way."

Laura could hardly believe it. They had arranged for this. Sidney had convinced this Vanese person to lie, so that she would go to jail. It was hard to comprehend it, to take it all in. It seemed as if she were surrounded by unfathomable wells of ill will, and she felt a surge of desire for revenge. What had she ever done to these people except to love their son? Their contempt for her rights, for her well-being, was monstrous.

Laura stared into Dolores's eyes, ready to lash out, summoning the words. Dolores looked back, ashamed but unblinking. Then, despite her fury, her righteous anger, Laura recognized the bottom line. Dolores hadn't had to tell. She could have kept quiet and let Laura remain in jail, but she hadn't. When push came to shove, she had acted fairly. She had done the right thing. Even for her enemy, the daughter-in-law she hated. What more could she expect of this woman?

Unsmiling, Laura reached her hand out, and Dolores flinched. Lightly, briefly, Laura rested a hand on her forearm. "Thank you," she said.

Dolores looked at her warily. "Do you want a ride home?" she asked in a harsh tone. "You can take your son home with you if you want."

A television van was pulling up in front of the county jail, and a female reporter in a raincoat and jogging shoes was emerging from the front seat, followed by a cameraman.

Laura thought quickly. "Can I ask you to keep him for me a little while longer?"

"Of course," Dolores said sharply.

"No," Michael wailed. "I want to go home with you."

Laura crouched down and held his face. "Listen to me. It's only for an hour or two. Go with Grandma right now, and when I come to get you, soon, we will never be separated anymore. I promise."

"Please . . ."

"Now. Before these people start hounding us. And Dolores, I need money for a cab."

Dolores began fumbling in her pocketbook, handing her bills.

"Please get him away from this," Laura said grimly as another car with a newspaper logo on the side pulled up. "I'll deal with these people."

"All right," said Dolores.

"But when I come for him . . .," Laura added warningly.

Dolores sighed. "He's your son."

"Please take him, then. I'll be there soon," said Laura, and she ushered Michael off with his grandmother as the reporters started advancing on her.

CHAPTER FORTY-SEVEN

Ron Leonard tried to keep his mind on his questions, but it was difficult. Ginger Cook, the head of the county summer youth program, was wearing red shorts and a white polo shirt, and her summer blond hair was arranged in a French braid, which was Ron's hands-down favorite for women's hair. The only thing was, she was chewing gum . . . Just as well not to show any interest, Ron thought, considering the reason he was here.

"Okay, these are the complaints we got," the young woman said matter-of-factly, handing Ron a few pieces of paper over the desk.

Ron couldn't help noticing that her tanned fingers were free of diamonds or a wedding band as he took the paper from her. Ron was investigating charges of sexual harassment against one of the county's longtime athletic coaches in the summer program. He hated this case. He considered it rinky-dink and a nuisance. But since it was a countywide program, it fell to him to look into it. He tried not to show his distaste, however. This Ginger person would probably jump up on a soapbox and start lecturing him about insensitivity.

Ginger crossed her arms on the desk and watched him scanning the complaints. "He said some things he shouldn't have to the girls. Apparently he used some pretty crude language, and these mothers complained."

Ron stifled a sigh. Here it comes, he thought, keeping his gaze on the pages in his hand. The speech.

"I'm not trying to make excuses for him," she said, "but he's from the old school, you know. Sometimes he's got that locker room mentality, and he doesn't care if he's talking to girls or boys. I mean, I can see where these mothers might object, but you might look at it that he just treats the girls the same way he treats the boys. It seems like that's the opposite of discrimination. He's a very dedicated coach."

Ron looked up at her with interest. These days he often felt that the war between the sexes had become nuclear. It was sort of surprising—refreshing, really—to hear a woman defend a man like that.

The phone on her desk rang, and Ginger picked it up, snapping her gum. Ron sighed and resumed studying the complaints.

"Just a minute," Ginger said. "It's for you."

Ron leaned over and took the phone, accidentally brushing her fingertips. "Ron Leonard," he said.

Ron listened as DA Jackson filled him in on the recantation of Dominick Vanese and the release of Laura Turner from the county jail.

Ron swore and then looked up apologetically at Ginger. She gave him a sly smile. He turned away from her and spoke quietly into the phone. "Well, I still think that bastard Turner was involved. It's time I took the gloves off." He and the DA agreed to confer when he got back. Then Ron looked at Ginger. "Can I make a call?" he asked.

"Sure." She nodded.

Ron dialed Vince Moore's office at the Cape Christian police station. When he got the chief on the line, Vince was apologetic about Vanese. "It's not your fault," said Ron. "It was all going to come out sooner or later. Listen, can you get a man over to that boat of Turner's, and make sure he stays there until I arrive?"

"I'll do it myself," Vince said before he hung up.

Ron turned back to Ginger. "Look, I'd like to talk to you some more about this, but right now I'm gonna have to go. Can we table this until tomorrow?"

Ginger nodded, and Ron stood up. "You be careful out there," she said with a smile, and Ron felt his heart do a queer little flip.

The cab pulled up to the dock, and Laura saw that they were stopped only two spaces from her own car, which was parked there. He was on the boat. She figured he was holed up there, cut off from the world. She paid the driver and got out. It was still drizzling, and the pier was empty of people. There were lights on at Boat People, but no one seemed to be coming or going on the dock. This was not one of those misty summer rains with the sun right behind it. This day was chilly and muggy at the same time, and there was no indication that it would clear.

She walked down the pier toward the boat, thinking about that first day they'd met. Michael had bounded aboard his boat—Ian couldn't have known that would happen. That had to have been an accident. And if he hadn't arranged that, then maybe . . .

Her head was pounding from thinking about it, from trying to make excuses for him. There was no more time for it. She reached the slip and climbed aboard. The deck was slippery. The minute she opened the hatch, she heard his voice shouting from below. She crept down the ladder. He was pacing the narrow confines of the main cabin, gesturing angrily as he spoke into the cordless phone.

"No, you listen, Stanhope," he cried. "I've been chasing you all over the goddamned Delaware Valley, and I'm fed up. For what we're paying you, I want you here, working on my wife's case. What? . . . No . . . No, I didn't hear." Ian stopped pacing and gripped the phone in both hands. "What happened at the jail?"

"Ian," she said.

Ian's head snapped around, and he saw her standing there. He did not speak. She could hear the squawk of

312

Stanhope's voice on the phone as Ian dropped the receiver onto the counter. He stared at her, and then he closed his eyes again, as if she were an apparition, her imagined presence a cruel joke. Then his eyes opened with dawning amazement.

"Laura," he said. "Oh, my God. I'm not dreaming." He moved toward her, his arms open. "How can you be here?"

She stepped back, away from him, into the galley, trapped by the teak lockers behind her, but he did not press forward. She studied his weary, bruised countenance. She felt the familiar quickening of her pulses at the sight of him. Even ravaged as he appeared, he exerted a sexual magnetism over her. It was a kind of madness, she thought. Lust.

"They dropped the charges," she said. "Vanese took back his statement. Told the police it was a mistake." Her tone was scornful.

"But darling," he cried. "Oh, thank God."

This time he did reach for her, and she backed away from him. "Don't touch me," she said. "Get away."

The look in his eyes was more startled than angry. "What's the matter? What is it? We couldn't have even hoped for this."

"Just get back. I mean it."

Ian read the fierceness in her eyes and stepped back, giving her some room. "All right," he said. "Okay. Okay. You've been through so much. Are you angry that I wasn't there to pick you up? I'm sorry. I didn't know. I just got through to Stanhope. I probably should have been listening to the radio, but I was so keyed up I put a tape in to try and calm down. Laura, if I had known . . ."

She looked at him skeptically. She was trying to see him in this new light, the light of all she now knew. He still looked the same, seemed the same. It was strange how that could be. His voice was still soothing.

"I didn't want you to know," she said harshly, and for the first time it was as if she had nicked him. The weary glaze in his blue eyes cleared, and he winced.

"Why not? Why wouldn't you want me to know? How did you get here?"

"It doesn't matter. I took a cab. By the way, I want the keys to my car. Now."

He did not protest or say "our car." He simply pointed to a dish on the countertop. "There," he said. His tone was cautious.

She picked up the keys and put them in her pocket. "I want the keys to my house, too," she said, grasping the extra set she had given him. "I don't want you there anymore. I'm going to be leaving this town, with Michael. With any luck, I'll be gone by tonight. Until then, I want you to stay away."

His face froze and his eyes turned wary. He leaned toward her, peering at her. The confines of the boat suddenly seemed frightening to her. She scuttled sideways and reached out for the ladder, as if to have one hand on the means of escape.

Ian shook his head. "God, I hate to see you look at me that way. You can let go of that step. I'll stand here." He placed his hands on the countertop between them. "Laura, I can see you're very angry. I mean, I'm sorry I wasn't there. I didn't know." He ran one hand through his dark hair, shaking his head. "This ordeal. It's been awful. But, now that it's over . . . Let's talk about it. What did Vanese say? Why did he lie?"

"I'm not here to talk about Dominick Vanese's lies," she said. "I'm here to talk about yours. Your lies."

"My lies?" he protested. "Wait a minute."

"Yes. Yours." There was a silence between them, and she saw his eyelid twitch. A guilty tic. "Your lies," she repeated. "While I was in the county jail, Marta Eberhart came to see me," she said.

For just an instant she saw it flash in his blue eyes—recognition, entrapment, guilt. And then it was gone. He looked away, and her heart plummeted. Because in that instant she knew. And she realized she had been hoping against hope that it wouldn't be true. That he would withstand her assault. Prove her wrong. But that was not going to happen.

"That's right," she said. "You know her."

"Isn't she your editor?" he asked evenly. "I'm sure you mentioned her."

"You're still lying," she said. "Goddammit."

He met her gaze implacably, but the muscle twitched again under his eye. Then he looked down at his hands.

"Remember now, Mr. Gerster?"

The only sound on the boat was the rain, tapping on the deck. Ian closed his eyes. "Okay," he said with a sigh. "Will you let me explain?"

"You knew me," she said in a low voice. "You pretended it was an accident. You pretended that you just remembered me, but you knew all the time. How did you arrange our meeting? What were you going to do if I hadn't wandered down to the dock that day?"

"Can I explain?"

"No, you can't explain," she cried. "You lied to me every minute of the day. You went to my editor and you masqueraded as someone else. No one would do that who was . . . There's something very sick about that . . ."

"Yes," he said. "I was sick. I was very sick. I was sick with grief and sick with loneliness. Don't you know what that feels like?"

"Oh no," she said. "Don't try to suck me in with the old sympathy ploy. I'm not buying it. 'Are you an author? Oh, how interesting,'" she mimicked him. "'Children's books. You don't say.' You knew my books by heart," she cried.

"How do you know all this?" he demanded.

"The police know it, too," she said. "They figured out your scheme. You thought you were too smart for everybody. Well, maybe you were too smart for me . . ."

"Ron Leonard," he said. "That business in Barbados."

"Ron Leonard has a theory about you."

"And you believe him. After the way he has come after you?"

"He's not a liar," she said. "You are."

"I knew I should have told you," he said. He sat on one of the berths and ran his hands over his face and then looked up at her.

She tried to meet his gaze, but what she saw there undermined her. Now that she was facing him, it was so difficult to fit him, the Ian she had married, into the scheme in Ron Leonard's scenario. Setting his house on fire, murdering his wife and son, hiring a killer to do away with Jimmy . . . You just don't want to admit to yourself that you would marry such a monster, she thought.

"I did know about you," he said in a shaky voice. "When Phillip was so sick, Andrea, a woman I worked with, brought him some books to the hospital. One of them was yours. It was his favorite. He wanted me to read it again and again. And I opened the book and there you were. Your beautiful face on the dust jacket. I recognized you instantly, even after all those years. That face that once leaned over the rim of a pit and promised to save me. My guardian angel. There to help me again. I can't explain to you what those days were like. I sat there beside him, watching him tortured by pain, slipping away from me. Your book, your picture, became like a mantra to us both. Your face. I clung to your face. And then, he was gone. His body gave up the fight, and he vanished on me."

Laura tried not to see Phillip, the child in the hospital bed. But it was impossible not to picture him. She looked at Ian, wanted to reach out to him. But the horror that Ron Leonard had instilled in her head pulled her back. Did you put him in that hospital bed? she wondered. Was that part of your madness?

"Sometime, in the days after that, I thought about finding you. I was just going to thank you. I think . . . I made this plan to pretend to be someone else, just to find out about you. Bob Gerster. It gave me a plan. Something to think about other than . . ." He shook his head, squinting at the past in his memory. "God, it felt good to be someone else, just for a little while. I know it sounds crazy now, but I had this idea about you . . . that if I could find you . . ."

He sounded so sincere, and she felt herself weakening. Wanting to believe him. He's hustling you, Laura warned

316

herself. Don't fall for it again. What about Jimmy? she reminded herself. Don't forget Jimmy. "Funny you never even mentioned all this when we chanced to meet."

"It *was* chance," he insisted. "Well, maybe it wasn't. All right, I knew you were here, in this town, when I got here. And I was lingering here. Okay. I intended to find you. Even though I knew you had a husband and a child. It wasn't as if I wanted to seduce you or something. I just wanted to see you—tell you about everything."

"What would have possessed you to think that I would care anything about you, or your problems?" she rasped.

"Nothing. I don't know. I couldn't get you out of my head. Maybe it was some sort of telepathy. I mean, I know that sounds crazy, but maybe I knew that you were suffering, too . . ."

"Yes," Laura said flatly. "That is crazy."

"I know how it sounds. That's why I couldn't tell you. You found me first . . . and then it was too late to tell you . . . I knew what you would think."

"You couldn't possibly know what I would think. You were a complete stranger to me. God, I walked right into your trap."

Ian glared at her. "Wait a goddamn minute. There was no trap. Call it fate or chance if you want, but it was not a trap. When you walked up to my boat, I felt as if my knees were going to give way. It was like it was meant to be. Don't try to pretend you didn't want me, too. I could feel it the moment we met . . ."

She remembered how she felt. And his insistence that she remember infuriated her. Not only had she believed him, she had desired him. God help her, she had married him. "And how is it," she asked through clenched teeth, "that my husband happened to be conveniently dead when you came looking for me? Was that fate, too? Or did you give fate a hand?"

Ian rose to his feet and stared at her. White surrounded the piercing blue of his eyes. His face was frozen into an expression of wordless rage. She stared right back at him. Somebody had killed her husband, and here was the man the police suspected. The man she had married. Oh, God, I've done everything wrong. I have nothing left to lose. Then, instantly, she thought of Michael.

"No," Laura cried. She backed up toward the steps. His eyes were blazing.

Ian came around the counter toward her. He grabbed her arms, gripping them. "How dare you say that? After I stood by you. Believed in you. No matter what the police said, or anybody said, I believed in you. And now you want to blame me? I'm going to try to forget you said that, Laura. For both our sakes, I'm going to do my best."

"Don't touch me!" she shrieked. "Let me go!"

"What's going on down there?"

Laura looked up. The uniformed figure of a police officer loomed at the opening of the hatch. As he started down the ladder, his large black oxfords squeaking on the rubber grips of the steps, she recognized Chief Moore. What a difference a day makes, she thought. She had never been so glad to see anyone. She had to restrain herself from throwing her arms around him.

"Chief Moore," she cried.

Instantly Ian released her. Vince Moore awkwardly made his way down the steep steps to the cabin. His bulky figure seemed to fill up the confined space. In his day, Vince had been called on to separate plenty of couples, locked in their raw, seesaw battles, but this one was different from others. Usually he saw resentment in the angry faces of the husbands and petulance in the teary, blackened eyes of their wives. But what he saw here unnerved him. Laura was looking at her husband in horror, as if she had seen a ghost, and Ian had the doom in his eyes of a man condemned.

Vince felt a certain guilty sense of protectiveness toward Laura. He understood what had happened with Dominick Vanese. Dolores had been roundabout, evasive in her responses, but he understood. Laura had been set up by her in-laws, and then they'd belatedly had an attack of conscience. Vince was beginning to think that this woman had been wrongly accused all along. After all, they had nothing on her. Wasn't that what justice was all about? Weren't the police supposed to protect the innocent? And as for this man, this Turner, Ron Leonard seemed pretty certain about him. If Ron was right, this man had a major mental problem. And from the look on Laura's face, Vince thought perhaps Laura had suddenly achieved the same conclusion. An urge to treat her like a daughter rose in Vince. It wasn't too hard. She was about the age of his own daughter. He tried to imagine how he would want someone to treat Katy if she were in this kind of trouble.

"What's the problem here, Laura?" Vince asked in a gruff, kindly manner.

"I just want to leave here, Chief," she pleaded. "Please don't let him follow me."

Vince nodded his head at the stairs. "You go along wherever you want to go. As for you, Mr. Turner, Detective Leonard has some questions for you. He's on his way here now. You're to stay put until he arrives. I'll be right up there on the dock to make sure that you do." Chief Moore turned chivalrously to Laura. "I'll help you up, ma'am."

Laura accepted the officer's proffered hand. She did not look back at Ian. All she could think about was getting away.

CHAPTER FORTY-EIGHT

Wanda turned off the clothes dryer, reached inside to check the clothes for dampness, and listened. She thought she had heard Gary calling her. But the house was silent, except for the hollow sound of the voices on the television.

"Gary," she called.

There was no answer. She gathered up some dry under-wear and socks and stepped out of the laundry room into the empty hall.

"Gary?" she cried, more urgently now.

"What?" he called back irritably.

"Were you calling me for something?"

"No," he insisted.

Wanda pressed his laundry, still warm from the dryer, against her chest and returned to her chores. It was like that whenever she did anything noisy—ran the vacuum, used the blender. She kept thinking he wanted her, needed her for some-thing. But he always denied that he had called for her. In fact, he seemed angry about it. Angry that she asked, as if he disliked her caring for him. All she was doing was the same thing she had always done. Making sure he was all right. Why should that suddenly make him angry? she wondered. Hadn't she been there for him every minute, every hour, since this all began?

Wanda folded the laundry on the folding table that had been provided for her. This house had everything, every convenience. It was sad to think that she would never have lived in such a comfortable house if it had not been for the accident and the insurance settlement. And none of it mattered to her. None of it. She would give it all up in a moment to have saved him from his pain and suffering. She would have done her wash on a metal washboard if that would have made the difference. That was why it troubled her so that he seemed impatient with her since his return. He seemed to have changed in his time away from her. He had become suddenly restless and agitated, less willing to abide by their routines. Sometimes when she offered him food he said he wasn't hungry or that she should leave it and he would have it later. She had to remind him, a little sternly on several occasions, that they did not live that way. Usually that was enough to bring him around. He had always been a good boy. Borne his suffering uncomplainingly. Just as she bore hers.

Wanda finished folding up the last of their clothes and the dishtowels, and she began to distribute them through the house. First she went to the kitchen and put away the towels and the pot holders. She stopped in the bathroom and hung up the bath towels. Then she went on to her own room. She hung her two wraparound skirts in the closet and folded her shirts into the drawer of the bureau. Gary's high school picture smiled out into the air on top of her bureau. His hair was still dark in that picture. It was taken before the accident. It was dark, as hers had been when she was young. Not blond, like his father's. Sometimes, not often, she wondered where Karl Jurik was. He had been handsome when she'd met him, and full of plans. But all his plans had ended in a bottle. Karl had left them so many times, left them so often, that when he finally left for good, it hardly mattered at all. Gary was nothing like his father, she thought. Thank goodness.

Wanda closed the drawer in her bureau and started back down the wide hallway to Gary's room. He was probably in his studio, painting, she thought with a sigh. Karl had always

liked to draw. Drew a picture of her once, when he was court-
ing her, and it was pretty good. That was probably where
Gary got it from. But that was all. Nothing else. She walked
into Gary's bedroom and started when she found him there.

"What are you doing in here?" she asked.

Gary shook his head slightly, as if somehow amazed by
her question.

"Did I say something wrong?" she asked.

"No, Mother. No," he said quietly.

"You don't usually spend much time in your room during the day. That's all."

"I know," he said.

"I brought your laundry," she said. She came around the
dresser and was about to open the top drawer when suddenly
she noticed a bag on the bed. It was a soft-sided gray suitcase.
She stared at it as if snakes were writhing around the handles.
She had never seen the bag before. When he left, he left without anything. That was one reason she had been so sure . . .

"Whose bag is that?" she said.

"It's mine," he said. "It's packed."

"I can see it's packed," she said. "What's it doing there?"

"Mother, don't get upset."

"What in the world is this doing here?" She clutched the
laundry to her breast and stared at the bag.

"Mother . . ." He hesitated. Then he said, "I'm going
away. These are the things I'm bringing with me."

"Going away? Going away where? You just got home."

"I've been . . . I'm thinking of moving to another place."

"What are you talking about? Another place? You might
as well say another planet. Gary, you're not making sense."

"A city, Mom. I can't tell you more than that right now."

"Can't tell me," she said incredulously.

"It's . . . it's confidential for now. Until things are
settled."

Confidential, she thought. The word scared her. It
sounded like something out of a spy story. As if he were not
quite in touch with reality. Wanda sank onto the bed and

322

put the laundry carefully beside her. She smoothed it absently with her hand and tried to phrase her thoughts carefully. "Honey," she said, "you can't go to another place. I mean, you can't manage, you know."

"I managed all right while I was gone," he said.

"And I thank God each day that you came home safely. You had a little adventure . . . and luckily you were not killed in the process. But you're home now, and we just have to try to forget all that."

"Mother, stop talking about it that way. I am going to go. I'm leaving here."

Wanda reared back and stared at him with livid eyes. "You can't go away from here. You can't manage by yourself. You have special needs that have to be seen to. This house was custom-made for your problems. You need looking after. Who would take care of you?"

He avoided her gaze. "There is someone," he said.

Wanda sniffed. "Who?" she demanded. "Who would take on this kind of burden? You don't realize the trouble you are. No one would want that kind of trouble. You're lying to me, Gary. There is no one."

Gary seemed to be considering his reply carefully for a moment, reluctant to make his admission. Then he said, "I'm going away with Laura. All right? She needs me now. We need each other."

"Laura? Laura Reed?" Wanda did not know whether to laugh or cry. "Have you gone completely mad? Laura Reed? I don't think so." She began to shake her head. "I mean, besides the fact that she's married again. There were a few other developments while you were gone. For your information, young man, she's in jail."

"No, she's not," he said. "Not anymore. She got out today. And she's leaving. She's leaving her husband. And she wants me to go with her . . . and Michael. So, I'm going."

Wanda looked at him hopelessly. "My poor deluded child. This woman has destroyed your mind. You have to get over this. She's in jail. She's never going to get out."

"No, she's not," said Gary. He picked up the remote control and snapped on the TV opposite his bed. "See for yourself."

A commercial for laundry detergent was playing. Wanda looked sadly at her son. She reached out and stroked the side of his face. "Oh, sweetheart," she said. "This isn't real. What you're thinking isn't real. You are home here, with me, and she is . . . where she belongs." She studied his face worriedly. "You do know that, don't you?"

"I'm going to get my sable brushes," Gary said shortly. He maneuvered the chair around her and out the door of the room, in the direction of the studio.

Wanda put her hands to her face and looked around the empty room. What am I going to do? she wondered. She did not want to even consider the possibility that he was becoming unbalanced. But what else could she think? He had been acting strangely since his return. He never told her anything about where he had been or what had happened to him. Anything was possible. Maybe he was having some kind of a breakdown. It happened to people sometimes, when they had been under a lot of stress.

And there was another thing, something that filled her with a sick, fearful sensation in the pit of her stomach. The gun. She had found it one day when she was cleaning up. She had picked it up and stared at it. It was a real gun. What did he know about guns? Oh, sometimes he would read those soldier of fortune magazines, but she figured that was all just a fantasy to him. Yet there it was in the drawer. She had wanted to confront him with it, but it had been in a locked drawer, so she had to pretend that she didn't know it was there. Wanda felt a yawning helplessness inside. She had always known how to care for him. How to soothe him and make it better for him. But this . . . this was something different. She needed help with this.

Muttering to herself, Wanda ran down the hall to the kitchen and rooted around in the kitchen drawer for her phone book. Her hands were shaking, and she had difficulty turning the tissuelike pages. After a few frantic moments of searching, she found the number she needed. She dialed and growled at the receptionist to answer as it rang. Finally, finally, a woman's voice answered: "Dr. Ingles's office."

"Oh, thank God," said Wanda. "Mary, this is Wanda Jurik."

"Hello, Mrs. Jurik," said the nurse.

Wanda spoke softly into the phone. "I'm calling about my son, Gary. He . . . he's not doing well . . ."

"You sound very upset, Mrs. Jurik," the nurse said kindly. "Is this a critical situation? Is Gary all right?"

"Well, you know about his condition, Mary."

"Yes," the nurse said cautiously.

"I'm really worried about his mental state," said Wanda. "I think Dr. Ingles should see him. I think he needs some tranquilizers, or something to calm him down. He's very agitated and upset. I have some Valium I could give him, but I think he might need a shot or something."

"Now try to calm down," said the nurse.

"Calm down!" Wanda yelped. "Would you be calm if your child was acting this way?"

"Dr. Ingles is with a patient right now," said the nurse. "I will have him call you the minute he is free. Meanwhile, don't give him any medication that hasn't been prescribed for him. That could be dangerous."

"All right," said Wanda. "But tell him this is very important."

"I will," the nurse reassured her.

Wanda hung up the phone and went out to the studio. She knocked at the door. "Gary," she called. "Gary, honey?"

There was no reply. She opened the door and saw that the studio was empty and quiet. She could not tell if anything was missing. He had so many sets of pencils, boxes of paints. It was always like a child's playroom to her, this studio. There was no need to keep track of crayons. You could always get more. But she had a sense that some were missing. Perhaps it was just that she feared it. Feeling the panic rising in her heart, she ran back down the hall to the bedroom. He wasn't there. And the suitcase was gone from the bed.

"Gary," Wanda cried, "where are you?" She raced down the hall in the other direction to the living room.

The living room was empty. The television was running, as ever. The front door stood open. A reporter was facing the camera on the television screen. "As we've been telling you all this afternoon," he said, "Laura Reed Turner was released from the county jail this morning after a witness recanted testimony that she had solicited a hired killer to murder her husband. This tape of Mrs. Turner was made as she left the county jail."

Laura's face appeared on the screen. "What are you going to do now that you're free?" a reporter asked her.

"I'm going to leave this town," she said. "I don't want to stay here a moment longer than I have to. I have nothing further to say."

Wanda heard the roar of an engine firing up in the driveway. She looked at the coat rack by the door. The jacket that he always wore, even in summer, was gone. She spun toward the window to see the blur of his van going by.

"Gary!" she screamed. "Come back! . . ."

CHAPTER FORTY-NINE

Well, darling, Laura thought, here we are. She crouched in front of the granite headstone and placed the bunch of hydrangeas she had just gathered from the bush beside their house into the vase implanted on Jimmy's grave. On her way to the cemetery she had stopped by the house to collect them. Pam Garrity had been out picking up Louis's toys in the yard and spoke kindly, almost apologetically, to Laura as she watched Laura break off the branches, gathering them into a large bouquet.

Laura knew that Pam had finally come to doubt her innocence in Jimmy's murder after she was arrested. It was not as if anything were said—just a tone in Pam's voice that put distance between them. At first she felt a little like Caesar, as amazed as she was hurt that even her closest friend would turn on her. But she knew Duane must have gloated over her arrest. And it was human nature to believe the official version of the truth. Never mind the presumption of innocence. Once a person was arrested, most people started thinking of them as guilty.

Besides, Laura thought, she was getting used to steeling herself to these injuries. Betrayal had become her daily bread. She thought of Ian and then put him out of her mind. It didn't matter about Pam, she told herself. She and Michael would soon be gone, and Pam and her family would fade into memory. She and Michael would make new friends, in a new home. But she wondered, really wondered, whom she would ever trust again. She thought all these things even as she explained to Pam that she was bringing the hydrangeas to Jimmy. He always loved it when the hydrangeas bloomed. They were so extravagant in their blowsy beauty, a storm of blue-violet flakes against their flat, deep green leaves. He said the flowers matched her eyes. Laura would accept the compliment, although she knew good and well that her eyes were gray, not that sky blue purple of the blossoms. But perhaps to him . . .

Now, as she knelt at his grave, the misty rain made all the sky the same gray-granite hue of Jimmy's headstone. The cemetery was empty in the rain. No other mourners trod on the carpet of grass that glowed mossy green in the gloom of the day. Laura said a prayer and touched the headstone. Jimmy was buried beside his father, James Reed Sr. Laura said a brief prayer for her unknown father-in-law, too. After all, his blood ran in Michael's veins. Although she had never met him, they were forever connected, she and Jimmy's father—Dolores's first husband.

Your mother came through for me in the end, Laura thought, speaking to Jimmy as if he were hovering there, hearing her thoughts. She really did. I thought I would never get out of that jail. I don't know exactly what happened. I'll probably never know. But I know that Dolores was the one who got me out. When everybody else turned on me, she was fair. You always said that about her, didn't you? I told you that you were shrewder about people than I was. Well, I promise you, no matter where Michael and I finally end up, I'll make sure he always knows his grandparents.

Laura sighed. Oh, Jimmy, Jimmy, she thought. How did we end up separated this way? By a distance we can never cross. It will be a whole lifetime until I see you again. And even as she thought it, she wondered. Would he want to see her again, after what she had done? Married a man who had . . .

Laura did not want to complete the thought. She could not seem to get her mind to take it in. Will you hold it against me, darling? she wondered, looking at the name *James Reed Jr.* carved in granite. Laura did not have a well-formed concept of the hereafter. She liked to think of it as a place where souls met with no rancor or regrets. As if the events of life on earth had not been that significant. All grudges and sorrows diminished and all that mattered was the love you had felt for that person on earth. If that was the case, then they would meet and rejoice in their meeting.

I'm going to be gone for a while, she thought to him. I won't be able to come here. I'm going to take our son far away from here, where we can shake off the memories of these last months. I'll come back and testify if I have to, if there's a trial . . . She thought again of Ian, that terrible last look on his face, and shuddered. Could she leave his memory here and only take Jimmy's memory with her? Her true husband. Oh, Ian had been her husband all right. Her face flamed at the thought of her longing for him. She felt guilty even for thinking of it, here at Jimmy's grave. But bitterness was already crowding out any love she might have felt for Ian. Soon there would be nothing left but a hard little nugget of cold vengeance. She was sure of it. And the sooner the better.

Jimmy, she said, forcing her mind back to the only man she wanted to remember. I don't really believe that you are here. This is just a place to come and think about you. I believe that you'll be with us wherever we go. I'll try to raise Michael to be the man you would have wanted. He lost his father so young, just as you did. But you turned out so well. Such a fine man. If I can just do half as well as Dolores did . . . She smiled ruefully at that thought.

"I'll never let him forget his father, darling," she whispered aloud. "I promise."

She touched the headstone again, her fingers lingering on the cold granite. Then she turned and began to walk back toward her car. She noted with disinterest that another vehicle was parked at the curb, beneath the drooping branches of an ancient elm. Someone else whose sorrow was undeterred by the rain. She walked over to a trash can and threw away the withered flowers she had replaced in the vase. Then she walked slowly, head down, toward where she was parked. Just as she reached the car and started for the door, she heard a whirring sound behind her.

"Laura," said a familiar voice.

Laura let out a little cry and turned, startled to hear her name spoken in this place of ghosts. She could hardly believe her eyes.

"Gary," she cried.

Gary Jurik sat in his wheelchair, blocking the door to her car. "Hello, Laura," he said.

* * *

Ron Leonard turned off his windshield wipers and fumbled around on the floor of the front seat for his umbrella. He hated weather like this. Your suits got all wet and wrinkled, and you had to make an extra trip to the cleaners. Through the gloom, he could see the black-and-white parked on the pier, all its lights blinking, only a few feet from Turner's yacht. He assumed that Vince was waiting inside the car, keeping out of the rain.

Ron popped open his umbrella and started down the pier. His shiny loafers were rain spattered and tended to slip on the shining planks. Carefully he made his way to Vince's car, wondering absently how much weight these docks could hold. A squad car was no lightweight item. It probably wasn't very often that a car drove down this way. A small crowd of curious onlookers had gathered under the overhang outside of Boat People, wondering what the unusual presence of the police car indicated. Ron ignored them, although he was conscious of his semicelebrity status as he made his way to the chief's car.

As Ron approached the car from behind, the driver's door opened, and Vince Moore stepped out into the rain. "I saw you in the rearview," Vince explained. The two men shook hands briefly.

"So, where's our suspect?" Ron asked.

Vince nodded toward the boat. "He and the missus were having quite a row when I came in."

"Really?" Ron asked with interest.

"I believe the young lady has come around to your point of view," Vince said, but there was no relish in his tone. The whole thing seemed somehow sad to him. But he could see that Ron was eager to get back into the middle of it. "He wanted to know if I was arresting him," said Vince.

"What did you say?"

"Well, I said no, of course, but I told him to stay put, that you were on the way. And I've been right here ever since."

"Good," said Ron.

"You really think this guy is a nut, don't you?"

"Hey, I spent a lot of time up in his old hometown. There's something very fishy about the fire that killed his wife and kid. Add to that a little murder for hire, a man who is pretending not to know things about a woman he knows all too well, and yeah, I think you've got a nut. I think he was obsessed with Laura Reed, and willing to do just about anything to get her."

Vince shook his head. "Poor Laura."

Ron looked at Vince in mild surprise. Even though he was beginning to suspect that Laura might be innocent, he didn't feel any real sympathy for her. After all, she married this guy of her own free will. He looked toward the boat. "So, he's just sitting down there stewing."

Vince shrugged. "I guess. Look, I think maybe I better come down there with you. He's had time to think about this. He might be dangerous."

Ron smiled and patted the gun in his shoulder holster. "Don't worry. I'm ready for him. I'm going to invite him back to the office. I don't want to spend any time on that boat. Boats give me claustrophobia."

"I agree," said Vince. "I prefer terra firma myself."

A squawking came over Vince's radio in the car. Vince excused himself and answered the call. He emerged from the car with a worried look on his face.

"What is it?" Ron asked.

Vince shook his head. "A holdup on Main Street."

"You go ahead," said Ron. "I'll be fine."

"You sure?" Vince asked. "I can direct somebody over here."

Ron considered the offer, but the prospect of waiting out here in the rain was unpleasant. "No problem," he said.

Vince sighed. "All right. I better get out there."

"I'll talk to you later."

The two men nodded, and Vince got back in his car and began to back it slowly up the pier. The curious onlookers stared at the black-and-white as Vince straightened it out and then turned on his siren. They all jumped back at that, and Vince sped off toward the scene of the crime.

Ron boarded the boat, treading carefully in his leather-soled shoes. He did not draw his gun until he was out of sight of the gawkers on the dock. But he did draw it once he'd reached the hatch and put one foot on the rubber treads on the stairs. He did not intend to walk into some kind of trap. He'd been around a little too much for that. "Mr. Turner," he said, "this is Detective Ron Leonard from the DA's office. I'm coming down there." There was no answer from below.

Ron took a deep breath and felt his heart beating faster. This wasn't going to be straightforward. He could see that already. Turner wasn't answering. He tried to picture the worst. The man, seated in wait at the foot of the stair ladder, opening fire as the detective came into view. Ron clenched his jaw and readjusted his weapon in his hand. He would be ready for him, no matter what. Still, for a moment he regretted his macho posture of having sent Vince on his way, leaving himself with no backup.

"Mr. Turner," he repeated loudly, "I am coming in to talk to you." Well, Ron thought, it would sound stupid to request backup for a routine questioning of a suspect. They'd laugh at him. It was just that these days—the things you heard about. How little these criminals seemed to regard a human life. They'd kill you for a can of Coke. And not the narcotic kind. "The pause that refreshes" kind of Coke.

Stop thinking this way, Ron ordered himself. He gripped his gun tightly and descended the ladder into the cabin. There was no sign of Ian Turner.

"Turner," he demanded, "where the hell . . .?" He looked around the cabin. He'd been on a few fishing boats, but this baby was something else again. It had regular rooms. Cautiously, his gun raised, he explored the boat. He switched on the light in the head and checked the shower. No one. Feeling a rising sense of panic and fury, he went around to the small stateroom off the galley and tried that light. All that was inside was a large, trapezium-shaped berth with a foam mattress, surrounded by lockers. Ron backed out of the small, empty cabin and made his way forward. The cabin under the bow had a raised double berth, with storage beneath it. It was neat, and tidy, and empty.

"What the fuck?" Ron cried. "Where the fuck is he?" He looked about helplessly. Vince had been on the dock the whole time. He was getting old, but he wasn't blind. Turner couldn't have gotten past that car.

Ron started up the ladder, toward the hatch. There was only one other way off this boat. As he climbed the steps he saw what he feared. The stern of the boat was somewhat lower than the bow. If Turner had crept up these steps and slithered over the stern, he could have gotten into the water without being seen.

"Son of a bitch," Ron cried. He shoved his gun back into his holster and clambered up the steps. He was furious, thinking about Turner getting away like that.

"Should have arrested the son of a bitch when I had the chance," he muttered as he scrambled across the deck.

Furious at the turn of events, and vaguely worried now about Laura Turner and her son, he was careless as he went. He was hurrying. His leather-soled shoes hit the slippery surface of the rain-washed deck, and he slipped and fell backward. He was aware of a wrenching in his back, and he cried out in pain as he landed in the cockpit. He tried gingerly to move, but the pain in his back was excruciating. "Goddammit," he cried. Even the vibration of his voice hurt his back.

The cluster of onlookers under the eaves at Boat People had thinned, but there were still a number of curious people there who had nothing better to do on this rainy day of their vacation than watch and see what developed down by the large sailboat. One twelve-year-old girl with the eagle eye of youth saw Ron's fall, saw him lying sprawled on the deck of the boat. "Daddy, look!" she screamed. "That man fell on the boat. He's just lying there . . ."

It took her a moment to convince the others. It took them a few moments of conferring to decide what to do. Then, ordering the children to stay back, a few of the men and one woman, in an apprehensive cluster, started down the dock toward the boat and the inert man crumpled on the deck.

CHAPTER FIFTY

"Surprised?" Gary asked.

Laura stared at her friend, reaching out to gently touch the side of his face, to be sure he was real. "More like stunned," she said. "God, I'm glad to see you. Where the hell have you been?"

Smudges of pink surfaced in his pale cheeks. "We've both been through the mill," he said gravely. "I heard about what happened to you on the news. I still can't believe it."

"It's been . . . a nightmare," Laura said with false cheerfulness. She crouched beside his wheelchair and pressed one of his cold hands to her face.

They smiled at each other ruefully. "I never believed you did it," he said. "Not for a minute."

"Well, thanks. You're about the only one. You . . . and of all people, my mother-in-law, Dolores. In the end she went to bat for me. Talked Vanese into telling the truth. You never know." She shook her head. "You know, I am so sick of thinking about this. But you. What ever happened to you? Where have you been? And what are you doing here?"

"I stopped by your house. Your friend told me where to find you."

"My friend . . . Oh, you mean Pam," Laura said thoughtfully. "I think you're my only friend I have left. You are still my friend, aren't you?"

"Of course," he said, gazing at her.

"Where have you been? Your mother has been frantic. You know she told the police that you left because of me. Because of my remarriage. I felt so guilty. It wasn't because of that, was it?"

Gary stared at her sadly. Then he nodded. "In a way. Yes, it was."

Laura looked away from him. "I'm sorry. More than you'll ever know."

Gary shook his head. "No, it's all right. It was just the jolt I needed. Look, it's raining on us here. Do you want to get in the van?"

Laura glanced at her watch and then at Gary's van, parked up the road a way. She was surprised she hadn't recognized it in the first place. Well, surely she could spend a few minutes with him out of the rain. Dolores would keep Michael a while longer. "Okay," she said.

She followed him to the van and resisted the urge to assist him as he raised himself into the vehicle. He didn't need help, she reminded herself. He was perfectly capable of managing himself. She climbed onto the passenger seat as he wheeled himself onto the driver's seat. She heard a click as he flipped the switch that locked all the doors, she looked at him quizzically.

"Force of habit," he said apologetically. "I guess I feel more vulnerable than some people."

Laura nodded and looked out through the mist on the windshield, which turned the graveyard with its tended lawns and ancient trees into an indistinct mass of gray and a brackish green. She could feel Gary's gaze on her, and she sighed.

"So the marriage didn't work out, eh?" he asked.

"Gary . . . the marriage was based on a lie. Maybe on something worse than a lie."

"What does that mean?" he asked.

Laura shook her head. "It means I have to get away from him. And this place."

"I know," he said. "I heard you on the news."

She was quiet for a minute, listening to the rain thrumming on the metal roof of the van. Then she said, "The police think that Ian may have been the one . . ."

"The one what?"

Laura shook her head. "I guess it was the loneliness . . . the utter loneliness I felt that clouded my judgment."

"The one who killed Jimmy?" he asked.

She leaned her head back against the seat and closed her eyes. "I can't bring myself to believe it. Every time I think about it my mind keeps veering away from it, you know, I can't believe that I could have married . . . made love . . . with the man who . . ."

There was a silence in the van. Laura felt a certain peace in the dark, quiet vehicle, her friend beside her. She turned her head sideways and looked at him.

"You never told me where you were," she said.

Gary was staring blankly through the windshield. "I was running away," he said. "Your marriage triggered something in me."

She waited for him to explain. Something in the tone of his voice made her shiver.

"I just started driving north. I ended up in Boston. I almost . . . I thought about killing myself."

"Oh no."

"I was ready to do it. I came close."

"Gary, why?" Laura asked. Don't say it was because of me, she thought. Please, don't say that.

Gary cocked his head, resting it against the driver's side window. "Ever since Jimmy died I was like someone who was lost . . . I went to Boston because that's where he wanted me to go. When he was helping me with that grant proposal. He kept telling me about the museum there, and how I would love the city . . ."

"He had such faith in you," said Laura.

Gary gave her a wry smile. "I loved him, you know. He was my first and only love."

Laura frowned. "I'm not sure I understand. You mean . . . loved, as in, love? . . ."

"You're shocked, right?" he asked, a shade of bitterness creeping into his voice. "It's been known to happen."

Laura nodded, holding her breath. Gary's confession was an undeniable shock. She felt slightly embarrassed at his admission. But she realized instantly that it was far more difficult for him to make that admission than it was for her to absorb it. She didn't want him to regret his decision to confess. "I know that," she said. "Don't take it that way. I didn't know. I'll admit, I even thought . . ."

"You thought it was you."

"Your mother said . . . she told the police . . ." Laura shrugged, embarrassed.

Gary shook his head. "My mother. She never knew, either. No one knew. Pining for him was a way of life for me. My secret life. When he went off to college, and then he moved on to California, I would see him on his occasional trip home, but I figured he was gone for good. I had all these rationalizations about how I would be content just to have loved someone. You know, better to have loved and lost . . . And it wasn't as if I had a social life to take its place," he said ruefully.

"And then, when he moved back here from San Francisco, married, with a young son, I could see that he was happy, that you loved each other very much. But for me, all the old feelings came flooding back. He never knew how I felt. It would have embarrassed him. It would have been awkward between us. Jimmy was so straight. Straight and good. The best man I ever knew . . ."

"Yes," she said feebly. "He was good." I must have been blind not to see it, she thought. And Jimmy, too. She knew that he never realized. Never.

"I guess I kind of decided that the next best thing was to just be a part of your family . . . of your world," said Gary. "And it was like that, wasn't it?"

"Yes," she said solemnly, remembering. "It was."

"He built those ramps for me at your house. You don't know what that meant to me. It was like saying that I belonged there, too." Tears filled Gary's eyes at the memory. Laura reached out and clasped his cold fingers. "It was a secondhand life, but after this"—he waved his hand at his legs in the chair—"and those long years when there was no one, and nothing else, I didn't expect much more than that. It seemed like enough . . ."

"He expected more for you," she said fiercely. "He always believed that the whole world would open up to you if you would let it. That's why he wanted you to get into that program in Boston so much."

"I know," said Gary. "I know. Although to tell you the truth, I didn't really want the grant. I didn't want to go away and leave him. Anyway, after he . . . was killed, I guess I was sort of hanging on to my sanity by thinking of you and Michael. You know, what he would want for you. Sending you the flowers, almost as if they came from him through me . . . I felt like I was doing something for him . . . you know." Tears were running down his cheeks, but he made no effort to stop them. "And then, when you dropped that bombshell, that you'd remarried, so soon . . ." Gary shook his head. "I don't know. Something snapped. It was like I finally realized that he was gone forever. That I had nothing left . . ."

Laura swallowed hard and nodded. "I know. I'm sorry."

"Don't be sorry. It wasn't your fault. It was my hang-up," he said shortly.

Laura studied his tearstained face but felt no pity. There was a certain nobility to him that moved her deeply. "What brought you back?" she asked softly.

"I went to Boston, and I got a gun, and I was sitting in a motel room with the thing pointed at my brain when somebody knocked on the door. A man I'd met in the park. He came after me. He seemed to know . . ." Gary looked at her in amazement and smiled. "I think Jimmy sent him to look out for me."

"He might have," Laura agreed.

Gary nodded. And they were silent again. Then he spoke, and his voice shook a little. "His name is Aaron. He's a psychiatric nurse. He works with teenagers. We've become very close. I feel like I have known him all my life. I'm going back up there to live with him. I just came home to tell my mother and get my things."

"It's like your own personal miracle," said Laura, and involuntarily she thought of how she'd felt when she met Ian. As if providence had sent him. But that had been a lie. For her, it had been a lie. "This is going to be the right thing for you," she said sincerely. Then she added, "Jimmy would be so pleased. Really. He only ever wanted the best for you."

"Thanks," he whispered.

"I hope you will find some real happiness. You deserve it," she said.

"I hope the same for you," he said.

She was going to deny the possibility. But that wouldn't be accurate. "I have Michael," she said. "I'll be okay."

He nodded, and they embraced impulsively, awkwardly, across the gearshift of the van.

"Speaking of Michael," she said, pulling back, "I've got to get him so we can be on our way, too."

"Miles to go before I sleep," Gary quoted, smiling.

"For both of us," she said.

Gary nodded, and Laura unlocked her side and started to step out.

"By the way," he said, "you may get a call from my mother."

"Your mother? Why?"

Gary took a deep breath and looked sheepish. "I couldn't bring myself to tell her about . . . you know . . . Aaron. I tried, but . . . She wouldn't understand. I mean . . . no way."

"Probably true." Laura nodded.

"So I told her I was going away with you."

"With me?"

"It just kind of popped out. I was watching you on TV, saying you were leaving, and I thought, 'Why not? She'll buy it for now. There's plenty of time to tell her the truth once it's done.'"

Laura shook her head. "You're bad," she said wryly.

"Will you cover for me, temporarily? As soon I get settled I'll level with her. I promise."

Laura laughed. "Sure. What are friends for?"

"Stay well, Laura," he said. "I'll miss you. And Michael."

Laura slammed the door on the van and blew him a kiss. She watched him as he drove away to his new life. You be happy, she thought. Then she turned and walked back toward her own car. It was time to get Michael and get moving.

CHAPTER FIFTY-ONE

"Okay," Laura said briskly, opening the front door of the house and ushering her son inside. "We've got to get our stuff together that we want to take, and get going." She deliberately did not look at Michael's face. Getting him away from Dolores and Sidney had been tough enough. She had called it a "little trip" that they were taking, but no one had been fooled. Michael had cried and clung to his grandparents. Laura had felt like an ogre taking him away, but she had reached the point of no return.

"When are we coming back?" Michael demanded. "I don't want to go unless I know when we're coming back."

"I don't know exactly when," Laura said carefully, not wanting to tell him any more lies. "I don't think this is the place for us to live anymore."

"You mean we're not going to live in our house?" Michael asked, incredulous.

"We'll get another house. An even nicer house."

"I like this house," he insisted.

Laura looked warningly at her son. "Look, I know you have been through the wringer. Believe me, this is not what I wanted for either of us. But the time has come to cut our losses here."

He did not know what she meant. He was on to the next problem. "What about Ian?"

Laura opened the hall closet and pulled out the empty suitcases she had stored in there. "Ian is not coming with us," she said, rummaging blindly among the snow boots on the floor of the closet.

"I thought we were going sailing this summer," Michael whined.

Laura turned on him and grabbed his shoulders. "Honey, stop. I know this is hard for you. Believe me, I do. And I'm sorry. But this is what we're going to do." Even as she said it, so firmly, she didn't know exactly what she meant. She thought about California. Maybe they would head out there. She still had contacts with people there. And it was far away from here.

"Look, we'll drive and drive," she told him. "We'll stay in motels on the way, and see the sights. It'll be fun. I'm looking forward to just being on the road after being cooped up in that horrible jail." That was true, in part. It was also a ploy, to remind him of their separation, of the ordeal they had just been through.

But, in the way of children, he was not concerned with what had happened in the past. His concern was for now, for right now. "I'm not going," he said. "You keep changing everything. I want to go back to Grandma and Poppy's. I don't want to go with you."

The truth of his accusation stung her, and rather than admit it, she got mad at him. She shoved an empty backpack at him and glared. "You get up those stairs this minute and get your things together in this bag. I don't care what you take, just take what you want and don't give me any more back talk, do you hear?"

"I hate you," he cried, running up the stairs, dragging the backpack in his wake.

Laura closed the closet door and leaned back against it, her eyes closed. Oh, God, she thought. Am I doing the wrong thing again? She had reached a point where she doubted her every choice. And why not? Every choice she made seemed to be the wrong one. Get a grip on yourself, she thought. It will all be simpler on the road. This route or that. This motel or that one. By the time they got to California, she would be in control again.

Clinging to that slender hope, she let out a sigh and pushed herself away from the closet door. At least her house was pretty well in order. Many of the rooms had been cleaned out, the contents boxed already. After all, they had been planning to leave with Ian, she thought, her mouth twisted into a bitter smile. Only a few things remained. She would go and clean out the refrigerator, throw out everything perishable and pack a bag of snacks for the road. Then she could get her clothes. She walked down the dark hall into the kitchen and opened the refrigerator door. There, on the shelf, neatly wrapped in plastic, was the leftover chicken and a few slices of garlic bread from the barbecue he had made that night. The night they'd come to arrest her. The night the court had given custody of Michael to Dolores. Their last night in this house, playing cards, unsuspecting. Sometime during that night Ian had wrapped up the food and put it away. Like a thoughtful husband. A perfect husband. Laura felt numb inside, like someone who had been battered to the point where she was senseless. With the tips of her fingers, she picked up the packets of old grilled chicken and bread and tossed them into the depths of a large dark green garbage bag. She poured half-empty bottles of juice and colas down the sink and walked the empty bottles and cans to the recycling container. It was empty now, but she could visualize Jimmy's photos there the night of her hasty second wedding. Ian probably did do it, she thought. It probably was him and not the florist. That was all she intended to remember about that night. She did not want to remember the other part—the part that had happened in the tiny room at the back of the house, in the dark. It made her hate herself just to think of it.

"Michael," she called out automatically. "Hurry up."

There was no answer, but she was not surprised. He was probably up there in his room, flung on the bed, not a single item yet put into the backpack.

"I'm coming up there," she called out.

She tied up the handles of the garbage bag and hauled it toward the door, to take to the trash can next to the back porch. It was getting dark, although the whole day had been gloomy. We probably should sleep here tonight and get started in the morning, she thought. But she knew she wasn't going to spend another night here. She wanted to get away before Ian got free of the police. Talked his way out of trouble once more. She wasn't going to take the chance of a knock at the door, of Ian showing up, trying to force her to listen to more lies.

She walked to the back door and reached to open it. The doorknob came loose in her hand. She looked down and saw splinters of wood surrounding the lock where the door had been pried and forced open.

Chills coursed up her spine, ran up and down her legs. For a moment she just stared at it, trying to absorb the fact that the house had been broken into. Then, her eyes wide with fear, she whirled around, expecting to see someone behind her. The room was empty, the house silent. Her gaze darting around the room, she tried to think, When, why? It could have been anytime in the last few days, she thought, trying to steady herself.

"Michael," she whispered, and then her son's name caught in her throat. It was quiet in the house. Perhaps too quiet.

She dropped the bag by the back door and rushed through the kitchen toward the hallway. As she went she slipped and caught herself from falling by grabbing the edge of the table. She looked down at the wood floor. Now she saw it: a trail of water leading from the back door, across the kitchen, and into the hallway, as if something dripping wet had made its way through the house. The sight of it made her feel weak with fear. Someone had come in here. Were they here still?

345

Avoiding the pattern of little puddles, she edged down the hallway to the bottom of the stairs and looked up. "Michael?" she cried, but her voice was small, and, as her chilled heart expected, there was no answer.

She looked around herself frantically. On a table in the hallway, flanking a vase of dead flowers, were two heavy brass candlesticks she had bought at a flea market. She pulled out the candle of the closest one and gripped the brass holder upside down in her sweaty hand. The weight of the base in her hand made her feel slightly more secure. Maybe it's nothing, she told herself. Michael often didn't answer when she called him. Kids got lost in their own little world. That door could have been forced days ago, when no one was here. But that did not explain the water. Maybe Pam had come in the house to check on things, during the rain. But no, she thought hopelessly. Pam wouldn't leave that mess. The thoughts were not reassuring, but they occupied her brain, enabled her to go forward, to move, her shallow breath coming in pants, up the staircase.

At the top she looked around. The house was still. She went immediately to Michael's room and looked inside. The door was open, and nothing was disturbed. Not even his backpack was there. As she stood staring into the empty room, her heart beating a tattoo against her chest, she heard a thud. She turned her head.

It came from down the hall, from her old bedroom. Hers and Jimmy's. Laura gazed down the gloomy hallway. The door to the bedroom was slightly ajar, and it was dark inside. But there was no doubt in her mind. That's where the sound had come from. Maybe he's in there, she told herself, going through his father's things, and he feels guilty and he's afraid to answer.

"Michael," she said again, "answer me," and her voice shook.

But there was no answer. And when she looked down she saw that the puddles of water, much smaller now but still shiny on the floor, led to the bedroom door. Part of her wanted to

346

run, to phone the police and say she suspected a prowler. To wait in some safe place for them to come. But there was no way. Not without Michael. You have to go, she told herself. Whatever it is, you have to go in there and get your son.

She walked to the doorway, and it seemed as if all her pulses were pounding as she went. She gripped the candlestick in one sweaty palm and reached out. She did not want to open this door again. Michael, her mind chanted, giving her momentum. She forced herself forward, pushed open the door, and stepped into the room.

The last gray gloom of the rainy twilight came through the windows and formed a dim pattern of leaves and branches on the white bed. The sheets and covers were disheveled, and some had slipped to the floor. And splayed out across the bed, half on, half over the edge, like the memory of her worst nightmare, was the body of a man.

His clothes were dark and bunchy, as if they had just come out of the washer, and the bedclothes beneath him appeared soggy. His hair was wet also, slick and stringy strands, black against the white spread. Blood oozed from the man's chest. As Laura stared in horror, the man turned his head and gazed at her blankly. It was Ian.

Laura clapped a hand over her mouth to stifle a scream. Suddenly, from behind her, she heard another thud and a strangled cry. She whirled around and stared at the sight that met her eyes.

Michael was on the floor, seated, his legs stretched out in front of him. His brown eyes were wide with terror. His little backpack lay open on the floor beside him. Some kind of cloth was stuffed in his mouth. He was pinned there, a gun pointed at his head, by Wanda Jurik, who crouched behind him.

"What in the world . . .," Laura breathed. "Let go of my son."

She started toward them, but Wanda jerked the boy up in her arms and pressed the barrel of the gun into Michael's soft flesh.

Laura froze, terrified. "Mrs. Jurik, please," she whispered. "Why are you holding my child? Please, put that gun down. It might go off." She glanced over at the bed. Ian was watching her, his gaze wistful and faraway. He had his hand over the wound in his chest, as if to stanch the flow of blood. His fingers were red and sticky.

Laura looked frantically back at Wanda. "What are you doing, Mrs. Jurik? What's wrong? What happened here?"

"I've been waiting for you," said Wanda. She nodded toward the bed. "He came nosing around and found me."

Laura turned to Ian, feeling weak with confusion.

"I wanted to see you . . . talk to you," Ian whispered haltingly. Each word made him wince. "Back door was broken in. Scared me. I came upstairs. She was waiting . . . shot me . . . Sorry . . ."

Wanda flashed a thin smile. "I fixed him."

The agonized expression in Ian's eyes made Laura feel faint with fear. How close to death was he? she wondered helplessly. She tore her gaze from his face and stared in disbelief at Wanda's satisfied smile. Pull yourself together, she thought. You've got to get control of this situation.

"Mrs. Jurik, what do you think you're doing?" Laura demanded. "Let go of my boy. Come on. Let's go. I'm sure it was an accident, but . . . my . . . Ian needs a doctor. Right now. Please."

Wanda shook her head. "It was no accident. And we're not leaving. Now where is Gary?"

"Gary?" Laura asked. "He's gone . . . What . . .?"

"Don't try to fool me, missy. I know all about your plans. And you are not going to get away with it. You are not taking him away from me. No, no."

"Taking him away . . . What in the world?" Then, through her confusion, Laura remembered Gary's words. *You might get a call from my mother*. Oh, my God, she thought.

"Wanda," she said, trying to sound gentle, trying to control the fury she felt at the sight of Michael struggling against her fierce grip, at the thought of Ian lying bloody behind her. "This is all a misunderstanding. I . . . I just talked to Gary. He's not going with me. He only told you that. I'm not going anywhere with him." She glanced frantically at Ian. The blood from his chest was beginning to seep into the soggy bedspread, making a pink stain that spread out around him. "Please," she begged, "my husband—" Her voice caught on the word. "He needs help."

Wanda shook her head. She had no interest in the fate of the man she had shot. "Lies and more lies," she said. "You can't fool me. You may have been able to fool my innocent boy. He's gullible all right. He doesn't know anything about the world. He's been confined to that chair. But I know . . ."

Laura looked desperately at Wanda. She could see the fear in Michael's eyes, and something else as well: his trust in her. He trusted her to get him out of this. She had to do something, say something.

"Look, Wanda. Gary's already gone. He's gone without me. He only said he was going with me because . . ." She hesitated, automatically reluctant to break a confidence. But then she looked at Michael, held prisoner there, heard the raspy breathing of Ian on the bed, and she didn't care. "Gary's going to Boston to live with a friend he met there. It's a man, Wanda. A man he cares for very deeply. He didn't want to tell you because he didn't think you would understand. He loves this man, Wanda. He just wants to go back there and . . . and start a life with him. But he couldn't bring himself to tell you. Not yet. I just saw him, not an hour ago. He was on his way back there. He promised me he would tell you the truth once he got settled."

But the expression in Wanda's eyes was fixed, glassy. "I'll never understand what this power is that you two have over him. First it was Jimmy Reed. And now you. Always trying to take him away from me. Did you cast some kind of spell on him? Why couldn't you leave him alone? He almost killed himself over you. He bought this gun," she announced, waving the weapon recklessly before returning it snugly against Michael's temple, "all because you got married again. Did he tell you that? But do you care? No. Now, suddenly you decide you want him to go with you. That's all you have to say, and he jumps at the chance. He's like a puppet to you."

"That's ridiculous!" Laura shrieked, suddenly furious. "Stop blaming it on me. Haven't you heard a word I said? Let go of my son. Put that gun down right now." She took a step toward Wanda, brandishing the candlestick.

"I wouldn't," Wanda said ominously, jerking Michael up closer to her. The ropy muscles in her forearms tightened below the rolled-up sleeves of her blouse. "You won't be stronger than me. I am used to lifting. Used to carrying the weight of my son. My weight. My Gary," she insisted.

"I don't care what you're used to," Laura cried, the candlestick hanging useless from her fist. "I am getting my son out of here."

"I should have killed him after the accident—when I wanted to," Wanda keened. "Then none of this would have happened. Why did I wait?"

"Gary?" Laura said softly, appalled by her words.

"*Gary?*" Wanda demanded. "Why would I kill my own child? I live for that boy. Don't be stupid."

And then Laura understood. With a rush of horror, followed by a freight train of regret, she understood. Wanda meant Jimmy.

"You?" she cried. "You did it? Why?"

"Gary didn't want to leave me," Wanda whined. "He was only doing that grant thing to go to Boston because Jimmy Reed wanted him to. Pulling his strings, manipulating him. But Gary would have gone. I know my son. He was helpless in the face of Jimmy Reed. He did whatever Jimmy Reed told him to. That's why he's in that wheelchair. Because Jimmy Reed made him get into that car that night. It was icy. I told him. But Jimmy Reed got his way. He was always trying to take him away from me. I had to do something. And I thought once Jimmy Reed was gone, that curse would be lifted. But no. You took over. Why couldn't you just have left him to me?" Wanda wailed.

"You killed Jimmy," she said slowly, trying to let it sink in, and her heart twisted at the memory of her lost husband, who wanted only to help his friend.

Then she thought of Ian, lying there wounded on the bed behind her. And she felt almost faint with shame and regret. Ian had found her when she needed him most, believed in her innocence, and stood by her. His only crime had been to search for her. And, in return, she had accused him of Jimmy's murder. Her face burned at the thought of it. Her heart ached. She wanted to run to him, kneel beside him, and beg him to understand. But he would never forgive her for that. Who ever could? Besides, it could hardly matter to him now. Because of her, because of his faith in her, he was lying there bleeding to death . . .

"Well, you can't have him," said Wanda. "I won't allow it . . . not this time."

Laura stared at the woman holding her son prisoner, her graying hair disheveled, her eyes filled with a kind of triumphant madness. You did it, Laura thought. You deluded, grasping witch. You ruined us, all of us. And for what? You had it all wrong. It filled Laura with rage, but also an eerie kind of peace. Peace of mind. She had to think. She had to stop this madness. No more doubts.

"No," said Laura. "Not this time."

CHAPTER FIFTY-TWO

Think, Laura said to herself. Think. But it was hard to think, staring back at the serpentlike eyes of the woman with the gun. She had to tear her mind away from the fear of that gun, poised to explode at Michael's head. Of Ian, lying on the bed, life oozing out of him. The only reasons she had for living surrounded her, steeped in the threat of death, and she had to find a way. Some way.

Get a grip on yourself. Think of what she wants. Think of some way to promise it to her. That's the only way out of here, Laura told herself. Make her think that you are giving up. Yes. Somehow you have to convince her.

Laura took a deep breath. "All right, Wanda," she said as gently, as calmly, as she could. "Perhaps you're right. I have been selfish. I've been thinking only of myself, and not about what's best for Gary."

"Well, it's about time you realized that," Wanda said with a sigh.

"I made up that story about the man in Boston," said Laura. "There is no man. There never was."

Wanda sniffed. "Of course not. That was a vicious thing for you to say. Trying to imply my boy was involved in something perverted . . . well, it's just ridiculous. Gary doesn't have any kind of feelings that way. He's like a child. It's all crushes with him. You know, he gets heartsick. The way he is about you. It figures, though." She shook her head. "You'd say anything to get what you want. But I never believed it for a minute. You think a mother wouldn't know something like that about her own son? You've got a lot to learn about being a mother. I feel sorry for this one," she said, poking the gun into Michael's hair, "with a mother like you."

Laura felt the band of tension pain tightening around her head, and she dug her fingernails into her palms to keep from lunging at the woman. Steady, she thought. At least she's talking.

"Wanda," she said, "tell me exactly what it is you want. I'm willing to do anything . . ."

A pleading note had entered Laura's voice, and Wanda was immediately on her guard. "You'll say anything. I know that much about you. But doing it is another matter."

Don't beg, Laura reminded herself. She's enjoying it too much. Make a plan.

"All right," she said with a firmness she did not feel. "Here's the deal. Gary and I made arrangements to meet. He's prob . . . he's waiting for me right now. Michael and me."

"Waiting where?" Wanda asked curiously.

Where? Laura thought frantically. And then she shook her head. "Oh no," she said. "I'm not going to tell you everything. Not while you're threatening my son like that."

Wanda jerked the boy up tightly, and her voice was a growl. "You tell me everything or I'll kill your boy in front of your eyes."

Laura fought to control the trembling that had broken out all over her body. It was as if she were trying to reach Michael across a thin sheet of ice. At every step she heard cracking all around her, and icy depths waited for her if she made a wrong turn.

Think, think, she told herself. Pretend it's true. What then? "All right, listen, Wanda. There is only one way that

Gary is going to believe I am through with him, that I don't want anything more to do with him. And that is if I tell him myself. He's not going to believe it if it comes from you. After all, you're his mother. Mothers always want to shield their children, right? He knows that about you. He must know you don't approve of me. The only way is if I tell him myself."

Wanda smiled as if she found Laura's argument amusing. "Nooo," she said slowly. "The only sure way is if you're dead."

Wanda enjoyed the expression on Laura's face. "Well, you didn't think I would leave you alive, did you? Now that you know about Jimmy Reed."

"I wouldn't tell," Laura pleaded. "I swear to you."

"Your word. What good is that?" said Wanda. She gazed around the room. "I'll have to make it look like you did it. Or he did," she said vaguely, gesturing at Ian with the gun. "I'll leave the gun. They'll think there was a big fight. He is your husband, after all. These things happen every day."

Something molten inside Laura's heart suddenly turned to steel. Oh no, you won't, she thought. You may have a gun, but you won't win. I won't let you. "When I don't show up, Gary will come looking for me," she said.

Wanda sighed. "Yes, he probably will . . . He never learns."

"You know the police always suspect the person who finds the body. Did you know that?" Laura asked. "I'm very familiar with all this police stuff by now."

Wanda shrugged but looked at Laura with narrowed eyes. "So what?"

"And it's Gary's gun," Laura said coldly.

Wanda frowned at the gun in her hand, as if it had suddenly developed a voice that had to be silenced.

"They'll blame him," said Laura. "They'll say that Gary did it. And they'll put him away in prison. Or maybe they'll execute him. What will you have then?"

"Shut up," said Wanda. "Shut up. They'd never blame him. He's in a wheelchair."

354

"He's perfectly capable of shooting a gun," said Laura. "You said so yourself."

"You are a devil," said Wanda. "You don't care what happens to him, do you?"

"They'll take him away from you for good," said Laura. "You can kiss your son good-bye forever."

Wanda's eyes were filled with hatred and confusion as she glared back at Laura.

Laura looked at her watch. "Think it over," she said. "I'm late for our meeting. He'll be here soon."

Wanda looked around frantically, trying to decide, and then, suddenly, her panic subsided and a wide, Cheshire cat smile spread across her face. "I don't think so," she said.

"You don't think what?" Laura demanded. "They will blame him, you know. He has a perfect motive. You've told the police yourself that he was in love with me. You told them over and over that he was ready to kill himself over me. Believe me, that's all the motive they'll be looking for."

Wanda shook her head. "Sorry, dear. It's a nice try, but they're going to find the bodies on the second floor. That would be quite a trick for my son to manage."

Laura flinched, but she did not waver. This is it. This is the sticking point, she thought. She had to convince this woman by appearing completely sanguine. Triumphant, even. Steady, she thought. Believe it. Make it true.

"Not really, Wanda," Laura said. "Not much of a trick. We have a stair lift."

Wanda's eyes widened. "No. No, you don't."

"Oh yes," said Laura. "You saw the ramps outside. Jimmy put those up for Gary."

Wanda's mind was working furiously. "Anybody can put up ramps," she said. Then she felt a shaky sense of confidence. "I came up those stairs. There was no lift."

"This old house has a back staircase," Laura said coolly. "It's wider than this, and it goes straight up. That's why Jimmy put the lift back there. So that Gary could have the run of the house."

"You're lying," said Wanda.

"Oh, am I," said Laura. "Come and look."

Wanda hesitated, and Laura held her breath. But Wanda had to know. She didn't dare carry out her plan without knowing. Not if it meant that Gary could be blamed.

"Put down that thing in your hand. Throw it on the floor."

Carefully Laura crouched and put the candlestick beside her.

"Kick it away," said Wanda.

Laura did as she was told. The candlestick rolled in an arc and landed against the leg of a bureau.

"Now get up," Wanda said to Michael. Michael scrambled to his feet. There were tears on his face. Laura deliberately did not look into his frightened eyes for fear it would unnerve her. As Wanda rose to her feet, clinging to Michael by the neck of his shirt, Laura glanced over at the bed.

Ian was gazing at her, trying to speak. But he couldn't. There was blood all over the bed by now.

Don't die, Laura thought. Hang on. She held his gaze for a moment, read the words he could not say. Don't die, she thought again. We need another chance.

Okay, steady now, Laura thought as Wanda herded her and Michael out of the room, the barrel of the gun bobbing somewhere above Michael's ears.

"Where are these back stairs?" Wanda asked skeptically.

"This way," said Laura.

She felt herself moving in slow motion down the hall. She had only one hope, one moment to act, and she couldn't afford to fail. When they reached the staircase, she would step down instead of forward and then pivot, try to take Wanda by surprise, grab her by the arm that held the gun. She was counting on Wanda to react as she expected, and there was no other hope. Because Wanda was right. There *were* no back stairs, no lift, and no other way out.

"Hurry up," Wanda said in a cranky tone. "Move."

Laura reached the top of the center staircase and said a silent prayer. She was about to make her move when suddenly

Michael, whose hands were now freed, reached up, pulled the rag from his mouth, and began to wail. "No, Mom. There's no steps back there. She's gonna see. She'll shoot you . . ."

"Hey," Wanda cried, and Laura froze. "No steps are there?" she demanded, prodding Michael with the gun.

Laura turned and looked at them helplessly. Michael was sobbing loudly now and shaking his head. "Please don't shoot us. My mom didn't mean to tell a lie."

Wanda looked up at Laura, who stared back at her defiantly. "Good little boy. Always tell the truth. Now, shut up."

But Michael was yelling now, his sobs turning to hiccups, his face bright red. "Please don't hurt my mom," he wailed. His cries filled Laura's ears, and the stairwell, and Wanda shook him roughly, trying to make him stop.

"Let me hold him," Laura pleaded over his cries. "Can't you see he's terrified?"

Suddenly, behind Wanda, she saw something looming in the bedroom doorway. Her mouth fell open as she realized it was Ian, struggling through the door, one hand scarlet as it gripped his bleeding chest, his eyes fierce as he used the other hand to propel himself toward them along the wall.

"Ian," she breathed. "Don't."

Wanda cuffed the screaming child on the ear and looked at Laura with narrowed eyes. "Don't make me laugh," she said, not looking around. "Do you think I was born yesterday? Can't you get this kid to stop screaming?"

Laura shook her head, dumbstruck at the sight of Ian staggering toward them. What was the use? What did he think he could do? He could hardly hold himself up. But his valiant effort tore at her heart.

"Oh, spare me the act. Fool me once, shame on you," Wanda chanted bitterly. "Fool me twice, shame on me."

The words were scarcely out of her mouth when Ian, who had by this time dragged himself near enough to her to grab the banister, placed one sticky, bloody hand on her upper arm. Wanda felt the tug, looked down, and screamed.

The sight of the bloody hand on her arm startled her into raising the gun from Michael's head.

In that instant Laura saw her chance. As Ian collapsed in the hallway, Laura stepped down, pivoted, and grabbed Wanda's outstretched arm that held the gun. Laura yanked down with all her strength, pulling the other woman forward, over the railing.

Wanda flailed in the air for a second, trying to regain her balance, to find the landing again with her feet. But Laura's movement had been sufficiently swift and unexpected. With a shriek of fear, Wanda lurched over the railing and fell.

Laura jumped back against the wall and watched the other woman's descent as she banged against the twisting banister and fell to the floor below. As she hit the parquet floor in the hallway below, there was a tremendous report. The gun fired as it banged against the floor.

"Mommy!" Michael screamed. Laura looked up at her son and then down at the woman crumpled by the foot of the stairs. She half expected Wanda to rise to her feet, but then, as she watched, she saw a burgundy pool spreading out across the floor beneath the spot where Wanda lay.

"Mommy, is it okay?" Michael sobbed.

"It's okay," cried Laura. "It's okay." She vaulted up the steps and scooped him into her arms, kissing his ear, his hair, his wet cheek. "Are you okay, baby?"

The child nodded bravely. But his little body was shuddering with sobs.

"But what about Ian? She killed him," Michael cried.

"No," Laura gasped sharply. "No." But she knew, as she said it, that the old horror was replaying in his mind, in hers. "Wait here," she said, planting him beside the nearest door—the one to her studio. She raced in, fumbled for the phone, dialed for an ambulance, and cried out her address, begging for help. Then she put down the receiver and rushed back into the hallway.

There was blood everywhere, on the walls, on the Persian runner, on the spindles of the banister. Ian's eyes were closed, his eyelids waxy pale.

"Ian," she whispered. She knelt beside him and gently wound her arm under his neck, lifted his head. His eyelids fluttered, and he looked at her.

"Help is coming," she whispered. "You have to hang in there."

He peered at her as if through darkness, and her heart was filled with fear. "Don't die on me," she said. "Please don't die. They'll be here any minute. All you have to do is hang on for a little bit. I'm so sorry for everything. I never should have doubted you. Please stay. Please stay, and we'll have another chance. I need you with me. I do. Please hang in there for me." She grasped his sticky, bloody hand and stroked it. In the distance she heard the fire horn sound three times—the signal for rescue—and the wail of sirens.

"They're almost here," she said. "They'll be here any minute."

"Mom, can I come?" Michael sobbed from the doorway of her studio. "I'm not afraid."

She looked at the bloody mess surrounding Ian. Michael had already seen it. What was the use of trying to protect him from what he already knew?

"Please, Mom," he pleaded.

"Yes, come," she said, and he barreled over to her, wiggled in between her and Ian. He gazed wide-eyed at the man crumpled on the floor.

"Don't die, Ian," he said seriously.

Ian licked his lips slowly, with the tip of his tongue, and his gaze fell gently on Michael. He opened his mouth, and a soft whisper came out. "I won't," he said. "Promise."

"You better not," said Laura, gripping his hand, kissing his forehead. And she felt him return the pressure of her fingers.

As the doors to the house banged open below and she heard the police and the rescue team swarming in, yelling, pounding up the stairs, she looked anxiously into his face. His lips were contorted with pain, but deep in his eyes there was something peaceful, joyful almost. Something that gave her hope. He looked as though he were waiting for rescue in a safe place. He looked like a man cradled in the wings of his guardian angel.

THE END

ACKNOWLEDGMENTS

Special thanks to my experts: Jack Sayre, who took this landlubber out to sea; Cape May County First Assistant Prosecutor Ted Housel; Sergeant Ray Lewis and his colleagues at the Cape May County Court House; and, especially, the Honorable Carmen Alvarez, who patiently, thoughtfully, answered all my questions and arranged for me to have a look behind the judicial scenes.

Any distortions of fact or procedure, either nautical or legal, are strictly my own.

Thank you for reading this book.

If you enjoyed it, please leave feedback on Amazon or Goodreads, and if there is anything we missed or you have a question about, then please get in touch. We appreciate you choosing our book.

Founded in 2014 in Shoreditch, London, we at Joffe Books pride ourselves on our history of innovative publishing. We were thrilled to be shortlisted for Independent Publisher of the Year at the British Book Awards.

www.joffebooks.com

We're very grateful to eagle-eyed readers who take the time to contact us. Please send any errors you find to corrections@joffebooks.com. We'll get them fixed ASAP.